S0-BNZ-688

"Tell me, Ricardo," Dr. Gregori asked, "what is all this talk I hear about a rash of new agents in Asunción?"

Caffetti studied the Doctor through narrow eyes, as if he were weighing the wisdom of telling the man everything he knew. At last he spoke: "As you know, in the past year or so certain Israeli operatives have been able to insinuate themselves into the Jewish community in Asunción. They pose as jewelers there and tailors, petty tradesmen. We think they are Mossad, but what their specific mission is, we cannot say. Some of the reports speak of—"

"Vengeance." The Doctor completed the sentence for him.

"One group they watch particularly call themselves 'Al Tishkakh.' Hebrew for 'We will never forget.' "

"Tishkakh." Grigori's eyes twinkled merrily. "Never forget, ay? How romantic. How heroic."

"Perhaps," Caffetti frowned, "but thank your stars that Arganas knows a good deal about these Mossad people in Asunción."

"I note that whenever Arganas wishes to extort higher protection fees, the tiger is somehow always at the gates." Gregori brooded thoughtfully. "Let the tigers come then." He hefted his Mauser. "I'm ready for them."

Books by Herbert Lieberman

Brilliant Kids
City of the Dead
The Climate of Hell
Crawlspace
The Eighth Square

Published by POCKET BOOKS

The Climate Of Hell

Herbert Lieberman

PUBLISHED BY POCKET BOOKS NEW YORK

POCKET BOOKS, a Simon & Schuster division of
GULF & WESTERN CORPORATION
1230 Avenue of the Americas, New York, N.Y. 10020

Copyright © 1978 by Herbert Lieberman

Published by arrangement with Simon and Schuster
Library of Congress Catalog Card Number: 78-17094

ISBN: 0-671-82236-5

First Pocket Books printing October, 1979

10 9 8 7 6 5 4 3 2 1

Trademarks registered in the United States and other countries.

Printed in the U.S.A.

For Georges and Ann Borchardt

ACKNOWLEDGMENTS

The following narrative is a fiction based upon fact. The details of Doctor Grigori's exile are drawn from actual episodes in the life of an infamous Nazi camp doctor still living as a fugitive in Paraguay today. Imagination has been used to stitch the known facts together. Only names have been changed, for the obvious legal reasons. The Doctor is still represented by one of the most prestigious law firms in Frankfurt, and his family remains one of the most powerful and litigious in Bavaria today.

I should like to express my gratitude to Mr. Ladislas Farago, who so generously permitted me access to his excellent files on Nazi war criminals still living in Latin America; to Mr. Isser Harrel, former Chief Executive of the Israeli Secret Service; to Mr. Tuviah Freedman of the Haifa Documentation Center; and to Mr. Simon Wiesenthal of the Vienna Documentation Center, for assistance and encouragement, as well as fascinating insights into a world I never knew.

And I shall be a fugitive and a wanderer on the earth, and whoever finds me will slay me.

GENESIS 4:14

Prologue

They say I'm dead.

One report has it I've been shot in a café in Asunción. Another states that I've been lured across the Paraná into Brazil and mowed down there by an Israeli assassin team. Another claims that a plane I've been flying in has been sabotaged and gone down in flames in the jungles of the Chagras. They say my body has been dredged up out of a cataract at the bottom of the Iguaçu Falls, apparently pushed or thrown from the top, my throat slashed from ear to ear.

When these reports are disproved, as they invariably are, they then say that even if I'm not dead now, I will be soon—that I'll wind up like Stangl or Eichmann, or like Cukurs, stuffed into the trunk of a Volkswagen in a back alley of Montevideo, my body pulped and bloody, with a small, neat calling card dropped upon it, signed compliments of the "Blue Falcon" or "Those Who Cannot Forget," or "Al Tishkakh," or some such nonsense.

Oh, they're clever, all right. I don't deny it. They're professional and they have style. They're audacious and persistent. Willing to take time and risks and do it over and over again until they get it right. They've already managed to dispatch all my old friends—Hoess, Viertz, Werner Roehde, dear old Fritz Klein; and with me they keep right on trying. Once or twice they nearly succeeded. Like the young Israeli with his flawless Spanish, and his ridiculous serape and sandals, who

1

befriended my housekeeper. And then there was that poor buffoon Erico, who still goes around insisting he's killed me.

Yes, they've come close, but in the end they always miss. I'm always one step ahead. I have my style too, and I always have the last laugh. Like the time I had myself buried at a mock funeral in Santiago with the name Cerillo Flores Chávez marked on the wooden cross of my grave, and flowers and grieving relatives all about. What splendid fun that was. For a year they came around, puzzled, bewildered, scratching their heads. Yes, they're clever, but not clever enough. The headwaters of the Paraná around Pedro Caballero are choked with the bodies of these romantic avengers; these beardless, pink-skinned infant assassins with their smoldering eyes and their heroic gestures. Let them come, I say. Let them come if they have stomach enough. I'll bury them all.

Part I

THE FALCON
AND
THE ANGEL

CHAPTER 1

Gregor Grigori
March 16, 1911—March 16, 1977.
Scientist. Physician. Soldier.
Patriot. Traduced, maligned, and
vilified in life, he died on his
birthday in a state of sanctity.

The young man stood in the overgrown, untended ruins of a small cemetery near the Indian village of Ita and read the epitaph scratched crudely there on a plain wooden cross. Dressed in a rumpled, dusty woolen suit that was too warm for the weather. His eyes were clear, icy blue, and his lips moved ever so slightly as he read.

The cemetery was a rough, simple place dotted by two dozen or so plain wooden crosses set randomly about to mark the final resting place of those Tupi and Aché Indians who had been converted by the Jesuits from the old mission at San Damien. But the young man was not interested in these other crosses. Eyes fixed solemn and unmoving on the curious epitaph, his lips and eyes read the words once again.

Carlos Danillo, the gravedigger of Ita, had told the young man that some Germans had paid him half a pig and two pairs of shoes as a fee for burying a German doctor in his mid to late sixties in that grave. There was no doubt that a body was buried beneath that cross, because a number of Indians in the area had seen

the earth spaded over it that afternoon during a sweltering heat spell of 38 degrees centigrade. However, when
the young man questioned them closely, they had grown
evasive.

The two Indians standing with the spade and shovel
behind the young man watched him impassively. They
waited with a kind of stolid, unquestioning patience,
like beasts of burden in their yokes.

At last the young man stepped backward and nodded
at them. They moved forward at once, stripping off
their shirts and falling instantly to their work. The
young man had given the drowsy old sexton a handful
of *guaranís* so that he would take a long nap that afternoon. Therefore, there was no need to hurry. The only
other creature around to witness their curious activity
in the cemetery was a solitary dove cooing mournfully
in the branches just above.

The Indians were strong, and they worked swiftly.
Shortly a wide, elliptical trench several feet in depth
had been carved out of the earth. The young man
waited in the shade of a tree, while the Indians, spading red dirt, sank lower and lower into the ground.

At a certain point the Indians abruptly stopped
spading and began to chatter and point at something
they had uncovered in the earth.

Now the young man sauntered forward out of the
shade and crossed a scorched, narrow space to the lip
of the grave and peered down.

The first thing he saw was what appeared to be a rib
cage. Not that of a human being, however, but, as it
turned out, that of the largely decomposed carcass of a
donkey. The young man was certain it was a donkey,
for the carcass could not have been buried too long—
several months, perhaps—and sizable strips of pelt and
flesh still clung there, matted down like a pair of mothy
flannel pajamas, to the skeleton. The entire skull, how-

ever, was clean, gleaming white in the shimmering sun, the eye sockets empty, and the huge crushing mandibles locked and frozen into a leering grin.

Frowning, the young man peered down into the grave a moment longer, pondering it. Then suddenly, he threw back his head and roared with laughter.

CHAPTER 2

"Oh yes," the old Paraguayan, Felix Nachtmann, laughed with twinkling eyes and told the young man who said he was a journalist and had good papers— "Paraguay's a naughty place." He had no objection to talking. Besides, the young man was buying the drinks.

"A thieves' carnival," Nachtmann went on in his comfortable German, warming to the subject. "The capital of fugitives and outcasts. The bunghole of the world." He threw back his head and laughed. "America says, 'Send me your tired and your poor.' Paraguay says, 'Send me your riffraff. Your scum of the earth.' What no civilized nation will accept, Mother Paraguay will open her legs to. Our major industry is smuggling. Our chief export, crime. Our leading citizens, pimps and *contrabandistas*. When there's no place left in the world you can run to, when no one else will take you in, come to Paraguay. We will welcome you."

Once again the old Paraguayan threw back his head and laughed at the purpling twilight sky above Asunción. It was one of those suffocating airless nights typical of summers on the Tropic of Capricorn. The evening laid a moist, hot palm against their faces and they sat beside the river on the dirty wooden benches of a little waterfront café where people sipped warm beer and ate *camarónes* out of little cones of brown paper. The river, at low tide then, exhaled the faintly repugnant odor of diesel fuel and sewage. Occasionally, river boats, gaudily lit with strings of lights hung in their shrouds, chugged past like tiny toys on a child's birthday cake. The young man ordered them two more cognacs.

"Civilization has always needed her Paraguays," Nachtmann continued. "Cities of Refuge they were called in the Old Testament. That's how we got our Nazis."

"But what about Grigori?" the young man asked. The hour was moving on, and he was growing impatient with the garrulous old man.

"Oh yes, yes." The old man waved his hand and underwent a sudden spasm of coughing. He coughed till his rheumy old eyes leaked and he had to wipe them with a handkerchief. "There's no doubt. No doubt at all that Doctor Grigori is here. Everyone knows that. I used to see him regularly. He would come and go quite freely. Once I saw him at a party in the Obligado colony. He was dancing with a young Belgian girl with splendid thighs. If you'd told her that this was actually the infamous Grigori, *Den Schönen Doktor,* the Death Angel of Auschwitz, who castrated children as an amusement, she wouldn't know what the devil you were talking about. Nor would she care. Well, why the devil should she? He looked an absolute prince at the time.

"Oh yes," Nachtmann drained his cognac. Two bright roses had bloomed at his cheeks, and he waited there smiling enigmatically at the young man. He had the look of the old roué—the impecunious boulevardier, preying upon an unsuspecting tourist. He refused to continue until another cognac had been ordered and the young man had lit his cigarette. Then he waved his hands expansively, pushing smoke out of the way, as if it had some palpable weight that he could shove against.

"Grigori is here, all right," he said. "You can see him in Bariloche at the gaming tables; or in Hohenau at the Tirol, dancing with young girls; in Asunción you're likely to find him at the Ali Baba or Las Acacias with Werner Jung or Hans Rudel, or in Puerto Stroessner in the marketplace shopping for groceries. He has a beautiful villa in Puerto Stroessner. They almost succeeded in burning it down one night. Finally settled for burning up one of his Mercedes.

"But the man's nomadic. He can't sit still. Or possibly he's afraid to pause in any one place too long. For his kind, immobility can be very dangerous. He never sleeps in the same place three nights in a row. One day he's reported in Encarnación, the next day Foz do Iguaçu, the next day Posadas. Then someone says they've seen him crossing the Brazilian border at Doña Ema, or shared a place with him on the Paraná ferry going up to Eldorado, or that he inhabits the old Jesuit ruins beyond the Tebicuary River in the southernmost region of the country. Around here they never call him by his real name. Rather they call him *El Gran Fugitivo* or *El Doctor Misterioso* or Don Gregor. Sometimes simply *Fugitivo*."

Nachtmann went on for some time, talking freely. And the young man continued to probe him with questions. The old man knew he was far too old for it to matter what the authorities might do to him for talking so openly with an outsider. His eyes twinkled mischievously, and that pair of roses bloomed like rouge at his cheeks. He wore a dark suit with a carnation in his lapel, and with his dark glasses, his pasty waxen features and yellow dentures, he had an oddly funereal look—tawdry, sinister, and farcical all at once.

"As you know," Nachtmann continued, rubbing his nose contemplatively with a long, crooked finger, "Doctor Grigori never seems to lack for money. A close friend told me that every month he receives by special post fifty percent of the profits of a metallurgical enterprise in Buenos Aires called Hierro–Fabrofarunk—with a capital of four million German marks. He lives quite comfortably. But they say the Eichmann business scared the hell out of him and he's grown a little more wary."

"But where is he now?" the young man persisted.

Nachtmann smiled and shrugged. *"Quién sabe?* The last address I have for him in Asunción is Fulgencio Moreno Street #507. But this is a false address, or rather merely the address of Doctor Sonabria."

"Sonabria?"

"Caesar Sonabria—Doctor Grigori's lawyer." Nachtmann winked slyly. "No, I wouldn't say where Don Gregor is now. But every two or three months the world press reports that he is captured in Argentina or Peru or Brazil. I just read a report that claimed he was apprehended by the Mexican authorities in Puerto Vallarta. When they fingerprinted this alleged Doctor Grigori, he turned out to be a fifty-year-old bank teller from Stuttgart who was running away from some minor bookkeeping peculations and the wrath of his wife." Nachtmann's head rolled back and he hooted at the moon, which had just risen above the smoky city. Several people in the café looked up, and the old fellow quickly composed himself. "So you see, dear boy, most of these stories turn out to be apocryphal. No one really knows where Grigori is. For all practical purposes, he's gone off the map. He's certainly not in Asunción. The government is no longer quite so cordial to the old party *Bonsen.* It's not as profitable these days to be so cozy with them. But take my word for it. The Doctor's about. Still in the country, that is. Still depending on *El Jefe*'s protection. Yes, it costs him dearly. He's had to paper the whole government with deutschemarks. Everyone is on his payroll—the police, the judges, the ministers of justice." The roses at Nachtmann's cheeks glowed brighter than ever, and once more he hooted at the sky. "Rather costly business, ay?" The old man winked. "This playing the *Gran Fugitivo?*" Old Nachtmann smiled, holding out his hand. "I'm afraid I have nothing more to add."

The young man who called himself a journalist frowned. His curiosity had not been satisfied. Nevertheless, he counted off several hundred *guaranis* and, smiling, laid them neatly on the outstretched palm before him.

CHAPTER 3

Somewhere down on the Tebicuary in the southeast corner of the country, at that point where the Paraguay and the Paraná flow together, a half dozen or so Paraguayan gunboats lay at anchor, tied up to the dock of the small river town of Desmochados. For the most part leaky scows and fossil World War II PT boats, this ragtag armada of small vessels, bristling with their gunmounts, comprises roughly half of the Paraguayan navy. That a nation the size of Paraguay should require any navy at all is perhaps mystifying; even more so when one considers that it is completely landlocked.

The navy's mission, official spokesmen of the Paraguayan government will tell you, is to regulate traffic on the vast intercoastal waterways. But, in reality, the actual mission of this navy is to lend comfort and support to the huge multimillion-dollar smuggling trade, the nation's number one industry, which plies freely up and down the waterways—a trade that consists chiefly of contraband drugs for the huge American market and, most lucrative of all, the traffic in human beings.

The small jovial Paraguayan official smiled approvingly at the commercial traveler who was an *Inglés* and called himself Hereford. Hereford had told him he was traveling through Latin America as the representative of an American pharmaceutical concern. He pointed to his sample cases, which he said were crammed full of brochures and drug samples.

"*Derecha . . . Derecha . . . Derecha . . . Izquierda . . . A la derecha . . .*"

Their attention was suddenly diverted from small talk to the excitement taking place down on the dock, where just then literally hundreds of Aché Indians were milling about waiting to embark on the gunboats.

"*Derecha . . . Derecha . . . Derecha . . . ,*" came the shrill cry again. Hereford's heavy-lidded green eyes gazed down from the road above the quay and found the source of the voice to be a small slight man with salt-and-pepper hair, and eyebrows and a beard that didn't match. He was dressed in a short-sleeved poplin shirt, Bermudas and knee socks; one of his eyes, the left, squinted, appearing to sit slightly off kilter, and when he smiled, as he frequently did, a wide triangular gap appeared between his front teeth.

The Achés lined up obediently in single file—men, women, children, each with all of his pitiful possessions balled up in a rag—waiting to approach the gentleman with the squinting eye.

*"Derecha . . . Izquierda . . . Derecha . . . Izquier-
da . . . Derecha . . ."*

"What does he say?" Mr. Hereford inquired.

"He merely waves them right and left. *'Derecha'* for
right, *'Izquierda'* for left."

"I see." The Englishman pondered. "And what do
the directions signify?"

"Ah." The small swarthy official beamed pridefully,
as if the *Inglés* had asked him precisely the question he
was so eager to answer. "It is a system, Señor Hereford,
of segregating the old and infirm from the young and
able. You see, it is only the young and able who are
in a position to take advantage of our Indian Cultural
Reclamation Program."

"I see," Hereford said again in his laconic, noncom-
mittal way. He had heard all about this cultural reclamation program for the Indians, paid for largely with
U.S. foreign-aid dollars. Monthly forays of ruthless
bushwhackers hired by the government would range out
into the forests of the Chagras and the Gran Chaco,
rounding up the Aché, guaranteeing them food and a
livelihood while supposedly educating them for a trade.
The Aché would be herded down to the river, there
packed and crammed like cattle onto the gunboats, and,
for the price of fifty or one hundred dollars a head,
sold to buyers outside the country. The male Aché were
immediately dispatched up into the appalling nightmare
conditions of the Bolivian tin mines. The women were
sold into domestic work, generally the rich hotel tourist
trade of Argentina and Brazil. The young and pretty
ones often wound up in the brothels of Rio and Montevideo. The children could bring, depending on their
general condition, anywhere from seventy-five to two
hundred dollars, condemned to labor ten to twelve
hours a day in the fish canneries of Ecuador and Peru
or the sweltering cotton fields of Guatemala. Often, the

little boys would be sold as catamites to wealthy, jaded Latins.

"And what becomes of the old and infirm?" Hereford asked, unable to resist the slight taunt.

"Not to worry, Señor Hereford. They are well provided for. Our methods are humane. You see, these poor devils have become a huge problem for us here. They're filthy, uneducated, diseased. They reproduce like fruitflies and will not learn the most simple methods of contraception."

"Are they told that they're to be separated?" Hereford inquired.

At first the official appeared a bit defensive, then he smiled, winked slyly, and put a finger to his lips as if to say hush. "I'm afraid that wouldn't do. You see, they're very close, very inbred. Strong family ties, you know. No, I'm afraid it wouldn't do at all to tell the poor devils. You see"—once again he flashed his wide, beaming, self-congratulatory smile—"we have adopted scientific German methods here to deal with the Indian problem."

"*Derecha . . . Derecha . . . Derecha . . . Derecha . . .*" Once again the shrill cry wafted up from the dock.

"Yes, I see," Hereford replied somewhat distantly, his eye traveling back to the natty gentleman down on the dock who was bristling with efficiency and even a courtly solicitude as he ordered these near-naked, gullible savages forward for examination. He carried a swagger stick and used it to lead them about like a conductor on the podium. The supreme mockery was that he even whistled while he worked.

"Who is he?" Hereford asked rather coldly.

"Who?" The official was momentarily puzzled. "Oh, forgive me. Of course, you mean Doctor Neiditch, the fellow in charge down there. He's a German. A physician. Several university degrees, you know. Frankfurt and Munich, I believe. He examines the Indians to certify their physical fitness."

"I see." Hereford's gaze narrowed. He had noted that Doctor Neiditch had eyed the children slowly, taking rather more time and care with them than their parents. Several of the smaller ones he'd pull out of line away from the terrified grief-stricken mothers. He'd prod and poke and handle them a bit. His assistants, big, strapping fellows, would then isolate them and lead them off to a little shed at the end of the dock.

Now, at this moment, just such an episode was taking place. The doctor had ordered one of these bruisers to lead a small boy off to the shed, but the mother refused to be separated from the child. A long, pitiful wail went up—a high, keening sound as of someone mourning. As the assistants got rougher in their attempts to separate mother and child, the wails turned to shrieks of terror.

In the next moment, Doctor Neiditch, who had been all courtesy and smiles, suddenly waded into the crowd wielding his swagger stick. The mother had fallen to the ground, and the child started to scream. While the assistants held her down, the doctor proceeded to club her brutally with his baton. The stick went up and down in wide, graceful threshing motions. From where he stood, Hereford could hear the whiplash whistle of it cutting through the torpid air and the sickening thud of it impacting on the woman's flesh.

The spectacle of such an action had terrified the timid Indians. Restive and suspicious, they now fanned out around the dock, some of them even trying to leave it while the guards stationed there attempted to shove them back on with the butts of their bright new Kalishnikov rifles.

A long, pitiful wail issued from the mother. Hereford stiffened as the guards prized the child from her arms and hustled it off into the little shed at the end of the dock.

"Good God," Hereford murmured, half aloud, half to himself. Smiling rather queasily, the Paraguayan official felt obliged to explain. But Mr. Hereford was of no mind to wait around for explanations. He glared at the official a moment, then turned abruptly and stalked off.

CHAPTER 4

The most powerful man in Encarnación is Alban Krug. Once a powerful figure in the NSDAP hierarchy, he settled, as many of his brethren did, in Paraguay, thirty years ago, at the conclusion of the war. Krug is what you'd call a gentleman farmer, although he has a number of subsidiary and less clearly defined interests. He knows everyone in Paraguay, particularly those living in the large German community, and indeed is thought of as the spiritual "godfather" of all Paraguayan Germans. If one were looking for a German in Paraguay today, any German, a logical place to start would be with him, and this was where the young man came next.

Alban Krug's offices in Encarnación are on Mariscal Estigarribia Street #378. It was quite easy to find the place, but by walking in there one could scarcely tell what kind of business Alban Krug was engaged in. There was no sign above the door describing the nature of the premises, nor was there any hint from the rather perfunctory furnishings within as to precisely what went on there.

The moment the young man entered he found himself surrounded by four large men with pistols flaunted brazenly on their hips, inquiring politely but rather forcefully about the exact nature of his business. This time he identified himself as Gerhardt Kunstler, a Bavarian, and he spoke German flawlessly without an accent. His clothing, too, one could see, was tailored in Germany. He said he was from Günzburg and was looking for Doctor Grigori. He had a message from his family there.

Krug's office itself was one room consisting of a typewriter, a telephone, and a long wooden trestle table littered with file folders, ashtrays, and a surfeit of empty wine bottles. Beyond that table was a cord hammock strung on hooks between two wooden posts. As this was a typical working day, the hammock was occupied by a dwarfish barrel-chested individual in his sixties with a long flowing, tobacco-stained beard and an enormous head. His shirt was open down the front, revealing an enormous tangle of gray, woolly tufts erupting from his chest. There was an automatic pistol tucked up rather ostentatiously in his belt, right beneath his beer-distended belly. And from his mouth hung an enormous white meerschaum, out of which periodically the grossest of sucking sounds would issue.

While the gentlemen surrounding the young man continued their methodical inquiry, Herr Krug, swaying ever so gently in his hammock, puffed circles of smoke from his pipe reflectively at the ceiling, all the while pretending to be oblivious to the visitor's presence there.

Once the guards had examined the young man's passport and identification and ascertained that his motives were not hostile, he was permitted to talk with Herr Krug. He was well aware that the gentleman could be extremely dangerous. It was fairly well known in these parts that a number of overly curious people who had offended Herr Krug had either died or disappeared mysteriously. The Indians around here called him *El Apagador;* the translation into English is clumsy, but it means something like "the extinguisher."

Krug questioned the young man closely and shrewdly about Günzburg, interrogating him about old friends there and deliberately inserting from time to time a bit of erroneous information, which the young man would immediately correct.

When he had drunk enough grappa and was feeling expansive, Krug suddenly fixed the young man with a yellow bilious eye and started waving his great smoking meerschaum in the air above the hammock.

"So, you're here looking for Grigori?"

"Yes, sir," replied the young man, and withdrew a letter from his inside pocket. "I bring this from his son Rolfe, who plans to visit him shortly."

"Where did you hear that?" Krug's head snapped around and the bushy brows squinted above his eyes.

"From Herr Hupfauer himself," the young man replied, knowing that this was the name Doctor Grigori's son now preferred to go under. "I also have regards from Frau Grigori."

"Ah, yes," the dwarf said slyly. "You saw her in Günzburg, then?"

"No, Herr Krug"—the young man smiled tolerantly, knowing he was still being tested—"in Merano—where she's been living for several years with her new husband. As you know, the federal police in Germany have made her life miserable."

Krug sighed and lay back in his hammock.

"Why the devil can't they leave them alone? No one has ever proved a thing against Grigori. He's not a criminal, and I don't permit anyone to suggest that he ever was."

"But," the young man argued, "as you know, Herr Krug, there's a great deal of evidence to suggest that ..."

"Lies, all lies of the Zionist press," Krug shouted. His face had grown a bit red by this time, and his voice was hoarse from shouting. At that point, a Paraguayan major stuck his head in the door and inquired if everything was all right.

"Yes, yes. Perfectly all right. He's a friend of mine. Get the hell out of here." Krug rose, fuming and coughing in a cloud of smoke, from the hammock and chased the officer out of the room. By this the young man was given to understand that the Paraguayan government worked very closely with Herr Krug.

"Grigori *was* here for a while," Krug said. Then he started pacing up and down the room, pausing every now and then to wave his pipe in the young man's face. "But no one knows where he is now. He's gone off the map."

"He's probably up around the Chaco," the young man suggested, pushing the angry dwarf a little harder.

"Where the hell did you hear that?"

"From an Indian in Foz. He told me there was a cross-eyed German doctor living up that way in the jungle, just below the Bolivian border."

"Indians?" Krug spat with contempt, then flung himself down on the trestle table, knocking off bottles and cans as he did so. "Don't believe anything an Indian tells you."

"It could be."

Krug squinted at his visitor sideways through a halo of smoke, more wary than ever. "Possibly. Possibly. But who knows?"

"I hear there's a Japanese colony of laborers," the young man continued, "some four thousand or so, living in the jungle near Pirapo." Then he remarked quite casually that he'd heard through reliable sources (not an Indian) that a German doctor lived far back in the jungle behind them, in a small but very well guarded *estancia*.

"Possibly." Krug shrugged again, feigning indifference, but now he regarded his visitor somewhat more intently and paid closer attention to what he was saying. At this point, the young man pulled back a bit, sensing that caution was the byword here. He'd gotten in too far with the man.

But, just to wind things up, he asked Krug what would happen to the Jews of Paraguay if they came and took Doctor Grigori as they took Eichmann.

El Apagador suddenly rose from the table like a specter. His red face darkened and he glowered at the young man. The other four gentlemen in the room moved ominously forward, but Krug waved them off, scowling all the while. Then, pounding the table with his little mallet fists he shouted, "If anything were to happen to Don Gregor, then we will *fracasar* all the Jews in Paraguay. And that goes for you too, you son of a bitch, if you don't get the hell out of here right now."

CHAPTER 5

Toward nightfall, the young man came to the Hotel Schweitzer in Hohenau, a small river town on the Alto Paraná. However, this time he bore not the slightest resemblance to the journalist who had interviewed Nachtmann, or to the young Bavarian who had dropped in so unexpectedly on Alban Krug that afternoon at Mariscal Estigarribia #378.

Checking into the Schweitzer late that day he identified himself not as Gerhardt Kunstler from Günzburg but rather as a Mr. Rabinovich from Asunción; and instead of appearing young and vigorous, in his twenties or so, he now wore a great long beard, flowing gray side whiskers, and a pair of cracked bifocals taped together at the bridge of the nose. He was attired in an old black frock coat and a beaverboard hat such as the kind worn by the old Orthodox Sephardim. He looked frail and worn—the perfect Hebrew septuagenarian.

He took a light supper at the hotel, and, since a steamy tropical rain was just then pelting the street outside, he sat in the small, nearly deserted lobby with its meager, shabby decoration—sat beneath a potted palm tree and with palsied hands read a copy of *La Correa de Buenos Aires* through his funny cracked bifocals.

Presently two men came into the lobby and swaggered over to the desk. The young man recognized them at once as two of the strapping thugs he'd met at Krug's that afternoon. Two of Herr Krug's bully boys.

Their manner was rude and gruff. The desk clerk, a gentle Paraguayan of Guaraní extraction, was quickly intimidated. He kept nodding his head as they barraged him with questions, and his voice trembled when he spoke. The young man, still scanning the sheets of his newspaper, bent his head to listen.

They were looking for a Herr Kunstler. A young German of such and such a height and such and such an appearance. Had he, or anyone matching that description, been in?"

"No, *señor*." The desk clerk shook his head. "We have no such person here."

One of Krug's men glanced over at the elderly Jew reading the newspaper in the dim light of the lobby.

If he were to come in, the other man proclaimed, the desk clerk was to notify them immediately at the following number, which the fellow then scribbled down. But under no circumstances was the desk clerk to tell the young man that anyone had been looking for him, or, indeed, that he had sent for anyone. Then they swaggered out.

Shortly after, the young man rose and, taking his key from the badly shaken desk clerk, shuffled over to the elevator and retired to his room for the evening.

What he had deduced from the little episode in the lobby was simply that Krug by now had had time to wire Günzburg and get a reply—a reading on one Gerhardt Kunstler that must have been sufficiently disconcerting to rouse the suspicion of the canny dwarf and cause him to send his people out looking for the impostor.

There was a distinct danger in remaining in Hohenau, the young man realized, but he felt sufficiently safe in the hotel room for the night. The desk clerk, it was certain, had no suspicion about his true identity. His papers had been in perfect order—and so Krug's two hired baboons would doubtless not be back.

Before retiring for the evening, the young man withdrew from the small haversack in which he carried his possessions a manila portfolio. It was crammed with papers and photographs. An adhesive sticker pasted across the face of it carried in ink the simple identification label "Doctor Gregor Grigori."

Lying there in bed now, the night lamp burning on the small rattan table beside him, he began to read and pore over for the thousandth time the many hideous documents contained therein.

Doctor Helmut Gregor Grigori. Wanted by the Government of West Germany for atrocious crimes committed while serving as Chief Physician of the internment installation of Auschwitz-Birkenau 1943–1945.

Doctor Gregor Grigori. Wanted by the United States Government for the wanton commission of cruel and ghastly crimes against inmates of the Auschwitz–Birkenau concentration camps March 1943–August 1945.

Doctor Helmut Grigori. Wanted by the Government of the USSR to stand trial for heinous and despicable acts against humanity. For having fled his homeland with the intention of avoiding criminal prosecution during the term of the select Nuremberg tribunals.

Doctor Gregor Grigori, alias Karl Geuske [as the Interpol Red Alert out of St. Cloud described him], alias Gregor Schlakstro, alias Fausto Rindon, alias Jose Aspiazu, alias S. Alvez, alias Edler Friedrich Von Breitenbach, alias Lars Balstroem, alias Heinz Stobert, alias Stanislaus Proske, alias Father Capezius (Order of Carmelites), alias Doctor Josef Neiditch—or whatever name or disguise he is presently going by—is a man with a multitude of identities. Innumerable sets of forged documents have permitted him until only recently to move about over national borders with impunity.

The physical description of the man as given out from captured medical records of the Waffen–SS—in which he served as an *Obersturmbannführer*—may be set down as follows:

Height 174 cm (5 feet, 10 inches). Weight 85 kilos. Straight forehead. Light brown eyes, the left with a pronounced squint. Straight nose. Medium mouth. Prominent chin. Medium ears with distinct lobes. Small triangular gap between front teeth. Mustache thin, carefully cultivated.

In social gatherings Doctor Grigori has been known to affect a monocle so as to diminish the "grotesque" effect of his squint, which is said to give his features an off-center, distinctly out-of-kilter cast. The monocle is more for cosmetic purposes than for either therapeutic reasons or disguises. Doctor Grigori is a vain man. Please treat all above information as confidential.

BONFI FOFKO EGVED REBDI [The Interpol Red Alert concluded with a line of inscrutable garble from the Organization's secret cable code book.]

The young man proceeded to read selected portions of the voluminous Bill of Indictment compiled by the West German government and the Bundes Kriminalen against the Doctor during the Nuremberg tribunals.

Helmut Gregor Grigori, Doctor of Philosophy, University of Munich, Doctor of Medicine, University of Frankfurt. Born March 16, 1911, Günzburg, District of Swabia, Land of Bavaria, West Germany. Formerly residing at 87 Sonnhalde in Freiburg, the son of manufacturer Karl Grigori, and his wife Walburgia, is hereby ordered into immediate custody on emphatic suspicion of murder. Specific charges include the following:

1. The Accused killed the newborn baby of Frau Sussman of Vienna 19, Sievering Strasse #107, by throwing the infant into an open fire before the eyes of the mother.

2. The Accused killed a fourteen-year-old girl

by splitting her head with a cleaver (or bayonet?), her death occurring after excruciating pain.

3. The Accused killed innumerable pairs of twins of Gypsy, Jewish, and Slavic parentage, either with his bare hands, or by mixing lethal poisons into their food. He murdered thousands of other children by injection of phenol, benzine, or gasoline directly into their heart for the purpose of conducting specious and wholly questionable studies in genetic medicine on their bodies during autopsies. Twins in particular were dissected alive.

4. The Accused sterilized thousands of women by injecting caustic agents directly into the uteri, cervices, and ovaries. He castrated untold numbers of men and young boys in sex-altering surgery without the use of anesthetics.

5. The Accused injected pain-causing solutions into the eyes of infants with the intention of changing the color of their eyes. As a result of which many died.

6. Among the Accused's other "scientific" experiments was the liquid force-feeding of prisoners in order to determine how much fluid a stomach could hold. Compelling inmates to bathe in hardening ice, then placing them in cubicles of scalding steam in order to test tolerances to extremes of temperature. Testing the effects of phosphorus bombs on live subjects. Operating without anesthetics in order to determine the levels of pain people could endure.

The specific charges of the indictment went on for some seventy sickening pages, a catalogue of horrors which the young man flicked through, each one incredibly surpassing the next in atrociousness, concluding with the astonishing fact that "it is estimated that Doctor Grigori in his capacity as SS *Chef-Arzt* in Auschwitz–Birkenau, and *Chef der Sonderkommando,* identified as one and the same with the infamous Death Angel of Auschwitz—one of whose prime duties was 'selection' of inmates for either forced labor or the gas chamber—was himself responsible for the death of nearly one million of the innocent and defenseless—men, women, and children alike."

The young man lit a cigarette, then scanned through reports from the Israeli Mossad and the Italian Questiore, which told of Grigori's desperate itinerary following his flight from Germany to avoid prosecution—a route of flight known well to every SS officer and NSDAP official who'd found himself in the same situation—the BB-Axis, code name for the Bremen–Bari route, which took Doctor Grigori over the Brenner Pass into the South Tyrol, from there down into Rome, where travel papers were arranged for him through the offices of the Vatican. From there he traveled as Doctor Karl Geuske, a podiatrist from Bremen; a Mediterranean shuttle then took him to Barcelona and ultimately to La Coruña on the northwest tip of Iberia, where the Nazi underground railroad, Der Spinne (The Spider), had arranged for his passage on a packet boat to Argentina.

A secret report of the Guardia Civil in Barcelona went on to tell of Doctor Grigori's arrival in Buenos Aires in 1952, his prosperous practice as an abortionist, and his hasty, somewhat panicky, migration to Paraguay after the successful spiriting off to Israel of his old friend Adolf Eichmann.

When the young man looked up again from the assorted intelligence reports, it was well past midnight. He returned his papers to the manila portfolio and that in turn to the canvas haversack. Then he flicked out his light. Early the following morning he would be leaving directly for Asunción to keep an appointment with General Alfredo Stroessner, the president of the Republic of Paraguay, who had unwittingly deigned to see him.

CHAPTER 6

I suppose the fact that my work demanded that I use exclusively children for experimental purposes makes it peculiarly horrific to the laity and the uninformed. People have imputed vile and disgusting things to my preoccupation with these children. Some have dared to suggest that I was a child molester—an ogre—a homosexual, even. . . . They speak of me as if I were some mad monk out of the twelfth century, a Gilles de Raiz. That is laughable. The count was a perverted aristocrat, a lunatic diabolist. I was—I am—a scientist seeking only truth. It is true I experimented with children. But these children were under sentence of execution anyway. Doomed regardless of whatever I did. So why shouldn't I have used them? Why not, if the end result is enlightenment?

Science is not moral and it is childish to think that it is. The pursuit of knowledge is often ruthless and, indeed, it ought to be. It was that very ruthless *need to know*, to stop at nothing in order to know, that hauled man up out of the quadripedal position and made him walk upright.

Therefore, I will not apologize or make excuses. I did what I did because I believed it was right. I still do. I was never a war criminal. I was a scientist. What I did then I would do now. Unhesitatingly. If anything, thirty years of history as written by the egalitarian theoreticians of the post-war West has convinced me more than ever that I was right. Pigs are loose in the streets today. Genetic monstrosities and racial mongrels abound. Civilization, as we know it, is burning. The world lies in moral tatters. Pornography and degradation abound. The universe is contaminated with industrial filth and human waste. Governments are run by moral pederasts. International law, or what passes for it, is a shambles. All human institutions are in disarray. Anarchy and terror are everywhere. Shortly we return to the conditions of the Pleistocene. . . .

Doctor Gregor Grigori looked up suddenly from his writing. He was sprawled on a battered plastic garden chaise in the scruffy grass before his shed. The chair had several sprung slats, the ends of which dangled like serpents from its bottom in the grass below. In his old terry cloth robe of faded blue, at that hour of the afternoon the Doctor appeared slightly disreputable—an old pensioner in a transient hotel, down at the heels and living out the frayed ends of his life.

Putting aside his writing tablet now, the Doctor ate an orange and spat the pits and watched the detestable *cuchilleros* (knifers) swagger along the wire with the brace of drooling Dobermans in tow. As they passed he muttered an epithet beneath his breath, then cleared his throat and spat phlegm. Then he rose and hailed them. "Scum. Come here, scum." He smiled amiably at them, knowing they didn't understand a word of German. Smiling frostily, he slouched toward the wire, where he handed them fruits from the sagging pockets of his robe, afraid they might go. He knew, of course, they would go. The moment there was trouble they would turn tail and run, this swaggering, boastful scum with their pistols and rifles. These mule droppings flushed out of the sewers of Tembuco prison were his bodyguard. His corps d'élite.

"*Muchas gracias, Doctor,*" one of the curs with a huge lousy beard leered at him and waved through the wire.

"*Muchas gracias, Su Excelencia,*" the other crowed, bowing deeply and sweeping his hat mockingly before the Doctor.

"*De nada, de nada,*" Doctor Grigori smiled, thinking how slovenly and unkempt they were. What a far cry from the quality of soldier he had served with on the Russian front. The crack Viking Division—all spit and polish. These buffoons strode about in dirty fatigues with missing buttons, their boots fouled with dog-merde. Not at all the caliber of trooper he'd been accustomed to. Those were men—proud of the service. Proud of the calling. Proud of the sacrifice. These were low creatures. Criminals mostly. Genetic slime. Pederasts and unsalvageable refuse. Cannon fodder that *El Jefe* sent him, with all his great protestations of cordiality and support, while charging him extortionate prices for each, like heads of cattle. But, of course, they were the only ones available to do such filthy work.

"*Buenos días, soldaten,*" he saluted them with an equally mocking flourish.

"*Aiee, compañero,*" they cried. "*Adios. Adios.*"

Their voices rang down the jungle path where they strode along, already wolfing the fruit he'd given them, moving in their untidy, diurnal circuit around the mile-long barbed perimeter. The Doctor knew that once they got into the forest out of sight of the shed, they would snigger and make jokes about *el señor doctor, el gran fugitivo, el cobarde maricón.*

"Filthy swine," he muttered and lurched back to the chaise.

Ludo was there now with the decanter of cognac and a carafe of water—the predusk aperitif, taken with two small spansules, one of amyl nitrite and the other indiral, both of which bobbled now in a saucer on the tray. There, too, were his newspapers, flown in from the Fatherland. (Ironically, he still thought of Germany as that, even though they had disowned him long ago, banished him forever, uttering his name only in whispers and disgrace. Hypocrite pigs. They loved him when they were winning.) But here now were the tabloids and chronicles—a blessed whiff of home—*Stern, Deutschen Soldaten, Deutsche Zeitung Nationale.* Photographs of a park in Munich. The St. Pauli in Hamburg. A track meet at a stadium in Bonn. People taking the waters at Baden Baden. A Fasching festival at Heidelberg. Ah, blessed Deutschland—HOME.

He asked Ludo to turn up the phonograph, and shortly *Rienzi,* his favorite, came booming out over the crackling loudspeakers, crashing among the cypress and conifers in the forest, drowning out the awful din of crickets and crepuscular creatures that made his flesh crawl. He had a loathing of insects, particularly the great fat moths that came at twilight and collided at his windows and drummed at his screens, entered the shed and divebombed the lights with sickening thuds. Shortly the bug lights would go on in the garden, luring the creatures with sugary essences to a bright glowing electrical wire that would then fry them with loud, satisfying cracks.

Now, leaning back in the chaise, Doctor Grigori read until the twilight shadows crept across his page. When he looked up, the garden had gone purple and shortly the fireflies flickered about him like phantoms in a haunted garden.

The great red disc of dying sun hung tangled in the treetops over the Doctor's left shoulder. Staring down toward the river, he noted how the water had turned then from the color of coffee to the color of blood. After the rains, when the banks along the river swelled and the current quickened and roiled the red mud on the bottom, he saw the Paraná at sunset as a river of blood flowing past his door. It became a Phlegethon of the tropic zone, and in its swift tumultuous currents he often had a vision of innumerable heads, faceless and disembodied, bobbing swiftly past him on the choppy tide. What these phantom heads were, he could only guess. But it was a question he had learned to avoid. The image came to him, of necessity, only after the rainy season, early April, around Eastertide and the spring solstice when the sun lingered longer in the twilight sky. He had learned in the three years that he had been confined to Zone 540 to avoid the river during those times, for the image was profoundly unnerving. But otherwise he found the river a place of recreation, and a source of solace and renewal.

Ludo reappeared. Now that dusk had come on he wore an automatic pistol strapped on his hip. In his outstretched arms he carried tenderly, as if it were an ailing child, the Doctor's violin case. With punctilious ceremony he laid the case lengthwise on the table before the Doctor, then retracted his steps as noiselessly as he had come. In the next moment he had vanished utterly into the harsh white glare of the shed.

Alone again, presently the Doctor rose. He took the violin from its case and plucked the strings several times, his head tilted down toward the instrument, tuning it while its plangent strains struck hard against the hot, still air of the garden.

Standing there and tottering slightly, the violin tucked beneath his fleshy chin, his spindly bowed legs, white as parchment and scored with varicosities, sticking out from beneath the frayed terry robe, he made a curious sight. Shortly he turned and faced the river. The broad Paraná stretched languid and still before him, a gaudy red ribbon strung between Paraguay and Brazil. It was already dark on the Brazilian side where the forest lay like a wall of black. In that forest he imagined the panther crouching at the water hole where the deer had stooped to drink. He thought he could hear the creature's husky bark carrying across the water. It was from that direction that he knew his death would come.

Now with the violin clamped firmly beneath his chin, Doctor Grigori faced the encroaching darkness, palpable and violet, creeping over the muddy water toward him, and he proceeded to play.

CHAPTER 7

Every morning, including Saturdays, *El Jefe, El Supremo, El Presidente,* General Alfredo Stroessner arrives at the Government Palace at 6:30 AM and goes directly to his "White House" located next to the Palace on the Plaza Constitución in the center of Asunción.

The General arrives in a chauffeur-driven Chevrolet Impala. When his car pulls up to the Palace gates, the military police snap to attention, clicking their heels and thrusting smartly out from the chest their bright new Russian-made AK–47s. Instantly all other pedestrians are cleared from the area. Shortly the gates are thrown open and the Chevrolet glides through the two big white marble stanchions and onto the Palace grounds. Some time later the ministers begin to arrive, also in Chevrolet Impalas, and for each arrival, pedestrians are similarly swept from the site.

If the President should deign to see you, your audience will no doubt be early, say around eight AM. You will find him in his office seated behind an enormous desk of mahogany above which hangs a portrait of Francisco López, Paraguay's greatest warrior and hero.

President Stroessner is a large-boned man, beefy yet muscular, approximately 1.80 meters in height and now in his mid to late sixties.

He has gray eyes and reddish-brown hair. Very often it is his custom to affect the same uniform as that worn by López, hanging there so imperiously above him, and to carry a cane like Marshal Goering. He has a corps of personal bodyguards, all strapping big fellows, all 1.80 meters in height just like him. They are commanded by a former Waffen–SS man by the name of Lieutenant Otto H. Buechner. Every morning, as Stroessner has his breakfast in the office, the elite guard plays for him records of "Mi Viejo Amigo," followed by highly spirited Bavarian marching music, of the thudding, "um pah pah" variety.

Alfredo Stroessner is a native-born Paraguayan of German descent. His grandfather, of whom he is very proud, was a Bavarian cavalry captain. His own parents emigrated to Paraguay after World War I and never again returned to the Fatherland.

Stroessner is the twenty-second president Paraguay has had in the last twenty years. He was an artillery commander in the army and came to power at the age of forty-three after a particularly bloody coup d'état. Since his ascendancy to the supreme executive position of the country, he has built factories and roads, reformed the incredible bureaucratic corruption, and made Asunción one of the cleanest and most efficient cities in Latin America. Also one of the most repressive. Today the people sing heroic songs about him, such as "Onward, Onward, My General," while looking uneasily over their shoulders for the ubiquitous *federales*.

Everything in Paraguay is named after the General —the streets, the ports, the schools, the parks, the boulevards. Some are called Colonel Stroessner, some Major Stroessner, and some General Stroessner or Presidente Stroessner. They describe perfectly the trajectory of *El Jefe*'s meteoric ascent in Paraguayan affairs. When you ask why this is so, people will tell you that it is quite simply because *El Presidente* ordered it so.

The only newspaper in opposition to the *Jefe*'s Red Party ("Red" has nothing to do with Communism here, quite emphatically the opposite) was *El Día de Asunción*. In one of their more acerbic editorials they had the egregious bad taste to suggest that "all we need now is Baby Stroessner Boulevard." Shortly after that impudent suggestion, the paper was dismantled and closed down.

This morning, however, *El Presidente* was wearing a brown tweed suit of fine English cloth. When the young man was ushered into his office, the General was just then signing a number of documents at a dizzying speed while a steady flow of people interrupted him and the phone rang incessantly.

Stroessner himself was very spry and alert, even though the night before he had drunk six full glasses of Vat 69 scotch whiskey and innumerable bottles of Kulmbacher Munchoff, his favorite beer. He'd probably had no more than three hours of sleep at the most.

At a certain point in the interview, a butler in starched livery entered and served coffee in small Meissen cups.

The young man had introduced himself as David Bar Levin, a historian from the Hebrew University in Jerusalem. He was attired that morning in the typical manner of an academic—coarse tweeds and frayed linen—clean, utterly correct, and slightly seedy. Along with the normal documents of identification, he had also presented to the President's first secretary top-priority diplomatic papers from the Israeli *chargé d'affaires* in Asunción. His particular period of interest, the young man said, was the Nazi era, and he had come to Paraguay to study firsthand the "Diaspora" of Nazis throughout Latin America following the war. He used the word "Diaspora" quite ironically.

The President was flattered to be interviewed by such a brilliant young scholar, but the subject matter made him distinctly uneasy. When they started to speak specifically about the "fugitive" question, the President suddenly switched from Spanish to German so as not to be understood by the clerks and secretaries who flowed constantly through the room.

"It is a lie that my government protects former Nazis," he remarked curtly. "Anyone who so believes should go out and try to find them."

He went on to tell the young man how he had cooperated with the Bonn government, the United Nations, and the War Crimes Commission to bring to justice those war criminals who might have come to Paraguay for sanctuary.

The President proclaimed this solemnly, with great force and sincerity. He was convincing. But then the young man asked him what would happen if Stroessner were to cooperate with the West Germans and the Israelis, the Russians and the Americans in the matter of extradition of Nazi fugitives seeking asylum in his country? What would happen to the broad support he gets, both moral and financial, from the wealthy and powerful resettled Germans living in Paraguay?

"Absolutely nothing," the General said huffily, waving the question aside as if it were irrelevant. He then went into a lengthy explanation of the long-established tradition of the "host" nation as it applied not only in Paraguay but in all Latin American countries.

"In my country if a man is a guest in your home, even if you have known him to have done wrong, his position in your home is sacred, and you are honor-bound to protect him. Once he leaves there, however, that's another story." The General smiled, much pleased with the logic of his paradigm.

"Where then," the young man asked point-blank, "is Doctor Grigori?"

For a long while the General gazed at the young historian, his features as impassive as if he were staring at a wall. At last he cleared his throat and said, "Doctor Grigori? I know no Doctor Grigori."

"Well then," the young man had the temerity to persist, "would it be possible for me to examine the files of the Policía Central de Paraguay in the matter of Doctor Grigori?"

"No," the President snapped emphatically. "Secret police files are privileged information. *Chito*," he said, meaning "quiet" or "top secret," then rose and extended a hand to his visitor, at which time the young man was given to understand that the audience was over.

CHAPTER 8

"On 25 NB3 there is no other defense against the threat of 26 N–Q5. It is possible to compel a piece sacrifice by 26 B–B1, R×R; 27 R×R, N×KP; 28 P×N, Q×P, but there is no need to give sly old Fritz any swindling chances, particularly when 26 B–B4 ch, K–R1; 27 Q–K6 has forced Black into a lost ending."

It had gone full dark now and all the lights in the clapboard shed were turned up. Outside the shed the small jungle clearing glowed like a jeweled tiara, harsh and white under the 16,000-watt floodlights illuminating the compound. The dogs, unleashed by their keepers and set free for the night to roam the grounds, had commenced their baying, while the *cuchilleros* caroused and laughed richly in the shadows around the barbed wire perimeter. It sometimes amused Doctor Grigori, twitted his sense of irony, that his survival now depended upon his ability to live in an establishment that resembled nothing so much as an internment camp.

Inside, Doña Esmeralda, the ancient mestizo housekeeper, was cleaning up after dinner. Grigori sat back now in a lounge and lit a cigarette. Björling's "Nessun Dorma" crackled on the phonograph. After dark his taste in music tended more toward the sentimental than the heroic, which he reserved for the dazzling light of day. The music wafted softly through speakers into the Doctor's library, where he sat now before the chessboard which had been set up before the fire. The game he was preoccupied with just then had been going on for several months—a long-distance correspondence match, a mortal struggle between himself and his old friend Fritz Streckenbach, like himself a fugitive war hero, spurned and discarded by the Fatherland during the shameful period of the capitulation and, like himself, forced into hiding, holed up like a rat somewhere in Lima.

Doctor Grigori had bathed and dressed for dinner. He bathed every night with almost hieratic zeal, scouring in soapy, steaming water, priding himself on his impeccable personal hygiene, even under the most trying of circumstances. It was his custom to dress formally each night and to require his two young companions who joined him at table to dress that way as well.

This evening, Doctor Grigori wore a white linen jacket with a pale blue shirt of chambray and a black bow tie. He sat now before the fire in his library drinking cognac and meditating on the chessboard before him. It was mostly after sunset that he commenced his drinking.

Champagne—Roederer '53 during dinner; then afterward in his library, listening to Verdi or Puccini or Mahler, he would drink fine old cognac—all flown into 540 twice a month from Asunción, courtesy of the Paraguayan Army. Then he would write letters or talk into his Dictaphone, ever adding to his voluminous memoirs. With the posthumous publication of these memoirs he felt certain his name and reputation would be vindicated. But, more importantly, the scientific work of four decades would be hailed as a boon to mankind rather than a scourge. He was engaged now on a manuscript that he believed to be his crowning achievement: "Morphological Differences of the Jaw in Four Distinct Racial Types."

Doctor Grigori glanced up out of his reverie to find

young Ludo Von Rattenhuber standing there above him, unwilling to break the Doctor's thread of concentration.

"We're ready to go out to the airstrip now, Herr Doktor," Ludo announced with almost hushed awe.

The Doctor stared at him blankly, rather like a man who'd been rudely jolted from sleep. "Ah, yes," he sighed, and slapped both knees as recognition flowed back in upon him. In the next moment he rose stiffly from his seat.

CHAPTER 9

"Five Johnnie Walker."

"Five cases Johnnie Walker."

"Five cases Roederer."

"Five Roederer."

"Three cases Hennessy 5 Star."

"Three Hennessy 5 Star."

"Ten cartons Marlboro cork-tipped. Eight cases Rameses supreme, extra dark."

A short time later that evening two men stood in the clammy shadows of the jungle shouting numbers at each other. One scribbled hastily on a wire clipboard. The other, using the illumination of a small pencil torchlight, cried out descriptions and numbers from a bill of lading.

They stood at the edge of a small landing in a makeshift jungle clearing while a small Beechcraft Twin, its motors idling, its props pinging, waited like an impatient grasshopper at the edge of the runway.

The plane's cargo hold was open, and three Indians from the Macá reservation a few kilometers to the north bowed and stooped and, grunting with the effort, passed crates and cartons down from the yawning bay doors and out to the surplus U.S. Army field truck parked just beneath the plane's wings.

Within the warm roseate glow of the cabin, the head of a large black man could be seen. The gay red epaulettes of a police uniform were visible just above the line of the fuselage. He wore a large pair of headphones on his ears and, from the satisfied expression on his face, he appeared to be listening to music. From time to time he leaned forward, pressing his face against the cabin glass and grinning toothily down at the people on the runway as if he were pleased with their progress.

At the northernmost extreme of the clearing, in the cool, moist shadows of the forest, a half-dozen or so *cuchilleros* stood casually smoking and chatting, observing phlegmatically the action on the runway while moonlight glistened from the metal of their gun barrels.

"Three cases pâté de foie gras."

"Three pâté."

"Three bushels strawberries."

"Three strawberry."

"Five kilos Iranian, extra-fine malassol."

"Five kilo Iranian."

The two men carried on their antiphonal shouting above the cough and ping of the plane's engines. The one crying out descriptions and numbers from a bill of lading was Colonel Félix Arganas, *Jefe de Policía de Seguridad*. The one answering him and scribbling onto the clipboard was Horst Matschke, the Doctor's other young companion.

Arganas was dressed in jodhpurs, riding boots, and the tunic of a Paraguayan Army colonel and, although the night was suffocating, he wore the tunic buttoned

to his throat. He was a small, fierce-looking fellow with
a cold smile frozen unchangingly into rather handsome
features. Consummately military in his demeanor, he
held himself with the rigidity of a man who'd lived ac-
cording to the tenets of some stern personal code for
the better part of his life. He carried a riding crop,
too, although he rode no horse. And, while he was
much decorated for bravery, he affected neither medals
nor ribbons. At forty he was unmarried, and there was
something distinctly austere, even jesuitical, in his manner. A born Paraguayan, he was fiercely proud of his
heritage.

Standing quietly in the shadows just behind Matschke
was Doctor Grigori, dressed somewhat incongruously
for this wild place in his formal dinner attire, as if he
had just come from, or was possibly just on his way to,
a dress ball. The orange glow from his cigarette in-
scribed long, leisurely arcs against the inky dark.

"Ten cases quinine water," the Colonel cried. "Ten
cases Coca-Cola. Ten cases Vichy water."

"Is that it now?"

"That's it."

"Any pastries, cakes, fresh croissants?"

"Not this time. My infernal bakers were arrested last
week."

Matschke shrugged and screwed the cap back onto
his fountain pen. "Too bad. Doña Esmeralda will be
disappointed."

The Colonel folded his invoice and handed it to
the young man. "Convey to Doña Esmeralda my regrets. I'll try to do better for her the next time."

Matschke handed the invoice to Doctor Grigori, who
had stepped suddenly out of the shadows to take it.
Sauntering slowly toward the others, he glanced over
it. When he reached the Colonel he stared up at him,
smiling a little sardonically, out of the monocle he

wore to mitigate the crooked cast of his features. "You do not want to disappoint Esmeralda too often, Colonel. As we all know, that can be bad luck, ay, Horst?"

The young man laughed along with the Doctor. The laugh was overly hearty and a trifle forced—the laugh of a man who knew he was obliged to be greatly amused.

In the next moment the Colonel cracked the clipboard against his thigh to signal the conclusion of their meeting. He extended a small, rather delicate hand to the Doctor. "We'd best be off now. The weather control people are predicting electric storms all the way down to Asunción this evening." Colonel Arganas turned on his heel as if to start back for the plane.

"Colonel," the Doctor called after him.

The Colonel turned and stared back at Grigori, who had just then withdrawn a thick white envelope from the inside pocket of his jacket.

"Aren't you forgetting something?" the Doctor asked.

The Colonel smiled, and his hand rose at once to accept the monthly stipend. As he did so, he held the envelope for a while in the palm of his hand as if he were mentally calculating its weight. Then he smiled apologetically. "I'm afraid it will be necessary to discuss cost adjustments again with you very soon, Doctor."

As he regarded Arganas in the dim glow of the cabin lights, Doctor Grigori's crooked features grew suddenly even more crooked. "But did we not just have a cost adjustment only two months ago?" His voice was husky and low. Inside the cabin of the plane he could see the grinning black man lean forward to watch. He was aware, too, of Horst at his right turning to observe the anticipated scene.

"Ah, yes," Arganas sighed. "Quite true. How distressing this disease of inflation. Everything is so costly these days. Particularly protection, Doctor. The gunboats that we send up here. And the munitions. Not to mention the *cuchilleros*."

"The *cuchilleros* are worthless," the Doctor fumed openly. "Lazy. Undisciplined. Rude . . ."

Arganas preferred to ignore these cavils.

"And, of course, the operation of my own personal plane at this remote stretch of the river."

"May I remind you, Colonel, I did not ask to be banished to this filthy swamp."

The Colonel's eyebrow rose. "Swamp? That strikes me as ungrateful."

"Ungrateful?" The monocle dropped from Grigori's eye and dangled loose for a moment on its chain. "Am I not grateful enough? Do I not express sufficient gratitude each month to every official of this nation from His Excellency on down to the lowest thieving petty official?"

"I don't think you appreciate what a high cost in terms of money, not to mention world opinion, this nation has paid for the luxury of keeping you here."

"Only too well do I appreciate it." Grigori struggled to control his rage. "But I refuse to be fleeced every month by a lot of grasping officials, who . . . What about my son?"

The Colonel stared at him. He knew this was where his leverage lay.

Grigori persisted. "Have you discussed the matter of my son with His Excellency, as you promised you would?"

A peeved, slightly impatient expression played about the Colonel's lips. He sighed wearily before he spoke. "His Excellency wishes you to know that he is personally delighted about your son's impending visit. Having sons of his own, he is extremely sympathetic to your request."

Doctor Grigori began to seethe. This elaborate and

careful phrasing sounded to him like the preamble to a refusal.

"But while His Excellency is sympathetic," the Colonel continued, savoring the painful prolongation of his reply, "he also wishes to stress that our nation is presently in the midst of very delicate credit negotiations with the governments of West Germany and the United States. Having denied for so long to both embassies in Asunción that you are in Paraguay and that we know anything of your whereabouts, you realize it would be extremely embarrassing for His Excellency . . ."

"Embarrassing?" Doctor Grigori felt his cheks flame.

". . . were you to suddenly appear in Asunción."

"May I remind you—" the Doctor stiffened and the *cuchilleros* shuffled forward out of the shadows the better to overhear—"there are many people in this country to whom I am still a national hero. I am sorry that His Excellency considers me an embarrassment. He is, however, never too embarrassed to accept my money."

The Colonel frowned and wagged his finger as if to caution Grigori against any further disrespect.

"So, he denies me," the Doctor continued bitingly.

"I did not say that. What I was about to say before you interrupted me was that His Excellency is a very generous man. He grants you two days in Asunción and two days in Encarnación at the end of this month. His Excellency only wishes to stress that you be discreet. Stay out of public places, particularly those frequented by the diplomatic corps. Make certain to call no attention to yourself and keep, as the Americans say, a low profile."

Doctor Grigori nearly leaped into the air. He was like a small boy granted a precious privilege.

"I will," he enthused gratefully and seized the Colonel's hand. "I will. Tell His Excellency he can depend

upon me. I shall be quiet as a church mouse. No one
will see me. No one will know I'm there. Thank His
Excellency for me."

The Colonel withdrew his hand abruptly, feathers
still ruffled, refusing to be placated.

Grigori went on now anxiously. "I shall be delighted
to discuss the matter of all necessary increments to your
monthly retainer, Colonel. Here, let me add something
to that." He plucked the envelope from the Colonel's
hand, proceeded to stuff a number of additional bills
into it, and quickly thrust the envelope back at him.

"I don't want it, thank you," Arganas snapped and
started for the plane.

Grigori followed quickly after him. "Come. Take it.
Don't be foolish. I put an extra thousand in."

"I cannot accept it, since you obviously feel you're
being cheated."

"I never said I was being cheated."

"Your manner suggests it."

"Take the money." Grigori pursued him toward the
plane, forcing the envelope into the Colonel's tunic
pocket. Once again Arganas swept it aside.

"You're being ridiculous," Grigori muttered.

"Perhaps." The Colonel put his foot on the boarding
ladder and started up. "But I cannot accept fees from
a dissatisfied client."

Just then they saw the black man in the cabin. He
appeared to be laughing and pointing at the Doctor,
making inaudible sounds behind the glass of the fuselage.

"What does he want now?" Grigori fumed.

For a moment the black man disappeared into the
nether regions of the plane, only to reappear at a side
door which had swung open, revealing the man, a giant
of nearly seven feet, standing behind yet another figure.
Upon closer inspection Doctor Grigori observed that

the second figure was that of a woman. She was young, possibly twenty or so. Small, dark, pretty, and probably Indian or mestizo, she was something Arganas had no doubt collected during the course of one of his numerous sweeps through the bars and brothels of Asunción. She was attired only in a light slip and she appeared to be cold and frightened.

"It appears, Doctor," Arganas sulked moodily, "that *Negrón* has brought you a little something to have with your pâté and champagne." Without further ado, the Colonel swept coldly up the boarding ladder and climbed into his cabin. He was clearly unhappy, and it was not good for Arganas to be unhappy, the Doctor knew only too well.

Grigori's eyes strayed to the side door where *El Negrón* just then was guiding, or rather pushing, the young girl in the slip ahead of him. Now he more or less shoved her directly at the Doctor. *"Buena salud, Doctor."* His voice was sonorous and lilting. His eyes twinkled with impudence—a huge, playful fellow, but with an undertone of something distinctly dangerous. "May I have the honor to present to you Señorita Ibis?"

Once again he thrust the girl toward Grigori, who stood there impassive, the fat white envelope drooping in his hand.

"She will give you much pleasure." *El Negrón* laughed, and as he did so he swept the envelope out of the Doctor's hand. *"Buenos días. Hasta luego. Buena salud, Doctor."* He grinned, bowed in a most courtly manner from the waist, and tipped his hat. Then he turned and scrambled back up the ladder and slammed the door of the plane behind him.

Shortly the little Beechcraft Twin was bouncing and rattling down the dirt runway, its wings flapping hectically like a fat, squawking goose unable to get itself aloft. Gradually, however, with a dark bank of conifer rushing ominously toward it, the plane lifted its wheels and rose, barely clearing the treetops lining the dark river.

Once up over the forest, the plane banked and circled the runway, shining below like a great cross in the wilderness, lit by kerosene flambeaux. From his place in the cockpit, the Colonel watched the two yellow beams from the jeep's headlamps sweep about as it started to back off the runway. The Beechcraft now veered sharply right, climbing all the while into the huge, starry vault above the water, the red radio light pulsing in her nose, beaming them southward, back toward Asunción.

If there was a semblance of order in Paraguay, it was due to these two gentlemen—Colonel Félix Arganas and his enforcer, *El Negrón*. Together, they were the backbone of Paraguayan justice.

For instance, if you had a penchant for revolutionary or otherwise seditious activity in that small nation, or if, for some reason, you were dissatisfied with the present regime and sought reforms, you had inevitably to deal with Arganas and his first mate, *El Negrón*. In short time the Colonel, no doubt, would cool your ardor for change by having you taken to Tembuco prison, there stripped naked, beaten with rubber truncheons, and dipped into a tub of ice cold water, while a near-lethal current of electricity was passed through your body. Or possibly he would have you submerged headfirst into an open cesspool, ripe and pulsing with feces, and leave you hanging there upside down for several hours. That generally served to stanch one's zeal for social justice. At least, very few such people ever saw fit to disturb the peace again.

Or if you had a grievance in Asunción—any grievance whatever—it was well known that you could seek redress by applying directly to Arganas. Assume you were a businessman and you had an outstanding debt you were unable to collect. When all known methods of civilized persuasion had failed, your next recourse would be to take the matter up directly with the Colonel.

The Colonel would listen politely to what you had to say, all the while nodding his head sympathetically. At the conclusion of your appeal he would rise, put his arm comfortingly about your shoulder, and walk you to the door, adjuring you as you went to put the matter out of your head. The debt would be retired and, although no collection fee would be mentioned, it was understood that it would be in the neighborhood of fifty percent of the outstanding sum.

Shortly after your visit to Arganas, *El Negrón,* the collector himself, would be sent round to visit the derelict account. At first *El Negrón* would smile and chat cordially with the person, inquiring after his health and his family. Then he would turn to the business at hand. Generally, the mere appearance of this laughing giant at one's door would be enough to make the most recalcitrant of debtors relent. But if cordiality failed, the collector would then break fingers, one at a time. For the more stubborn accounts, he would move on to the legs. The most intransigent would suffer concussions or have their backs broken, but in the end they would always honor their debts. For this service *El Negrón* would levy a collector's tax of ten percent. A part of his service would be to return the outstanding debt to the client personally. Thus, justice would be served in Asunción, even if it did cost you as much as sixty cents on the dollar. But it was well known from this display of swift judicial redress that in Papa Stroessner's Paraguay, there was no room for welchers.

For some time after they had departed from Zone 540, no words had passed between Arganas and *El*

Negrón. The small cramped cabin had grown stiflingly hot from engine heat, and everything in it vibrated wildly.

A grim, darkening scowl about his face, Arganas sat at the controls smoldering with anger. It was a mood that most of his colleagues and subordinates, those that lasted anyway, knew enough to be wary of. When that sort of thing was afoot with the Colonel, these people knew enough to scurry down the nearest hole and cower there till the storm blew over. Only his old, and possibly closest, friend, *El Negrón* (no one really knew the origin or basis of their improbable alliance), had the temerity to approach the Colonel during these stormy episodes.

El Negrón had been sitting stolid and silent like a large granite boulder for the past three-quarters of an hour. Silence, however, was not his forte. Suddenly he leaned forward and, with Doctor Grigori's thick white pay envelope, he tapped Arganas on his epaulettes, causing several bills to spill out and onto the Colonel's lap. Partly startled, partly outraged by such insolence, Arganas whirled about, ready to rail and snarl. But then he saw the big envelope resting lightly on the epaulette of his tunic and, behind that, the great shiny moon of *El Negrón*'s face grinning amiably at him from out of the cabin's shadows. A great load lifted from the Colonel's heart and suddenly the two men were laughing—roaring and hooting, bellowing merrily, all the way back down to Asunción. For Arganas, the successful bilking of Doctor Grigori was a source of the deepest personal pleasure.

CHAPTER 10

Doctor Grigori woke suddenly from a dream. He did
not recall the content of the dream, but something
within it had bolted him sharply upright. Bathed in
sweat and panting, he sat in bed now, flanks heaving
like a hounded animal. He thought for a moment that
he'd heard the sound of screaming but he wasn't at all
certain if these sounds, now faint and receding, came
from outside somewhere in the dark, encroaching forest
or from inside, within his dreams—strange, indeterminate sounds—sometimes shrill like someone screaming. Sometimes the sound seemed to originate from a
single source; sometimes from a communal one—many
people screaming.

It was nearly two AM and all the lights burned in
Doctor Grigori's bedroom, for the Doctor would not
sleep in a darkened room. He insisted that all the
lights be lit at dusk and not extinguished until dawn.

In the next moment he heard a sound outside his
room. Breathing or snuffling, it was, as if someone were
standing out on the verandah there in the pale moonlight, observing him through the windows. Then he
heard the unmistakable whisper of footsteps moving
through grass.

The Doctor sat there paralyzed. Once again it came,
that sound of something moving outside just beyond
the window. He made a small, whimpering sound like
a child on the verge of tears, then suddenly he shouted
at the top of his lungs, waving his hands wildly above

his head, as if he were fighting off some invisible intruder. The mestizo girl, who had been sleeping beside
him, bolted up, her eyes wide with terror. In the next
moment, Horst and Ludo, both brandishing Lugers,
burst into the room. *"Was ist?"* They peered round,
yanking open closet doors. Esmeralda in a nightcap
and belting her robe followed soon after, perplexed and
moving her lips soundlessly.

"Outside," Grigori gasped, and pointed to the window. He was still sitting upright in the dishevelment of
his bed, flailing his arms and gesticulating wildly.
"Someone outside there. Looking in."

The two bodyguards streamed out of the bedroom,
out the front door, and into the night.

"Kill them," Grigori shrieked after them. "Get them.
Kill the bastards. Blow their goddamned heads off."

The young girl sitting in bed cringed beneath the
sheets, as if she wanted to cover either her nakedness
or her fright.

Outside, they could hear the barking of the dogs and
the shouting of the *cuchilleros* running on the footpaths
around the shed. Shortly there was a pistol shot and in
the next moment Matschke tramped back into the
room, a huge grin upon his face. He carried a huge
furry gray-brown creature, a capibara, hefting the giant
rodent upside down by the tail. It had been shot in the
back and its spine broken, but it was still alive and in
terrible pain. As it thrashed and flailed against
Matschke's leg, it made a fierce, chattering sound.

"Here's your intruder, Herr Doktor." Matschke
beamed triumphantly. Ludo stood behind him with a
smoking Luger. "He was into the trash pits."

Grigori gaped at the jerking, twisting, panic-stricken
thing dangling there before him. Outside the windows
of the room, two swarthy *cuchilleros* grinned toothily

and pointed fingers at *"el doctor cobarde maricón"* and the naked girl cowering beneath the sheets.

Dangling inverted by the tail, the huge rat dripped blood through its mouth onto the rug. Its anguished stricken chatter made an awful racket.

Grigori put his hands up before his eyes. "Get it out of here. For Christ's sake, get it the hell out of here."

When they had at last disposed of the animal, Horst and Ludo came back to the room to make certain that everything was in order. By that time Grigori appeared to have recovered some of his composure and most of his arrogance. He blustered now and grew abusive. "I knew it was nothing." He laughed and made a series of grunting noises. "I knew it was only an animal. Did you think I didn't know that? I just wanted to see how alert you all were. How fast you could get in here."

The two young men looked at each other knowingly. That was unfortunate, for the Doctor caught the exchange of glances and it infuriated him.

"You were slow," he sneered. "Much too slow."

The young men stood there, heads lowered, like mischievous puppies accepting chastisement. When the Doctor had vented his spleen sufficiently, they murmured good night and left.

"Too goddamned slow," Grigori bellowed after them, and shouted for cognac.

Several hours later, when he awoke in the predawn chill of his bedroom, he had no recollection at all of the events that had transpired only hours before.

Doctor Grigori lay back in his pillows then, shivering a little and rubbing his eyes to adjust them to the gray, nacreous light. His head throbbed, for he had drunk too much the night before. Shortly, the comfort of familiarity was rushing back in upon him and he peered into the shadow-shrouded room about him.

Looking backward and above his head, the first thing

his still-woozy eyes discerned was an old wood crucifix of Indian design hanging above his bed. One foot was broken off the Christ and its nose had vanished, leaving only a vacant, termite-ridden hole in its place. It bore a sorrowful expression—full of infinite pity.

In the corner, rumpled, balled up, and wadded, where they'd been tossed, were his trousers with the braces dangling like serpents on the floor. Atop that was his shirt, ripped down the back. A chair was overturned and there was some broken crockery. He remembered at one point flinging a vase and a door slamming, then a woman screaming. Then, off to the side, he saw a small grayish pile of feminine undergarments strewn in a sour heap across the back of a chair; further on, to the right of that, a pair of ladies' stockings dangling like filmy threads from the rim of a lampshade.

It was then he remembered the night before and the Indian girl. One of Arganas' whores, Grigori thought bitterly. At least once a month the Colonel brought the Doctor a whore. Usually they were young Indian girls from the nearby Macá reservation a few kilometers to the north. Tired, drab, utterly dispirited creatures, there was little they would not do for a few paltry *guaranís*. But occasionally the Colonel would scrounge up a European, a stranded dancer who'd come to Buenos Aires or Asunción to dance, so she thought, at the Opera House or the ballet, and wound up, instead, performing "exotic" dances in the disreputable saloons along the Estrella and trying to work her passage back to the Continent.

Now suddenly the sight of the woman in his bed beneath the crucifix disgusted him. Her face was badly bruised. The eye had been blackened and swollen shut. Her lower lip was split in the center and crusted over by an unsightly scab that dangled revoltingly. In addition, there were ghastly purple welts about her head.

Even in her sleep she appeared to cower at the edge of the bed as if she feared being struck again.

Aware of his own discomfort, Grigori gazed down at his hands. The knuckles cut and painfully swollen caused in him a sudden urge for contrition. He wanted to pray for forgiveness. He knew it was he who had beaten the girl the night before, but exactly why or how, he had no recollection. It was after the filthy business with the capíbara, he knew. He'd been edgy and unsettled, unable to get back to sleep. He remembered calling for cognac and Esmeralda's bringing him a bottle. Then he recalled sending everyone away but the girl and, together, the two of them, draining off in swift, resolute draughts nearly two-thirds of the bottle. Lastly, he recalled the shattering glass and the screams, then waking several hours later in the morning with the poor, battered thing cringing there beside him.

It had happened often enough in the past for him to know the pattern of it—Arganas bringing him some *puta* from the stews of Ascunción, presumably for his pleasure; and then the lengthy, almost ritualistic preamble to the brutal mess that was predestined to follow. Before dinner, he would insist that she bathe and that she anoint herself with all manner of cosmetics and fragrances. Esmeralda would lay out a fresh wardrobe for her—everything from undergarments and hosiery right up to a long white evening dress curiously suggestive of a bridal gown.

The puzzled girl would be offered cocktails in the library and then taken into dinner. Throughout the course of the meal, recorded music would play softly in the background and the Doctor would be assiduous in his attentions. His manner with such women was invariably gentle, solicitous, even courtly. He would attend to their every need. But, as the evening wore on and he continued to drink more and more, this manner would slowly change. There was no question of sex with such women. Women of this stripe revolted him. However, the act of administering physical punishment to such a woman accomplished for him the same thing as sex. Such bouts generally lasted from one half hour to an hour and, at their conclusion, he felt himself spent, emptied, and wonderfully released.

Gazing down once more at the battered, sleeping form in his bed, he felt a vague twinge of pity, followed by a rush of horror. Like refuse, he wanted the thing swept quickly and efficiently out of his sight.

He was about to prod her, rouse her, and send her off but just as he raised his hand to do so, a fly strolled out of her ear onto the pillow, where it sat for a moment rubbing its forepaws. A wave of revulsion swept over him. *"Puta,"* he muttered, slipped from the bed, then washed and dressed quickly.

Doctor Grigori's daily regimen began with nearly a half hour of calisthenics. Finally, at 6:30 he slipped into a pair of bathing trunks and rubber thongs, threw on his old frayed terry cloth robe and stepped out into the hazy morning sunlight. As soon as he emerged into the light of day, he was joined by Horst and Ludo, who'd been outside, jogging, warming up, and waiting for the Doctor to make his appearance.

Horst Matschke and Ludo Von Rattenhuber were Doctor Grigori's protégés. They lived together with him in his several residences and traveled inseparably about the country with him.

Referred to euphemistically as "companions" or "houseboys," Horst and Ludo were in truth bodyguards rigorously trained and bred to a hair-trigger readiness in the pursuit and execution of their duties. Doctor Grigori referred to them affectionately as *"Meine zwei Wachenhunde,"* and, indeed, they were very much like two watchdogs, affectionate, loyal, vigilant, fiercely protective of their master, and lethal to all potential intruders. Needless to say, they were a source of profound comfort to the Doctor.

Now Doctor Grigori and his two young *Wachenhunde* jogged out of the barbed-wire perimeter of the compound and onto the dirt serpentine that led through the forest down to the river. The Doctor looked strangely incongruous trotting between the two strapping youths.

A few yards down the path they came upon one of the *cuchilleros,* who was supposed to have been on guard there all night. Sprawling on the ground and dozing against the bole of a tree, he stirred in his dreams, swiping at a fly buzzing desultorily about his nose. Shortly he fell back into a deep snoring sleep, an Uzi submachine gun cradled lovingly in his arms.

The three men paused there for a while and gazed down at the sleeping figure. It was impossible to judge from the blank, impassive expression on Doctor Grigori's face what thoughts ran through his head as he viewed this untidy sight. He stood there for what seemed an unnaturally long period of time. Then, quite suddenly, he nudged the man gently with his foot.

The eyelids of the *cuchillero* fluttered. He gasped and started up. But in the next instant Horst had snatched the gun from his lax grip, then kicked him hard in the ribs. The man grunted and doubled up in pain and came fully awake. With his eyes now opened fully, the first thing he saw was the cold hard barrel of his own submachine gun pressed hard against his temple, and then the three figures looming above him.

Grigori said nothing to the slovenly guard—the look of disgust on his features said all that was necessary. In the next moment the Doctor turned sharply on his heel and proceeded down the dirt path, followed by

Ludo. Horst, still hovering above the sprawled figure, waited a moment, then placed the barrel between the terrified man's eyes. The guard whimpered slightly, then started to tremble.

But instead of firing, Horst drove the gun barrel heavily down into the man's groin. There was a bellow of pain, then Horst turned and strode quickly out through the mist-hung forest after the two figures moving toward the river.

Once out on the white plank dock, Horst and Ludo quickly peeled off their clothing and dove in naked. The water was still cool from the night. Shuddering, Doctor Grigori dropped his robe and slipped from the dock ladder into the brown slick current. He was not a strong swimmer and he paddled about, breast stroking, his chin elevated high out of the water, several feet from the dock like a retrieving dog, quarry in muzzle, looking for a place to land.

The boys darted and swam about him. There was much laughter and horsing about. Shortly, Grigori slipped off his suit as well and flung it up on the dock. Then all three cavorted about in the oily water.

Twenty or so feet out from the dock, the Doctor's huge pleasure launch, the *Viking,* named after his SS division, bobbed gently on the current.

Grigori paddled about, kicking and splashing, trying not to feel the vague twinges of pain in his chest, ignoring them and testing them at the same time. Were they real or imaginary? He couldn't tell. Nevertheless, he swam about vigorously, keeping up with his young companions, seemingly as youthful as they. For several moments he lay on his back watching warily for the large alligators that occasionally drifted downriver from the swamps of the Chagras above. Then he gazed across at the low, huddled line of forest that marked the Brazilian shore. A gray, hazy light hovered above it, making it seem oddly forbidding. His feet struck a cold pool beneath him and he shuddered. Suddenly, he turned, swam back to the dock, and lumbered, dripping and weary, out of the water.

8:20. Having showered and shaved, Doctor Grigori, still in his robe, lingered over breakfast. He ate a dish of guava and cold mangoes, then black coffee and croissant served by Horst on the sun-flooded patio at the rear of the shed, while the strains of *Tannhäuser* booming on the phonograph inside wafted out over the jungle landscape. He smoked one of his small pastel Egyptian cigarettes, drank another coffee, and proceeded to write a letter to his son.

It was a long, rambling letter, full of cheer, gossip, and good will, recording fully the Doctor's successful meeting with Colonel Arganas the night before. The long-desired, long-awaited trip had at last been sanctioned by *El Presidente*. There were no further obstacles to their reunion. They would be together again in a matter of weeks and, oh, what pleasures they would enjoy together. They would travel about the country and sail the *Viking* upriver into the Chagras—fish and possibly hunt. But mostly they would talk and drink and be together like old friends.

"So, Rolfe, my dearest boy," it concluded,

when they ask you in Günzburg or Freiburg, or wherever you go, "How is your father?" "Any word from your father?" "Is he well?" Don't be frightened. Don't be ashamed. Throw up your head and shoulders and tell them your father is very well indeed. Tell them your father's work goes on. Even as an exile in this godforsaken country, with its heat and rain and degradation, my vitality

is high; my brain is alive. Tell them Grigori is
alive. Grigori lives.

With love to your dear wife and my beloved
grandchildren. I look forward to our reunion in
Encarnación at the end of the month. All I ask is
that you be discreet. Tell no one where you are
going. The walls have ears. My enemies are everywhere.

Come quickly, my son. Nine years is too long to
wait to once again hold my dear boy in my arms.
Ever yours, Vati.

Grigori looked up just then, as if to pause from his
writing. Suddenly he saw Doña Esmeralda on the porch,
standing there in her large, floppy sunbonnet squawking
and pointing a long, bony finger in the direction of the
forest's edge. The Doctor looked that way, into the
sun. Momentarily blinded, he saw nothing. But when he
covered his brow with a hand and stared again, he
saw a tall, tatty figure wrapped in rags and standing
silent at the bottom of the garden.

Doña Esmeralda's squawking grew shrill and more
frantic. In the next moment, Grigori started up, spilling
pencils and pads, as if he were about to run.

Pistol in hand, Ludo dashed out of the shed in the
direction of the figure, only to stop dead in his tracks
moments later. "It's only the old priest," he called to
Grigori, who was slouching quickly toward the protection of the shed.

The Doctor turned to look again. This time the figure
had taken a step or two out of the shadows and stood
now out in the open, in bold relief with the wavy haze
of the late morning heat radiating upward from the
earth all about him.

Grigori muttered disconsolately. He had not seen
Sabané, the old Aché cacique, for several months now,

and he knew that the appearance of the fellow invariably coincided with distasteful chores.

"Tell him I can't go today," the Doctor instructed Esmeralda. "Tell him I don't feel well. *Enfermo. Enfermo,*" he cried at the old man coming toward him and put his face on his cheek to mime his meaning. The old man continued to move toward him, hand out, grinning toothlessly and jabbering, an apparition in rags, mindless of Esmeralda squawking Guaraní and darting all about him like an impudent fly.

"*Padre. Padre. Buena salud, Padre Capezius,*" he said.

"No *padre.* No Capezius today," Ludo said grimly, and planted himself between the old cacique and the Doctor. "No *padre* today. You understand? Go home. Go now."

"Capezius. Capezius." The old man grinned amiably, his eye fixed on the shrinking Doctor, and danced a little ballet with Ludo in an effort to dodge past him. "Capezius. Come."

The tall, wiry savage, with the white wire-brush hair and the ceremonial scars on his cheeks was now so close that the Doctor could see the bilious yellow whites of his eyes and smell the acrid stench of his rags.

"What is it now, for Christ's sake," Grigori moaned.

Still the Doctor's crossness could not mar the old priest's amiability. He grinned. "You come up reservation, Capezius. Today."

Grigori shook his head and waved his hands. "Not today."

"Sick today," the old man went on in his dogged, unhearing way. "Many children sick today. You come, Capezius. "

"Not today. Not today. *Estoy enfermo.*" Once again Grigori started toward the shed.

Sabané made a gesture of commiseration but kept

right on coming. Esmeralda flew at him, an old witch on her broomstick, a string of Guaraní invectives streaming from her.

Ludo set a restraining palm on the old man's chest. *"Hoy no. Comprende?"* he said. *"Hoy no."* But the old fellow pressed forward. He neither paused, nor slowed his step, nor even attempted to step around the young man. He simply moved through him like a cyclone—mindless and unswerving—cutting a wide swath as he went.

"You may as well go, Doctor." Esmeralda threw up her hands in despair. "He won't leave here unless you do."

"Ach scheiss." Grigori flung his cigarette aside. "What is it this time? Dysentery?"

Doña Esmeralda and the priest jabbered back and forth at each other. Shortly she turned back to the Doctor. "He says they're all throwing up. Can't keep their food down. Can't stop shitting."

The Doctor shook his head despairingly, his hands plunged deep into the pockets of his robe. "All right," he sighed at last. "Tell him I'll be right along. Ludo—go get my bag. Tell Horst to get the jeep out."

Grigori disappeared into the shed. A few minutes later he reappeared, carrying a doctor's bag, but this time dressed in the long white flowing robes of a Carmelite monk. The big, scarlet Maltese cross emblazoned on his chest glowed with dazzling radiance in the light of noon.

"Padre. Padre." Old Sabané grinned and clapped his hands. "Come—come—quick. Something special for you."

CHAPTER 11

Doctor Grigori, the one in the white Carmelite robes, the one they called Father Capezius, squatted on the dirt floor of the hut, above an ailing, howling child. It was a little Aché boy, five or so, stunted and malnourished, with the scabrous legs and bloated abdomen so typical of kwashiorkor syndrome.

Father Capezius swabbed the leg lesions, chanting softly to the yowling child, while the naked mother straddled and pinned him between her legs, her thin, oddly conical breasts swaying in circles above him. Several additional squawling children crawled around the dirt floor of the manioc hut, while a father attired only in a straw hat and wearing a kind of codpiece made of reptile skin lolled about in a murky corner of the room babbling to himself and sipping maté from a gourd.

Grigori had come down from the north to the Aché reservation. Led by Sabané they had come as far as they could by jeep, then by a small river ferry, switching for the last several miles to foot (the only way to reach there) through the great steamy conifer forests. Stumbling along behind the old cacique, they wound their way through a Carboniferous landscape of soaring trees, of tortuously tangled shrub and liana, still intact and unchanged for millions of years.

The Aché were a miserable lot. A stone age folk living at the loincloth level of civilization. Mongolian in type, they were small, lightly built, with broad, flat faces, prominent cheekbones, yellow skin, narrow eyes, straight black hair worn long to the shoulder, and their bodies almost entirely hairless. A timid, gentle folk, they were patient, trusting, pathetically cheerful and even optimistic in the midst of the most abysmal squalor. They thought of Father Capezius as a white divinity.

The children of the Aché were filthy and had lice. They suffered from malaria, malnutrition, tuberculosis, and a whole host of the most horrible and disfiguring fungal diseases. Infant mortality alone had greatly decimated their numbers. The adults suffered from all the same diseases in addition to syphilis and rampant alcoholism.

Their huts, when Grigori entered them, made him physically ill. Grouped in villages of from five to six dwellings, they were rudimentary things raised up out of manioc leaves. Chiefs and priests lived somewhat more elaborately in structures consisting of a square palisade of palmetto trunks bound together with tough, fibrous vines of liana, and roofed over with banana leaves hung from the walls. But it was also possible to see the pitiful spectacle of a whole family, six or seven people, barely subsisting under nothing more than a branch-hung awning. Outside these huts there was always some mothy captive creature destined for the pot—a wild hog tethered to a stake, or a wormy goat with sunken, cavernous ribs, bleating dolefully in the hot, dusty afternoon.

The insides of the huts were a masterpiece of disorder. On the bare earthen floor were strewn all the Aché's earthly possessions—clothing, food, tools. There were the husks of discarded food, the maggoty, moldering remains of meals consumed days ago; rags, litter, axes, knives, pots, pans, needles, threads, ropes, bottles, gourds; then occasionally something totally incongruous like an umbrella. In those extremes of temperature and humidity, the entire mess combined to produce one vast and suffocating stench.

The furniture, if there was any, was of the crudest. A few low wooden stools, baskets of all sizes, sieves for flour, mortar and pestle for maize, and gourds of every conceivable size and shape strewn everywhere.

When Doctor Grigori would arrive to treat the sick, he would find the family all assembled in one room, waiting in line to greet him. They appeared to eat constantly the sweet potatoes that lay roasting in the ashes at all times of the day, plucking them out with long pincers of bamboo. All night they would lie about on miserably thin pallets of corn shucks, each with his feet pointed toward the fire—poor protection against the intense cold that came down there after sunset at those 3,000-foot elevations.

Doctor Grigori despised the Aché. Their filth and squalor. The patient acceptance of their plight roused in him something comparable to rage. Yet, he was drawn to them for very specific reasons. And when he entered their villages and they came rushing out of their huts, laughing and jabbering and swarming about him like frolicking children, kissing his hand, he would seethe with contempt. His cheeks burned. He felt a curious effulgence of blood in his head and chest. And when they brought the small, sick children for him to heal and bless, he grew feverish with excitement.

Doctor Grigori had now been in the reservation treating the sick for almost seven hours. Trachoma. Erysipelas. Diarrhea. Tape worm. Fungus. They'd come one after the other—the aged and infirm, the young with the drowsy eyes and swollen bellies. He was nearly finished now swabbing the open, running lesions of the yowling child. At last he signaled the mother to release him. She did, but still the child screamed.

The Doctor murmured softly to the child, tucking

his finger under its chin, then tickling its armpit. But the child bellowed all the louder. Slowly he permitted his hand to caress and stroke the overwrought child, cooing softly at it all the time.

Finally the Aché child was pacified. Grigori rose and, shutting his bag, gave the mother tubes of antibiotic ointment with instructions conveyed to her by the sorcerer, Sabané, who stood by the Doctor's side during the entire visit. Then the monk reached into his cassock and took out a handful of red gumballs, pressing them into the hands of the malnourished child, who lay whimpering and prostrate below him.

When they saw the candy, the other children in the hut crowded around him. They had been eating koro worms out of clays cups. Scores of the fat white creatures writhed and squiggled in the cups they held out to the monk in offer for the gumballs.

The koro, a large, round worm that breeds in the trunks of pinheira trees, was a great delicacy among the Aché. It is said to have the smoothness and consistency of butter and the flavor of coconut.

One of the children pressed his wriggling cup on Doctor Grigori. *"Padre—mio—mio,"* he cried, pointing all the while to the bright red gumballs in sign of trade. A wave of nausea overcame Grigori as the boy impassively cut off the head of a worm and held it out to him. The decapitated koro still writhed, and as it did so, it oozed a thick whitish substance.

Grigori, momentarily stunned by some irrational terror, was unable to turn or avert his gaze. Still the headless worm writhed and slithered before him. He heard something cry inside himself. Deep inside and far away over the space of years. Another wave of nausea overcame him, a sense of self-loathing and disgust. Suddenly he struck the headless wriggling creature from the boy's hand and strode quickly from the place.

Outside Sabané walked with him to the entrance of the compound. They stood there for a moment talking until a wild-eyed, desperate-looking Aché woman came running up. She tugged two small, scruffy-looking boys behind her and jabbered excitedly to the old shaman. Instantly Grigori observed that the boys were twins— an almost perfect example of identical multiple birth— very rare among the Aché and looked upon by them as a sign of great holiness. The mother offered to sell them to "Father Capezius" for a price of two dollars apiece. In the past, Father Capezius had paid money for other Aché children, she had heard, and she assured the Padre, clutching his hand tearfully, that *los pobre niños* would have a better chance with him than with her.

Grigori feigned disinterest. Sabané jabbered something at the woman in Guaraní and she quickly dropped the price to one dollar fifty. Still Grigori hesitated. Distraught and frightened, the woman scarcely noted the excitement in the monk's eye. Sabané jabbered at her again. She burst into tears and dropped the price to one dollar. This time Grigori accepted. He paid her the two dollars in *guaranís* and wondered how much of it the sorcerer would take as his commission.

At the compound entrance the mother hugged the boys and wept bitterly when Matschke came and led them off.

CHAPTER 12

Mariscal Rondon in the state of Boquerón is a dusty little village with a hotel, a post office, and a general store with a single gas pump that has been out of operation for years. It sits in the center of a flat disc of arid earth stretching monotonously in an unbroken line to the sky. A narrow ribbon of third-class road leads abruptly in and out of the town. Indeed, one is out of the town before one realizes one has been in it. The place invites no stops.

The principal population of Mariscal Rondon is Indian. But outside the town in the surrounding hills lie the *estancias,* the prosperous cattle ranches. These are owned and operated exclusively by Germans, who live there in almost ducal splendor. Like old feudal lords they exist with a set of laws unto themselves and they employ their own personal armies of mercenaries in order to strictly enforce them.

These "ranchers" have little interest in Mariscal Rondon except that the place suits their purposes well. The region is remote and isolated, without the encumbrance of any effective police force. Hence it is a perfect place to avoid detection and arrest, for at least ninety-five percent of these "ranchers" are either still wanted by the War Crimes Commission of the West Germans or are on the hit lists of the Israelis. Without exception, they have all been fugitives since late 1945 when they were spirited out of postwar Germany, com-

pliments of the underground railroads run by such
organizations as ODESSA and Der Spinne.

Today these men have banded together in tightly
guarded federations of mutual defense in such out-of-
the-way places as Mariscal Rondon and Mariscal Estigarribia. The pattern of operation is always the same.
They come. They intimidate the frightened, defenseless
natives, eventually divesting them of all they own. These
outcast Europeans are understandably fearful and very
suspicious of outsiders.

Once a week in Mariscal Rondon, the State Agricultural Committee meets in the bare offices above the
Post Office. Very little in the way of agriculture is discussed there. Rather, it is an opportunity for a number
of paunchy, middle-aged men to don their old military
uniforms, replete with swastikas and jackboots, and
strut their stuff. There is a great deal of swaggering and
heel-clicking, much talk about the glories of the old
order and the coming of the new. Huge, wall-size
poster photographs of the Führer are displayed all
about. Then someone invariably has a story of how
Bormann was seen up in Lima or Freddie Schwend in
La Paz. They've managed to raise billions in deutschemarks, the story goes, and have managed to pipeline it
back into the Fatherland, where it's being used to re-
cruit a new "Fourth Reich." Democracy has failed in
Germany, they tell each other, and the time is ripe for
them. They drink a great deal of beer and clap each
other on the back. "Soon we'll be number one again,"
they say, while the dry wind soughs mournfully across
the vast, empty waste outside the Post Office.

To one of these meetings above the Post Office had
come a young German nobleman by the name of Baron
Gottfried Von Türlow. Many there had known his father,
General Büller Von Türlow, who had commanded the
SS Viking Division during the war. The General was

old now and ailing. He was not expected to live much longer, but before he died it was his wish to locate his old friend Doctor Grigori, who had served with him as chief medical officer on the Russian Front. Von Türlow had a number of documents and secret reports that he had managed to withhold from the Allies in those awful last days of the capitulation. These documents were vital to Grigori's safety and well-being. The General had heard through the grapevine that Grigori might possibly be found on one of the *estancias* outside of Rondon.

Little in the way of firm information was exchanged at that meeting except that young Von Türlow was given the wary assurances of several of the elders there that the matter would be looked into and that they would get back to him.

Late in the evening of that same day our young man was in Hohenau, but he was no longer Baron Von Türlow. Now he was Commander Bar Lev, the Israeli naval attaché in Asunción. Turned out smartly in an Israeli commander's uniform, he had a diplomatic portfolio and a full set of papers to attest to his august identity. Türlow, or Bar Lev, or whoever he was, had come up to Hohenau to speak with a cashiered Reuters correspondent by the name of Correns who was stranded there without a sou and who had "things to tell" for the right price.

It was nearly eleven PM when the young man reached Correns' hotel, the Alte Berliner, a seedy, disreputable place frequented by the *contrabandistas* on the outskirts of town. Bar Lev roused the dozing desk clerk and asked to be announced.

"Announced?" the clerk grumbled, unhappy to have been woken. Then he smirked. "No one need be announced here. Go right up."

The young man went up and knocked on the door of

Correns' room. There was no answer, but a crack of light shone beneath the door and he could hear a radio playing softly from within. The wood along the door-jamb, he noticed, had recently been splintered and there was also a peculiar odor seeping over the transom.

Several times the young man knocked but with no success. Then he went downstairs and roused the clerk again. He felt there was something strange going on in the room and insisted that the door be opened. The desk clerk refused, maintaining that he had no authority to do so. The young man showed him his diplomatic papers. Still the clerk refused.

"Fine," the young naval attaché said curtly. "I'll be back shortly with the police."

It was at that point that the clerk relented.

Moments later they were back upstairs, the young man and the grumbling clerk with a huge ring of clanking keys. A half-dozen or so were tried before the right one was found. When the door was opened, the first thing they were conscious of was the stench. Directly in front of them, not ten feet away, stood a cheap, rickety iron-frame bed, above which a naked light bulb depended from a long electric wire. On the bed lay a gray, heavy-set man. He wore an undershirt and trousers, with no shoes or socks. There was several days' growth of beard on his face, and his eyes stared straight ahead.

A necktie and leather belt had been tied into a noose, one end looped round the man's neck, the other end hitched to a rung of the bedpost above him. The upper torso was propped against the bedpost and the head listed queasily to one side. With the tongue slipping from the mouth, the face was twisted into the rictus of death. The man had obviously been dead for several days.

If it was someone's intention to create the impression

of suicide, the results were comically deficient. Very few people with serious suicidal ambitions attempt to hang themselves from a bedframe three feet off the ground.

Momentarily awed by the spectacle of death, the desk clerk muttered some oath and crossed himself, turning then at once to Bar Lev for guidance. But the young naval attaché was no longer there. The outer door was still open, the corridor outside was empty, and the young man was gone.

CHAPTER **13**

If you take the boat upriver from Hohenau the boatman of Encarnación will tell you all about Doctor Grigori, whom he too calls "Don Gregor." He used to carry the gentleman up the Paraná in the ancient ferry *Esperanza,* with its pink-painted sides peeling flakes into the river and its tired diesels coughing and wheezing. "A very fine gentleman," he said over and over again. *"Un caballero muy distinguido."* Don Gregor would pay him 500 *guaranís* to take him to Puerto Stroessner, where he was said to live then in a large white villa on the waterfront with two strapping young men and a corps of armed guards.

The boatman is an ancient, wizened Bolivian from Cochabamba with the leathery face of an Indian. He longs someday to leave the river and return to his village high in the Andes. Unaccustomed as the boatman was to conversing with his passengers, the young Spaniard going up to Eldorado was a pleasant exception. What in the world, the old boatman wondered, could such a fellow be looking for in Eldorado? The young man claimed he had relatives there, but the old boatman doubted it. No one had relatives in Eldorado. And why all the questions about the German doctor? He knew the man, of course, but a more bland and un-assuming fellow one could scarcely imagine. In any event, the boatman did his best to satisfy the young man's curiosity. He told him how Don Gregor always traveled with at least three or four men, although he never sat with them. They were rough, uncouth-looking fellows, the boatman averred, and the Doctor preferred to sit alone. So Grigori-Neiditch—as they called him up around there—Doctor Neiditch, would sit by himself on a small wooden bench below the wheelhouse and read a newspaper. His companions would play cards up forward and drink beer and laugh raucously at bawdy jokes. Often, they would annoy the other pas-sengers. Though he traveled with these fellows, Grigori preferred to dissociate himself from them.

The German always carried a small black bag, by which the boatman first divined that he was a physician. Often in the fall and winter months when it grew raw and drizzly on the river, he would wear a woolen shawl of Indian design across his shoulders. In that blustery season on the river, most of the passengers would crowd themselves into the warmth of the noisome little cabin below with its stench of diesel fuel and cat urine. But not Grigori. He would prefer to sit above on deck wrapped in his shawl, rain streaming from the wide brim of his soiled white plantation hat, and stare out over the water toward the shoreline slipping ever back-ward. Toward the end of the trip he generally appeared nervous and tired, and the shawl, the boatman said, made the good doctor appear far older.

Several hours later when they would reach the dock

at Puerto Stroessner, Doctor Grigori would disembark before the others. Carrying his black bag and always seeming in a rush, the doctor would press a few additional *guaranís* into the boatman's hand and wish him well in his gruff, slurred Spanish. Then he would hurry down the dock.

His companions, reeling from an excess of beer and a trifle boisterous by this time, would follow at a respectable distance, never losing sight of their charge. Because they had been drinking, and their clothing was usually open and in some disarray, the boatman maintained that it was often possible to see the glint of pistol handles carried in the belts about their hips.

The *Esperanza* had reached Eldorado by late that afternoon. The old boatman himself came down from the wheelhouse and walked with the young man out along the decaying wharf with its crumbling spiles. They conversed a while longer in their comfortable informal Spanish, and when they parted the boatman told the young man when he would be coming back through that way. The little ferry then blew its whistle, backed out of the dock, and continued its journey farther north upriver.

The young man was then left there, quite alone on the dock, with no one about to greet him or give him any directions. Eldorado is far up into the Chagras and quite desolate, but once the young man reached there, he began to sense the ground starting to warm up with the Doctor's presence.

Far upriver in the jungles of the Chagras the Indians say that a white man passes through the small village there of Eldorado. In their characteristically terse fashion, they describe this man as an "ugly man." *"Un hombre feo."* German. About sixty years old, 1.73 meters tall (they show you the height by placing sticks against a wall or tree). Front teeth gapped. Left eye crossed with a pronounced squint. Hair closely cropped with graying hairs at the temples, and a small bristly mustache. They say he comes from Coronel Oviedo, 130 kilometers from Asunción. His visits are regular, and rarely with exception. The local shaman up there maintains that they can predict with remarkable accuracy the day of the month and the time of the day he will arrive. Dressed in the robes of a mendicant White Friar and calling himself Father Capezius, he goes to the Aché Indian reservation just north of there to treat the sick free of charge. They say mostly he is drawn there by the children.

There is only one small hotel in Eldorado. In addition, there's a German bank (Banco Mostes), a telephone office, and, oddly enough, a small importing business which deals in agricultural machinery. Odd because there's not a great deal of agriculture carried on in that forlorn region except, of course, the very primitive kind practiced by Indians, picturesque and quaint, but still functioning at the stone-age level of efficiency, who would scarcely know a tractor from a plow.

This small importing enterprise is an Argentine firm called simply Hierro–Fabrofarunk, Ltd. S.A. The proprietor is one Ricardo Caffetti. Señor Caffetti, a naturalized Argentinian, is the sole representative in Paraguay of the distinguished Bavarian firm of Karl Grigori & Sons Ltd. of Günzburg, Germany.

Señor Caffetti was not in just then, the scruffy Macá assistant told the young man. He was traveling on a business trip that would take him to Valparaiso, Antofagasta, and Santiago de Chile. He was not expected back for at least a week. Could he, the Indian, be of any assistance? No, the young man assured him. He was going out now to take a look around. He had business further north, and he might be back through there in a few days.

In the northernmost reaches of Paraguay, just below the Bolivian border, in the province of Boquerón, lies a broad swath of jungle about three hundred square miles in size. Triangular in shape, it sits snugly between the borders of Argentina, Bolivia and Brazil.

It is a dismal and forlorn place pullulating with insects and wildlife—jabbering monkeys, screaming parrots, tapir, ocelot, capibara, puma, the maned wolf, which the local Indians call *zorro colorado,* and the big jaguar, which they call *pantera onça,* "the king of the Gran Chaco Woods."

It is a steamy, festering, godforsaken hellhole of a place, part swamp, part bramble and bracken, with giant, untracked conifer forests that look today just as they looked twenty million years ago. The temperatures there at midday run to between 115 and 120 degrees. You can't stay indoors and you can't go out. The sun in that subequatorial zone can kill. It beats down like a hammer, and when you stand still you can feel it start to devour your flesh.

The humidity is monstrous. It smothers the earth there like a huge sodden blanket beneath which there is no breath of air. You can't get away from it—and there's no place to hide from it. It is simply everywhere. The rainfall runs to a staggering 52 inches annually. It is a world where fungus and lichen abound; where the vegetation is profligate and choking. Everything there is mutant and outsized—even the animal life—great bats, huge rodents, and anacondas of several hundred pounds in weight, running, some of them, ten inches through the middle. You come upon them in the forest there, coiling and drooping from the branches of trees, looking like some allegorical serpent in a mythic land.

The people who live there—the white people anyway—are there because they have to be. They are of
two orders—criminals and priests; the former because
of the commission of sins, and the latter on some private quest for atonement of sins. The old priest, Father
Minheiro, missionary in the area for several decades,
asked to describe the place, merely shakes his hand,
repeating over and over again the words: *"um pais
ruim, muito ruim, mais ruim que qualquer outro. . . ."*
"A ghastly country, simply ghastly, more ghastly than
anything anywhere. . . ." A country they all say to stay
the hell out of. The region is heavily patroled and forbidden to all foreigners. It is called simply "Zone 540"
on the geodetic and topographical surveys and only
the Paraguayan military is allowed access to it.

In rainy weather you can't get through 540 because
the earth turns into a pestilential swamp—a quaking,
lethal ooze. There are no roads other than a few rudimentary jeep tracks and small trails hacked out by
the Japanese lumbermen working even farther back in
the deep mahogany forests behind 540. They say that
there are a number of small wooden houses back in
there, actually sheds set deep into the scrub, and that
the identity of the occupants of these sheds is a rather
carefully guarded military secret. *"Chito,"* as they
say. *Muy chito.*

Only with a helicopter or a small plane could the
young man reconnoiter the area. Producing his pilot's
license for the agent there at the tiny airport in Eldorado, he rented a small Cessna and took with him the
Indian called Humberto. He found him lounging on
the town square, just as he was told he would. He's
there at almost any time of the day, the young man was
informed, but try to get to him before nine in the morning, however. He's seldom sober after that. For a few

guaranis one can have his company all day. He is good company and also an excellent guide.

Humberto was quickly able to guide the young man up to the small white shed where the elusive Doctor Grigori had come to spend his final days. When Humberto the Indian and the young man reached the place, they flew low and circled about. The young man could see the shed, which was quite spartan, with its small verandah and white picket fence and its few rickety lawn chairs scattered randomly about in the garden out back. The white shutters were closed against the heat of day. It all seemed quite inoffensive and anticlimactic. No doubt a great disappointment. More like the modest residence of an Indian farmer or possibly a squatter. But certainly not the secret lair of one of the most wanted fugitives in the world.

There was no one about of any importance—just the dozen or so *cuchilleros* who patroled the barbed wire perimeter of the shed with their large dogs and their walkie-talkies. These *cuchilleros* are a rough lot. A kind of quasi, unofficial, paramilitary force, serving as Doctor Grigori's personal armed militia. The Doctor is free to go wherever he wants in 540, but whenever he ventures outside the barbed wire perimeter of his shed, the *cuchilleros* must accompany him. They are paid out of government funds, though strictly speaking they are not soldiers, but merely a cadre of thugs drawn from the lower depths of the Tembuco prison in Asunción. They are the criminal element of the country, recruited to do the unsavory tasks that even the military would balk at carrying out. All such regimes as "Papa" Stroessner's require the services of just such a force of men as the *cuchilleros*. They help to remove constitutional obstacles, or at least neutralize them so as to enable enlightened despots like *El Jefe* to get on with the business of good government.

So, there it was at last—the great secret hideout, the ogre's awful lair, revealed. The young man studied the place. He took his time and circled about the site at his leisure. Studying the topography and making mental notes. But at a certain point he flew too low over the area and suddenly the *cuchilleros* opened with a terrific blast from their Uzi submachine guns. Humberto's eyes opened wide like blooming peonies. At that point the young man concluded, and wisely, that it was time to go. He was not unhappy, however. He had got what he'd come for.

CHAPTER 14

Several days later, four men moved briskly up a hill. It was just after dawn and they had been trudging for several hours. They did not speak. The only sound they made was the crunch of their boots and the harsh throaty rasp of their breathing. They carried rifles—Mausers—and large-gauge shotguns, and as they pushed through the waist-high grass of the broad savannah, the cane and cattails pushing against them made a dry rattling sound.

The four moved in a wide flank, spread out at intervals of nearly fifty feet or so. As they moved up the steep acclivity with a kind of stolid, remorseless forward motion, flocks of birds fluttered up and out of the tall cane before them. Up ahead the Macá beaters shouted and banged pots and pans with old wooden ladles. They rattled gourds and tin cans loaded with pebbles. The din was awful.

In the next moment they breasted the top of the hill, all four reaching the crest at once and pausing there, four black spots against the sky. Suddenly one of the beaters screamed. Something up ahead coughed, then growled in the deep grass. A flock of doves rose clattering out of the cane, and circled wildly above a point in the moving grass. In the next moment a vivid shock of yellow streaked across an open space and plunged into the tall cane beyond it. The beaters shouted, banged their pots and ran about in circles. One of the four hunters raised his Mauser and took aim at the clump of cane. The other three put up their guns and waited, almost dutifully.

"Aiyeeeee." One of the beaters screamed an unearthly wail and came tearing out of the cane in the direction of the hunters—a great blaze of yellow bounding and leaping after him. The man with the Mauser fired—a thunderous sound that rolled like an avalanche over the wide, empty disc of space and bowled like falling ten-pins on up into the purple infinitude of distant surrounding hills.

Still screaming, the beater came bounding on toward the four, but the splash of bright yellow in hot pursuit suddenly faltered, then veered off its course, plunging, bellowing once more into the tall damp grass.

"He's hit."

"How bad? Could you see?"

"No. There was too much dust."

"I think you caught him on the shoulder."

From somewhere deep in the high grass they heard a hoarse barking. It was the sound of something stricken, nevertheless dangerous.

"*Ach, scheiss.* We'll have to go in now and get him. Horst. Ludo," snapped Doctor Grigori. The two young men quickly unstrapped canteens and hip holsters, then each scooped up a handful of cartridges and reloaded their Mausers. In the next moment they went thrashing off, disappearing into the grass with the excited beaters streaming after them. The other two lit cigarettes, crouched on the dew-damp earth and waited.

Shortly there was another sharp report. Then a brief period of silence. One of the beaters who had gone into the grass reappeared about fifty yards off, waving a red handkerchief frantically at the others. They rose, shouldered their guns and came on, following the frenzied beater into the grass.

Fifty or so feet in, the beater suddenly started jumping up and down and yelling: *"Pantera—pantera."*

They peered into a narrow tunnel of grass full of the fresh droppings of large animals and proceeded quickly down that way. The place reeked of the warm sharp musk of big cats. Shortly they came upon the two men hovering above the carcass of the fallen jaguar. One already had a tape out and was measuring the animal. Its great emerald eyes were still open and staring; the tongue had slipped out of the muddy muzzle and blood oozed slowly at its nose. It had a posed, rigid quality as if it were already stuffed and mounted.

Grigori, who'd shot the cat, knelt down now beside the fallen animal. "Where did I hit it?" He flicked a fly from its bloody muzzle.

"In the jaw, Herr Doktor," said one of the young men who'd gone in after the cat. "A perfect shot."

"Slightly over two meters," announced the one with the tape. "About two hundred kilos, too, I should judge."

"Another trophy for your wall, Don Gregor," said the third man.

Crouching, the Doctor looked up into the sun and frowned. A few points higher in the sky, he realized, and shortly the place would be a blazing inferno.

While the two young men and the beaters began to

skin the jaguar, Grigori and the other hunter squatted in the grass and lit cigarettes. The Doctor produced a flask of cognac and soon that was passing back and forth between them.

Doctor Grigori's companion that morning was a short, square gentleman, solidly built, with thick, toadish features and a completely bald skull. His name was Ricardo Caffetti.

With the beaters and the two young men skinning his prize, Grigori took a long pull at the cognac and wiped his sweating throat with an immense scarlet kerchief. "I suppose," he said a trifle whimsically, "if there's really such a thing as Hell, it will turn out to be remarkably like Paraguay."

Caffetti frowned. Momentarily at a loss for words, he permitted his gaze to stray across the shimmering savannah where a tepid breeze soughed through the tall grass.

"I imagine Hell will be a great deal hotter," Caffetti remarked blandly and lay back on the damp earth.

For a brief time the Doctor pondered the climate of Hell, then lit one of his small pastel cigarettes and stretched back, too, with his hands cradled behind his head, squinting up at the sky.

"Tell me, Ricardo, what is all this talk I hear about a new rash of agents in Asunción?"

"Agents?" Caffetti appeared surprised.

"You know very well what I mean."

Caffetti was a cautious man. Inward and laconic by nature, he had little in the way of small talk. As a man of commerce, facts, figures, and strictly verifiable data were his stock in trade. "I know as much as you do. We've seen this sort of thing before, and we know how to deal with it."

"With what?" The sun flashed blindingly off Grigori's monocle. "Specifically?"

Caffetti studied the Doctor through narrowed eyes, as if he were weighing the wisdom of telling the man everything he knew. At last he spoke: "As you know, in the past year or so certain Israeli operatives have been able to insinuate themselves into the Jewish community in Asunción. They pose as jewelers there and tailors, petty tradesmen. You know the sort of thing. We think they are Mossad, but what their specific mission is, we cannot say. Some reports suggest it is merely intelligence gathering. Others are a little more ominous. They speak of—"

"Vengeance." The Doctor completed the sentence for him.

Caffetti watched the Doctor wipe more perspiration from his throat with the big red kerchief. "One group they watch particularly call themselves 'Al Tishkakh.' "

"Tishkakh?"

"Hebrew for 'We will never forget.' "

"Tishkakh." Grigori's eyes twinkled merrily. "Never forget, ay? How romantic. How heroic."

"Perhaps," Caffetti frowned, "but thank your stars that Arganas knows a good deal about these Mossad people in Asunción."

"I note that whenever Arganas wishes to extort higher protection fees, the tiger is somehow always at the gates."

"That may well be," Caffetti cautioned, "but still—there's no guarantee that there aren't a few tigers out there watching you at this very moment." He waved his short, stubby arm in the direction of the long, low expanse of savannah stretching to the sky.

Doctor Grigori's gaze followed the direction of Caffetti's arm, and he brooded thoughtfully.

"Let the tigers come then." He hefted his Mauser. "I'm ready for them." In the next moment he rose and strode forward, staring hard at the pale line of distant mountains. Hands on hips, jaw thrust forward, there was something more than just a little jaunty and defiant in his pose. Suddenly he threw his head back and he was roaring merrily out at all that vast uncaring space.

Just then, only some three hundred yards away, a fair, slim young man lay prone in the dense marshy underbrush. So deep, so profligate was the vegetation there, that he could not be seen by the hunters whose voices traveled up to him on the scorched breezes.

The young man lying there in the grass was part of a seven-man surveying team that had been sent up into the forests of the Paraná as part of the multinational, multimillion-dollar Pan American Highway project. The name on his passport was Carlos Ondivos. The nationality given there Brazilian, and his occupation, it said, was that of surveyor.

At this moment, the other members of the surveying team accompanying Ondivos were working several miles northward, and so the young man lay in the grass by himself, prone before a surveyor's transit, his eye screwed hard to the lens. Though he had been living out in the forest for several weeks now, where conditions were primitive, his face, nevertheless, was cleanshaven and his clothing immaculate. He had a lean, doglike face, flared by too much sun, and the expression on it just then was one of impassive, almost frozen, calm. Periodically he lifted his eye from the transit to scribble notes in a pad lying in the grass beside him. His movements were spare and economical, as if each had been carefully premeditated. There was no wasted motion. He was meticulous.

Hearing that wild unearthly laughter carried upwind, the surveyor swerved his transit several points in its direction, murmuring numbers aloud to himself and jotting them down into his pad. The transit, mounted on its tripod, was actually a powerful, long-range camera with telescopic lens. The glass now suddenly fixed upon the figure of a man standing hip-high in the grass and apparently laughing. The man was wearing a white basque shirt open at the collar and had his back to the surveyor.

Another man, bald, paunchy and short, sprawled in the grass just behind him. Suddenly the man in the white basque shirt turned. At once his features floated airily into the telescopic lens field, filling it completely.

It was a face the young man knew well, and though the features had been altered by time, there was no doubt in his mind as to the true identity of the fellow.

For several weeks now the surveyor had been observing the movements of this man. In his pad he had noted the fellow's daily routine. His comings and goings as well as those of his companions. He had sketched in his book the anchorage point of the gunboats opposite 540, plus innumerable views and elevations of the white shed set back deep in the forest, along with details of the topography surrounding it. He now took several additional photographs of both hunters drinking and chatting in the tall grass. Then, snapping the pad shut, he tucked it into an inside pocket. Carefully he dismantled the telescopic camera, storing it finally in a white canvas haversack. The roll of film he had taken from it he tucked into the wide cuff of his jeans, rolling the flap over it several times for safekeeping.

He would be returning to Asunción that night with the rest of the surveying team, but he would not be going back to the hotel with them on the Calle Sarmiento. Tonight he would be going elsewhere with his rolls of film and his information. The young man's name was not as his passport attested, Carlos Ondivos. It was Ian

Asher. He was Israeli and, within certain intelligence circles, he was known as the Blue Falcon.

While Horst and Ludo completed the skinning of the jaguar, Grigori and Caffetti sat in the grass and continued their sporadic conversation. There was an uneasiness between the two, a tacit antagonism that roiled the air about them. Caffetti pretended to be interested in the activity of the Macá beaters now playing a form of mumblety-peg in the grass. Shortly he spoke again. "You haven't mentioned your forthcoming trip to anyone?"

"Absolutely not."

"There's no chance Rolfe spoke indiscreetly to anyone about it?"

"Rolfe? My God, no. He's completely reliable."

"You didn't call or attempt to wire him?"

"Certainly not." A red blotch had erupted at Grigori's throat. "What kind of idiot do you take me for?"

"Please don't take offense . . ."

"I take no offense . . ." the Doctor replied, deeply offended.

"Odd," Caffetti mused aloud. "I'm convinced that these people in Asunción just at this time have something to do with your upcoming trip to Encarnación."

"How could anyone possibly have learned of the trip?"

"I haven't the slightest idea," Caffetti replied. He appeared troubled.

"What would you suggest I do?" Irascibility crept back into the Doctor's voice.

"I'd suggest you postpone your trip."

"Impossible. I've postponed it three times already because of alerts," the Doctor snapped. "I will not postpone it again. I want to see my boy. Besides, I've already cleared everything with the President."

The tone of Grigori's voice brought Caffetti up sharply. He shrugged and rose. "As you wish, Gregor." He took a long pull on the cognac flask, finishing it at a single gulp. "So then, it is all set for Rolfe? He's coming?"

"Yes. Of course. You'll meet him in Buenos Aires."

"And bring him to Encarnación?"

"Yes. That's right."

"By boat?"

"That's the plan. Arganas didn't tell you?"

"He told me." Caffetti nodded. "But I wanted to hear it straight from you. And also warn you—"

Grigori looked up. The squint of his bad eye had grown more pronounced.

"Be careful, my friend." Caffetti stared back at the Doctor. "Observe the signs."

"Aah." The Doctor waved a disparaging hand at his friend. "You talk too much with Arganas. He's an old woman. Come—have another drink and then let's get some lunch."

But Caffetti persisted. "Where do you go now?"

"To Asunción in the morning." The Doctor rose and wiped his forehead with the handkerchief. "Then Bariloche with Krug and Rudel for a few days' vacation. From there, on to Encarnación."

"Be very careful, Gregor."

Suddenly Ludo, who had been skinning the jaguar, came forward smiling with a bloodied knife. They had by now separated most of the pelt from the carcass. "Do you want the head, too, Herr Doktor?"

Doctor Grigori looked slowly up at him, a little peeved, as if the question had been an impertinence. "What do you think, fool? Yah, yah, of course I want the head."

"Be very careful, Gregor."

*   *   *

Later that evening in the small shed behind the main house that served as his laboratory, Doctor Grigori slipped into his immaculate white surgical gown, and the first of the Aché boys he had taken on the reservation was brought in to him. The child's large, fawnlike eyes were wild and staring, and he was clearly terrified. Doctor Grigori patted him on the back, spoke gently to him, and mussed his hair. Shortly the boy relaxed. He sat on the Doctor's lap, and the Doctor gave him candy and told him funny stories. The child had cut his knee playing outside that day, and now the Doctor washed the wound and bandaged it. They laughed and joked some more, and when Grigori pricked the boy behind the ear with the hypodermic needle, it was done so skillfully that the child scarcely felt a thing. Moments later, he had fallen into the deep, unfeeling sleep of morphia.

In the next moment, the Doctor rang a bell. Von Rattenhuber, also attired in a white gown, entered and carried the sleeping child into the adjoining surgical suite. Once in there he would prepare the child for an operation from which he would never awake.

Almost simultaneously, Matschke would bring the twin brother in, and Doctor Grigori with his bag of candy would begin again the gentle seduction of his next victim.

With children the Doctor was always the soul of kindness.

But once these hapless little creatures were deep under anaesthesia, the kindly, avuncular gentleman with his bag of sweets was quickly left behind, and the cold dispassionate scientist stepped forward, ruthless in his quest for truth. Or so the Doctor saw himself as he prepared his instruments to dissect alive these small, malnourished children strapped to his table. It was crucial to his observations that the dissection be carried out while they still lived and breathed, for he was determined to learn exactly how much could be taken from them in terms of vital organs before the onset of actual clinical death.

Afterward, he would carefully weigh and measure pancreas, liver, spleen, lungs, heart, brain, and cranial index, comparing not only each twin with its opposite, but with a file index of like figures compiled over his years of study in the forests of the Paraná. The files were quite impressive—all broken down in terms of age, height, weight, and even tribe.

It was these figures, compiled over nearly two decades, upon which his monumental work would be based. Once this work was published and its significance finally understood, history, he knew, would exonerate him completely.

At the conclusion of these researches, Horst and Ludo would gather the remains and bury them several hundred yards back in a clearing in the forest. The vital organs were preserved in formalin and stored in jars in the Doctor's laboratory. How many such children were buried in the back of the shed of 540 no one could say, but the Doctor had been in residence there for nearly a dozen years, and his work had gone on quite diligently right from the beginning.

Part II

TRAVELERS

CHAPTER 15

On the Kärtnerstrasse in the heart of Vienna, workers streaming out of office buildings were starting homeward through the violet dusk. The broad, gracious linden-lined boulevards were lit with street globes and a soft diffusion of orange-yellow lights emanating from innumerable shop windows. The department stores, the booteries and haberdashers, bakeries and wine stalls, the elegant salons and boutiques were jammed with late shoppers, and the Viennese, garrulous and sociable as ever, were thronging into the smoky little coffee and tobacco shops to munch and gab and sip before returning home to dinner.

On the crowded avenue outside the Graben, the dial of the great clock high in the baroque steeple of Saint Stephan crept imperceptibly toward seven. When the minute hand, pointing like a great finger of Destiny, finally nudged across the román numerals of XII, the first of seven great gongs tolled a leaden circle into the cloudless evening sky. Instantly a covey of pigeons roosting in the clerestory beneath the cathedral cupola wheeled outward in a wide half-circle, flapping over the boulevard.

A young woman, tall, angular, with a loping, almost masculine, gait, swept past the cathedral and on up into the pleasant din of the Kohlmarkt and into the Michaelerplatz. She carried a small suitcase, and her stride was swift and purposeful, with a decided air of

91

urgency about it. Clearly, she was in a hurry. She had business and a destination.

At a certain point she stepped out of the shadows into the harsh glare of a news kiosk, put down her suitcase, and stood there a moment, slightly breathless against a lurid backdrop of newspapers, periodicals, and sex magazines.

In that rather tawdry setting, the casual observer passing by might have seen a young woman in her mid to late twenties with the sharply delineated look of classic Nordic beauty. It was the kind of beauty one associates with a highly paid mannequin in an expensive salon, yet the ungainliness of posture and the seeming indifference to her own beauty belied that impression. On reconsideration, one might have guessed that she was an athlete—a swimmer or, possibly, a runner.

Her face was one of striking linearity, and the eyes, wide and intelligent, were of a soft green like the patina of old copper—a color one associates more with Mediterranean peoples rather than those of northern climes.

The hair, which was long and smoke-blond, had been tied back severely in a bun, and the wool navy merchant seaman's cap pulled down hard against her skull served to accentuate the high cheeks and the splendid bone configuration of her face.

It was a chill night in late spring, and the young woman wore a denim skirt and jacket with high brown boots. Around her neck she wore an amulet of Egyptian design. It was a chunk of tourmaline—grayish-blue and cut in the shape of a falcon.

Glancing up and down the boulevard, she bought a *Deutsche Zeitung* and a pack of Gauloises. Tilting her head sidewards, she lit one and glanced at her wristwatch.

After a moment, she pulled out from the inside pocket of her denim jacket a long tissue-thin envelope. It was

postmarked Asunción and studded with an array of the
18.15-*guaraní aeropostal* stamps in which the faces of
John and Robert Kennedy appeared along with the
melancholy countenance of Lincoln brooding in the
background.

The letter, addressed to P.O. Box Number 6403,
Wien, had already been opened. Actually, it appeared
to have been opened for some time and the contents
inside well-thumbed.

Now the young woman opened it again, lifting the
torn flap backwards and, with impatient fingers, extracting the contents. These were simply a Braniff Airlines ticket, round-trip, first-class from Vienna to Buenos
Aires, via Dakar, a stack of Argentine currency, and a
small square of pale blue tissue. On this was scrawled
in bold, untidy letters the following brief missive:
"GREETINGS FROM THE LAND OF INFINITE
OPPORTUNITY." There was neither salutation at the
opening nor any identifying signature at the conclusion.

For a long while the young woman gazed down at
the message, pondering it. The somewhat cryptic contents, however, did not appear to puzzle her in the
least. Several times she touched the tip of her finger
to her tongue, then ran the dampish skin over the untidy
calligraphy until the letters smudged and ran.

In the next moment a black, vintage Mercedes cab
pulled up at the curb beside the kiosk and gave two
short blasts of its horn. The young woman looked up.
Recognizing at once the shadowy occupant in the back
seat, she jammed her airline tickets back into her jacket
pocket, hefted her suitcase, and with her long, loping
stride, made for the cab.

CHAPTER 16

June 1, 1976
Günzburg, Bavaria

Dear Vaterchen:

Thank you for your letter of May 22. All of my arrangements are now made. I depart for Buenos Aires on Lufthansa Flight 430 out of Munich on June 17. I understand Ricardo is to meet me in Buenos Aires on the 18th. We are to attend to company matters for several days, then proceed by river steamer to Encarnación on the 27th. I shall enjoy the one-night cruise up the Plata, recalling everything you've ever told me about how lovely the river is at night. Then we shall be together again. I too have missed you. Nine years is a very long time.

At that point Rolfe Hupfauer's pencil snapped from the inordinate pressure he had been exerting on it as he wrote. In the next moment he snatched up the sheet of foolscap he'd been writing on, tore it up into a dozen pieces, and flung the scraps at the wall.

"Rolfe."

When he looked up again he saw the quiet gray eyes of Hedi, his wife, regarding him reproachfully.

"So?" he snorted at her and stared down at his hands. "Go on and say it if you have to."

"I don't have to say anything." Her voice was very calm. "You say it all with your actions. If it is going

94

to make you sick, if it is so repugnant for you to see your father, then don't go."

He laughed and shook his head ruefully. "As if I had a choice. As if I could write back . . . let me see. How would I phrase it?" He snatched up another piece of foolscap and started to scribble with an elaborate and spiteful glee. "Dear Vaterchen . . . I will not go to Encarnación to see you. I will not go now or ever again. The truth of it is that I don't care to see you. The sight of you is abhorrent . . . disgusts me . . ."

At that point, Hedi crossed the room, snatched the paper from him, and crumpled it in her fist. "Hush— the children will hear."

"You mean they haven't heard already?" Rolfe's eyes opened wide in a parody of shock. "Amazing. I would have thought by this time that every German from age one to a hundred had heard. How long can the children be protected?"

"As long as it's humanly possible, I shall protect them."

"Why?" Rolfe snarled. "I wasn't protected. Nobody protected me. From the age of ten on, I heard about the esteemed Doctor, my father, from everyone. The newspaper. Radio. Periodicals. They even taught about him at school." Rolfe Hupfauer laughed spitefully. "I shall never forget the professor ranting at the podium. 'Monster. Ghoul. Grigori the Death Angel' he called him. Since for obvious reasons I'd adopted my mother's maiden name, the poor fool didn't realize I was the same Grigori. Son of the ghoul. My little friends made jokes about it. Later, when I was older, I recall being called to the prosecutor's office in Frankfurt, summoned there like a common criminal and forced to listen to the indictment—to that hideous document with all its horrid, carefully catalogued detail. They read it out loud to me. All sixty-three counts—one by one. One more ghastly than the next. 'Is this your father?' they asked. 'Is this he?' "

Rolfe Hupfauer rose and walked to a large expanse of windows that looked out over the tall tips of wavering pine trees to a spectacular prospect of a lake below. He gazed down on the sparkling blue-white disc of pine-girded water and out across to the distant shore.

How much he resembled his father, Hedi thought, as she watched him there. The thin, slight frame. The dark, moody, attractive look . . . only at thirty-seven, he seemed older than his father had at that age. Grayer. More haggard. More driven. Gregor Grigori, her cele-brated and infamous father-in-law, had seldom looked haggard or driven. On the contrary, he was generally spry, dapper, mischievous, eager for fun. In the fifteen years of her marriage to Rolfe, she had only met the Doctor three times, and those under very curious and trying conditions. Once, at the funeral of his father, Karl Grigori, when the Doctor returned from Argentina to Günzburg disguised in an outlandish blond wig and calling himself Fausto Rindon. A second time she met him at a night club in Rio de Janeiro, introduced to her then as Gregor Schlakstro. It was Carnival. The room was crowded and noisy. Horns blared. People about them were all drunk and disorderly. Dressed in out-rageous costumes, she and Rolfe sat miserably in a blizzard of confetti and spilled wine, and several times during the confusion and hilarity Herr Schlakstro tried to slip a hand up his daughter-in-law's skirt beneath the table.

The third time was in Acapulco at a hotel out of town near the Pied de la Cuesta. Alois, Grigori's young brother and titular head of the Grigori empire, had died suddenly and unexpectedly. Papers had to be signed very quickly. Transfers of deed had to be con-summated, and Rolfe, a lawyer himself, was very hastily given his father's power of attorney. On that occasion, Hedi recalled, her illustrious father-in-law was not quite so playful. He seemed haggard, driven, and worried. He kept looking over his shoulder, just the way Rolfe did at this moment.

"Do you want me to go with you?" she asked. "Would it help?"

"No. I have to go by myself."

"It's only for two weeks."

"Yes. I know. Just two weeks." His fingers drummed idly at the window panes. He stared down at the two little children—a girl and a boy—playing in the garden below. "He'll take me out everywhere. Spend money lavishly on me. Introduce me to all of his old cronies. The goosesteppers and all the old party *Bonsen.* 'This is my Rolfe. My son. My attorney. My good right hand.' We'll drink a lot of champagne and get drunk. I'll look at him there, laughing and drinking, his eyes sparkling, people smiling all around him, fawning over him as if he were some kind of hero. And I'll say to myself, Is this the monster? The ghoul? The castrator of little boys? The celebrated Angel of Death? This silly, sentimental, weepy old man? Hardly what one thinks of as quintessential evil.

"He'll take me fishing on his boat. We'll go out on the river for two days. He'll have those two thugs with him. They'll sing songs and tell lewd stories, and he'll try to apologize to me. Justify himself. 'You know, Rolfe,' he'll say, his voice husky with cognac, the way it gets when he drinks too much, 'it wasn't all the way they say it was. Not at all as bad as the way they've painted me. We had a cause,' he'll say, and he'll get that drunken beatific look in his eye, as if he had just come from a chat with God. 'Oh, I don't say we didn't make mistakes. There were some excesses—oh, yes, I admit it. Unfortunate—lamentable—but—we had prinziples then. Prinziples . . .' " Rolfe tried to imitate his father's grandiose Bavarian elocutions. He waved his finger like a comic strip demagogue. " 'Our duty— Duty—' And I shall hate him all over again. And he'll see that in my eyes. And he'll look hurt. That hurt puppy look he gets. It's not sincere. It's fake. I know that. And he'll put his arm around me and kiss me and start to cry. How I loathe that tendency to bathos in him when he drinks and starts bawling. And that slavering contrition he reserves just for me. I know it's just for me. When he's with his cronies, they revel in the past. They sing the 'Horst Wessel' and he boasts louder of his deeds than ever. And I'll come away from there again sick with hating him."

Hedi watched her husband for a long moment, then knelt and proceeded to pick up the scraps of torn paper. "If it is all so distasteful to you," she said, "don't go. And"—she hesitated, momentarily flustered—"don't accept any more money from him either."

His features froze and he shot her a look of pure hatred. Then he turned abruptly from the window and limped slowly back toward the desk. Sitting down heavily with a great sigh, he took up a fresh sheet of paper and proceeded to write: "Dear Vaterchen," he began with trembling hand. "Thank you for your letter of May 22 . . ."

A short time later, Rolfe Hupfauer was out tooling up the *Autobahn* toward Günzburg in his small Porsche. He drove fast, with a quiet, self-directed rage. A month ago he had been full of hope and plans for the future. It was as if after many years a pall had lifted and he was at last emerging from a smog of recrimination and guilt. He had begun to once again enjoy himself, to find pleasure in his family. Then suddenly that letter in its small tissue envelope, postmarked Asunción and littered with bright gaudy stamps depicting native Paraguayan fauna—jaguar, ocelot, tapir, capibara. Before he'd even opened it he could feel his bowels grind. He sensed trouble. Then the letter in Caffetti's small, precise hand, and the words "erratic," "unpredictable," "sick," "matter of some urgency," leaping out at him from the page. He had to sit down before he could finish reading it. "Your presence here most necessary," it continued. "Would be best he never knows I wrote—Let it seem you're coming simply out of affection—"

Rolfe laughed bitterly as the final word trailed off in his mind's eye, and he turned off the *Autobahn* at the Günzburg exit. In the distance it was possible to see the spires of the old Rococo church and to the left of that the sprawling Renaissance castle with its turrets and machicolations.

Driving into the small medieval town of twelve thousand inhabitants on the banks of the Danube, he crossed the bustling market square and recalled that his father had grown up in this town, and that Grigori & Sons Industrial works, renowned throughout the world for its fine agricultural machinery, had dominated the financial life of this small Bavarian city for nearly two centuries. Eighty percent of the town's working force was employed by Grigori, and so, despite the horrors of the past, the Grigoris remained unassailably heroes here.

Crossing the old market square Rolfe drove up the narrow cobbled road to the large, ancestral home built high on the rocks overlooking the Danube. With a twinge of melancholy, he recalled that here had been his birthplace. Here he had been weaned, had played and thrived, attended elementary and high school. Then later, like his father, had been sent to Munich for his professional degrees.

The Porsche turned through two stone stanchions and rolled up a gravel path for several hundred yards through a vast expanse of parklike grounds. The car wheeled slowly around several sharp turns on the drive; then, looming suddenly, unexpectedly, before him up ahead at the end of the poplar-lined drive, was the sprawling villa with its stucco and timbers, its towers and steeply pitched gables.

Built nearly three centuries before by his great-great-grandfather, Karl Grigori, the place never failed to fill Rolfe with some inexplicable unease. As a child, he had dreaded the house. Its dank, musty corners, its vast shadowy wings, its corridors of empty rooms, one leading almost compulsively to the next. So easy for a little boy to lose himself within its labyrinthine complexity. As a lonely, unsettled child, he had peopled those rooms with terrifying phantoms and ghosts. Even today, coming back to it, three decades later, he felt himself dwarfed and overcome by the size of it, the sense of ever-present menace. It reeked of his father.

Otto, the old family retainer and valet for some forty years, met him at the door. Nearly blind now, he still wore full livery and supervised the activities of a staff of four—an upstairs woman, a cook, a porter, and a chauffeur—all simply to maintain old Grandmother Grigori in a style to which she declined to become un-accustomed.

Now into her nineties, Madam Grigori was the last of the Grigoris. With her grandson Rolfe, who called himself "Hupfauer," the line would expire. Over thirty years ago she had seen her beloved husband Karl die brokenhearted by revelations at Nuremberg of his son's wartime activities. At first the old man stubbornly refused to believe any of the charges leveled at his son, Gregor, certain that the tribunals would completely exonerate him. When they didn't, old Grigori one day simply turned his face to the wall and gave up.

In the years that followed, Madam Grigori was to see her eldest son, Kurt, die prematurely of an embolism on the brain, and her youngest, Alois, of a tragic "accident" many believed was not all that accidental. Alois had always been thought of as the "sensitive" one, and the disgrace of the revelations at Nuremberg had unsettled him greatly. But the Grigoris were devout Catholics, and a determination of suicide was simply unacceptable. On the subject of her middle son, Gregor, Madam Grigori had sealed her lips thirty years ago. Within her presence the topic could never be broached, and for all intents and purposes in her mind that son no longer existed.

Chatting reminiscently and laughing, Otto had led him up the winding sweep of stairs to the top of the house where Granny Grigori resided now in splendid isolation. She occupied the entire upper story, never going out, taking all of her meals in a large canopied and richly carved oak bed—caustic, dictatorial, and abusive to all those about her. Standing there before her door, Rolfe felt a spasm of desolation. He was not at all certain why he had come.

Entering, he found her in a beaded peignoir, seated at a small card table, involved in a game of bezique with herself. The old gnarled hands bedizened with gaudy rings fanned out sets of cards on the green baize table-top. Around her swirled mists and rags of cigarette smoke.

She did not look up when he entered, although he was certain she knew he was there. She had never forgiven him for dropping his paternal name. Considering it a betrayal, she had all but disowned him, dividing his portion of her estate among other, less conscience-stricken grandchildren.

Madam Grigori kept her grandson waiting for several long moments, refusing to acknowledge his presence until she had finished out her hand. Then, scribbling numbers onto her scorepad and without looking up, she merely said, "Come."

He walked forward, it seemed, out of one circle of shadows into another, more smoky and penumbrous. It was late afternoon and a mote-filled shaft of late spring twilight slanted through the tall leaded windows and fell across the tabletop. Somewhere behind her a large white cockatoo standing on a brass ring squawked its harsh elocutions into the deepening shadows.

"You wanted to see me, Rolfie?" she said and dealt herself another hand. The "Rolfie" had struck him as pejorative. It was what she had called him as a little boy. Her sudden reversion to the name now was quite pointed.

"*Grossmutter,*" he said, settling into an old cane *bergère* that creaked beneath his weight. She appeared now much smaller and slighter to him. Her face was heavily made up in a ghastly maquillage, and it occurred to him that she was wearing all of her jewels.

The skin stretched taut against the bones of her cheeks was waxen and translucent. An intricate blue filigree of veins shone just below the surface of the skin, and below that one could see clearly the conformation of the skull. Yet, even now, there was still something of the coquette about her . . . some vestige of the great beauty she had once been. It suddenly struck him how much his father resembled her.

She lit an ivory-tipped cigarette from the nearly expired ash of another. "Everything all right at home, Rolfie?"

"Yes, *Grossmutter.*"

"Hedi and the children?"

"Fine."

The cockatoo squawked a garble of indecipherable words. She glowered and shook a hand in the creature's direction. "Oh, shut up, Zigi." She turned back to him.

"You look tired, Rolfie. Your business—your practice going well?"

"Fine. Just fine, *Grossmutter*."

"Old Handelmann tells me you're very good at your work. That's nice."

"I try, *Grossmutter*."

There was a pause in which she appeared to be waiting for him to start whatever it was he had come there to start. She knew he was there to start something.

"*Grossmutter?*"

"Yes." Her eyes narrowed shrewdly as she leveled them at him.

"I'm going to Paraguay."

Her hands paused over the cards, and something like a cloudy film passed momentarily over her eyes. "So nice to see the good warm weather return. It was a filthy winter, wasn't it?"

"*Grossmutter*." Rolfe leaned forward. "I'm going to Paraguay." He repeated the words—this time louder, more insistent.

"All that snow." She started dealing cards again. "And then the rain this spring."

"*Grossmutter*. I'm going to see Papa."

"Appalling," she muttered. "Truly appalling." She glared at her cards and the bird squawked. "Shut up, Zigi."

"I have a letter from Caffetti. He's not well. They're very worried about him. They say I must go."

The ancient, arthritic, gem-encrusted fingers paused. Her tongue darted out, reptilian-like, across her thin, bluish lips, then retraced again.

"I don't want to go," Rolfe went on heatedly. "But I think I should."

"Did you know that your cousin Rudy is a father again?" She cackled, and, flustered, she dealt her cards again. "Seven children. Imagine that. What splendid fertility. What's the matter with you and Hedi with only two?"

"*Grossmutter*—" he appealed. He pleaded. But she would not be drawn in.

Later, Otto returned with a tray of tea and cakes, but Rolfe excused himself without taking any. When he leaned over to kiss her goodbye, she clasped his hand in her small, cold, prehensile claw, which had the feel of cold marble. "Rolfie." She stared up at him and the musty odor of tobacco and cologne wafted out of her clothing. For the first time that day her eyes appeared childlike and frightened. "Be careful."

At the door he gazed back over his shoulder to wave goodbye, but she'd forgotten him already, lost as she was in the joy of putting bits of cake from the tray into the cockatoo's large, snapping beak.

CHAPTER **17**

At 35,000 feet up the world looks better. You don't see the pockmarks and the pustules. You don't have to smell the bunghole that is civilization. Up here in the still, uncluttered blue, staring at the gauzy configuration of clouds, Mr. Baumstein began to feel better. At least he thought he felt better. A little more himself. The stewardess brought him a scotch, but twenty minutes later he was in the rear of the ship, straddling a steel potty, vomiting chyme into a fetid hole of blue-tinted water that was little better than an outhouse cucking stool. Such is civilization, he thought. You press a button and all the vileness is flushed off in a frothy blue whirlpool of disinfectants while the interminable Muzak croaks Jerome Kern down upon you from overhead. It took thirty million years of evolution to reach this point.

A few moments later Baumstein was back in his seat, the sour taste of eructed enzymes coating his tongue, his feverish forehead pressed hard against the cold panes of window. A gaunt, greenish visage peered back at him from the glass, its expression haggard, querulous, and a trifle injured, like a puppy slapped unjustly, for no apparent cause. He thought to himself now how ill-equipped he was, how poorly suited, for embezzlement and grand larceny. Mr. Peter Baumstein—J. Peter Baumstein actually. (He was part of a mercantile culture that flourished on the claptrap of image fabrication. Insert an initial—any initial—before a Christian name, and lo and behold, one becomes a titled captain of industry.) Baumstein felt like a silly ass, calling himself J. Peter. But he was not an icon smasher. Whatever he thought of them privately, publicly, at least, he subscribed to corporate rituals, as asinine as they were. Baumstein was now a fugitive. He was fleeing home and family, career and a former life upon which he'd squandered youth and health—all to no significant gain for anyone, least of all himself.

At the conclusion of thirty years at hard labor in the marketplace, he was ulcerous, hypertensive, and nearly sixty thousand dollars in debt—a victim of those same chimerical hopes he, as an investment counselor, had helped to foster in the venal hearts of myriad gullible small investors as a means of effectively separating them from their life savings. Many had been effectively separated, including himself. A spider caught in his own elaborate net.

But there was a time in Baumstein's life when things had been decidedly better. He had been, for most of his professional life, a highly prized, richly remunerated economist with degrees from the University of Vienna (the city of his birth) and the Harvard Business School in Cambridge, where he had emigrated as a refugee after the war. Attractive, bright, neither brash nor distastefully aggressive, he was shortly a partner in one of New York's most prestigious brokerage houses. That's when the "J." was prefixed augustly, like a royal title or a papal seal, to his name.

But that was so long ago. The world was bright and fresh then. Full of opportunities. Now he was departing—fleeing to be more precise. He'd stuck a note for Edith on the piano and bank books in the urn on the mantel where he knew she'd find them. There was enough to sustain her for several months. After that, she was on her own. He could do no more.

Why he found it imperative to leave just then was hard to explain, least of all to himself, and he had at that moment neither the time nor the inclination to do so. He was at a point where he sensed that introspection could be crippling, that his badly shattered ego could not and would not sustain the battering of a careful self-scrutiny. All he knew, or cared to know, was that he had to get out. And get while the getting was good.

Still, what a ghastly little joke it all was. A man his age, exhausted from so many years of coping, of contending with the awful drudgery of "getting ahead," suddenly having to decamp now, like some brigand, and steal off into the night, with a dispatch case full of purloined negotiable paper—bearer bonds, stolen traveler's checks, and the like—all jammed in with dentifrice, mouth gargle, a pair of unlaundered pajamas, several bottles of liquid Maalox, and a variety of green and blue pills for the management of elevated blood pressure. At a time of life when one ought decently to be looking forward to a bit of rest, respite from obligations, quittance from all further strife—a small but adequate pension and a quiet retreat at the end of the road—Baumstein was now suddenly confronted with the grim prospect of covering his tracks and starting out all over again.

The engines droned. Night came on and the lights went up in the cabin. Lights too began to flicker upward from below, thick clusters of them marking the placement of large cities; small sporadic ones designating the more isolated outposts of mankind. Each stood for a life, Baumstein thought, an existence—a feeble pulse of light, like a firefly stabbing a dim mote of illumination out into an ever-encroaching darkness.

A baby cried up ahead. Several men were playing cribbage across the aisle, and a stewardess was staring at him oddly.

After supper the dirty steel trays, the miserable little packets of condiments and unused cream, the tiny envelopes of granulated sugar, the crumpled paper napkins were all collected, heaped in a sodden pile, and carted off on a rattling trolley. In order to get to the toilet again he had to wait for the trolley to get past his seat so as to clear the aisle. He was certain he was going to be sick in his seat.

He thought of Edith for a while, having supper just then with her mother in Greenwich, still unaware of his action. And Joel, up at school, not having the faintest suspicion that the golden interval of his insouciant boyhood was rapidly and fatefully drawing to a close. He'd take it hard, but what of it? He'd given Joel sixteen of the best years the boy would ever know. Now he could do no more. Where is it written that the mere deed of procreation is so heinous a sin as to condemn a man to economic bondage for the rest of his life? And if he knew Joel, and he did, the boy was undoubtedly going to spend the next sixteen years of his life on the couch of some particularly venal psychoanalyst—the two of them mutually damning him for all his paternal failures. Baumstein had no illusions, you see. Joel was a selfish, ungrateful little swine, and, while his father was going down, he knew Joel would be kicking him all the way.

The stewardess came by again, this time offering Baumstein a pillow scented with a fragrance reminiscent of pine, but a kind of cloying, thoroughly bogus laboratory pine—a scent manufactured in a vat stowed in some warehouse in New Jersey, or possibly some other state famous for warehouses containing vats of scent. Baumstein took the pillow, punched it despairingly, dimmed his light, and went to sleep.

"Anything to declare, señor?"

"Nothing."

"Ceegarettes? Wheeskie?"

"No. Nothing." Baumstein smiled queasily and held his bag and dispatch case up to the customs inspector. He was a drowsy little Paraguayan with drooping mustaches and an outsized rumpled gray uniform. With its epaulettes and frogging and its big tinny badge, he looked slightly ridiculous, rather like a bit player in an *opéra bouffe.*

The little inspector stabbed with a chalk poker at Baumstein's luggage. The completely fortuitous scrawl left there on the leather surfaces of the two bags resembled broken stars.

"Pasaporte, señor," proclaimed the inspector, and as Baumstein handed it to him, his fingers trembled.

"Señor Gales? You are Señor John Gales?"

"That is correct." Baumstein's voice sounded unnaturally high—strangely distant from him.

While the inspector consulted a master list of names —presumably criminals, undesirables, and those deemed to be political enemies of the Republic—a loudspeaker

Travelers 109

crackled destinations and departures overhead. A blur
of passengers and porters whirled past Baumstein's
swimming vision. Leaning on the customs counter just
ahead of him were two brown-helmeted, jackbooted
policías sporting shiny new Russian AK–47s, slung
raffishly across their shoulders. They laughed and caroused with a blowsy Lufthansa stewardess while Baumstein, heart thudding in his chest, waited breathlessly
for the customs man to finish with his inspection.

"Very good, Señor Gales," the inspector snapped, and
returned his passport. "Hotel?"

"Beg pardon?"

"Your hotel in Asunción, please, señor?"

"Oh." Baumstein glanced uneasily at a gentleman
hovering there close behind him, passport at the ready,
waiting to pass next through customs. He turned back
to the customs inspector. "The Guaraní."

"El Gran Hotel de Guaraní," the inspector scribbled
importantly on a card. *"Muy bueno, señor. Bienvenido
a Paraguay."*

Baumstein moved numbly through the din of the
terminal beneath a wall-sized mural photograph of Alfredo Stroessner. He was in uniform and smiling bene-
volently like God Himself down upon the new arrivals.

Outside the swinging doors, beyond the sanctuary
of air-conditioning, the heat hit him like a sledgehammer. It was palpable and immense, like walking into
the maw of a blast furnace.

The parking lot was choked with cars. Horns blew
and a miasma of exhaust fumes blanketed the place.
More jackbooted police with machine guns piped shrill
whistles and waved menacingly at drivers.

Baumstein stood wilting in the scorched air beside
the mud-spattered, flyblown airport bus, reluctant to
board it, for the temperature within was at least fifteen
degrees hotter than outside on the frying pavement. Al-

ready a row of pale, damp faces appeared at the windows like strange, puffing subaqueous creatures trapped within aquatic tanks. So Baumstein waited there outside, swallowed up in sickening waves of engine exhaust, while two diminutive men of Indian extraction, grunting and sweating, wrestled luggage into the broiling baggage hold beneath the chassis.

Then, finally out of the airport precincts, the old bus groaned southward toward the city, through a haze of poisonous yellow phosphorescence hovering like a fatal toadstool above the landscape. Someone up front had opened a window and, at once, the choking stench of sulphur and burning rubber was everywhere.

The turnpike from the airport into the city had a surrealistic quality—a broad uninhabited vista in which tall nightlamps spaced at regular intervals stretched like gallows all the way to an indeterminate horizon, rather like a de Chirico landscape. Along the road stood chemical works, oil distilleries, high-tension towers, labyrinthine structures forged out of swirling pipes and cylinders, unearthly white spheres circled by steel ladders spiraling ever upwards. Domes and minarets slid backwards past Baumstein, putting him in mind of a postcard his father had sent him forty years ago from Istanbul: "Dear Jake. Here I am in Turkey. The weather's fine. Sorry you can't be here." The bastard. Goddamn his eyes.

He had a sudden vision of them all at the office. He could see old Priestly, her beady, vigilant gaze like a famished vulture fastened on his vacant desk. And Battersby, grim and carping, wattles all aquiver beneath his chin, the spray of veins at his nose, redder, more agitated, fishing out a watch fob, ringing Baumstein's line every fifteen minutes to see if he'd come in.

Surely they've called home by now, Baumstein thought, and Edith has told them everything. She'd probably read his letter to Battersby over the phone, sniveling and daubing a rumpled handkerchief to her mouth to keep down the sobs. And that old sour-breathed bitch, Priestly, swelling with self-righteous indignation, clacking her yellow dentures and handing Battersby the key to his desk with that triumphant "I told you so" look in her eye.

And then all the hushed whispers. The rush of feet trampling back and forth over the pile carpets. Battersby's door opening and closing with uncommon frequency; the minatory ring of phones, and the old fool in and out of his office every minute with that lackey Caruthers right at his heel—bowing and scraping, sycophantic, wringing his hands, full of weasely nice-guy regrets about one's "fall from grace" all the while his eyes lingered hungrily on the buttery yellow leather of Baumstein's brand new Eames chair. And outside, all about the clerks' and tellers' cages, uneasy glances; the fidgety tremulous air of "something's up."

He wondered how long it would take them to start the audit. Surely they'd start at once. That nasty business with Smythe a few years back. It didn't take them more than twenty-four hours after they'd found him belly up in the river—floating near a piling of the bridge from where he'd jumped—for Battersby to bring in the accountants and call an emergency board meeting at two AM. Hauled everyone out of bed and dragged them down there. Christ, he's got his nerve, though, Baumstein brooded. Well, he wouldn't go Smythe's way. Although they'd both succumbed to the same temptation, both of them having a key and combination to the vault, and both being, regardless of high salaries, impecunious in the way most seemingly high-salaried people are impecunious nowadays. And then, of course, all those things—what do they call them?—negotiable instruments, just lying around there. Just waiting to be plucked. There were all those debts, you see; Joel's tuition, Edith's hypochondria and her costly habit of treating it with daily visits to demented specialists of every calling and persuasion. And then that damned farm in Connecticut. Fifty acres of prime meadowland for which the bank caused him to hemorrhage money every month. What the hell did he need a farm for? He, Jacob Peter, who didn't know the front end of a cow from a fire hydrant. It had become a swamp for his money. And those things just lying about in the vault, faintly mocking and come-hither. Like a tart they were. A whore. Just daring him. Try me. Come on, just try me.

"Well, I won't go Smythe's way," Baumstein thought to himself. "I won't give them the satisfaction." And anyway, Smythe was a fool. A real amateur. It would take at least a dozen accountants and two or three of those big new 242s going twenty-four hours a day for a month before they'd unscramble the riddle of the books. "Good," Baumstein mused as the bus rumbled on. "All the more power to me. Make the bastards work for their money. Goddamn their eyes."

El Gran Hotel de Guaraní, just off the Jardin Botanico on the Independencia Nacional. Mr. Fuentes, the manager, searching the register for Baumstein's reservation; a man of suave amiability, the vinyl cordiality of the professional hotel administrator. He was at pains to show his English off to Baumstein. He too now examined the passport.

"A mere formality, Señor Gales." He pronounced the name with careful elocution, rolling the "r" of "Señor" ever so slightly. "Ah, yes, here we are. I have you down for the 16th through the 19th."

"That's correct."

Mr. Fuentes' long, palsied index finger strayed up

the mahogany aisles and rows of little pigeonholed mailboxes just behind the desk. He paused finally at one. *"Trecientos noventa y cuatro,"* he murmured to himself, and plucked down an old bronze key of immense size. It clattered noisily onto the desk, the number 394, stenciled deeply onto its face, coming up at Baumstein like the roll of a die.

"Is there another room I might have?" Baumstein inquired, swallowing audibly as he did so.

"Another room?" Mr. Fuentes appeared puzzled.

Baumstein faltered, his mind gone blank for the moment. How could he tell the man that the digits 394 added up to a total of sixteen, and that sixteen was an unlucky number for him. Had always been. Would always be. Hadn't his brother David died after sixteen months in the camp? Hadn't his very own daughter, barely two years old, died on the 16th of October? And wasn't it on the 16th of April, 1955, that he went to work for Battersby & Co., Ltd., too? A dark day, that.

"Is there something wrong, Señor Gales?"

"No—nothing."

"The room is quite excellent, I assure you. Spacious, with a balcony and a splendid view of the city."

"Yes, of course. I just wondered if you had something else?"

"A little less dear, perhaps?" Mr. Fuentes' eyes twinkled sardonically.

"No, no, the price is fine. I just wondered if there might not be something else," Baumstein murmured again feebly.

Mr. Fuentes smiled his commiserative smile. "I'm afraid not. You see, this is our heavy tourist season. The house is full up. We have many parties going out to San Bernardino and Iguaçu do Foz. I have a huge tour coming in tonight from Buenos Aires. Perhaps in two, three days—"

"Yes, yes," Baumstein sighed impotently. A small, sharp pulse began to throb at the base of his skull. He gazed around the completely empty lobby looking for the alleged glut of tourists. Somewhere nearby in the cavernous shadows beyond the desk he could hear the high, lonely whine of a vacuum cleaner and smell the slightly acrid stench of cold cigar ashes moldering in lobby cuspidors that had not been emptied for weeks.

"Will 394 be all right, Señor Gales?"

Baumstein sighed. "I suppose it will have to be."

"*Bueno.*" Mr. Fuentes thumped a desk bell, and in the next moment an ancient bellman, stooped and wizened, shuffled out of the shadows of the loggia as if he'd been crouching there for all eternity, and limped forward now to the desk.

"*Trecientos noventa y cuatro,*" Mr. Fuentes proclaimed imperiously to this poor battered old devil.

The bellman nodded and took the key, then groaned slightly as he hefted Baumstein's single suitcase. When the man then reached for the dispatch case, Baumstein snatched it back violently. Mr. Fuentes took note of the motion, shaking his head slightly. Baumstein was uncertain whether the silent condemnation in that shake was for him or the bellman.

Once inside the elevator, the bellman flicked a switch, the overhead light dimmed, and the motor purred instantly into motion. Baumstein could feel vibrations in his feet and head. Enclosed within the brass ribs of the narrow coffinlike cage, pressed nearly chest to chest with the ancient bellman, slowly he began to rise. As the compartment swayed ponderously upward, the damp, whitewashed walls of the shaft slid past and Baumstein could smell the stench of sewage wafting up about them from somewhere below, at the bottom of the shaft.

For an instant, Baumstein caught the poor old bellman glancing furtively at him from beneath lowered brows. When he stared back, the old man quickly averted his sad, rheumy eyes and pretended to busy himself with driving the machine.

Once inside 394, the bellman limped across a dusty rug, drew open a pair of heavy chintz drapes and, with a great clatter of tin louvers, drew up a pair of blinds, revealing a skyline scene of downtown Asunción. Instantly a mote-filled shaft of sunlight streamed across the room, and the old man, obviously impressed, as if he had just unveiled the "Primavera," stepped deferentially aside to permit Baumstein to enjoy the scene as well.

Baumstein followed the man into the bathroom where, with a flourish of officiousness, toilets were flushed and spigots spun. This was followed by a brief altercation involving an exchange of *guaranís* and execrable Spanish between them.

As the old man was leaving, Baumstein asked him to send up a bottle of plain Vichy and some ice.

"*Una gaseosa?*"

"*Si, una botella y hielo.*"

"*Ah, si, si,*" the old man said, still holding the *guaranís* in his leathern palm, nodding his head sagely.

The door whispered shut behind him. Then Baumstein was alone in the great shabby decrepitude of 394 with its bogus-gilt department-store Louis Quatorze, its dusty rugs and frayed linen. He was certain the sheets on the bed had not been changed. They had a soiled and rumpled look, and in the bathroom the scent of face powder and cheap toiletries was cloying. The whole place had the desecrated feeling of cheap, hasty assignations—that melancholy air of innumerable bodies continually slinking in and out.

Odd that, Baumstein thought, how in hotels, particularly sleazy ones, some sad emanation of prior occupants lingers on there; some aura of grief and transient desperation clings to the curtains and the shabby upholstery like a sour breath.

It was, however, in all fairness, a thoroughly serviceable room. Suitable, if not ideal, for his purposes. It was not his sort of place, to be sure, but he was a fugitive, and Asunción, lacking extradition treaties of any sort with the rest of the civilized world, was the world's capital of fugitives. Absconding financiers, political criminals, cutpurses and desperate men of every caste and persuasion made the unavoidable hegira there. So why not him? He would remain in Asunción until something better presented itself. After a time, when things cooled down, he might slip into some more civilized setting—something more to his taste, London or Paris, or possibly Zurich—and with his forged papers and shiny new identity cards find himself a cushy little niche on any one of a half-dozen bourses of the Western world. Who knows?

He prided himself on how smoothly things had gone so far. It had been remarkably easy. But he'd planned well. Covered every point. His credit cards, driver's license, passport, and birth certificate, down to the last detail, were all first-rate. And the new social security number was pure inspiration. It was almost too easy, he chuckled. But, then, these Latins were a torpid lot. Characteristically lax. Climate made them that way, he reasoned. It would not be so cinchy in Zurich beneath the icy, vigilant gaze of Swiss bankers.

There was a pair of sliding glass doors behind the open draperies, and beyond that a balcony lined with pots of wilting hibiscus and bougainvillea, upon which ashes sifting down forlornly from the ever-glowing incinerators above had quietly settled. Out on the balcony in the choking air of the street, three floors below him, little dark figures swarmed up and down the tessellated pavements.

From where he stood, Baumstein could peer down at the entrance of a large European café called Las Acacias where just then a truck was pulled up and deliveries were being made. Excitable little men waved their arms and chattered frantically at one another, while they hauled crates and burlap sacks of produce in and out the side entrance of the café.

Alone now, left to his own devices, Baumstein turned immediately to his dispatch case. It was as if he had to gaze on it almost constantly to assure himself that it really existed. With trembling fingers and a mouth dry from fear, he unlocked the case, flipped the clasps, and lifted the lid. Then, breathless, and with eyes burning, he gazed on the splendors shimmering there like rare gems below.

He murmured some exclamation in the argot of his native Austrian tongue, then, with a squeal of delight, plunged his arms up to the elbows into all of that gorgeous, priceless parchment, flipping it wildly into the air and roaring merrily, insanely, while it all cascaded down upon him.

He planned to spend the better part of the next two hours counting, tabulating, recording serial numbers in a small black book and inventorying his take. When at last he tired of that, like a small boy weary of his tin soldiers, he would lock his treasures away in the dispatch case and bury them in the back of a deep wardrobe closet.

It occurred to him now that he was tired, but not in the least unhappy. Neither contrite, nor rueful of the future. He was even optimistic about the possibilities for a new life with his sheaf of magical, instantly transforming, new identity papers.

He missed home and hearth. He could feel the blood

hammering at his temples and clammy sweat pocketing his armpits. But there was something else too—and that was a curious sense of exhilaration at finding himself in a strange city, alone and suddenly free.

Just then the doorbell rang. That in turn was followed by a knock—rude and peremptory. The tone of it made Baumstein's bowels grind. He had a sudden vision of blackbooted policemen standing outside his door, pistols at their hips, a warrant in their pockets for his arrest, and proclaiming aloud to him his rights as an American citizen. His panicky eyes swarmed around the room for a quick way out. Then suddenly, with relief, he recalled the old lame bellman who had scurried off to fetch his *gaseosa*. Probably they had no *gaseosa*, he thought, and absolutely no ice. Would he prefer instead a *limonada?*

Prepared to be unpleasant, Baumstein crossed at once to the door and yanked it open. There, indeed, was the old man. He stood just beyond the threshold now, gaping in at Baumstein and holding in his palsied hand a tray on which rattled a small, bead-frosted bottle of Vichy water. The sudden motion of the door being flung open had startled the old fellow, causing him to step back, the tray to dip, and the bottle to teeter perilously. Both men lunged for it at the same moment, and their hands scrambled for it together on the rug; it was then that the old bellman saw the numbers—all seven of them—tattooed in faded and wavery blue figures on the area just above and on the inside of J. Peter Baumstein's wrist.

Part III

ASUNCION

CHAPTER 18

"Education?"

"BS–MS, Hebrew University."

"Profession?"

"Electrical engineer."

"How old did you say?"

"Twenty-four, twenty-five. Very promising career."

"Pity. Young fool. Height?"

"Six-two."

"Weight?"

"Oh, twelve stone, I should judge."

"Military experience?"

"Israeli Special Tactical Forces. Five years. Decorated for valor during the '73 campaigns. Demolition and light weapons expert."

"Then he's dangerous."

"Exceedingly." The Israeli Ambassador sat back behind his capacious desk on the top floor of the Embassy building on the Avenida Choferes del Mar in Asunción and regarded the small, intense uniformed gentleman who sat there questioning him.

Colonel Arganas looked up from the pad into which he'd been scribbling. "And this curious aberration of mind, you say?"

"Began, I should judge, shortly after the Sinai campaign. Mind simply snapped. Battle fatigue. Nerve strain. Disillusionment. Possibly a combination of all three. Whatever—in any event, he set out on this God-given mission of . . ."

121

"Extermination?" Colonel Arganas supplied the word, then scribbled it into his pad.

"I'm afraid so." The Ambassador cleared his throat.

"Do you know under what name he entered the country, Your Excellency?"

"It could be any one of a dozen aliases. He has forged papers in several nationalities and speaks at least a half-dozen languages perfectly. He's a master of disguise."

The Colonel flicked his pad closed and tucked it into his tunic. "And he chooses Paraguay as his theater of operations?"

"Let us be frank." The Ambassador opened a humidor of cigars and extended it across the wide, paper-strewn expanse of desk. "You happen to have here in your country a rather heavy concentration of precisely the kind of individual Ian Asher is compulsively drawn to."

"Are we talking about thieves or fugitive Nazi war heroes, Excellency?" The Colonel winked mischievously and thoughtfully selected a cigar.

"I gather quite frequently they're one and the same." The Ambassador reached across the desk with his flaming lighter. "But for simplicity's sake, I'd say more the latter than the former."

"Ah, I see." Arganas rose, puffing his cigar, and proceeded to pace thoughtfully about the room. "As you very well know, I have little sympathy with this kind of 'individual' myself."

"But, nonetheless," the Ambassador went on tauntingly, "as a nation you find it highly profitable to serve as a sanctuary for them."

The Colonel stiffened. His finely attenuated nostrils flared. "That is most unkind, Excellency. Personally, I abhor the lice. But as long as they are guests within these sovereign borders, this country is sworn to protect their rights."

"Yes, yes." The Ambassador waved impatiently. He had heard it all before. "But we have now the question of a deranged young man who's come here with the avowed purpose of assassination. To the best of my knowledge, he's already liquidated three people."

"Three?"

"One in Luba. One in Memel. Both known Nazi war criminals. The third"—the Ambassador lowered his voice and eyes simultaneously—"was a case of mistaken identity."

"He killed the wrong man?"

"Regrettably."

"And his target here is Doctor Grigori?"

"Undoubtedly."

The Colonel paused in his perambulations, folded his arms, and mused for a moment in a haze of smoke. "Tell me. Does he mean to kill Grigori or bring him back alive to Israel for trial?"

The Ambassador sighed and rolled his eyes heavenward. "Let me put it this way, Colonel. If Asher were to come across the Doctor today, I can assure you, he'd shoot him on the spot. And that we cannot permit to happen. My government has no wish to see the thousand and some odd Jews living today in Paraguay pogromized by the German community here as a result of the actions of some crazed assassin. We don't want another bloodbath such as we had during the Eichmann affair."

The Colonel nodded his head sympathetically. "And, of course, *El Jefe* has every reason to wish to preserve the delicate balance that exists here between the Jewish and German communities."

The Ambassador smiled. "It is to our mutual benefit, Colonel."

"Precisely. And if that is *El Jefe*'s wish, we shall of course honor it."

The two men beamed at each other like a pair of conspirators who have agreed on satisfactory terms.

"I should add," the Ambassador went on, "that the Mossad has even more reason to wish to see Asher run to ground. As you know, he is an ex-Mossad agent."

"Cashiered, I gather, for disobedience and recklessness."

"Yes—and now he has the temerity to go about with forged papers, still posing as an active Mossad operative, still privy to state secrets." The Ambassador unfurled an immense handkerchief and wiped his brow. "That could be embarrassing."

"And very dangerous as well," the Colonel taunted. "The fellow must be mad."

"As a hatter. With beatifying missions, no less. Pretensions to sainthood and calling himself the 'Blue Falcon' or some such rot."

"The Blue Falcon?" Arganas laughed. "How droll."

The Ambassador glowered. "If he succeeds in his mission here, my dear Colonel, I can assure you, you won't think it very droll." The Ambassador sighed and folded his pudgy hands across his capacious middle. "Quite frankly, as for Doctor Grigori, I'd love to see the bastard strung up by the heels and gelded. That would be fitting justice. I'm sure the world would rejoice. Then my government could make a suitable fuss over the outrage, charge Asher with treason and murder, and put him safely behind bars."

"And, after several months, release him and declare him a national hero with a fat pension for the rest of his life." Arganas clucked his tongue snidely. "How cynical we have all become, ay, Excellency?"

"Yes, Colonel." The Ambassador winked. "Not the

least of which is a government calling itself a democracy which protects the likes of a Grigori up in Zone 540, while at the same time protesting to the world that he's nowhere to be found in the country."

Arganas and the Ambassador glared at each other for a moment, then burst into laughter. When the Ambassador rose, it was to take down from a nearby shelf a carafe of whiskey and two glasses. He poured two double shots and passed one over to the Colonel. "Tell me, Félix, where will you start your search for the Falcon?"

The Colonel drained his glass with a single draught. "Why, in the Jewish community right here, Excellency. Where else? With the many excellent paid informers I maintain there."

CHAPTER 19

"That's him."

"You're sure?"

"Of course I'm sure."

"It's been thirty years. Faces change, you know."

"Not that face. That face will never change for me. It will always be just as it is there."

In a small basement apartment in Mompox in Asunción's Bahia district, two men sat in a darkened room observing gray-white flickering figures projected on a wall. The filmed figures were walking in the high grass of what appeared to be a vast rolling plain. The pale, somewhat imperfect quality of the film gave them a rather ghostly appearance as if they were people long-since dead.

"Run the film back for a moment."

There was a click, and the high whirr of the projector made a reversing sound, as the figures in the film slid backward across the wall. Then another click and they marched forward again.

"That's him, all right. There's no mistake."

"Who's the other fellow? The bald man."

"Caffetti. Ricardo Caffetti. A business associate of the family."

"Dangerous?"

"Extremely. Stay far away from the man."

"And the other two?"

"The young chaps up front, you mean?"

"Yes. You can barely make them out." The man speaking was Ian Asher. He strode up to the wall now, where the figures flickered eerily, and thrust a hand, suddenly black and immense, into the illuminated square. "Right there. With the Mausers."

"That would be Matschke and Von Rattenhuber. Rattenhuber's the taller of the two."

"Bodyguards?"

"Yes, but referred to euphemistically as 'companions.' Actually, they're just thugs. Hired killers. Very bad business. Stay far away from them too."

"Don't worry about them. I'll take care of them."

Just then two of the Macá beaters loped across the apartment wall in slow motion, rattling gourds and pots.

"Here they come again," said the other man, slumped there in the darkness, his feet propped on a chair, great puffs of smoke from his cigarette curling upward through the beam of the film projector.

For a moment they sat silently watching a view of a

large jaguar bounding through the grass and one of the hunters raising his rifle and firing at it.

Suddenly the wall went white. A series of numbers starting from ten and descending to one were flashed there, then darkness, followed by a light going up in the room.

For a while the two men sitting there were silent. They continued to gaze at the wall as if they could still see figures moving across it.

"Well, that's it, then," said the other man, rising. "When do you go?"

"When he leaves for Encarnación."

"Undoubtedly he'll travel by boat," said the man who had been talking throughout the film. His name was Arturo Rubens. He was about forty-five years old, a naturalized Paraguayan. Short, stocky, powerfully built with sandy hair beginning to gray, Rubens had come to Asunción via Buenos Aires via Auschwitz, from which he had been liberated by the Russians in 1945. "In the past he's always gone down there on his launch."

"How long a trip is it?"

"About three days downriver."

"I'll need to be advised a few days before he leaves," Asher said. "Time to get there. Put myself in place. May I see a copy of that letter again?"

The man called Rubens handed him a Xerox copy of a letter written several weeks before from Paraguay.

" 'With love to your dear wife and my beloved grandchildren,' " the tall man read aloud in his quiet, ruminative manner. " 'I look forward to our reunion in Encarnación at the end of the month.'

"The end of the month?" Asher frowned. "That could be any time in the next two weeks." He screwed out his cigarette in a glass jar. "There's got to be a new letter soon with more specific details."

"We've got every message and transmission coming

out of there covered," said Rubens. "Letters, phone calls, telex cables."

"And you say he goes now to Bariloche?"

"That's right. That's our information. For at least five, six days. He goes there every year at this time. Meets with an old friend by the name of Krug. Alban Krug."

"What sort of place is Bariloche?" Asher inquired.

"Luxury resort. High up in the Cordillera. Very popular with the chiefs and the old hardliners. When there, Grigori stays at the Llao Llao."

Rubens slipped into his jacket. "They all do. Stroessner himself stays there. It's their playground. Fancy casinos. Expensive ladies. That sort of thing. We have information that Schwend and four or five more of the big boys will be checking in at the same time. Grigori likes the swimming there, and hiking the mountain trails on the Tronador peak. Plays a lot of bezique at night and flirts with the young girls."

"I see," said Asher pensively. He appeared to be calculating something on his feet.

"Why not hit him there?" Rubens asked.

"No good." Asher shook his head from side to side. "Too much security around. The place will be crawling with bodyguards and there are routes of escape. The boat's the place, all right. I've only the crew to contend with there, and a couple of guards. There's no escape route unless you swim, and the river is a mile across at either point. No, I'll stick with the boat."

Rubens pondered a moment, then shrugged. "In any event, the houses in Puerto Stroessner and Zone 540 are both under twenty-four-hour-a-day surveillance. We have the son's residence in Günzburg covered too. We know he's recently applied for a renewal of his Argentine visa."

"I see," Asher mused thoughtfully.

"We won't be able to give you much in the way of assistance. We're watched very closely here and I'm afraid we're plagued by informers within our own small community."

"Whatever you provide will be fine," Asher replied quietly. He smiled to himself. "The moment the son leaves for Argentina, so do I. He'll lead me right to the old man."

"It can't be soon enough for me," said Rubens. He rose.

"You're much too impatient, my friend," said Asher gently. "You know, at least a dozen people have died trying to get to Grigori. They were all impatient like you."

Rubens buttoned his topcoat. "I've waited a long time for this. I have the scars to show for it."

Asher came forward now. Smiling, he took Rubens' hand. "Don't worry, Arturo. This shall be done. I promise you. Put it out of your mind now. Go back to your job in the postal service. Continue to monitor all of the Doctor's correspondence. And keep me informed."

Asher put his arm around Rubens, guiding him slowly toward the door. "And don't worry about me. I'll be in Bariloche within the fortnight."

When they reached the door Rubens turned suddenly, agitated and worried. "Don't think it will be easy. Don't think you're going to walk into Asunción or Puerto Stroessner and find him waiting there for you. He's wily. He's shrewd and very dangerous. He's a cat with nine lives. His instinct for trouble is uncanny. He has an elaborate and well-paid ring of personal informers—policemen, magistrates, immigration officials. The moment they smell something funny—if they get even one whiff of you—he'll be out of the place forty-eight hours before you can set foot there. He'll lose himself

in the Chagras or in the jungles up around the Gran
Chaco. He has at least a dozen hideouts up there and
a bunker in addition to the one at 540. It's all un-
charted and impenetrable country, patrolled and protected by the nastiest bunch of plug-uglies you've ever
set eyes on. And all at his beck and call. If he gets back
up into there, you wouldn't get within a hundred miles
of him before you'd be shot or have your throat slit."
Rubens paused at the open door. "How will you do it?"

"It?" Asher was puzzled.

"Kill him? How will you do it? Tell me the actual
way." Rubens' eyes glowed a little madly.

The young man was silent for what seemed an unnaturally long time. Then slowly he shook his head
and smiled sadly. "Whatever I do, Arturo, I promise
you won't be disappointed." The young man's eyes
were beady and riveting with the kind of steely blue one
associates with frigid weather.

"When does Dovia arrive?" Rubens asked.

"Tomorrow evening—I'm on my way to Buenos
Aires tonight to get her."

"Go with God then," Rubens said. His eyes were
troubled. "And be careful."

Sometime after Rubens had left, Asher sat by himself
at the small kitchen table of the apartment in Mompox.
In the dying light of afternoon he drank milk from a
cardboard container and ate sugar cookies and played
eagerly and delightedly with a child's top.

He was a strange young man, Asher. Hard to get
close to and almost impossible to know. Of the bare-
bones facts of his life, very little was known, but the
fullest and most complete dossier on his activities is to
be found in a restricted section of the files of the Israeli
Secret Service. A cursory study of those files, assuming

you had been vouchsafed clearance to review them, would reveal the following:

Ian Asher was the son of a Jewish Irgun hero and an Irish Catholic mother. His father died in the Negev of machine-gun wounds inflicted by the Egyptians during the '57 campaigns, at which time his grieving mother took him back to Ulster where, at the age of sixteen, he had become passionately involved in the tragic politics of civil warfare there.

At the age of twenty he was back in the Holy Land attending university. In between extended bouts of military service, he took a degree with honors in physics and electrical engineering.

No one knew very much about Asher. He had no family and he did not cultivate friends. Though a highly attractive young man, in that rather surly, inaccessible manner that many women find alluring, he was seldom, if ever, seen in the company of a female.

Now, at the age of twenty-four or -five (no one is certain), he spent most of his free time reading Jewish law and the hagiography of Christian saints, all supplemented with zesty dollops of T. E. Lawrence, whose memory he revered. Often he would dream that he was with Lawrence in the desert, dynamiting Turkish ammunition trains bound for Jiddah. But mostly he would imagine himself some mutilated and transfigured saint sizzling on a pyre in a transport of ecstasy. And though his father and his paternal grandparents had never been within a thousand miles of a concentration camp, nevertheless, in his more heightened states of consciousness, he would imagine himself an internee of such a camp —for were not these tortured and incinerated people the contemporary counterparts of martyred saints?

Ian Asher, it seems, was the child of calamity. In a quarter-century of life, the very blush of youth, he'd already fought and killed in Ireland, Angola, and Israel;

in the first as a Catholic guerrilla, in the second as a mercenary paid out of the coffers of a government whose identity he did not know, and in the third as a commando, highly decorated for bravery in two wars, as well as innumerable clandestine actions taken deep behind enemy lines. In whatever theater of war he served, it was always in behalf of some patchwork of vague, inchoate causes, which one would be hard put to reconcile into any single governing principle, be it political, moral, or otherwise, save that he told himself, and those who had the temerity to inquire, that what he did, he did for the "common good" and that was surely enough.

He was a man given to causes, though he could not precisely articulate them. His instincts were more for action than for introspection. Not that he did not brood a great deal and dwell inwardly on questions of motivation and "right," but had he truly examined what it was that led him each time into the din and fray of battle— drew him in as on some long, invisible leash across oceans and continents toward devastation and holocaust—he might have been forced to concede that even more than the "common good" as a call to duty was the tingling sense of excitement he invariably felt when in the presence of impending violence. This was where he felt exhilarated, supremely alive. Without the gorgeous nighttime incandescence of artillery fire overhead, without the stink of cordite in his nostrils, and the ghastly cries of mangled men groaning all about him, life was a very bland, apathetic thing indeed.

Within Israel, his activities were well known to the police and the Mossad, who had good cause to watch him. Outside of that small nation his name appeared on the records and dossiers of at least a half-dozen law-enforcement agencies throughout the world, including the NKVD, the CIA, Scotland Yard's Special Branch, the Bundes Kriminalen, the Questiore, and the central headquarters of Interpol at St. Cloud. In all dossiers he was invariably described as "professional," "unbalanced," and "dangerous." Within intelligence circles he was referred to as the "Blue Falcon." No one knew precisely how or why the title became associated with him. An older breed of man than those running police and intelligence agencies today, however, would have quickly recalled that the Blue Falcons were an Irgun brigade. Closer study would have revealed that Asher's father had at one time led that brigade—a small, elite group of men whose specialty was execution —a talent at which, as the British came sorrowfully to learn, the Blue Falcons excelled.

Asher is a very secretive man. He travels about a lot, in and out of Israel, and he never seems to want for money. Some people hint at ties, albeit clandestine, to the Israeli government, particularly the Mossad, for whom, it is rumored, he might be an agent. None of this is verifiable, at least through the Israelis, who have long ago disavowed Asher, at least publicly. What private arrangements existed between the government and Asher, or more specifically, the Mossad and Asher, people joked, was another matter entirely.

One further detail might be added to Asher's brief history. At the conclusion of the Yom Kippur War, in which he had served with distinction, Asher was sent to a military hospital in Haifa. The record, if one bothers to consult it, maintains that he was sent there to recover from exhaustion and fatigue. However, the particular hospital in which Asher was interned for nearly three months is well known in Israel as a center for the study of mental disorders. The inmates are kept under strictest surveillance, the windows are barred, and the perimeter of the place is secured by the presence of a high cyclone fence.

It was from this institution that Ian Asher had escaped, and he has been at large ever since.

CHAPTER 20

Catedral de Cristo Rey—Asunción

"*. . . Spiritus sanctus . . . Nomine patris . . . filii . . .*"

Doctor Grigori on his knees took communion. "Forgive me, Father, for I have sinned." The wafer dissolved to a thin watery pulp on his tongue. "Forgive me, Father . . ." Grigori on his knees in the confessional. "I have been in vile company again, Father. With low women . . . I have cohabitated. Forgive me, Father. Why this need to degrade myself? To humiliate myself —over and over again? This loathing I feel. O Father, I regret . . ." Grigori cried out in high, anguished tones. Then, as he remembered his place, his voice trailed off and he shifted on his knees in the cramped confessional. It was a small space, airless and stifling, lined with bombazine. "But I have also gone three times since my last confession to the Aché to treat the sick," he added, by way of balancing the books. "I am tired, Father. I miss my children and my home. I long to see my land once more before I die. I am weary, Father, and frightened. I was not frightened before. But I fear now I will never see my son and grandchildren again. All these years, I have not been frightened. Now suddenly . . . what is it I fear, Father? Not my avengers, surely.

That's child's play. Fools and heroes and vain gestures. I will smash them all as I have before.

"But if it is not my avengers I fear, then what is it exactly that I do fear? I have a dream, Father. I dream it over and over again. I am in a strange, desolate land. Full of small children. There are no adults there. They run and scamper all about me. Play and sing. They tug at my clothing. They beseech me to play with them. Their eyes burn brightly and they seem scarcely human. Wraithlike—small dead creatures. Only they're animated and dancing all about me. One rumples my hair. Another pulls a button from my coat. I'm terrified. Then I see that there are not only children there, but dwarfs as well. Little homunculi, hunched and grotesque. And there are the filthy little gypsy children, too, all running naked and yammering. All waiting for me, and I'm frightened."

10:30 AM   *The Café Flores*

Behind dark glasses Doctor Grigori passed through the narthex door of the cathedral and out into the dazzling sunshine of Asunción's morning. He wore a white tropical business suit and a yellow poplin shirt open at the collar, and a wide-brimmed slouch hat to protect him from the sun. Squinting, he covered his brow as he emerged from the shadowy arches, for even with the protection of his glasses and hat pulled far forward and down, the sudden bright sunlight hurt his eyes. Then he was out among the people, strolling in the square before the church, hordes of scruffy pigeons wambling and purring about his feet.

Followed at a short distance by his two young companions, the Doctor strolled to his favorite barber shop on the Estrella where he had a haircut and shave. He chatted about the national lottery in demotic Spanish with his hairdresser, Carlos, while great foamy clots of shaving cream were carved from his face.

Thus shorn and anointed, redolent of ointments and cologne, he sauntered out once more into the Calle de Lillas. Horst and Ludo, like devoted hounds, trailed at his heels. His feet carried him in no particular direction. He merely drifted through the Estrella, a look of remote abstraction about him. From time to time he paused to gaze in a shop window.

At a certain point a ragged, scruffy Indian boy of six or seven years walked past him. He was barefoot and there were running scabrous sores on his legs. His palm was extended in the age-old gesture of the mendicant. Grigori proffered a few coins, pressed into the small dirty palm. The boy looked neither right nor left. He said nothing, nor did he bother to acknowledge the charity. He merely walked on through the crowds like a somnambulist.

Walking thus unencumbered in the bright morning sunshine, people flowing all about him, he felt a strange exhilaration, an unaccustomed oneness with all the others moving about him in the street. A sense of being human again, as opposed to being in 540, where he felt like a mole in its burrow.

At a small variety shop called the Casa Inolvidable at the end of a quaint mews, the Doctor paused to admire a little German music box that sat in the window amid a clutter of puppets and figurines, cheap jewelry, and brummagem. The music box made him think of his mother in Günzburg. He recalled precisely where it sat in the old house on a Biedermeier card table with a green baize top. He smiled down at the box, scarcely aware of the two lady shop proprietors gazing back out at him.

Esther Lederer and Sonia Halevy stared at the face

looming suddenly at their shop window, a faint, curious smile playing about its lips. Their blood ran cold and they were filled with a horrible sense of loathing. They had seen that face before. Not only at their shop window, but thirty-three years before in a cold, drizzly prison yard at Birkenau, for he was the great *Selektor* then, who gave them candy when they were children and gassed their parents. Today in Asunción they knew him as Doctor Neiditch. But in Birkenau they knew him as *Den Schönen Doktor,* Doctor Grigori.

With three-quarters of an hour to go before his doctor's appointment, Grigori sat down at one of the outside tables of the Café Flores in Chávez Street, at the same time inviting an old blind man to join him for coffee.

"Will you have a cigarette?" the Doctor asked in his thick, inelegant Spanish after the coffee was served. Most solicitous of the aged figure who reminded him of Tiresias, the old blind prophet, he placed a package of Egyptian cigarettes in the calloused, scaly palm, which looked like reptile skin. With palsied fingers, the old fellow fumblingly extracted one, then handed the package back to the Doctor, who lit it for him.

"Beautiful morning," the Doctor remarked offhand-edly.

"Yes, sir," the old man nodded. "That it is." He sipped his coffee and they were silent for a while, enjoying the warmth of the sun. Nearby, Horst and Ludo were having a beer and flirting with a waitress. Grigori turned back to the old man.

"What would you do if you knew you were sitting with a murderer?" he asked.

"A murderer?" The blank, lightless eyes stared directly ahead.

"Yes." Grigori twinkled with amusement. "At this

very moment you are sitting having coffee with a murderer."

"Oh, sir." The old man was flustered and incredulous.

"It's true. I have murdered hundreds—thousands of people with a flick of my wrist. I have tortured and cruelly misused innocent children."

"I swear to you on the Holy Cross," Grigori pleaded. "I have done despicable things. I am a beast—beneath contempt."

"Oh, sir. Why tell me? There's no need. No need . . ."

"Your voice is kind, I cannot believe—"

"Believe it, my friend," the Doctor pleaded softly. "What I tell you is true."

The old man's palsied hand fumbled across the table until it found Grigori's hand and topped it. "Even if it were true, to acknowledge such sins as you just have is the beginning of absolution. Pray for forgiveness."

Doctor Grigori gazed blankly at the old blind man and shook his head. It was a gesture that mingled both despair and contempt. Suddenly he asked: "Is the darkness frightening to you?"

For a moment the old man seemed puzzled. Then he laughed. "Oh, you mean my eyes."

"Yes. Do you see any light at all?"

"No. None at all. Simple blackness. It's not at all frightening."

"You've been that way since birth?"

"Yes. I've never known anything else." The old man laughed. "I'd be frightened if suddenly I saw things. I think that would be terrifying."

"To see things?" The Doctor's laugh was ironic. The blood-red Paraná with its disembodied heads flashed in his mind's eye. "Yes, I suppose. Most terrifying."

11:15 AM *The Office of Doctor Enríquez*

"A little more. A little more. That's it. That's it. Fine. Very good."

Doctor Grigori on an examination table. Crouched over on all fours, he submitted, grunting and red faced, to Doctor René Enríquez' proctoscopic scan of his lower colon.

"There's nothing there. It's absolutely clean."

"Don't tell me there's nothing there. I know there's something there—a polypoma. A tumor. I feel it on elimination. There's blood in my stool."

"Hemorrhoids, my dear Doctor. No more, no less. Eat soft, laxative foods."

"You're a fool, Enríquez," Grigori snarled. "You must be blind. There's a lesion there. Undoubtedly cancerous."

Doctor Enríquez sighed with a weary futility. "There's no sign of cancer in your colon, Neiditch. I don't know what I can do to convince you. If you do not trust my opinion, you're perfectly free to seek another."

"From whom?" Grigori hauled on his trousers. "Who would trust any of these Latin quacks? I wouldn't give you a nickel for the whole goddamned pack of them. They're all inept. Poorly trained. What I need is a good German doctor."

"By all means. Be my guest." Enríquez peeled off his rubber gloves.

"Believe me, my friend," Doctor Grigori glowered, "would that I could. Would that I could just get on a plane and—"

2:15 PM   *Café Bavaria, Calle de las Mariposas*

"Number 22. Fräulein Giselle Kletzburg."

A voice boomed into a megaphone and a squat, dumpy girl in a one-piece bathing suit teetered out from behind a beige curtain to the strains of "Countess Maritza" scratched out on a stridulous café fiddle. There was the pop of Taittinger bottles uncorking. Platters of wurst and smoked fish, trays of strudel and sachertorte, sherbets and berries in kirsch all rolled past on a steel trolley. The air was drugged and clouded with the smothering fragrance of expensive Havanas. Two hundred or so people sat about at a number of circular banquet tables, waiters scurrying in and out of the aisles to serve them.

There was a great burst of applause as Fräulein Kletzburg, of Asunción, a hometown sentimental favorite, sauntered off. Then a drum roll, and once again the voice boomed into the megaphone. "Number 19— Fräulein Ursula Sharmscraft from Iguaçu do Foz."

The master of ceremonies who introduced the girls was a man of about fifty in a shiny tuxedo, with rouged cheeks and an execrable toupee. The girl he had called forth this time was a strapping young Swabian with equine features and bulging thighs. She tripped tentatively forward on high heels across the small elevated platform. She too sported an outdated one-piece bathing suit. Her eyes were lowered and she was blushing profusely.

"Oh la la," ogled the master of ceremonies, and as the girl completed her twirl at the edge of the platform a red swastika armband worn on her bicep flashed into view.

At the judges' table, a dais set up front not far from the platform, Doctor Grigori sat with a panel of seven other men—cronies from the old country, party *Bonsen, schwere Fälle,* chiefs of the Kameradenwerk. They sat all about him in old SS uniforms, pressed and spruced up for the occasion. They wore their division medals and campaign ribbons. There was a great deal of "Sieg Heiling" and heel-clicking and stomping about in jackboots that had been tucked away in attics for thirty years. Amid the euphoria engendered by kirsch and and fine Havana cigars, people reminisced nostalgically about the glories of the Third Reich and the awesome puissance of the Fourth, whose appearance, they all agreed, was imminent. They had come there—emigrés, fugitives, and criminals at large—from hiding places as far-flung as La Paz and Quito, Rio de Janeiro and Santiago de Chile. Some owned luxurious *estancias* in San Carlos de Bariloche or rich cattle spreads up and down the fertile Pampas. Others ran taxi fleets in Montevideo or cargo ships out of Antofagasta and Guayaquil. They had come there seeking the comfort and reassurance of familiar faces; to sing old party songs; to see how this one had fared and what time had done to that one.

Doctor Grigori had come there too, as he had for the past several years, as one of the honored judges in the annual Miss Nazi Beauty Pageant of Latin America. But as of late he had not enjoyed the occasion as much. He found himself tired and irritable. Now he sipped from a flute of champagne and scribbled scores onto a pad.

"Number 12. Frieda Hochmuth from Encarnación."

The drum rolled again and the fiddle scratched. A pretty Guaraní Indian boy poured another flute of Taittinger '59 Blanc-de-Blancs for the Doctor.

"Ask her to turn once more," cried out Freddie Schwend, who'd come down there from Lima.

The girl, robust and fair, twirled confidently, smiling boldly at Schwend.

"How do you score that one, Gregor?" Schwend asked, red in the face and panting with excitement. The master of ceremonies crooned behind the girl.

"She's a seven out of ten." The Doctor scribbled onto his pad.

"She's worth at least a nine. Those thighs alone—"

"Very well, Freddie." Grigori laughed. "Ask her to pass the dais again."

Once again the girl was brought forth and, while the master of ceremonies moaned "Vienna Nights" into his megaphone, Fräulein Hochmuth executed a number of clumsy pirouettes.

"Come now, Gregor, is that not perfection?" Schwend sighed. "That's at least a nine out of ten."

"It is not," snapped Otto Huensch from Santiago, sitting on Schwend's left. "And I object, Schwend, to your goddamned pushiness."

"Pushiness?"

"Exactly," Huensch fumed on. "Every year you come down here promoting one of your tarts."

"I?" Schwend's hurt eyes opened like blooming peonies. "Promote tarts?"

"Yes. You promote tarts," Huensch persisted. "And I object. It's disgusting. An affront to everyone here. Gregor—surely you see—"

Schwend, swelling, rose from his place. "How dare you?"

"Gentlemen—gentlemen—"

In the ensuing moments there was an altercation between the seven judges, centering around Schwend and Huensch. Fräulein Hochmuth stood wringing her hands helplessly before the judges, while the master of ceremonies, totally unfazed, continued to croon "Vienna Nights" into the megaphone. In the midst of all this melee, Schwend tossed a flute of champagne into

Huensch's face. Instantly both men were cuffing each other.

Suddenly and quite unaccountably, Doctor Grigori giggled. Shortly he was howling with glee, gales of laughter erupting from him. His whole body was convulsed and shaken with strange hootings. Tears streamed down his cheeks.

For a brief time the Doctor's laughter was contagious, and several of the judges laughed right along with him. But their mirth was forced and nervous. It could not match the Doctor's in volume or duration. Also, there was a curious undercurrent of something to the Doctor's laughter—something indefinable, nevertheless unsettling, that was not present in that of the others. The girl, forgotten and humiliated on the small stage, stumbled off.

Schwend and Huensch ceased their squabbling and the other panelists all gazed at the Doctor uneasily. Much of the laughter and chatter in the room now broke off abruptly too. The master of ceremonies at last fell silent and even the stridulous fiddle trailed squeakingly off, isolating finally the awful sound of Doctor Grigori's strange, harrowing, mirthless laughter.

CHAPTER 21

Flutes, harps, marimbas. Timbals quavering in the smoky violet air of a neon-lit café. The motor of a large air conditioner rumbled noisily, sending chill, wet waves of air wafting outward from it.

Outside the window of the Café Las Acacias on the

Avenida Choferes del Chaco lay the purple sweltering dusk of Asunción. A great blaze of lights glowing beyond the glass marked the white porte cochere of the Gran Hotel de Guaraní.

Mr. Baumstein devoured a small steak, then asked the waiter to bring him another. Only an hour before he had been standing on his balcony at the Guaraní and wondering where he would dine. He gazed down and saw the lights of the small café twinkling in the dusky street below. The sign glowed a warm, festive orange, putting him in mind of the holiday season in New York. It was extremely inviting. A short time later Baumstein was ensconced within the ample curve of a leathery banquette in a shadowy, candlelit corner of the Acacias, turning his attention to a large, bead-frosted double martini.

For a brief while Baumstein dwelled ruefully on visions of old Battersby closeted with hordes of Treasury agents, and then Edith dismembering the remains of his estate with vulturous lawyers.

The appearance of his second steak and another double martini quickly banished all further gloomy speculations. When he looked up he heard the pop of a champagne cork and a burst of laughter. A number of waiters scurried back and forth before his table, all streaming like magnetic filings to a tenebrous little corner a dozen feet or so beyond him.

Several red-vested waiters were just then buzzing around three gentlemen seated at a table there. In all the café there were perhaps a dozen or fifteen people, yet most of the staff appeared to occupy themselves only with the needs of the three gentlemen. Baumstein watched a maitre d' bow from time to time in response to the murmur of a voice giving orders in a firm, deliberate tone. Though the murmur was low, it was peppered liberally with a stream of piercing sibilants that he heard quite distinctly from where he sat.

Baumstein could not see the occupants of the table. (There was too much activity around them.) But he could hear their voices. At first he imagined they were speaking Spanish; then it occurred to him that it was German, or possibly a combination of both. He had not heard his native tongue spoken in a number of years. He himself had consciously avoided speaking it since he had been naturalized, but hearing it now, spoken with such gruff, clipped authority, and in such proximity to himself, was oddly unsettling. A short time later he heard a voice snarl "Roederer '53" and the name "Don Gregor" repeated over and over again.

Shortly the maitre d' and the waiters all withdrew and suddenly the three gentlemen seated at the nearby candlelit table were in Baumstein's full view. They were all in evening dress, as if they were going from the Acacias to the theater or the opera. The candlelight playing on their features gave them a curiously sinister appearance.

One of these gentlemen was small, slightly larger than a dwarf, with an unnaturally large head and an immense flowing white beard. Rosy, apple cheeks and a meerschaum stuck in the middle of his mouth gave him the quaint, almost toy-like appearance of a department-store Santa Claus. He wore a rose carnation in the lapel of his tuxedo and drank copious tankards of ale. When he laughed, he had a habit of pounding the table with his little mallet fists.

The gentleman seated beside him was tall and angular, rather saturnine, with dark, sleek unparted hair combed severely back from his brow. There was something rather Byronic about him—gaunt, stormy, and ill-starred, and though he laughed with the others, some unaccountable melancholy appeared to hover about him.

It was the third man from whom Baumstein could not unhinge his gaze. Undoubtedly, it was the extravagant Old World cut of his dress—the opera cape, the monocle screwed into his left eye, and the pearl-handled cane with which he fiddled incessantly at the table. Not only was it extravagant, it was bizarre. And it was to this third gentleman that the waiters paid most assiduous court. They bowed and scraped, genuflecting before him and backing off like lackeys as he sampled and evaluated each dish.

Baumstein watched this performance transfixed. Suddenly, a number of things were going on inside him for which he could scarcely account. That warm, slightly heady feeling of well-being that he'd been savoring only moments before was gone, replaced now by icy hands and a dry, thick tongue, a feeling as of a large fist closing over his heart.

The little dwarflike figure, it seemed, had just completed telling a story. He pounded the table with his fists. The gentleman in the opera cape tossed his head back and laughed out loud. Baumstein saw a bit of gold flash in his teeth. Then the monocle dropped from the man's eye and dangled back and forth hypnotically on his chest, suspended there from a long gold chain.

All of them were laughing heartily now, but Baumstein could only stare at the man in the cape, unable to fathom the depth of his feelings.

In the next moment, the dwarflike figure was again pounding the table with his fists. "Schwebe . . . Champagne . . . Schwebe . . . Christ . . . Where the devil . . ."

A cold sweat had erupted on Baumstein's forehead and he felt dizzy. The Indian musicians were once more playing lively rhythms, and a fiery little dancer hammered the bandstand with her wooden heels. A flood of images spun before Baumstein's eye. The room was suffocatingly warm and for a moment he thought he was going to keel over.

He didn't recall how he finally managed to get the check, pay his bill and get out of there leaving most of his second steak on the plate and the waiters gaping after him. How he made his way through a blare of speeding traffic on the Avenida Independencia Nacional back to the Guaraní and up finally to his room he had no way of knowing. All he knew was that he slept fitfully that night and that along toward dawn he had a nightmare, the details of which commenced with the shrill cry of the word *"Links."*

"Links . . . Recht . . . Links . . . Links." The words came flowing in upon his sleep like waves rolling back across the spate of years.

"Recht . . . Links . . . Links . . . Links."

Hundreds of prisoners shuffled down a makeshift plank leading from an open freight car. They were disgorged onto a concrete railroad platform gathering and huddling there in a cold drizzle. From open freight cars ahead and behind, hundreds—thousands—of other prisoners streamed out.

As they shuffled down the planks in long, untidy files, an orchestra comprised of men and women attired in the striped pajama garb of prisoners played polkas, tangos, and lively Strauss waltzes. The orchestra was composed of a saxophone, a clarinet, an accordion, several guitars, a cello, a piccolo, and a snare drum. They were led by a stern young woman violinist who used her bow as a baton.

"Links, Recht, Recht, Links, Links—"

The land around this strange phantasmal sight was flat and marshy, pocked with craters and ditches, and arid, like a lunar landscape. A ceaseless swirl of mist spiraled from the earth licking upward, like flames, around the legs of the prisoners.

"Recht—Links—Links—Links—Links—"

An SS captain dressed in a field gray Waffen-SS uniform with the white piping of the SS medical corps clearly visible on his cap cried out with monotonous regularity into the damp, chill air, vapor rising from his throat as he did so. Prisoners stood milling about, waiting to approach him. Once they reached him they fell away to the right or left depending upon where he directed them.

"Links—Recht—Links—Recht—Links—Links—"

Surrounded by bodyguards, the SS doctor stood erect, legs spread jauntily, ordering prisoners to the right or left with a perfunctory, yet graceful, flick of his thumb.

The doctor, an *Obersturmbannführer* by rank, was impeccable. As the selector on duty he cut a dashing figure in his smartly tailored SS uniform, with spotless white gloves, gleaming black boots, and swagger stick tucked under his left arm. One of the doctor's eyes, the left, had a pronounced squint to it, and when he smiled, a wide triangular gap showed between his two front teeth. He smiled quite frequently. Elegant and courtly, bowing rakishly to the attractive young female prisoners, the youthful doctor conveyed an impression of suavity and professional detachment. Only occasionally was the precise, unbroken rhythm of his work interrupted by a touch of glee or spiteful amusement.

He gazed coolly at each advancing prisoner, his swift glance evaluating the situation. *"Links"*—left: immediate death by gassing. *"Recht"*—right: temporary reprieve at forced labor. That swift unbroken rhythm of his thumb was metronomic, reminiscent of imperial Caesars, almost gladiatorial.

As the doctor worked he whistled softly to himself.

During the selection process while the orchestra played languorous waltzes and swooning tangos, he whistled Wagnerian arias. Now a young female prisoner stood before him awaiting the fateful flick of his thumb. He cocked his head sideways, his face creasing into an archly playful smile: "What melody was I whistling?"

The girl pondered a long moment, chewing her lower lip. "It's from *Tannhäuser*," she remarked, gravely.

The doctor shook his head reprovingly. "Wrong. It's *Lohengrin—Links*," he snapped, and flicked his thumb left.

An elderly lady now toddled up before him. Pushing her shoulders back with a kind of pathetic dignity, she tried to hold herself erect. The doctor smiled gently down upon her, a touch of playful malice in his eye. "Have you ever been on the other side, mother?" he asked. "Do you know what it's like?"

"I don't understand your question, sir," she replied.

"Don't worry, mother," he soothed her. "Soon you will. *Links*."

Now a young man being separated from his aged father left the line to embrace him in fond farewell. In an instant, with lightning speed, the doctor, face red with rage, smashed his swagger stick across the young man's cheek, laying it open in a trice.

There were these occasional outbreaks of irritation, very distressing for the doctor, but, for the most part, as he worked he was unruffled and debonair, courtly, even kind.

Now a mother cried out at being separated from her child, and the doctor graciously permitted her to rejoin her youngster on the left. A married couple balked at being parted. Smiling enigmatically at the chimneys of the crematorium belching smoke skyward, he kindly reassured the couple that shortly they would be reunited. He pointed them left.

A pair of twin boys, seven years old, were now marched up before the doctor by an SS corporal who had fetched them out of the milling throng. The doctor's eyes lit up. A radiance emanated from them. He bent down tousling the twins' hair affectionately. *"Recht und recht,"* he sang out merrily into the chill air.

At the completion of this trying labor, never once did the doctor appear one mote of dust or tiny crease the less elegant than when the grisly process had started. For truly, the doctor was a man of great passion and conviction. And he loved his work. *"Links."*

The dream ended as it had begun, on that word. When Baumstein awoke, it still echoed in his head, but of the dream, mercifully, he recalled nothing of the details. They had been too horrific, and his waking mind had blocked them out. But one thing he knew. He had dreamed once more, as he had not in nearly thirty years, of Auschwitz.

The following morning Baumstein, still queasy and profoundly shaken, resolved to leave Asunción. He did not know where he was going. Movement for him was still an activity fraught with peril, and he could not say why flight, immediate and unimpeded, was now so imperative.

He dressed and went down to the lobby where the Aerolineas Avianca maintained a ticket agency. He told the young lady in charge there that for reasons of health it was necessary that he get out of the city proper immediately. He needed to get to the mountains, he said. He had asthma, and for purposes of verisimilitude he coughed violently several times. In no time the young lady, deeply concerned for Baumstein's lungs, sold him an airline ticket to Bariloche, high up in the Argentine Andes. A short time later she called up to his room on the house phone as he was packing and re-

ported to him with a sense of beaming triumph that
she had, at great pains, been able to book rooms for
him at the most chic and prestigious hotel there—the
Llao Llao.

CHAPTER **22**

It was going on three AM, and the old night watchman,
Corrados, was making his rounds. His lonely nocturnal
perambulations took him customarily through Asunción's lower business district—through Remigio, Ten-
iente Ruiz, Boquerón, 22 de Septiembre, Manuel Perez,
and finally around the broad, cypress-ringed perimeter
of the Parque Caballero.

During the day these streets and boulevards, these
cramped and huddled plazas with their dung-spattered
benches and military statues, all teemed with a seamy
vitality. Merchants packed side-by-side into one dank
little *tienda* after the next lined the narrow cobbled
streets and choked the byways with innumerable carts
and displays of their wares. To here the citizenry of
Asunción flocked for their general needs. Food, produce, fabric, cheap furniture, bric-a-brac, and general
housewares were to be had in abundance and at nominal
prices.

At dusk, however, the carts would be taken indoors,
the corrugated aluminum blinds hauled down before
each storefront, the streets and gutters swept spotlessly
clean, and the merchants and pedestrians would all
have gone home.

That's when Corrados would come, hobbling on his

lame leg into that eerie solitude so recently teeming with life—now a stark, disquieting vacancy in which his footsteps rang out loud on the tessellated pavements as he made his appointed rounds.

Asunción is a city that goes to bed early. After ten PM it is rare to see a soul in the streets. Papa Stroessner firmly believes that working people should have a full night's sleep. He takes a dim view of late-night carousing among his children, the general citizenry, while indulging fully in his own insatiable passion for lively after-dark diversion.

It was Corrados' function in the course of these nocturnal vigils to check that each of the *tiendas* was securely locked, and to discourage any loiterers who may have lingered too long in the district with manifestly questionable motives.

Armed with a lantern, an antiquated revolver of American make, and a handful of cartridges of doubtful utility, Corrados would make a regular circuit of the area every three hours. Having eaten too heartily at supper, he was a little drowsy now and was therefore quite anxious to complete his tour. The appearance of the grand Parque Caballero up ahead was a welcome sight, for it signaled the last leg of the wearying circuit. A small barrack at the northeast corner of the park was his destination. Within its whitewashed adobe walls was a single large room with two cots, a privy, and a small electric cooker upon which one could brew hot coffee or soup. But even better, within those cramped, narrow walls was the man who would now relieve Corrados.

Seeing the small white building not far ahead, he moved on somewhat more briskly. It was a chilly night and a gusty breeze rattled through the leaves of the cypress overhead, causing the big blossoming *lapachos* all about the perimeter of the park to sway like phantom dancers in the dim gloom.

The big tower of the Guaraní was just up ahead now—a great slab of a silhouette plunged in darkness except for the few small sporadic lights scattered here and there across its granite face. At a certain point, as Corrados made his customary turn on a wide loop of the Sebastien Gabieto, he was aware of a slight disturbance in the park. Vague, indeterminate sounds; at first he thought they were merely the wind. Then something quite like the clatter of metal on pavement brought him up sharply, drawing his gaze to a gray blur of motion just over his right shoulder about two hundred yards into the park.

In the next moment, he had barged through the ring of cypress, emerging on a wide, grassy plain. About fifty yards off now through the gray gloom of early morning, he saw quite distinctly what he imagined to be six or seven people all running. Crying out at once, and commanding them to halt, he immediately gave chase. But undoubtedly it was he they were running from, and they had absolutely no intention of halting.

With a great surge of renewed energy, Corrados lumbered after them, shouting all the way, his great brass lantern banging wildly at his hip, waving his ancient revolver which he kept threatening to fire. But all to no avail. Whoever these park vagrants were, they knew that between the darkness and Carrados' rusty revolver, they had little to fear.

Shortly the band disappeared into a thicket of woods up ahead, and poor Corrados, panting and winded, hobbled from his brief gallop to a slow, rather desultory prowl around the area where he'd first spied the intruders.

Who were they? What were they up to? In a matter of moments, as he marched gasping up to the grand equestrian statue of Francisco Solano López astride a white, rearing alabaster stallion, and attired in full battle regalia, Corrados had his answer.

On the tarred footpath just before the statue a half-gallon can of upended black paint lay on its side, its contents leaking out onto the grass. Now Carrados raised the guttering flame of his lantern to the statue itself, and in that dim flickering light, he could see clearly the large, black wavering letters scrawled across the entire face of the alabaster pedestal. It read:

> PARAGUAY PROTECTS NAZI BUTCHERS
> LIKE GRIGORI FROM JUSTICE

And higher up, across the withers and heaving flanks of that splendid marble creature, as if by signature to the message, in bold Hebrew calligraphy, the words "AL TISHKAKH."

At that same moment another night watchman several miles away, making his rounds about the white-domed Pantheon, Paraguay's Tomb of Heroes, came across a similar defacement. Along one of the walls, just inside the huge marble pillars supporting the tympanum, indited similarly in large, black painted letters, was the following message:

> PAPA STROESSNER—FRIEND AND PROTECTOR OF
> THE NAZI BUTCHER GRIGORI

About two hundred kilometers northeast of Asunción, dawn was just breaking over the bustling little river town of Puerto Stroessner. The dusty streets were still empty there too—devoid of all life except for the few vagrant cats shivering and nosing hungrily in the alleyways.

A mile or so out of town on the banks of the broad

Paraná, a small white villa with its immaculately tailored lawn and white picket fence sat brooding and silent beside the new Highway 30 leading from the local airport all the way down to Asunción.

There were several newspapers still unopened on the side verandah, and all the shutters were drawn, giving the place a curious air of desolation. There was no sign of any occupant about, but on the new two-lane macadam running past the front of the house, a long chalk arrow extended some fifty feet parallel to the highway until it reached the front gate of the white picket fence where it then made an abrupt right turn pointing brazenly to the front door.

Along the fifty-foot shaft of the arrow written in bold, ragged white letters was the message:

THIS WAY TO THE HOME OF DR. GRIGORI,
THE DEATH ANGEL OF AUSCHWITZ

And beneath that, in Hebrew, the words "AL TISH-KAKH."

Back in Asunción it was going on to eight AM, and already the first sign of official cars could be seen drawing up to the Government Palace. Alighting from one of the first was Doctor Simon Nogues, Secretary of the Interior for the Province of Amambay.

Briskly acknowledging the salute of one of the elite Palace Guard, Doctor Nogues strode purposefully through the gates and bustled down a mosaic path that led through a series of formal gardens.

Feeling uncommonly well, he whistled as he swept on toward the impressive, tri-tiered white building—immaculate and gleaming like a wedding cake in the dazzling morning sun. It was just as his foot struck the lower stair and he started to ascend that he nearly stumbled, for his eye, at that moment, had risen to the level of the marble lintel above the side entrance where he saw emblazoned in huge, black letters the terse and blasphemous missive:

PAPA STROESSNER IS A PIG

Directly beneath that and affixed with all the pomp of an official seal was a huge, black Star of David.

By nine AM of that morning reports had come in from well over twenty locations, mostly official sites—museums, monuments, government buildings, and military installations—all similarly defaced, all linking President Stroessner with Doctor Gregor Grigori.

A short time later a dozen special cars of the federal Policía de Seguridad rolled one after the other up the ramps of the subterranean garage located in the basement of the Government Palace. They had been dispatched by Colonel Félix Arganas to a variety of points about the city. "Sensitive points" as the Colonel put it, but the majority of these points were located in the heavily populated Jewish district around the Estrella. The special officers of the elite internal security forces were now charged with the task of casting a dragnet through this "sensitive" area with the hope of apprehending the possible offenders. More specifically, each officer carried with him a list of a half-dozen prime suspects for interrogation—suspects thought most likely to be the architects of this heinous outrage—the most flagrant yet in what had been a long series of precisely such outrages.

Colonel Arganas had given instructions that these prime suspects were to be rounded up early that morning while most people still slept, so as to prevent, if possible, the insidious effects of alarm spreading wildly through the affected community.

The special forces moved with quiet and great dispatch. But not fast enough, for at just about ten AM of that morning, a band of young German boys was chased by guards from the Israeli Embassy in Asunción; however, not before they had smeared a great sprawling message on one of the outside walls. It read:

> JÜDISCHE BOTSCHAFT
> HANDE WEG VON GRIGORI.
> WIR BEFEHELEN.

To this was affixed a large, black swastika.

By noontime, swastikas had begun to twinkle like stars on the windows and walls of shops owned by Jewish merchants all around the Estrella. In addition, several display windows had been shattered, and an old rabbi, returning from the synagogue, had his beard pulled and was then pushed to the ground and kicked by young thugs.

Just before noon of that day security police arrested Arturo Rubens at the General Post Office in downtown Asunción, where he worked as a trusted upper echelon official.

Later that evening, after a particularly good dinner, Colonel Arganas lit a cigar and drank cognac with *El Negrón*. He had been very well pleased with the progress of the day. The ploy of using his own agents to perpetrate "the outrages and desecrations" of government property as a pretense for rounding up all "controversial and suspect" individuals had worked like a charm.

Just at that moment a Braniff 707 Stratocruiser was dropping through a light haze toward the lighted cruciform runways of Don Torcuato Airport twenty miles outside of Buenos Aires.

The girl in the rumpled denim suit had just emerged from the lav where she'd rinsed her face, put a brush through her hair, and freshened the pale coral lipstick she wore as her sole concession to cosmetic adornment.

Now back in her seat, she was a little breathless from anticipation and straining lightly against her overtight seatbelt. In her hand she clasped the small tourmaline falcon, fingering it, rotating it slowly in the palm of her hand, as if it were some talisman from which she extracted strong magical powers.

For nearly nine years now, Dovia Safid had been an agent of the Israeli Mossad. Born in Tel Aviv twenty-seven years ago to a high consular official who eventually became Israel's Ambassador to Sweden, she had been raised abroad, educated in Swiss schools and later English universities. She spoke six languages fluently and had lived everywhere. But for all of her internationalism, she remained fiercely and idealistically a Sabra. She was one of that late postwar generation that saw her destiny almost exclusively in terms of Israel's. Parochial, chauvinistic, belligerent to all whom she deemed outsiders—whatever was good for Israel was good for her.

In March of '67, she'd been on a skiing vacation to Kitzbühel when word of the Egyptian sweep into the Sinai came over. Immediately she cut her vacation short and returned home to don a uniform and take up arms with schoolfriends and coevals.

Dovia was assigned to an intelligence unit. She hadn't wanted that. She wanted a combat unit but, unknown to her, because of her father's high consular position, she had been remanded to something considerably less risky and, ironically, that's how she'd met Asher.

It was an accident and had not been meant to be.

She'd missed a convoy of intelligence units going up to the front and had to travel with one of the Special Tactical Units. It was then that she met Asher.

They got on awfully at first, and from there on the situation deteriorated. Where she was going was several hours away from the fighting; Asher resented having to miss any of it. They quarreled a good deal all the way out to Sharm al-Sheikh—first about the inconvenience of having to take her where she was going. And then, strangely enough, about politics.

He accused her of being narrow and childish, blind to the larger issue of the universal sufferings of humanity. She was full of platitudes and shibboleths, he claimed, like some mindless, idiotic Sabra singing and dancing folktunes out on the desert. Quite baldly, he charged her with having no mind of her own.

She, in turn, accused him of being an international adventurer, a mercenary, and only "half a Jew." What's more, he was a traitor to Israel whose pleas in behalf of the universal sufferings of all mankind were merely an excuse to dabble in violent political situations, which were his real passion.

Their mutual antagonism was, of course, primarily glandular, and that first night they shared a sleeping bag out on the desert. She found his lovemaking fierce, perfunctory, even mechanical, as if it were no more than some form of prophylaxis, like brushing one's teeth.

Being the child of a so-called "politically aware" generation, she associated his "uncommitted" lovemaking to a function of his staunchly "uncommitted" political ideologies. Needless to say, they started to see a good deal of each other. Her feelings with regard to Asher were confused. But one thing is certain—she never loved him. She thought he was crazy, volatile, unpredictable. But she couldn't stay away from him, drawn as she was to the nitroglycerine of his personality.

After the war they were both back together in Tel Aviv. He was studying engineering at the university, and she had gone to work for the Mossad. Dovia traveled quite a bit in the course of her work. It was not only risky work, it could also be extremely unsavory. She knew very well into what seamy situations that must inevitably lead her, yet she did not care particularly about the morals, or rather lack of them, inherent in her job. That was merely the way of intelligence work. There was no questioning its morality. It had none. What concerned her was the principle of justice, and especially Israeli justice, the justice of her people being served.

Once on the ground Dovia stood nervously in a queue of passengers in the aisle waiting for the boarding ladders to be set in place. Then in no time at all they were disembarking.

Clearing customs smoothly, she had no trouble finding him. She saw him at once and before he saw her—a tall, rumpled figure hovering near the carousel of swaying luggage. It was no surprise to her—she had wired him from the airport in Dakar to meet her there. Now—seeing him suddenly, dreamy, preoccupied, remote—it occurred to her for the most fleeting instant of time to turn round at once, get back on the plane, and get out of there. She was not ordinarily given to premonitions, but this was rather like one—a jab, it was, a preternatural awareness which told her to look sharp. She was coming too close to the edge of something. "Turn back," it said. And she almost did, but then it was too late, for he was looking up at her, waving and smiling, and the premonition had boiled off like a puff of bad air. She was smiling back too, and waving. And then he was there beside her, kissing her in that restrained and reticent way he had, and she was clinging to him, wildly and irrationally happy.

Later, at the hotel, it was not quite so reticent or restrained. His lovemaking seemed almost savage, like that of a man who had imposed celibacy upon himself for too long a time. He was rough and bruising, and yet not unkind, and while she winced, she also swooned deep in the warm spidery cage of his arms, her head full of the musky, slightly unwashed smell of his body. His arms held her like a vise beneath him and for a moment she had an image of something dark and primordial, a pair of rudimentary unthinking crustaceans coupling at the dawn of time. She was profoundly happy and grateful to be there.

Afterward they lay side by side in the warm dishevelment of the bed, spent and happy, smoking and laughing. He taunted her, made mildly derisive jokes about the young men in her life, about her work with the agency, about the soft, easy loyalty of her Mossad colleagues, who at one time had been his as well.

His manner piqued her and she sensed that he had intended it to. Still, she was in no mood for arguments. She told herself she would not spoil it all with arguments. At a certain point he reached across her to the package of Gauloises on the night table, and it was only then that she saw the series of cuts and weals along his exposed flank. They had formed scabs and appeared to have been freshly inflicted.

"Good God," was all she said and touched one lightly with her finger.

He looked away, trying to evade her searching gaze.

"Where'd you get those?" she cried. "What have you been up to?"

He started to get out of bed, but she pulled him back down. "Answer me. I don't hear from you for months. I don't know where you are from day to day."

"Since when have I had to report?"

She saw red. "I don't ask you to report. I never have. For all I care you can walk off the end of the earth. You and your goddamned missions."

He got out of the bed and she rose too, snatching the crumpled telex off the night table, pursuing him like a wraith with a flowing sheet wrapped round her. "GREETINGS FROM THE LAND OF INFINITE OPPORTUNITY," she read aloud. "What the hell is that supposed to mean? I get this in the mail. Only this and nothing more. And like an idiot I come thirteen thousand miles to find out."

She followed him around while he sought his trousers.

"What's all the secrecy, anyway?" she jeered at him.

"You know what this is about."

"I do, I suppose. But I don't really."

"You want to be part of it, don't you?"

"Yes, of course."

"You know who *he* is."

"Yes, yes, of course."

"And you're interested. You want to be part of us."

"Of course I do, idiot." She flung up her hands in exasperation. "I didn't come halfway around the earth out of casual curiosity."

"Then what more do you need to know?" He started to put on his shoes. "You know everything."

For a moment she was stymied. She'd run out of words. Then something like revelation flooded her eyes. "The agency was right. Absolutely right to have tossed you out. You're mad. Pathological—you bastard." She sprang at him and tried to slap him, but he pinned her arms easily to her side. "Bastard. Bastard. Bastard," she cried, tossing her head from side to side as if she could lash him with that splendid mane of ash hair.

"You want to go home?" he said quietly, still pinning

her arms. "You've got your ticket. Turn round and go home now."

"I never said—"

"I don't want this now," he muttered beneath his breath. "I don't need this now. The operation is too important to me."

"To me, too," she pleaded. "I want to be a part of it. You promised."

"And I've kept my promise. You are a part of it. But that's not enough for you, is it? You want something more."

"I don't—"

"You think just because you've come here, you're owed something."

"I'm owed nothing," she nearly shouted. "I want nothing from you. Bastard."

"Good." He smiled suddenly and chucked her under the chin. "Then everything will go well for us. Get dressed. We have a train to catch."

Shortly Asher and Dovia Safid were making their way by taxi from the downtown Hilton Towers on the Avenida Diaz Velez to the rail station on the Retiro. They had twenty-five minutes to get across the traffic-choked downtown section in order to make the midnight, high-speed Special Correntosa Express to San Carlos de Bariloche. There were sleeping cars on the train and richly appointed Pullmans as well as a restaurant with first-class cooking and a cinema. The twenty-nine hours between Buenos Aires and the little mountain village would fly past quickly.

Part IV

LLAO LLAO

CHAPTER 23

Doctor Grigori spooned up the last of his strawberry
kirsch frappé, daubed his lips lightly with an edge of
crumpled damask, and lit one of his fine Egyptian oval
cigarettes. Shortly, he knew, they would wheel a carriage into the dining room—a small carriage laden
with after-dinner liqueurs, sumptuous chocolates, and
fine Havana cigars, all of which he would partake of
heartily.

A small orchestra played on an elevated balcony
above the glittering crystal of the dining room of the
Hotel Llao Llao, world-famous spa high on the spine of
the Argentinian Andes—in San Carlos de Bariloche.
The orchestra was composed of six rather stiff male
musicians in tuxedos and a solitary lady harpist with
equine features in a gown of silk organza and a ruffled
sleeve that kept sliding off her shoulder. Strauss waltzes
were their forte, and the occasional short Liszt or Von
Weber. And then, of course, lots of light opera—*The
Student Prince, Naughty Marietta, The Merry Widow,*
and the like. Grigori ground his teeth at the banality
of it all. Its relentless thudding was an offense to his
ears. It gave him *Kopfweh.*

Krug and Rudel, seated with him, were chatting together—Krug gesticulating broadly, more red in the
face than usual; Rudel, solemn and funereal in his evening clothes, like a great black raven poised ruefully
on a branch. Grigori listened, or pretended to listen, to
the conversation. Actually he had heard very little of

what was being said, for at that moment, his attention was completely absorbed by the attractive young woman dining by herself at a nearby table.

Dovia Safid had arrived about a half-hour earlier that evening, led down that long sweep of center aisle by a bustling and officious Argentine maitre d', who bowed as he finally sat her at a small table obliquely across the aisle from Doctor Grigori's. She was attractive, the Doctor noted instantly—dramatically so—in the neighborhood of thirty, wore no rings, and was a recent arrival, Grigori surmised, for this was the first he'd seen of her. She was not the sort of woman one might easily overlook. Danish, he imagined—or possibly Dutch—with that ash-blond hair, those marvelous cheekbones, and that exquisitely thin patrician nose. Most simply dressed, she was, in an elegantly tailored gray pin-stripe suit, with that long, willowy body moving so liquidly beneath it. Oh, yes, if she'd been anywhere around, Grigori would have spotted her by now. In fact, he had begun to grow distinctly restive with the quality of available women at the hotel—dumpy widows, for the most part, and old maid school teachers. The Doctor smiled inwardly. Thus it had always been. *Den Schönen Doktor* had never had to go too long without attractive companionship. Sooner or later, he knew, it would turn up, as it had just now, drawn to him like small metallic filings to a powerful magnetic field.

Alban Krug turned to him and was asking something. The Doctor nodded, trying to bluff comprehension. But he'd not heard a word that was spoken. Nor did he care to. His eyes had been riveted on the young woman across the way—watching her all the while through the thick, slowly curling clouds of latakia wafting upward from his cigarette. Much to his irritation, she had not looked up once in his direction. In fact, she seemed oblivious to his bold, persistent stare.

The dreadful dinner music continued to thud, and Grigori's irritation slowly mounted. He fancied he looked quite well this evening—trim and fit—tan and astonishingly youthful. His brisk walks on the Tronador peak, and the long, strenuous afternoons spent fishing salmon trout on the cold glacial waters of Nahuel Huapí had had a felicitous effect upon him. And then, of course, he was splendidly turned out that evening in a white dinner jacket, with a pale tea rose at his lapel and the silver-rimmed monocle, which reduced the rather unsightly effect of his squint and lent him, he felt, an unmistakable aura of the genteel and aristocratic.

But still the woman did not notice—did not even deign to acknowledge his presence. Grigori was unaccustomed to such indifference. It was unheard of. He knew that women found him simpatico—that even under the most trying of circumstances, such as they'd all had to live under in the camps, *Den Schönen Doktor* could always manage to turn a female eye.

Now his gaze bore down on the solitary young woman, sitting not ten feet from him, excavating a chunk of lobster from a claw. He gazed at her as if the intensity of his oddly crooked stare could will her head to rise and turn in his direction.

"I say, Gregor. Wasn't it splendid?" he heard Rudel ask him, as if from a great distance.

He turned back, somewhat abashed. "What's that?"

"The salmon," Krug snapped. "The salmon I caught today."

"Oh yes," the Doctor murmured. "The salmon. Quite splendid." His eye wandered back to the woman. "Splendid creature."

Suddenly she looked up, trying to catch the waiter's

eye. But instead, she caught the glint of candlelight flashing from Doctor Grigori's monocle. He nodded, smiling faintly at her.

If he'd expected her eyes to drop demurely or, blushing and flustered, that she'd knock over her water glass, he was sorely mistaken. What he got for his trouble instead was a cool, unruffled, and frankly assessing gaze. It was not hostile, nor did it pretend any great injury. It was actually more a kind of resignation with which she regarded the monocled gentleman across the way, candidly disinterested—a mixture of boredom and impatience that produced on her strikingly intelligent face an expression that seemed to say—"Oh bother, what the hell is this now?"

Grigori was about to send over a champagne cocktail, but just then the Argentine maitre d', full of courtly flourishes, bustled back down the aisle, followed by another gentleman—pale, rumpled, prematurely gray, who hovered uneasily in the background while the waiter conferred with the young woman.

Doctor Grigori leaned forward, the better to overhear their conversation. The gentleman had just arrived that evening, the waiter explained. There was no other available single table. Would the young lady be kind enough to share her table with the gentleman, just for tonight. They would try very hard to arrange separate tables for each of them the following day.

Doctor Grigori flushed angrily as the lady smiled and nodded her assent to the new arrival. He felt betrayed.

"Very good, Fräulein Aldot." The maitre d' beamed as he turned to the gentleman standing beside him. "May I have the pleasure of introducing you . . . ?"

The Doctor leaned forward to hear the lady's name, and to his distress, he could now see the two of them talking there, rather animatedly, heads tilted toward each other, both obviously not in the least displeased with the new and happily fortuitous seating arrangements.

"I'm awfully sorry to put you out like this," the gentleman was saying, smiling a little foolishly. He appeared flushed and overcome.

"Not at all," Dovia remarked warmly. "I was just thinking," she said, lowering her voice and glancing across the aisle toward Grigori's table, "that this is not the best place for an unescorted lady. Is this vacation or business for you?"

"A bit of both, actually. And you?"

"The same. American?"

"Yes."

"I see your suit is American, but your accent isn't."

The rumpled gentleman smiled. "I'm a naturalized American. Actually, I'm Austrian by birth."

"Austrian?" Her eyes lit up. "Not really? So am I. I knew there was something about you. Where?"

"Vienna."

"Ah." She clapped excitedly. "Me too."

"You still live there?" he asked.

"No. Haven't been there for years. I live in Paris now. I'm a teacher."

"Ah—a teacher?"

They both laughed and started to chat together in the old language of their youth, like two small children suddenly discovering a mutual secret. They failed to note the grave and disapproving glare of the monocled gentleman sitting across the aisle from them.

"I'm afraid I didn't quite catch your name," Dovia went on, noting that the man seemed very tired.

"Gales," J. Peter Baumstein replied, somewhat flustered. "John Gales."

She frowned. "Gales? That's hardly Viennese."

Baumstein reddened. There was a pause while his

brain worked desperately. "I anglicized my name for business purposes. An English name is so much better in my line of work, you know."

"Ah." Dovia leaned back and regarded him rather coolly. "And what is your line of work?"

"Finance."

There was an awkward silence. Just then a waiter appeared, brandishing an enormous menu above Baumstein's head. "Ah, here we are." Baumstein seized it. Glad to be off the hook for a moment, he buried his eyes in it. "I'm famished," he went on, his eyes scanning the columns printed in three languages. "What are you having?"

"The pheasant," she remarked, inserting a Gauloise into a small silver cigarette holder. "It looks very good. I just saw them serve one across the way. Quite beautiful."

"Splendid." Baumstein nodded to the waiter. "Pheasant it is then. And I shall have oysters to start. Will you share a bottle of wine with me?"

"I should love it." Dovia smiled, leaning forward to permit him to light her cigarette.

When he'd ordered his bottle and the waiter had bowed and scurried off, he turned back to her.

"Well, this is an unexpected surprise," Baumstein remarked, looking round the glittering room. He felt himself beginning to relax and unwind; from the moment he had left Asunción two days ago, he had been in a state of nervous exhaustion, convinced that the authorities had discovered his true identity and were now in hot pursuit and bearing down upon him. Coming through the Argentine customs, he was certain he'd been recognized. Then, on the overnight train up from Buenos Aires, an American man looking very much like a federal agent—or what he imagined a federal agent to look like—kept staring at him. Or so at least he imagined. The moment he checked into the Llao Llao, he deposited his attaché case in the hotel vaults and hid the keys beneath the water tank lid of the commode in his lavatory.

Baumstein was about to speak again, but suddenly the orchestra, which sat directly above them, broke off from the Strauss München waltzes and into a long and portentous drum roll.

There was a mild stir at the head of the dining room, and several of the waiters appeared to stream in that direction. All at once the orchestra broke into a self-conscious and rather tinny version of the Paraguayan national anthem. In the next moment a spotlight hit the large, glass portals of the entrance way, and a tall, distinguished looking gentleman appeared.

"Stroessner," the young woman remarked.

"Who?"

"Alfredo Stroessner. The president of the Republic of Paraguay."

"Is he a guest here, too?"

"It would appear so." She smiled ironically, and Baumstein noted for the first time how pretty she was. For a moment it made him think of Edith and he was sad.

"It seems," Dovia went on in her slightly mocking way, "we are about to be greatly honored."

While the orchestra continued its thudding version of the national anthem, President Stroessner and a running phalanx of six or seven large, rather strapping fellows swept down the center aisles, moving toward a large banquet arranged for them somewhere at the rear. On the way, *El Jefe* paused here and there to shake hands with old friends and associates he recognized at various points in the dining room.

Baumstein watched the presidential party bearing down upon them like a juggernaut, and he had a sudden inexplicable desire to bolt. Ever since his wartime experience, officialdom continued to have that curious effect upon him. He was certain now that these men had come there with the express intention of arresting him. Almost in self-defense, he leaned away.

But in the next moment they swept past, causing the vase of anemones on the table to tremble as they did so. When Baumstein looked up again, he found the wide green smiling eyes of Dovia Safid directed at a point just over his left shoulder to where the President and his party had momentarily stopped—this time to greet the three gentlemen sitting diagonally across the way. One of them, she observed—the slight, rather odd-looking fellow in evening clothes and a monocle who had been staring so boldly at her—was now on his feet and shaking hands with the President.

CHAPTER 24

The big Lufthansa 747, Flight 506 from Frankfurt, was just then clearing the control tower at Buenos Aires Aerodromo de Don Torcuato preparatory to putting down.

Rolfe Hupfauer stared out the window down through a thin puff of scudding cloud at the myriad lights of nighttime Buenos Aires glittering below him like a vast undulant lake of incandescence.

He listened for a brief moment, not really hearing, the staticky chatter of a flight stewardess announcing in three languages the terms and conditions of their descent. For him the show was the staggering pattern of lights below him and the stark, brilliant cruciform that marked the appointed runway to which Lufthansa Flight 506 was inexorably beating its way.

There was a discernible bump as the wing flaps went down, then a slight roll of the ship as the left wing dipped queasily, causing a few nervous laughs amid the passengers just behind him. Rolfe had just finished his supper and now he thought, as the inveterate systematic burgher in his soul invariably did, of such things as whether or not he would have a difficult time clearing customs, whether or not all of his luggage had arrived safely, and whether or not Ricardo Caffetti would be there waiting below to meet him.

He had nothing to fear; the customs inspection was perfunctory; his luggage was already out and swaying on the carousel by the time he'd reached it; and Caffetti was most emphatically there, standing arms crossed beside the flight gates and smiling as he emerged.

In short order they had cleared the airport and were tooling down the big Highway 9, the Ruta Panamericana, streaming toward the great dazzling glow of the city in Caffetti's late-model Lincoln Continental.

Now sitting in the capacious leather upholstery of Caffetti's car, Rolfe felt the inevitable sense of soiled rumplement one feels at the completion of a flight of ten hours. His mouth tasted sour from the dreadful airline food and he was tired and wanted a shower. But the lights of the city glowing up ahead that had transformed the sky above it into a shower of molten red excited him strangely. It was a kind of romantic excitement—the sort of sensation very young men feel when cut loose for the first time in a large and strange city.

"Have you eaten?" Caffetti asked.

"Yes. On the plane. But I wouldn't mind a nightcap. How is my father?"

"Not well. I was with him two days ago. He wants

very much to see you. Wants to take you hunting. Buy you all kinds of presents."

Rolfe ground his teeth and smoldered quietly in his seat.

"He's in Bariloche right now," Caffetti went on. "In the casino I should imagine." He checked the luminous dial of his car clock. "We'll join him in Encarnación in three days. Meanwhile, you must let me see to your pleasures."

When they had crossed San Isidro and entered the posh suburb of Vicente López, Caffetti suddenly veered hard left off the Ruta Panamericana, causing the car to swerve and Rolfe to fall heavily against the driver.

"What the devil—"

"Sorry—just turning here."

"I thought we were going into the city."

"We were," Caffetti said curtly. "But I've had a change of heart." He stared hard into the rear-view mirror, where the pair of headlights that had been following them so doggedly out of Don Torcuato was now no longer visible. Happily, when he veered, he had seen his pursuer hurtle past, unable to turn in time, and unable to stop because of the heavy flow of traffic just behind him. He had no way of knowing if the lights he had seen behind them were really those of a pursuer. He was merely being cautious. Instinct made him wary of those particular headlights, and so he turned.

Now the Lincoln hummed south toward the luxurious waterfront district running out along the Avenida del Libertador San Martín on the Rio de la Plata.

"Where are you taking me?" Rolfe asked, slightly alarmed.

"To the Yacht Club at Olivos."

"But I have reservations at the Hilton."

"This is quieter than the Hilton. Very exclusive. I'm sure you'll like it."

"But they may have no room for me."

"Let me take care of that," Caffetti said grimly, and he glanced once more into his rear-view mirror. It was still empty.

CHAPTER **25**

"Veintidós. Veintidós rojo. Pongan sus apuestas, damas y caballeros."

The wheel spun to a white whirring blur. There was a suspended moment of hush while innumerable eyes, transfixed on the small white pellet, watched it spin and bobble from groove to groove, rattling and clicking as it went. Shortly the wheel began its deceleration. Its numbers and colors grew increasingly legible until at last the pellet bobbled into the red–9 groove, rose to the ledge dividing it from the adjacent black–10 groove, hung for an exquisitely protracted moment on the lip, then bounced back with an irrevocable, almost mocking thud into the red–9.

Groans of despair went up along with squeals of delight. *"Rojo, damas y caballeros,"* cried the croupier. *"Rojo nueve."*

The croupier was a tall, whip-thin Argentinian with a pencil-line mustache and shiny raven-colored hair. When he smiled, as he often did, his white teeth glittered, giving him the appearance of an evil wizard. Now, with a great wooden paddle he pushed a toppling heap of chips in the direction of the laughing, mildly intoxicated gentleman flushed with victory. Doctor Gregor Grigori opened his arms wide like an ascending angel in order to embrace the flood of bright red discs tumbling upon him. He waved at a waiter hovering nearby and bought champagne for everyone around the table.

"Otra vez," cried the croupier. *"El gran vencedor. Pongan sus apuestas, damas y caballeros. Vamos a jugar."*

Once again the wheel spun and an excited hush descended over the smoky glittering casino. Someone had set a fresh flute of Dom Perignon at Doctor Grigori's elbow. Horst, standing behind him, lit his cigarette. Krug and Rudel hovered protectively behind at either elbow, preventing anyone from getting too close.

Grigori had been playing at the wheel for the better part of three hours. A number of people had been playing when he'd first started, but as his winnings grew and his game became more flamboyant, they had gradually withdrawn—dropped out to become merely observers—intimidated and envious.

Now more and more people crowded about the table. Word had spread quickly through the hotel that Doctor Neiditch from Asunción was enjoying a fantastic run. Sensing the excitement of a big killing, they flocked in from the bar and the card rooms, from the salons and wide garden promenades outside. Other gamblers deserted their own games; the tables of *chemin de fer* and blackjack, *baccarat* and craps were suddenly all empty. Even the dealers had gone to watch. Everyone wanted somehow to be a part of it.

Alfredo Stroessner, *El Jefe* himself, appeared around ten PM amid an entourage of cronies and strapping bodyguards. Immediately a place was made for him at the table. The *Presidente* settled himself directly opposite Grigori, puffing an immense Havana while the jeweled index finger of his right hand lightly rimmed a pony of brandy. Each time Doctor Grigori won, Stroessner applauded.

Baumstein was there too, standing just behind Dovia Safid, who had managed to get herself a place up front.

"Isn't it exciting?" She smiled up at him over her shoulder. Before he could reply, she had somehow managed to pull him right up front beside her.

Doctor Grigori was now sitting with approximately sixty thousand dollars in winnings piled up before him. Quickly he wagered a thousand pesos on a *passe*.

"*Treintaidós*," the croupier cried.

There was a loud cheer as the Doctor raked in two thousand pesos. It was at that moment that he looked up from the table and saw the beautiful young woman from the dining room along with the newly arrived gentleman observing the game from the far end of the table. Flushed with victory and wine, he nodded and smiled brazenly, then raised his glass to her.

"He's toasting you," Baumstein said.

"Yes, I know."

"Do you know him?"

"I've never seen him before in my life."

"I have," said Baumstein after a moment.

Dovia gazed up at him. "Oh?"

Baumstein's voice trembled slightly. "At a restaurant in Asunción. Making an awful row. He was with those same two gentlemen standing just behind him."

Dovia appeared suddenly quite grave. "The funny little fellow and that rather tall, evil-looking chap?"

"Yes. That's them. I'm certain of it. I keep thinking I know the fellow with the monocle."

"Odd-looking isn't he?" She laughed.

"*Cinco*," cried the croupier. Another burst of applause, and once again the great paddle plowed a pile of chips into Doctor Grigori's ever increasing mound.

Several moments later a waiter appeared and served them two flutes of Dom Perignon.

"For us?" Dovia smiled at the waiter.

"Si señorita—cumplimientos del Doctor Neiditch."

"Doctor Neiditch?" Baumstein asked.

The waiter pointed across the table. They followed the direction of his finger and saw the monocled gentleman smiling at them, holding up another glass of champagne in their direction. Accepting the champagne, Dovia and Baumstein raised their glasses in turn and toasted the Doctor across the table.

Now that he felt he had the young lady's undivided attention, Doctor Grigori's play grew even more flamboyant. He played four thousand pesos on black. Several people around the table quickly followed suit and staked on black too. The croupiers exchanged glances with the house manager, who had come over to watch. The wheel spun.

"Negro," cried the croupier.

There was a prolonged outburst of shouting and applause. Someone set another flute of Dom Perignon at Grigori's side. Champagne had left him eerily remote from the excitement of the moment. He heard no applause, he heard no laughter or shouting. He had entered instead a realm of icy quietude, peaks and crevasses inhabited only by himself and the exquisite lady hovering there across the narrow green swath of baize cluttered with its chips and dice. It occurred to him that she was smiling at him now, that something infinitely seductive was taking place—a subtle but enormously potent give-and-take going on between them. He was now, quite literally, playing for her.

Several times Krug and Rudel pleaded with him to stop—walk away with his winnings. Instead, his laughter grew louder and he doubled and trebled his bets.

"Pongan sus nombres, damas y caballeros," cried the croupier. *"Vamos a jugar."* The large white teeth glittered beneath the hairline mustache, the oddly sinister

wizard smile radiated about the table, and the night wore on.

"Fantastic, isn't it?" Dovia remarked.

"Yes, fantastic," Baumstein agreed. "Quite remarkable." But he was not referring to the game at all or to the extraordinary thing that was taking place on the table. It was rather the player, this Neiditch fellow, who absorbed his total interest. And even as he watched the man with a horrid, almost trancelike fascination, he was aware that he was at the same time struggling to recall something, to dredge up some aspect of the remote past that he had long since buried and forgotten.

Just at that moment Baumstein's musings were interrupted by a tall, blond youth standing stiffly before him. He was a remarkably striking young man of Teutonic mien, Baumstein noted, with something defiant and faintly mocking in his eye.

"What does he want?" Dovia asked.

"I'll let him tell you," Baumstein replied curtly. There was something in the young man's manner that made him bristle.

Ludo Von Rattenhuber bowed and stepped forward, addressing himself directly to the young woman. "Doctor Neiditch conveys to you his good wishes and wonders if you would not afford him the great pleasure of accepting these chips with which to play the game." He carried on a small silver salver several thousand dollars in chips of varying denominations.

Dovia stared down at the chips. She appeared momentarily perplexed, then smiled at the young man hovering there above her. "You mean accept his money?"

"Precisely." Ludo smiled crisply.

The young woman glanced across the table in Grigori's direction. He was smiling at her and, as he did so, his unnaturally red lips moved as if he were saying something intimate or suggestive to her. Someone in the presidential party leaned toward *El Jefe* and whispered something in his ear. The President laughed aloud, and suddenly she was aware that he was staring with frank admiration at her.

"What do you suppose is going on here?" Dovia whispered at Baumstein.

"I believe they're watching to see what you'll do."

She smiled, a look of cunning flickering on her face. In the next moment, she turned to Von Rattenhuber and took the salver from him. Then she turned back to the monocled gentleman and, still smiling, nodded her consent, as if taking up a challenge. There was a small burst of applause from the Stroessner party as the Doctor bowed in the direction of the beautiful lady and resumed his play.

Baumstein was a bit taken aback. In his Old World way, he had naively assumed that she would decline. Now, oddly enough, he was miffed. Already she had started to play, and it seemed perfectly understood, without words having to be spoken, that she would play the same numbers and stakes as Doctor Neiditch.

The game went on thusly for an hour or so while Baumstein watched Dovia's pile of chips double and treble.

More people had flocked into the casino from outside, the news of this fabulous killing having spread like wildfire through the hotel.

Shortly after midnight, two immense glittering stacks of chips had mounded up before Grigori and Dovia. Baumstein, pleading exhaustion and a headache, excused himself and went up to bed.

CHAPTER 26

Baumstein had an awful night. Though he was exhausted, he was unable to sleep. He tossed and turned, rose several times to go to the bathroom, then lacerated himself with thoughts of Edith forsaken. Then, too, strangely, compulsively, the face of the monocled doctor—*el gran vencedor* of the casino—kept flashing through his mind. Unmindful that he was in a cold sweat and wringing his sheets until his knuckles had turned white, Baumstein struggled to suppress the disquieting image.

Still the more he tried to suppress it, the more stubbornly it persisted. This man whose champagne he'd drunk that evening—what was his name?—Neiditch—Doctor Neiditch he called himself—was undoubtedly the same man he'd seen along with the same two cronies in Las Acacias. There was certainly nothing strange in that. Many people—well-to-do Asuncianos—came down to Bariloche for the weekend. It was very much the thing.

And then, of course, there was the fact that Baumstein had fled Las Acacias, a very sick man, two nights before. Now here he was tonight, suffering that same awful malaise. It had come over him the same way— swiftly, unaccountably—the nausea, the sweating, the lightness of head, that trapped panicky sensation one experiences on the verge of blacking out. Why? Was it a bug? One of those famed Latin *turistas* that travelers make gross jokes about. Or was it possibly the altitude?

In these parts it was tremendous—8,000 feet at the very least and the air quite thin. Or was it just plain fright? The alien sensation of being a fugitive—a criminal at large. The sense of being hunted, the horror of imminent arrest, the humiliation of being clapped in irons in a public place and hauled out before a lobby of gaping guests.

Or was it Edith and Joel? His overriding sense of guilt for having somehow failed, betrayed, and even disgraced them? Even then he could imagine newspaper accounts of his crime; his face plastered all over the cheap tabloids with long and remarkably thorough accounts of all his peculations, and Mr. Battersby denouncing him to all the world.

Baumstein got up and started to write a long, rambling apologia to Edith, then tore it up, for not a single note of it rang true. Shortly he was thinking of Doctor Neiditch again. That face, sallow and waxen, yet undoubtedly handsome, but beginning to sag and soften and bloat a bit with time and self-indulgence. And the monocle and that slight crookedness of features. And that mouth with the too-red lips. What was there about that mouth that curdled Baumstein's blood?

At three AM he called down to the bar and asked the night porter to send up a bottle of scotch whiskey, along with ice cubes and a soda siphon. At dawn, in something of a stupor, his taut and twitching nerves at last relented and he sank into a deep and beneficent sleep.

Dovia Safid had not got to bed until four AM that morning. That's when the party in Doctor Grigori's suite had broken up. Many people, primarily Germans of a very wealthy order, had attended.

Dovia had nearly fifteen thousand dollars in her purse from winnings at the table, and "Doctor Neiditch," beaming with triumph, displayed her on his arm to friends very much as if she, too, were a part of his enormous winnings. When she left the party, it was nearly daybreak. Back in her room she locked the door, kicked off her shoes, and went directly to the phone. She dialed a local number she had committed to memory. The phone rang five times before anyone answered. Then a rather sleepy, masculine voice came on:

"Ian?" she whispered.

There was a pause. Then a reply. "Dovia?"

"Yes." Another pause, then: "Just calling to say everything looks fine here."

"Contact?"

"Yes, contact," she smiled.

"Fine," he replied quite simply.

For a moment they didn't speak, just sat there listening to each other breathe.

"Good night, darling," she said at last.

Dovia lay back in bed and closed her eyes. In spite of the hour and her lack of sleep, she was happy. Her work had gone well.

Baumstein awoke several hours later surprisingly refreshed. He shaved, showered, and went down to a breakfast that could have choked a horse. When he emerged about an hour later from the dining room, whistling softly to himself, the desk clerk handed him a message. It was written in a small immaculate hand and signed by Nora Aldot. It read:

Have been invited by Doctor Neiditch for a day of boating and fishing on the lake. Told him I had an appointment with you. Hope you don't mind the little white lie. Would you come? Please.

Will explain later.

Nora

Baumstein had not the slightest intention of accepting the invitation. Boating held no interest for him and fishing made him physically ill. No, he would spend the morning reading. Perhaps later he would wander down into town.

He asked the desk clerk for a piece of paper to jot down his regrets. But no sooner had he started to write than he felt a clap at his shoulder. He wheeled sharply, emitting a slight gasp as he did so, for there, standing and smiling amiably at him, was Doctor Neiditch himself.

"Sorry. I didn't mean to frighten you like that."

"You didn't frighten me," Baumstein almost shouted. He felt a sharp visceral spasm as he tried to smile back. Dovia Safid stood beside the Doctor and he was holding her arm. "I am afraid I have expropriated your lovely companion." Doctor Neiditch smiled broadly. "You see, you made the mistake of leaving her alone this morning at breakfast. So naturally—"

The Doctor chided Baumstein good naturedly. His English was impeccable, with an accent that was more continental than German. "—wondered if you might not possibly consent," Doctor Neiditch continued. Baumstein scarcely heard a word, so quickly did his brain spin in some feverish act of recollection.

"It would be such fun, John," Dovia chattered happily. Her hand was on his arm and he felt a slight but emphatic twinge of pressure. Her eyes implored him— "Won't you please? For me?"

For a moment he glimpsed the eye, greenish-yellow and hugely magnified, behind the monocle.

"Yes. Do, Herr Gales," the Doctor appealed most charmingly.

Baumstein felt a knot in the pit of his stomach and his palm sweated. "Yes, of course," to his amazement, he heard his voice reply. "That would be fun. I'd enjoy that."

Dovia sighed happily. Her eyes were almost grateful.

"I'm afraid I have no gear," Baumstein babbled on.

"Don't worry about that. I have everything you'll need on the boat. Splendid then—leave all the arrangements to me. Shall we say 10 AM?" Doctor Neiditch clapped his hands. The motion was so sudden and resounding that Baumstein flinched. Everyone laughed. So did Baumstein, but his blood had frozen. That sound, that sudden clash of palms, had for him an air of terrifying finality, like the clap of doom.

CHAPTER 27

"You who cannot forget—you Tishkakh people. You who have traveled here from far and wide—Asunción, Rio, Montevideo, Santiago, Buenos Aires—sent by your leader, Mr. Rubens, to participate in a holy mission. I want to tell you all at the start, this is a thankless task. The mission is dangerous. Our numbers are few. Each year our cause grows less popular. The world has a short memory. We have been given a chance here to make it remember once more, if only briefly—one chance only. We cannot afford to waste that chance. We have no place here for heroes. Everyone has a job. Every job is equally important. The distribution of duties will be as follows—"

Ian Asher stood in the center of a circle composed of fifteen people—thirteen men and two women—clustered together in the abandoned ruin of a farmhouse twenty miles outside of Bariloche. The farm itself had once been used for the raising of cattle. The barns and outbuildings still contained many of the original stalls, and there was a granary and a silo, albeit both a shambles, where feed had been kept. Now only birds and small rodents haunted the place. Over the past months, this ruin had been ruthlessly vandalized—fixtures ripped out of the walls, plumbing torn from the floors, beams yanked from the roof, so that the ceiling in many places had collapsed, leaving above the windy frame of the dwelling great patches of blue, cloud-strewn sky, through which the shadows of birds darted sporadically.

"The *Eden* squad will be the support. We'll want six to eight men. Missions, two. Tracking and surveillance of the target and providing the protective corridor through which *Ames* and *Basil* squads will withdraw from the country."

Where Asher stood now in the center of a bare, grain-strewn floor, a chalkboard had been erected, and as he addressed the group encircling him, he scribbled simultaneously on the board.

"*Chad,*" he went on, in his abrupt methodical way, designating squads by code names. "Communications. Two men. Missions, two: one to maintain steady contact with the team from a clandestine point near the scene of the operation. The other to serve as relay between our Embassy in Santiago and the Mossad central in Tel Aviv. Any questions?" Asher gazed around at the circle of silent, intent figures, waited a moment, then continued.

"*Dylan:* The cover. One man and one woman. Missions, two: to arrange for rental cars and all necessary logistical support. And to enable the rest of us to operate without detection. Since the *Dylan* squad will serve as front for the operation, the team chosen must be gregarious and outgoing in personality. They'll require carefully devised cover, possibly the pose of husband and wife, planted in a hotel or rented apartment, in order that they betray no hint of the Israeli connection. We already have one female in close proximity to the target."

Asher gazed round to see how his words registered. It was characteristic of the man to appear abrupt and somewhat peevish during the course of such crucial briefings. He continued:

Basils will be guards, of which there'll be two. They will operate as a unit in tandem with the *Ameses*. While *Ames* is performing its mission, *Basil* will protect the getaway route. Since we'll be in a major waterway, this will involve complicated sailing and navigational skills. The Paraná at the point where we intend to hit the target is heavily trafficked by both Argentine and Paraguayan gunboats. Neither will be particularly friendly to our cause. For this reason, *Basils* must be excellent shots and shall carry automatics. They must also have a thorough knowledge of the use of explosives."

Once again Asher gazed around, his steely blue eyes darting from man to man.

As he spoke, he seemed older at that moment— somewhat more haggard and gray. A man animated, yet wearied, by some fierce, uncompromising demon. Yet he enjoyed the faces encircling him, staring at him rapt and intense.

A small vireo had entered through a wide gash in the barn roof and settled in the peeling rafters above them. It dove and swooped from time to time across the vacant, windy space. Asher watched its flight somewhat intently, as if in its weird presence there, some special sign or portent had been revealed to him. Then he continued:

"So then, we are left with the last squad. *Ames*, the killing squad, of which there will be two men. Since

Ames will be executing with hand guns at close range, no doubt looking directly into the face of the target, *Ames* perforce must be either highly motivated or very callous. Preferably both. Any questions, gentlemen?" Asher snapped.

One of the men standing in the circle raised his hand. Asher acknowledged him with an abrupt nod.

"Are the *Ameses* and the *Basils* standing here now among this group?" the man asked.

"The *Basils* are. The *Ameses* are not."

"Who will make the final team selections?" asked a tall, willowy girl in fatigues.

"I will," Asher replied without hesitation. There was a note of slight belligerence in his manner. "And let us clear up this business of the *Ameses* right now before we go on. I feel this has become a bone of contention among us. This is a very important operation. You all know the target involved and it's a big one. Our plan of action here has been a long time in the making." Asher's gaze moved from one face to the next. "Most of you have come to me privately at one point or another and asked to be chosen for *Ames*. I admire your zeal, but you must all realize that cannot be. The signal honor of execution can only go to those two team members most likely to succeed, for it's certain we will never get another chance. As it is, we have been given this chance without the formal blessing of our government. It is understood that we have their informal blessings and full support, but for reasons known very well to all of us, the government may in no way be implicated with our activities here. It is also understood that, should we succeed, the government, for purposes of appearance, will surely have to disavow us. It is further understood that should we fail, should we be taken into captivity by either the Paraguayans or the Argentinians, we can expect little in the way of help from the government. We all have a fairly good idea of what a Paraguayan prison is like and what could very well happen to us in one. But we are all adults, are we not, acting in full knowledge of the risks implicit here? That is why we must all work, as of this moment, as a team; as one body. If any one part of that body is either weak or endangered, the whole body itself is at peril. So, who is *Ames,* who is *Basil,* and who is *Chad* does not matter. Each function as of this moment is crucial, and don't for a moment forget that."

"When do we move?" a small wiry man asked at the far end of the circle.

"The day after tomorrow when the target travels by riverboat to Encarnación." Asher looked around, smiling then for the first time. "If there are no further questions, ladies and gentlemen, I suggest that we get on with the business at hand."

CHAPTER 28

"Bend. Snap. Bend. Snap." The tip of the rod rose, spanned backward, quivered momentarily in midair, then with a sharp ping, snapped forward. A wide looping arc of filament line soared outward above the sunspangled water. Where its trajectory ended, thirty yards or so beyond the boat, a trout fly settled lightly on the surface of the water, bobbing there and radiating little watery circles outward. "Bend. Snap. Bend. Snap," Doctor Grigori chanted again, raising and snapping the rod as he did so.

"Now you try." He presented the rod to Dovia. His

face was flushed and his forehead glistened with sweat. It was barely past noon, but he had already drunk too much wine, and the presence of the beautiful young woman encouraged him in behavior that was more grandiose than ever.

"No, no," he fumed when she'd fumbled the cast and snagged his line. He stood behind her and placed his cheek quite close to hers, guiding her arm backward and forward, so that her lithely supple body moved within the contour of his own. Several times while they simulated casts Baumstein observed the Doctor's hand brushing her breasts. Grigori panted heavily from the effort. It was all blatant lechery.

They'd been out two hours. The sun was already at midpoint in the sky. The lake was a spectacular disc of icy blue. Where the depth was one hundred feet, they could see the bottom as if it were a yard away, all of which created the illusion of their boat hanging suspended in midair. Ringed all about them as far as the eye could see, the ice-capped peaks of the Andes, timeless and imperturbable, stretched far into a purple infinitude.

More champagne was opened. There was a great deal of nonsense and raucous laughter. Baumstein brooded, regretting his acceptance of the invitation. He believed he had accepted in a moment of chivalry because the girl wanted him there, or possibly even needed him there for reasons she was unable to disclose. Now the spectacle of her and the Doctor cooing over each other sickened him.

Baumstein pretended to fish with a kind of desperate good cheer. He thought only of the time when he could return to his room, lock the door, and soak in a hot tub with a double scotch.

Hans Rudel seemed annoyed too. Clearly he considered the girl an intrusion. Fishing boats were no place for women. He stood by himself at the rail, chainsmoking cigarettes and flinging them, half-finished, far out over the water. Occasionally, he looked up and glowered at the Doctor fawning over the girl, then he would peer, moody and sullen, back down into the frigid depths of Nahuel Huapí.

Hans Rudel was what people used to call a "man's man," and a "soldier's soldier." A Luftwaffe ace before he was twenty, and decorated twice by the Führer for extraordinary valor, his heroic reputation in the Wehrmacht was almost legendary.

More a man of loyalties than ideologies, his instincts were all for automatic patriotism rather than for self-questioning. When he came to Latin America in 1946, settling first in La Paz, then Buenos Aires, Rudel was not in flight from any war crimes commission. He was in no sense of the word a war criminal and there had never been any need for him to flee Germany. He came to Latin America, rather, to be among people whom he considered his compatriots—people with whom he felt he shared ideals and national aspirations. Besides, the Germany that was only just beginning to emerge in late 1945 and 1946 was no longer a Germany he cared to be a part of.

Hans Rudel never had any money to speak of. He came from a family of proud but humble Lutheran farmers. To compound his problems, he would accept no financial assistance from Der Spinne, and as a result, he found himself forced to live an exiguous, hand-to-mouth existence amid the social glitter of Buenos Aires' wealthy German community. An aloof and moody man living largely in the heroic past, he was not one to seek help. He was therefore frequently lonely, and when he met Doctor Grigori in 1952, each man was ripe for the union that was ultimately to evolve.

They met at a fashionable dinner party in the exclusive suburb of Olivos just outside of Buenos Aires. Grigori was already a vivacious social lion—just arrived and eagerly sought after. He was going at that time under the name of Stanislaus Proske, but everyone knew who he was, including the Argentine authorities who happily obliged the Doctor by looking the other way.

Thrilled by his military exploits and idolizing his legendary courage, Grigori was instantly drawn to Rudel. He was everything a good German ought to be. An Aryan test case. Always on the lookout for such talent and sensing the man's pride as well as his impecuniousness, Grigori immediately proposed a business arrangement. If Rudel would consent to be a "companion-cum-bodyguard" to the Doctor, he would immediately be placed on the payroll of Hierro–Fabrofarunk at a handsome yearly retainer. The work would be enjoyable—just traveling around with the Doctor. Hunting, fishing, and attending pleasant gatherings such as the one at which they presently found themselves. All expenses paid.

If Grigori had heard of Rudel, so had Rudel heard of Grigori, and everything he'd heard, the pilot-hero utterly despised. Rudel's concept of the soldier's code had very little to do with Doctor Grigori's. The work as a *Selektor* in the camps was despicable enough, not to mention the crimes against innocent people—particularly children. That was beyond contempt. Nevertheless, Rudel rationalized, he and Grigori had fought in behalf of the same glorious cause and under the command of the same transcendent leader. They were comrades in arms. As long as the Allies continued to hound the man, he, Rudel, would consider himself duty-bound to give him succor and protection. Of course, he also needed the money.

Alban Krug, at that moment, appeared to be having a splendid time. The imp of the perverse, he was delighted to see Grigori make an ass of himself over some tart half his age. For him it was all a kind of smutty joke. His face was red now from an excess of beer and grappa, and a great spray of capillaries had bloomed on his nose; the louder he laughed the more crimson it grew. Laughter made the great head on that dwarf-like body nod ponderously, like an over-large flower on a fragile stem.

As for Horst and Ludo, they too, were irked by the master's performance. They were helpful and scrupulously polite. They served drinks, they baited hooks, they removed the squirming, slippery salmon trout from the line, then later spread bright checkered tablecloths on a long refectory table and served lunch with punctilious aplomb. They were gracious at all times, but on several occasions as they hovered about the table, Baumstein caught their eyes on the girl. Though their civility never faltered, there was something cool and decidedly watchful in the manner in which they regarded her. As if they were biding their time. Waiting for a sign they knew would surely come.

At lunch Krug and Grigori imbibed heavily. A case of the Roederer '53 had come on with them at the dock at Puerto Panuelo and now the more they drank, the more loud and raucous they became. Krug told bawdy stories, pounding the table with his little fists and hooting wildly after each. Grigori roared heartily. By the time they had reached the dessert of strawberries and kirsch, the Doctor was slumped against Dovia, his arm thrown carelessly across her shoulder, pulling her roughly against him from time to time. Rudel scowled and sank more gloomily into himself.

Baumstein was more miserable than ever. And now there was something else—he was actually a little frightened. Who were these five men? What odd, improbable relationship did they share with each other? Clearly they all seemed to revolve about one man—the Doctor —like satellites around a single luminous planet. These two overly attentive and rather ominous young men and this funny, salacious little dwarf with his smutty stories, his cheap cigars and gross body sounds? And the other —the sullen, brooding one, Rudel? Saturnine, Baumstein had thought in the restaurant in Asunción, and saturnine he was. Then, of course, there was the Doctor, the center of this universe—cultured, refined, obviously wealthy—the stink of iniquity all about him. Never once had he mentioned a word about family or profession. What sort of doctor was he? There was still, too, that nagging familiarity Baumstein felt about him. But he could not quite put his finger on it. And where did the girl figure in all of this?

It was then that Baumstein decided that Nora Aldot was an adventuress. She was too clever, he knew, to be genuinely attracted to this fatuous old man. She had seen the Doctor's fabulous winnings the night before and, with that, an opportunity to cash in, and that is precisely what she was doing at this moment. But why did she need Baumstein along to witness it?

Grigori was laughing again, keeping his arm around her, periodically burying his face in the nape of her neck. At a certain point, he flung his head back, howling gleefully, and Baumstein found his eyes fixed almost hypnotically on the Doctor's mouth. The lips were full and sensuous with that unpleasant quality of being too red for a man. He was lighting one of his pastel blue Egyptian cigarettes, smiling broadly at Nora, and his teeth were—

Baumstein's train of thought was interrupted by Alban Krug tugging at his elbow and addressing him. "What sort of work did you say you were in, Herr Gales?"

"Finance," Baumstein replied somewhat evasively.

Krug's ears perked up. "Stocks? Bonds? That sort of thing?"

"More or less. I'm a market analyst. I don't actually do any selling. I advise foundations, large corporations."

"You tell them how to invest?"

"In a manner of speaking."

In the next moment Krug launched into a series of questions about his own portfolio. The sun was high now and they'd eaten well. Rudel excused himself from the table and went forward to stretch out for a nap on the sun-baked deck. Shortly Dovia and the Doctor rose and wandered out of sight of the others. While Horst and Ludo cleared the table, Baumstein and Krug talked finance. The little man at that moment was trying to sell him real estate in the Alto Paraná.

"Highly desirable," he babbled on through wreaths of choking cigar smoke. "Potassium . . . Manganese . . . Fantastic deposits . . . Fortunes to be made . . . Prices should treble within the next decade."

Baumstein nodded drowsily and sipped his coffee. Suddenly one of the rods that had been baited and left in a pole-grip up on the rail started to twitch and flail.

Krug rose and lurched forward. Baumstein, uncertain what to do, followed.

"Yi, yi, yi," Grigori shrieked, appearing suddenly round the wheelhouse and lunging at the whipping rod.

Rudel leapt up from the deck. "Hold him. Hold him. I'll get the net."

Ludo and Horst bounded to the rail, and Chuzito, Doctor Grigori's young galley attendant, burst up from below. Suddenly the entire boat was a blur of action.

Flustered, Baumstein watched the pole whip and jerk. Grigori, holding tight to it, made a series of small grunting sounds.

"Give him line. Give him line," Rudel shouted.

"Surubí. Surubí," Chuzito shrieked at the rail.

"More line. For Christ's sake, more line."

The Doctor grunted and struggled. He'd thrust a foot up on the rail for leverage and hoisted. The reel screamed and Grigori cursed. Dovia laughed and clapped her hands, shouting encouragement. The boy, Chuzito, howled with maniacal glee. *"Tira. Tira. Más cuerda."*

Ludo came streaming back down from the wheel-house with a large net. Matschke hovered at the rail brandishing a gaff. A great condor circled slowly overhead.

"Now. Now," Rudel snarled. "For Christ's sake, now."

The Doctor's face twisted in a grimace. "It's like trying to pull down a wall."

Fifty yards off, just below the surface, they could see a swirling movement on the water. Suddenly a shape, massive and black, breached, lifted out of the water, then flopped back with a great splash.

"Aiiiiieeee," Chuzito squealed and danced round the decks. *"Surubí. Surubí."*

"He's going to make a run for it," Rudel cried.

Chuzito danced wildly and pointed toward the spot where the fish had gone down. *"Se esta y endo."*

Grigori had wedged himself back against the wall of the wheelhouse. "Release the anchor," he gasped, his face a deathly white, his rod bent nearly in half.

Horst sprang to the stern and started hauling up the anchor. In the next moment, the boat rose on a choppy swell and, spinning slowly counterclockwise on her axis, came about.

"My God." Baumstein leaned far out over the rail. "He's pulling us upstream."

The *surubí* was about fifty yards up ahead of them now, and they could see it swimming close to the surface. Standing forward on the prow Ludo pointed to the

large dorsal fin and roared obscenities at the hooked
creature.

Rudel hovered just behind the Doctor, whispering
instructions into his ear. "Not yet. Not yet. Too fast.
Don't horse him. You'll lose him."

They let the *surubi* tow them upstream for nearly five
hundred yards until they could feel the big fish beginning to tire. Shortly the boat, which had been lurching
and bucking against the current, came to a dead halt,
just bobbing up and down on the choppy waters.

"I've got you now." Grigori grinned into the lowering sun. He started to reel in. "I've got you, you bastard.
You're mine now."

But the Doctor was to struggle for twenty minutes
more. At times he'd bring the fish within several yards
of the boat, then incredibly, the creature would make
another dash. The reel would scream and the micro-
filament line would fly out through his fingers. His brow
was covered with sweat and his flanks heaved from the
exertion. Finally, the fish was towed within reach of a
gaff, and after another ten minutes of grim struggle, the
creature was netted.

Its size was phenomenal—five feet from nose to tail,
and nearly one hundred and fifty pounds. Its black bullet mass made piteous thumping sounds as it flailed
about on the deck. Horst, who was nearly two hundred
pounds, sat on it and rode its slithering form as if he
were a rodeo rider. Then he lay prone atop it, making
a copulating motion while the others howled with glee.

"Don't," Dovia cried. "Don't hurt it like that."

Rudel knelt solemnly beside the fish and gazed at it
in mute wonder. Baumstein felt sick at heart.

Gasping and wiping sweat from his brow, Doctor
Grigori leaned against the wheelhouse and watched the
great fish whomping out the final moments of its life on
the deck. The Doctor's face bore a curious expression

—a peculiar, obsessive fixity about the eyes. Blood had begun to seep from beneath the creature's gills. The big hook that had snared it had driven itself up through the roof of the mouth and emerged quite near to the eye. From where Grigori stood, he could see the white panicky eye of the fish swiveling in its head. The eye appeared to him suddenly human and wise, sensing its destiny. It struggled to get out from under the cruel weight still straddling it, wanting desperately to return to the cool dark safety of the depths. Grigori reached for a nearby gill knife and tossed it to Horst. "Finish it for Christ's sake, will you?"

Horst rose, his legs on either side of the fish, straddling it, and holding the blade above his head. Then he thrust the fingers of his left hand hard up under the pink, bloody gills. In a flash of motion, he drove the dagger deep in behind the creature's white gaping eye, and swept the blade round in a perfect, unbroken circle, decapitating the head cleanly.

Dovia turned and walked slowly away. For several moments Grigori stood there among the others, staring in rapt fascination as the headless body continued to thrash and flail about on the blood-slicked deck. Baumstein, glancing up, suddenly saw Grigori shrink backward and cringe against the wheelhouse wall as if he were going to be sick.

"My God." Krug danced like a mad little troll around the fish. "It's a monster."

"Weigh it," Rudel said. "It must be weighed. It's a prize."

Shortly they were all struggling to lift the bloodied corpse onto a hook scale at the ship's stern. It was a messy business, accompanied by a great deal of panting and shouting as they struggled to hoist the slippery carcass high up onto the hook scale. Several times they nearly succeeded, but each time the creature would slip back down onto the deck, the men groaning and sagging beneath it. Only Doctor Grigori stood aside and aloof from the struggle, still panting and leaning against the wheelhouse as if for support.

Ludo and Baumstein were pulling together on one side, Rudel and Horst on the other, with Krug beneath everyone's feet, shouting orders. Slowly the great fish, silvery and bullet-shaped, rose, its great ponderous mass levitating like the emanation of a divinity above them. They groaned and hoisted and the fish rose higher. Baumstein, exhilarated by the struggle, laughed as he hauled, until suddenly he was aware that Ludo, standing just behind him, had ceased to lift. Instead, he was staring fixedly up at Baumstein's wrist, where, in the ensuing struggle, his sleeve had raised, revealing the series of seven jagged blue numbers tattooed there.

CHAPTER 29

"So you returned home at 10:40. Where had you been?"

"Buenos Aires. I told you I was in Buenos Aires."

Colonel Arganas raised a gloved hand and a uniformed guard cranked a large winch, which groaned and squealed while it slowly played out a heavy pulley chain. At the end of the chain Arturo Rubens' drenched and twitching figure dangled headfirst over an open pool of sewage. The pool was actually a large sewer line located in the stone floor of a dank and stinking oubliette in the basement of the Tembuco prison just outside of Asunción. The floors were covered with the slime of algae, and the air, suffocatingly hot, was saturated with the horrendous stench of raw sewage running from the center of Asunción into the basin of the Rio Paraguay.

The figure of Arganas, immaculate and cool, seemed totally incongruous within the setting of this fuming dungeon. Arms crossed, he watched imperturbably as the sputtering, twitching figure sank headfirst beneath that thick, horrific ooze until at last only the legs protruded, strung up and flailing rather comically like a man planted headfirst in a peat bog.

The huge shambling figure of *El Negrón* hovered at the edge of the pool. He carried a long white pole, and whenever the figure implanted in sewage slowed its twitching, he smacked it with the pole as if to galvanize it back into life. Now, grinning toothily, he smacked hard.

For a brief moment the water churned and frothed as the man at the end of the chain thrashed about below the surface, struggling to right himself. Gradually that frantic motion diminished into a sputtering series of plaintive little bubbles.

Colonel Arganas observed the bubbles expressionlessly, his face a mask of impassivity, until at last his arm rose slowly once more in the direction of the winch. The guard stooped above the great wheel, proceeded at once to crank it. Once again the cell filled with the awful reverberation of the heavy chain clanking over the winch, its sound magnified many times in that cavernous subterranean vault below Asunción.

Slowly the body of Arturo Rubens, sodden and dripping, rose from the fetid pool like a mass of nondescript ascending rubbish. It might have been a log or a bit of wreckage, long buried in a swamp, now grappled by hooks and raised unceremoniously to the top. It was certainly no longer anything human. Barely animate.

"Señor Rubens," the Colonel commenced once more.

"This is all so unnecessary. And very foolhardy of you, I must add." His voice had a gentle, almost reasonable quality. You might say it was commiserative. *El Negrón* jabbed the figure with his pole as the Colonel spoke.

"I have in my hand an Avianca passenger manifest, Flight 502 arriving here ten PM a week ago from Dakar." Arganas held the list up and flapped it feebly at the foul, inverted thing dangling by its ankles in midair.

"Your name appears on this list," the Colonel went on sympathetically. "I also know you did not board in Dakar. Dakar was merely your transfer point. The Avianca people who checked their passenger manifest for Flight 502 assure me that you reached Dakar via a connecting El Al Flight 601 out of Tel Aviv. Now why do you persist in telling me that you are not an Israeli operative when all of my sources assure me that you are? When I know that you have made six trips to Israel in the past year, why do you deny it? That really injures me. You must think me an awful fool."

By way of reply, the thing dangling at the end of the chain twitched slightly, the feeble movement causing it to rotate slowly on its fastenings.

The Colonel continued: "I also have here an application from the National Ministry of Immigration filed by you some time last month. It says that you and your family are planning to emigrate to Canada—the day after tomorrow, as a matter of fact. Now, what I would like to know is what you were doing in Tel Aviv a week ago; why you lied and told me you were in Buenos Aires; why it is so important for you to leave Paraguay so precipitately; and why all of this should coincide with the recent Jewish desecration of public and historic landmarks in Asunción."

Colonel Arganas studied the attitude of the dangling man and waited patiently for it to respond. He appeared almost deferential, like a suppliant in ancient times addressing questions to an oracle and waiting for it to proclaim incontrovertible truths. But the dangling man neither responded nor even moved. Only the pull of gravity and the figure's peculiar linkage to the chain caused it to rotate slowly—first clockwise a few degrees, then counterclockwise. It was a languid, almost hypnotic, motion accompanied by the slow, high squeal of rusting chain.

Colonel Arganas walked slowly to the edge of the cesspool and, stooping slightly, peered up at the features of the inverted man. The eyes were closed; the hair and beard clotted with fecal matter. A green ooze was streaming out of the nose and mouth and dribbling back down into the pool.

Arganas waved a hand behind him and shortly *El Negrón* came up with his long white pole. The Colonel murmured something and *El Negrón* stretched the pole across the short distance of the pool to where the figure hung. Several times he prodded it, poking it this way and that, until at last the figure's eyes fluttered; it shook its head and spluttered a bit.

"Are you all right—Señor Rubens?" Colonel Arganas inquired solicitously.

For answer Arturo Rubens belched loudly. Then vomited mouthfuls of the awful stuff he'd swallowed while submerged.

"Very good, Señor Rubens. That should make you feel much better. Now to return to my questions—"

CHAPTER 30

In the dining room that evening, the Doctor's table made a lively party. There were Rudel and Krug, the Doctor, and, of course, Dovia, looking more ravishing than ever. Baumstein had begged off, pleading exhaustion and too much sun.

At a nearby table, Horst and Ludo ate like a pair of ravenous young wolves. Between greedy mouthfuls of food, they observed the Doctor and the young lady. There was now something distinctly wary and uneasy in their manner. The thin line of Matschke's lips tautened like stretched elastic bands as he watched Grigori's fingers lightly stroking the lovely nape of the girl's neck beneath her upswept hair.

At the Doctor's table they were having coffee and cognac when the maitre d' appeared and summoned Krug to the phone.

Krug glowered up at the man. "What the devil now?"

"Long distance from Asunción," the man apologized. "A Colonel Arganas."

"Lonely . . . Regret having . . . Wish to come home . . . What a fool . . . To think . . . Futile now . . . All futile." J. Peter Baumstein's pen scratched across a sheet of bond with a Llao Llao letterhead. He lay in bed in pajamas and a robe, a tray of half-eaten supper, dirty plates, and rumpled napkins on the bed table beside him. His back ached from the exercise of the day, and he had smeared cooling unguents on his badly burned legs. "Please try to understand . . . Forgive . . . if you can."

He looked up, having heard what he thought to be a faint knock on the wall behind him. Or was it the door? Silence now. Probably the door of the adjoining suite.

He reread his last line, composing in his head some suitable conclusion. Apposite. Affectionate. Contrite, yet not groveling. He did not wish to grovel, even though he was consumed with the notion of how stupidly he'd acted. Punishment was certain, judicial as well as personal, but still, he did not wish to grovel.

Then it came again. This time louder. More insistent.

"Just a moment," he called from the bed, mortified to hear the quaver in his voice. Then he rose, fumbled into slippers, and went to the door.

"I beg your—" Baumstein gasped at the figure standing out there. In the next moment, Dovia Safid swept past him in a blur.

"Close the door," she whispered.

"What in God's—"

"Close the door, I said." This time the whisper had some of the harsh edge of a shriek.

"What is it now?" Baumstein whined, and before he could go on she'd pressed a finger to his lips. The proximity of her—that emanation of soap and cologne, of clean hair, and pure female scent—suddenly aroused him.

Then she was tugging him back across the room to a distant corner, her gaze fixed on the door, until they'd reached a small divan where she pulled him down beside her.

She was pale, he noted, agitated and slightly breathless, as if she'd been running. Her eyes kept darting about the room, and she was waving an envelope at him.

"Would you kindly tell me—" Baumstein made another attempt to speak.

"Take this," she said, pressing the envelope upon him.

"Look here, I—"

"Take it, I said. Don't argue with me."

"What is it?"

"That's not important. You're simply to take it. Keep it for me. Some place safe. The hotel vault will do quite well."

"But surely—"

"If anything should happen to me," she barged right past his protestations, "you're to mail it. Do you understand? Just mail it."

Baumstein glanced down at the envelope in his hand. Still, he recoiled from it as if it were lethal. It was already stamped and addressed to a box number in Santiago.

"Now take it," she said, trying to cram it into his robe.

Baumstein's fluttering hands pushed it off. "I have no intention of taking this—or for that matter, of taking anything."

Suddenly something came over Fräulein Aldot—something hard and ruthless which altered drastically her softly appealing expression. In a flash of motion, like a sword thrust, she snatched his hand and tore the sleeve of his robe back, revealing the series of seven numbers tattooed in faint, wavery blue lines there.

"As an economist, Herr Baumstein," she spoke through gritted teeth, "you're undoubtedly brilliant. But as a fugitive from justice, you're a disaster."

He sat there, heart thudding, stupefied. His lips moved, but little more than air came out.

"You're not a teacher then, are you?" he finally asked.

"Not any more than you are a Viennese or a financier."

"I used to be," he said mournfully. "Now no longer."

"In fact, everything you told me was a lie."

"Not everything." Suddenly tired, Baumstein paused, reflecting, stalling for time. "Are you the police?"

"I am not," she said emphatically. "And let me assure you at once that I have not the slightest interest in your pathetic little cachet of stolen bonds."

"How did you know my name?"

"I'm coming to that," she went on, talking very quickly and glancing each moment at the door. "While I am not, as you say, the police, I happen to have very substantial contacts among the police."

"I see," Baumstein said, not seeing at all. "Then, who are you?"

"Never mind that now," she rattled on, impatient with his interruptions. "When you told me the other night that your name was Gales, I thought that very odd. A man with an Austrian accent going around with such a blatantly English name. And then this afternoon on the lake, I happened to notice the tattoo on your wrist. You know," she said, a sardonic smile playing at her lips, "in a place like this, you ought to be a little more cautious about flaunting such a tattoo. I wasn't the only one who noticed."

He stared at her with a kind of idiot fixity, barely understanding a word of what she said. He understood only that for him, somehow, the jig was up. If the police did not get him now, something worse would.

"In any event," she went on, "through excellent sources of my own, I was informed that a man by the name of Jacob Peter Baumstein of New York City was being sought by U.S. Treasury agents for the theft of over a million dollars in bearer bonds, stock certificates, traveler's checks, and other negotiable paper. I was also informed that Mr. Baumstein, whose occupation is described as that of chief economist for the firm of Battersby, Rudge, and Pospisil, is believed to be traveling with a complete set of forged papers under the name of John Gales."

A curious calm had now settled over him. "And who are these sources?"

"Never mind who they are," she snapped, and extended an open hand to him.

He gazed down into her palm to see a small passport photograph of himself taken nearly ten years ago. "You'd have thought they could get something more recent." He smiled sadly. "Then you are the police."

"No, I am not," she flung out with exasperation. Then the harsh facade unexpectedly softened. "Look —I can't tell you anything more now," she went on. "You simply have to trust me. I have something you want, and you have something I want." She placed the envelope in his lap where it lay untouched by either of them. "If you do what I ask, I can forget about who you really are. I don't have to wire the FBI or the Department of the Treasury, or the Argentine authorities."

"Do the Argentine police know anything about me?"

"To the best of my knowledge, nobody knows that you're here. Except me. And you have my word that if you cooperate with me, you'll be perfectly safe."

Baumstein inhaled deeply and held his breath. "And if I don't?"

For reply Dovia merely shrugged her beautiful, well-tanned shoulders.

"I see." Baumstein let the air slowly out of his lips. She smiled not unkindly at him. "Understood?"

This time Baumstein shrugged. He was quite defeated. "But if you're not the police, and you're not interested in what I have, then who the devil are you and what precisely are you interested in? Does it have something to do with this Neiditch fellow?"

She sat there silent, not moving, the trace of a small smile flickering at the corners of her mouth. "Yes," she said finally, "it does. But let me say that if I succeed here, you won't be unhappy with the outcome." She took his hand and held it for a moment. Looking at her then he suddenly realized that she was undoubtedly even younger than he'd first thought. He could see how she'd got herself up to look older—more mature. To Baumstein, looking at her then, she seemed like a child. No more than her early twenties but with the worldiness and composure of a woman years beyond.

Still holding his hand, she raised it, then let her lips graze lightly over the area where the serial numbers had been burned into his wrist. "My grandparents bore those same marks," she said softly. Then she rose and quickly crossed the room. At the door she waited a moment, listening as if she could hear someone breathing there on the other side.

"Trust me," she said, smiling back at him. Then she was gone.

For a long time he sat there on the divan where she'd left him, a wave of panic clutching him. He thought about running. About packing and leaving there at once. Heading for some large city like Rio or Buenos Aires. Getting lost in the crowd. Or better yet, some desolate, godforsaken land—Eritrea possibly, or Tierra del Fuego. No one to commune with but the mute, uncaring tribal people, or the penguins, and his own ridiculous, self-inflicted sorrow.

He looked down and saw the envelope lying there in his lap where she'd tossed it. He started to open it, certain that its contents would at once clear up all confusion. Why not? It was not even sealed. It invited prying. He pushed the flap back and was about to withdraw the material inside. But, instead, he rose from the divan and crossed quickly to his bed. He pulled the drawer of the night table out and withdrew two Band-Aids taken from a first-aid kit inside there, then taped the envelope to the bottom of the commode lid in the lavatory as he'd done with the keys to his attaché case.

For a long while he lay in bed, unable to think or lay out a course of action. All the time the face of Doctor Neiditch smiled mockingly at him. When at last he turned out the light beside him he was exhausted, and shortly he fell into a deep but fitful sleep.

"Links . . . Recht. Links . . . Recht . . . Links . . . Links . . ."

His dream of several nights before returned, announced once again by that grim chant of the *Selektor*. Only this time he saw a small boy standing damp and shivering in his underpants in the immaculate, white-tiled anteroom of a surgery. The piercing cries of children issued from the experimental wing just beyond. The screams were horrifying. The hoarse shouts of the doctors could be heard above them along with the stamping booted feet of the SS men moving in and out of the surgery.

"You," the big SS officer snapped at the small gypsy boy huddled beside young Jacob Baumstein, who'd become his friend in the last week. The SS man snatched the gypsy boy by the shoulders, attempting to propel him toward the surgery. But the boy pulled back, struggling against the man, using his feet for braking. A shrill, panicky bleating ripped from the boy's lips as the SS man stamped with hobnailed boots on the child's bare feet, then lifted him squealing under his arm and carried him twisting and struggling into the surgery. In the next moment there was a prolonged, rending scream.

The other boy, young Jacob, eyes open wide like great saucers, ran to the *Kapo* attendant, moving back and forth in the anteroom, a dirty white surgical robe over his prison garb.

"My brother," the boy stammered, and pointed to the surgery. "My brother . . . my brother," is all he could say. Tears gushed from his eyes.

The *Kapo,* a short, bald man with a dirty, unshaven face and broken brown teeth, merely shook his head dumbly and shuffled past, trying not to hear.

Then the Doctor appeared in the doorway of the surgery. He too wore a white robe splashed horribly with blood. The rubber fingers of his surgical gloves were smeared with blood. He was a slight, dark man with an attractive face. The expression was not at all unkind. He was the one they called *Den Schönen Doktor.* He moved out of the surgery, smiling at the small boy shivering there in his dirty underpants. Now, tousling his hair, the Doctor stood above the child, tucking a finger playfully under his cheek and smiling. The boy peered upward into a smiling mouth—red lips encircling gapped teeth. Smiling, the mouth came closer and closer.

Baumstein was sitting bolt upright in bed, blankets wound around him, in a cold sweat. "Grigori," he whispered into the darkened shadows, waiting as if he expected some reply. But none came and he uttered the word again. "Grigori."

But that was impossible. He refused to believe it. Grigori was dead. Everyone knew that. He himself had read accounts of it in at least a dozen newspapers that had reported it in banner headlines over a decade ago. "Death Angel of Auschwitz Dead in Paraguay" or words to that effect. The story had told of how a grave had been uncovered in an Indian village in the jungles of northern Paraguay, just below the Bolivian border. How local tribesmen had led officials to it. How forensic experts flown in from Russia, Israel, and the United States had made positive identification from X rays of the skull and dentition. He recalled having read it with a quiet sense of justice done. His poor brother David's maimed and grieving ghost could now finally rest.

Grigori was dead. There was no doubt of that. How could he be alive now and here today? This man here— what did they call him?—Neiditch. Doctor Josef Neiditch didn't even look like Grigori, or what Baumstein recalled of Grigori's appearance. Of course, that was thirty years ago. Three decades will alter the features, and what time itself does not alter, the surgeon almost certainly can. Still, it was too preposterous. Too incredible. An uncanny coincidence—that squinting eye and that gapped tooth, that red, red mouth. All a coincidence. Nothing more. Still—

"Links . . . Recht . . . Links . . . Recht . . ." His dream came tramping back upon him. For an instant it occurred to him that he could even then hear the sound of thousands of feet shuffling out of freight cars, down bare wooden planks, onto railway platforms, marching inexorably over gravel to the crematoriums. *"Links, Recht. Links, Recht."* The sound echoed and roared back at him over the space of years. And suddenly there was his brother, David, a ghostly emanation, a wraith-like creature. Older than him by a year—but so close in resemblance to his younger brother that they were automatically assumed by strangers to be identical twins. A curious phenomenon, but it had saved Baumstein's life. In those awful nightmare years of holocaust, there had been no birth certificates. No available records of their past existed. The estimable Doctor Grigori, pursuing his blind passionate interest in the phenomenon of multiple birth, also assumed they were twins and there-

fore kept the Baumstein boys alive for experimental purposes.

It was early in 1945, with the Russians streaming across Poland, pressing hard on Auschwitz–Birkenau, that Doctor Grigori commenced his work on David Baumstein. The boy didn't survive it. Jacob was shortly to follow, but fortunately for him, the Russians got there first.

Now a presence, something numinous, a kind of aura of his older brother, seemed suddenly to fill the room all about him. He was suffused with a tangle of emotions—a kind of foreboding as well as a warm, comforting sense of someone—something—trying to warn him of impending danger. Baumstein was a pragmatic man. Eminently logical. He prided himself on that. He was not the sort of individual to indulge himself in chimerical speculations of the other world. But this night, high in the Cordillera, nearly ten thousand miles and thirty years beyond the place of David Baumstein's ghastly demise, Baumstein had a strong, incontrovertible sense of his older brother's protective presence all about him. When he rose finally from the bed, he did not even know that he was crying.

He reached for the phone and a night clerk rang through to Nora Aldot's room. He sat there in the dark on the edge of the bed, clammy in his nightshirt and listening over and over again to the ringing of the phone in her room. Of course she wasn't there. Nor was she meant to be. That was not part of the grand scheme he was beginning now to only dimly perceive. If she were anywhere that night, he knew exactly where that would be—in the arms of Grigori, lulling the infamous Doctor into a comfortable but fatal sense of well-being. It was an embrace, he knew only too well, that could prove fatal to her. "You won't be unhappy with the outcome." Those cryptic words of hers, first uttered several hours ago, now took on portentous significance.

He rose quickly, nearly leaping out of bed. His acquaintance with Fräulein Aldot, inadvertent as it was, he now realized, placed him in dire jeopardy. Surely if they began to suspect her, for any reason, they would most assuredly suspect him as well. He had a sudden icy recollection of Ludo that afternoon glancing down at the tattoo numbers on his wrist while they struggled to weigh the fish. He did not attach much significance then to the fact that Ludo had seen his internment number. Now, in the light of recent developments, these numbers marked him.

He must leave Bariloche at once. Get far, far away from all of this. Put some quick distance between himself and Grigori, Nora, and all the rest.

Shortly he was up and moving, tossing things into a small suitcase. But then he came up short. The attaché case with all its precious contents was locked below in the hotel vaults. He would not be able to get into the safe until the morning when the hotel desk reopened. He would have to stay then—at least for the night, unless, of course, he was willing to leave the case behind. To forget it. Write it off as a bad joke and go home and take his medicine after returning what he had been foolish enough to steal. He might then conceivably throw himself on the mercy of the authorities. Who knows? They might look kindly on his plight. He had lived an exemplary life up until then—voted and paid his taxes, even served on a local school board. He was a family man. Surely they would take that into consideration. The thought of going home suddenly buoyed him. He felt a warm surge of affection at the thought of seeing Edith. And even Joel—vile, ungrateful, wretched, puling Joel. He laughed momentarily and cherished a sudden mental picture of the boy. Then, recalling his danger, he was deadly sober again. At any rate, he must wait now till the morning.

At least he could warn the girl of her danger. No doubt she knew better than he. Still, he threw a robe on, not certain at all where he was going, but knowing somehow he must get to her and, if he could, help her.

He knew where Grigori's room was, and that was undoubtedly where she was. Unmindful of his wild appearance, he tore the door open and burst out into the darkened corridor. But in the next moment he ducked quickly back in and locked the door, standing there panting against the wall, his heart thudding in his chest. In the moment in which he'd stood in the corridor, he was aware of a presence—someone standing at the end of the hall some fifty feet away, regarding him. He had not seen the person full view, but in the moment in which he'd barged out, he'd seen a shadowy figure— almost an apparition—spin about and quickly vanish around the corner of an intersecting passageway. It appeared to him that what he had seen, and only fleetingly, was a profile, then a back. But in that split millisecond of time, he was convinced that the person he had seen, observing his own door, was none other than Doctor Grigori's young companion Horst Matschke.

CHAPTER **31**

Tronador

"If I were to go away now, would you follow me?"
"To the far side of the moon."

"Ah, you mock me. It's all a joke with you."

Doctor Grigori looked up, feigning injury. Inwardly he was delighted. That such an adorable creature should find him so alluring flattered him deeply.

"I mock you?" the Doctor protested. "My dear Nora, I can assure you . . ." They were strolling down a path deep in a forest called the Arrayanes. Situated on the tiny peninsula of Quetrihue, the place could only be reached by motor launch. They had started out quite early that morning with Rudel and Von Rattenhuber. Krug and Matschke had remained behind at the hotel with odds and ends to tie up before they could leave the next day.

Now Grigori and Dovia Safid strolled hand in hand beneath a canopy of century-old trees in a soft diffusion of green coppery light. Rudel and Von Rattenhuber had started out walking with them. But as the Doctor and the young woman penetrated deeper into the forest, the other two had fallen discreetly behind until finally, as if by some prearranged signal, they had dropped out of sight completely.

"But why must you leave tomorrow?" Dovia's voice had an appealing plaintive ring. "Just when . . ."

"Just when"—Grigori put his arm round her waist and laughed—"everything is going so splendidly."

"And you won't even tell me where you are going?"

"I told you, I am going to meet my son."

"Whom you haven't seen in nine years," she added impatiently. "Yes, I know all that. But here, we've only just met. And we've had such a good time. Haven't we? Last night was so lovely."

They meandered onward deeper into the forest.

"And now you simply pick up and leave," she fretted. "And you won't give me a forwarding address. I can't even send you a Christmas card. You make me feel cheap, Josef. As if I'd been used."

He laughed out loud and pulled her against him.

"You see," she pouted. "You do mock me. You laugh as if it were all simply an episode."

"I don't laugh, my dear. And I am desolate at the thought of leaving you." He kissed her eyelids.

She stared miserably up at him. "Promise me we'll see each other again."

"Of course we will, my darling." He kissed her eyes, thinking what a cunning little bitch she was. "I promise we will. But now, let us have some lunch and a brief rest. This afternoon we go up the Tronador."

"The closet," Krug snapped.

"I've already been through the closet."

"What about the shoe bag? And don't forget the Valpack hanging there on the door."

Horst Matschke shook his head breathlessly, his eyes a little frantic. "I've already been through both."

Krug watched the boy bolt into the bathroom. "Where are you going?" he barked.

"To check the medicine cabinet."

The dwarf snapped his fingers as if struck by a bolt of revelation. "Of course. The medicine cabinet." He stormed in after Matschke. There was something comical about the two of them there—Matschke, the young blond hero of a Ring Cycle opera, and Krug, the dwarf, the ugly toad of a Grimm's fairy tale—the two of them tearing hectically about, upending furniture, emptying wastebaskets, making a thorough mess of Dovia Safid's room, to which they had obtained a passkey from an exceedingly pliant and greatly intimidated house manager. The place had been subjected to a violent ransacking and still they had found nothing.

Now the two of them were in the bathroom, rifling through toiletries and medicines. Matschke opened a small phial of perfume and sniffed. "French," he murmured, lingering over it a moment. "And expensive."

Krug snatched the phial from him and thrust it back where it had been. "Fool—you're wasting time. Arganas is very alarmed about all this." He pored through a box of sanitary napkins beside the commode, scattering them on the floor and peering upward into the empty box. *"Nichts,"* he fumed. *"Immer nichts.* We're wasting time. Come on." He tugged the young man out into the sitting room. "Let's straighten up here. Next we check the hotel vault."

Shortly the room was restored to the precise order in which it had been found. Not even the most practiced and astute eye would have been able to detect that intruders had been at work there. Then, as stealthily as they'd entered, so they departed, back downstairs to the desk, where the house manager awaited their next request.

At that same moment Ian Asher was plucking a small steel spring from a jumble of newly oiled gun parts. They represented the innards of three stripped-down, semi-automatic, long-barreled Berettas which were just then undergoing modification.

Asher sat at a long refectory table in the kitchen of the abandoned farmhouse outside Bariloche. The table at which he sat was covered with an oilcloth upon which dozens of gun parts were strewn, along with oil cans, ramrods, and rags.

The young man worked intently at his appointed task—extracting a small part of the powder of each of the .22-caliber cartridges, then replacing the lead projectiles so that each shot would be relatively quiet. All this was preparatory to the next step in the operation, which was two-fold—to adjust the trigger mechanisms of the Berettas so the weapon could be fired more quickly. The second step was trickier and more delicate; it involved the reloading mechanism. Since the Berettas were going to be operated with cartridges that had less explosive force than normal, the spring in their blow-back mechanisms had to be fine-tuned accordingly. This was Asher's task. At the conclusion of all these modifications, he would have at his service a small-caliber, soft-spoken, and utterly lethal weapon.

Asher worked with almost surgical precision, a jeweler's loop screwed into his eye and totally unmindful of the chaos all about him. He was obsessed just then with the matter of time and whether or not he would have everything set in motion, ready to go, in the few remaining hours.

CHAPTER **32**

Baumstein called down to the reservations desk early that morning attempting to book a flight to Buenos Aires. He was told promptly that there were no flights to Buenos Aires that day. The earliest would be the following day. What about La Paz or Rio de Janeiro? Baumstein inquired, and received the same reply. Somewhat apologetically, the desk clerk reminded him that it was Sunday and that nothing of any consequence left the drowsy little Bariloche airport on Sundays save some inconsequential local mail flights. He could, however, guarantee him a seat on a flight out early the next day to Rio. Resigned to waiting another day, Baumstein booked the Rio flight and hung up somewhat apprehensively. He had no way of knowing that at that same moment Krug and Von Rattenhuber were down below, inside the safety deposit vaults of the Llao Llao with an extremely frightened hotel manager.

Had Baumstein known that, he might not have been so complacent about staying over the additional day. Instead, he might have elected to go by rail to Buenos Aires, or simply rent a car and get the devil out of there. But at that moment, he had no idea of the full extent of his danger. The presence of young Matschke in the corridor outside his door at three AM that morning should have been indication enough of that. They suspected something. But it would be too laughable to think they could imagine him in collusion with Nora Aldot. Him, an undercover agent for some undisclosed government, a member of an assassination team with the infamous Doctor Grigori as its target. Laughable indeed. Of course, Baumstein was sympathetic enough with their cause. God knows he had reason to be. Vengeance is sweet, but, oddly enough, he wanted no part in the exacting of it. Baumstein was not a vindictive man. Bloodletting was not his forte. All of his life he had had an abhorrence of violence. He feared guns and hated the noise they made. Long ago he had buried the awful nightmare of his past. He had no desire now to see it resurrected. He had lost a beloved brother— mutilated and tormented to death by a fiend whose work was legitimized by war. Now, thirty years after the fact, the fiend still walked free and lived in comfort and luxury. Where was the justice in that? The fitting vengeance? Baumstein had no stomach for vengeance. Let Nora Aldot and her zealous colleagues exact the vengeance. More power to them. He had problems of his own just then and he wished nothing more than to get far away from the whole business.

* * *

Even then, as Baumstein lay sprawled on his bed in his underwear contemplating the vagaries of justice, Krug and Matschke below were rifling hectically through Dovia Safid's private papers. Her safe-deposit box lay open on a desk in the manager's office at the rear. There, a Señor Ortiz, backed against a wall, wrung his hands and perspired freely, certain that the lady in question would return at any moment and call the police. He was certain to lose his job.

Krug, however, had no such fears. He knew very well that Fräulein Aldot would be kept well away from the hotel that day until such time as her real identity could be determined. She was certainly not the lady she claimed to be. Colonel Arganas had made that quite clear over the telephone the night before. From everything the Colonel had seen and learned in Asunción over the past several days, the indications were that Fräulein Aldot's presence in Bariloche just then was ominious. Under no circumstances was the Doctor to be left alone with her, unguarded.

"Dovia Safid," Krug read aloud from a set of identification papers. "Twenty-seven years old. Born in Tel Aviv." The other papers, the more damaging ones—the Grigori dossier with the official seal of the Mossad embossed on it, full of photographs and fingerprints of the Doctor, with copies of cable traffic between Interpol and the Mossad, dispatches to and from the Israeli Embassy in Paraguay and the Haifa Documentation Center—these are what really settled Dovia Safid's fate that day.

"I knew there was something rotten about her," Matschke muttered, kneading a fist into his palm. "And that worm, her accomplice . . . what's his name—Gales? Herr Gales, with his numbers tattooed all over him. I shall particularly enjoy dealing with him. How stupid to be so brazen. To flaunt it like that."

Matschke's fists clenched and his face darkened. "Let's get out there at once."

"Not yet." Krug replaced the papers very carefully in the metal box.

"But they may be in danger. God knows how many they have with them."

"I think there is no immediate danger," Krug remarked with impressive calm. "There will be plenty of time to take care of Fräulein Safid. Ortiz . . ." the dwarf snapped over his shoulder at the craven manager. "Return this box to the vaults, and when you return, be so kind as to bring Herr Gales' safe-deposit box along with you."

CHAPTER 33

"Over there directly west is Chile."

"That high ridge of peaks?"

"Yes—the tall, humped one is the Osorno volcano."

"Cruel-looking, isn't it?"

"Yes." Doctor Grigori smiled at the young woman who leaned so appealingly for support on his arm. "Very cruel."

They were standing on a rock ledge high up on the Cerro Tronador, almost at the summit of the Andes. The air up there was cold and thin; the views awesomely spectacular; everything so vast and overpowering as to reduce all pride and human vanity to mere dumb silence.

The climb up had been invigorating. Indeed, it had brought the color into Doctor Grigori's cheeks. He appeared very pleased with himself for having made the climb—a vindication of his indestructible constitution. The fact that he had accomplished it in the presence of such a bewitching female was an additional bonus.

Now the Doctor expatiated on salient points of interest within the landscape, while the winds whipped and snarled about them. They were standing several feet from the edge of the ledge which overhung the Valley of Vuriloches, several thousand feet below. Rudel and Von Rattenhuber cowered behind on the footpath, unwilling to venture out with them.

"And what's that over there, Josef?" She pointed to sheer, towering walls of ice that had frozen into rippling, undulant shapes. In varying tones and gradations of gray, they ringed the valley and soared high above it.

"The Black Glaciers, they call them," Doctor Grigori enthused, and pulled the girl closer to him. "That huge, gray chasm over there. You see it?"

"Yes."

"That's called the Devil's Gorge." Grigori tugged her out a little further, then looked back at his companions. "Come on out here, you jellyfish." He laughed at the two men, cowering fifty or so feet behind on the footpath. They waved back but refused to be coaxed out. Grigori and Dovia laughed.

The lack of oxygen at that extraordinary altitude had made her breathless and a little giddy. Yet, in some curious way she felt exhilarated. Even as the Doctor was speaking and she nodded, seemingly attentive, she had a sudden image of Asher somewhere out there— not more than twenty miles away—and she had to suppress a fierce desire to laugh.

She gazed up at the man hovering protectively beside her on the ledge and oddly enough felt a strange affection for him. Oh yes, she knew all about him—every ghastly, hideous detail of his dossier. She had committed the whole dismal chronicle to memory, yet she could not associate the ravening beast of that record— the castrator, the *Selektor,* the child abuser—with the kindly, attentive, exceedingly refined and avuncular gentleman who stood beside her now. Although last night in his bedroom avuncularity was the farthest thing from his mind.

"Over there, where you see that great cleft in the face of the cliff," the Doctor went on, his breath warm at the nape of her neck. She was absorbed in what he was saying. The voice was almost lulling. Yes, that was one of his most seductive features—the voice with its suave unbanity, its rich tones and hues. He could caress her with his voice.

He was holding her chin firmly between thumb and fingers, pointing her gaze in the direction of a purple ridge of distant peaks when, suddenly, out of the corner of her eye, she saw, or thought she saw, a movement, tentative at first and so slight as to be barely perceptible. She had no sense of alarm or impending danger, and when she felt Grigori's hands fall lightly from her shoulders, still nothing like fear registered. There was only a sense of separation, the departure of the presence behind her, and though she never knew how it had occurred, she was suddenly aware of her awful isolation on the ledge. It was then, still smiling, that she turned.

The first thing she saw was Grigori—or rather his back. He was still on the ledge but already several feet closer to the footpath and moving with a slow, ponderous deliberation toward the place where she had imagined Rudel and Von Rattenhuber to be. Indeed, Von Rattenhuber was still there, but now Rudel was gone and in his place stood Matschke and Krug.

Then she saw Rudel. He'd come around the side of the ledge and had extended a hand to Grigori, leading him gently back off the rock and onto the footpath. The Doctor turned for a moment and gazed back at her—a wistful, rather hurt, look that made her almost pity him. He appeared so vulnerable just then with his protectors —like an invalid or a full-grown idiot amid his keepers.

The other two, Horst and Ludo, waited at the end of the ledge—two lean cougars straining to get at a cornered deer. Krug waited too, just ahead of them, holding them at bay until the propitious moment. Nora Aldot, née Dovia Safid, did not even try to save herself. Even at that extreme moment, she was enough of a professional to make a quick assessment and conclude that her situation was hopeless. Strangely enough, she felt no fear.

Suddenly Grigori cried out, his features hideously contorted, as the sound rose from his throat. Something in German, she imagined it to be. An obscenity. Something vile. And for a long, horribly protracted moment, the echo of it reverberated through the chasm, bouncing back and forth off the rocks and still booming at her, even as she saw him charge. What came at her then was not a man. It was nothing human but, rather, only a gray, formless, onrushing motion, striking, cutting, slashing. She found herself gazing into his squinting eye. They held her there at the edge, arms outstretched, while he pummeled her over and over again with sharp, cruel little fists. Then he kicked her in the stomach. Oddly enough, she felt nothing. It was rather as if she were an observer standing detached outside the scene. Then finally the light, giddy sense of feeling herself lifted off her feet and tossed high in the air, the way she recalled her brothers tossing her upward in a blanket, then catching her in it. Sinking into the dark, comfortable warmth of the blanket. But now she was aware of being suddenly very cold and unable to catch her breath. And she could hear the awful reverberation of her own scream booming in her head.

Ian Asher gazed toward the Tronador peak and felt a cold, inexplicable shiver shoot up his spine. Over twenty miles away, the mountain loomed enormous and foreboding. At the summit he could see the flashing peak of ice and then the steep sprawl of its silhouette, dark and gibbous, dominating the entire northerly vista.

Asher hunkered down in the sand before the farmhouse, obliterating with a stick all traces of the map he'd etched for himself there only moments ago. He had committed details—routes and alternate routes—to memory. Now he was alone, desolate beyond words, the taste of ashes in his mouth.

It was late afternoon. The sun slanting toward the west had sent a golden spike of light directly into the majestic face of the Tronador. He wondered about Dovia, where she was at that moment, and with whom. It was an unsettling thought, and he sought quickly to change it. So he concentrated on the peak once more, trying to imagine the dizzying heights at the top, the icy blasts, the bleak, pitiless crags around which only the eagle and the condor soared.

A lowering cloud like a dirty thumbprint suddenly scudded over the peak, and he felt a spasm of apprehension—a feeling as if a fist had closed over his heart.

"Tonight," he thought. "I will see her tonight."

CHAPTER 34

It was past dusk when the overnight ferry from Posadas slipped out of the quay pointing her bright red prow northward up the Rio de la Plata, moving like a child's toy up a sluggish stream. Rolfe Hupfauer stood far back at the stern, hunched over the rail, eyes lowered to the frothy wash of water churned white by the propellers. He had not eaten that day, nor was he particularly hungry, and as the engines throbbed, he could feel their huge beat in the vacancy of his stomach. What occurred to him now more keenly than ever was the fact that the closer time and circumstance brought him to his father, the more despondent he grew.

Caffetti sat behind him, reclining in a deck chair, reading *El Correo de Buenos Aires*. People meandered up and down the decks, clustered in festive little groups, drank beer and aperitifs, and caroused. A solitary guitar played a doleful ballad. Lights flickered on and sprinkled the hills lining either shore. Overnight voyagers—those going up to Encarnación, or further north to Asunción—had quickly succumbed to the spell of boat travel by night, people clustering together within a large watery darkness. The sense of impending adventure.

A steward came by taking drink orders. Caffetti, sprawled in his deck chair, called over his newspaper to the young man at the rail. "Have an aperitif. You will feel better."

Rolfe accepted a Campari, and down below a small rhumba band had started to tune up in the dining room.

"Are you hungry at all?" Caffetti asked.

Rolfe merely stared at him. He looked ashen and disheveled. In his conservatively tailored worsted suit, starched white shirt, and necktie, he appeared stiff, uncomfortable, and terribly out of place. There was a sudden burst of laughter behind him. He winced and ground his teeth. Laughter, gaiety, lightheartedness, only magnified his despondency.

"You'll make yourself sick going on this way." Caffetti rose and took him by the elbow, guiding him tactfully away from the frivolity of that corner.

They strolled along the deck, sipping their drinks as they went, threading their way forward, where only a handful of people braved the gusty wind buffeting the bow and the steeply pitching cross-currents out at midstream.

"I wish we had accomplished more these past few days," Caffetti remarked offhandedly. He had settled on a course of evasive and untaxing conversation, avoiding anything too painful for young Hupfauer. Still he was shrewd enough to see that such tactics were fruitless, that the reunion with his father after nine years was going to be traumatic for the young man, despite anything he did. With a sigh of relief he let his guard slip. "I honestly don't know what we'll find once we get up there."

"I don't expect anything very different from my last visit," Rolfe muttered resignedly. "Lies. Boasts. Evasions. Drunkenness. Long rambling apologies. Protestations of innocence. Charges of being unjustly singled out for special punishment. In short, lunacy. Does he still have those thugs with him?"

"Horst and Ludo?"

"That's their names. Two jackals if I've ever seen

any. Swaggering about. Flashing pistols. Sucking around him. Stealing his money. I swear, Ricardo, I would never have come if you hadn't told me he was so sick."

The other man pondered awhile. "Shortly you'll have an opportunity to see for yourself."

"It's his mind, you say?" Rolfe mused. Stars had begun to shimmer on the water.

"No doubt of it. Doctor Enríquez maintains that physically he's in superb shape. But he's convinced he has a fatal malady. One day it's heart; the next day, cancer. He fears the dark. He will not sleep alone. He sees enemies hiding behind every bush. He thinks his food is poisoned and he hears voices at dusk. Children crying, he says. He plays the violin then so as not to hear them."

"What a charade." Rolfe laughed bitterly.

Caffetti shook his head. "I used to think so, too. But frankly, between you and me, I think your father is a very sick man. His behavior is erratic and more flamboyant than ever. Everything has been stripped from him—rank, station in life, professional credentials. He has no useful work to occupy his mind. The thieving officials steal his money. He's lonely and growing older. He's sick of Paraguay and has no wish to die alone in a swamp. In short, he wants to go home."

"But he never will." Rolfe spoke in a quiet, yet forceful voice. "Never again if I can help it. I still have a wife and children to consider—and I will not put them through that trauma."

Caffetti regarded him uneasily beneath his bushy, caterpillar brows.

Young Hupfauer lit a small cigar and tossed the still-burning match far out over the water. "When do I see him?"

"Tomorrow evening if all goes as planned."

"You've no reason to suspect that it won't?"

"None at all." Caffetti laughed sardonically and ordered another Kulmbacher beer. "But, nevertheless, we must be cautious."

"Cautious?"

"There are always the lunatics and fanatics. The mercenaries and the careerist avengers. The youthful romantics with the lofty ideals."

Rolfe puffed reflectively at his cigar. "Like the other night?"

Caffetti appeared momentarily confused.

"When we were driving into Buenos Aires from the airport," Rolfe went on, "and you swerved so sharply off the road." Rolfe fixed his eye sharply on the short stocky man with the shaved head. "Was that merely caution?"

Caffetti pondered the question. He did not wish to alarm the young man in any way. "In a manner of speaking."

"You're being evasive."

"I don't want to make more of something than needs be."

"You thought we were being followed?"

"I was only exercising caution, my dear Rolfe." Caffetti put his arm around the young man's shoulder. "The water has a salutary effect on my digestion. Suddenly I have the most ravenous appetite. Come—let's have a bottle of champagne and a steak. You know, as I look at you now, you look exactly like your grandfather. Old Grigori, bless his soul. The old chief. He'd be very proud if he could see you today."

Frowning into the great moist shadows of the night, Rolfe Hupfauer permitted himself to be steered toward the tawdry lights of the dining room.

The place they had just occupied now appeared strangely vacant. Only the moon, huge and toylike, sent a shaft of radiance down upon the spot where

Rolfe and Caffetti had stood. But shortly two other figures, a man and a woman, presumably lovers, stepped out of the nearby shadows. Arm-in-arm and laughing, they strolled toward the lighted dining room where the five-piece rhumba band was now in full swing.

CHAPTER **35**

Baumstein rose from his bed and once again commenced his pacing of the room. It was well past dusk now and he had not yet dared to venture out of his hotel room all that day. He was counting hours until his departure in the morning for Rio de Janeiro. He had a bad case of nerves. At any moment, he knew, the Argentine federal police could be banging at his door, demanding explanations and papers that he would not be able to provide. Surely by this time the FBI, special agents of the U.S. Treasury, and Interpol would have succeeded in tracing him here. They'd come and arrest him. Extradite him back to New York. He sighed wistfully, almost wishing they would. He wanted now nothing so much as to be apprehended, to be taken in hand and to be relieved of all further responsibility for himself. What could be more comforting than to be locked up in some quiet dark place where he would be called upon to do nothing? Where he could do no further harm to anyone, most of all himself.

Baumstein's heart leaped. A footstep passed his door, then receded quickly down the corridor, its swift, hollow click muting in the distance. But still his palms were wet, and sweat glistened on his forehead. He had been thinking of Nora Aldot again. If she was not a police woman, then she was damned well a government agent of some sort. Certainly not American or British or German. A light flashed in his muzzy head. But possibly Israeli. He snapped a finger. That would explain a great deal.

In the next moment he was moving back across the room to the lavatory. Striding. Nearly running. Barking his shin on the corner of a bed, he spat epithets into the stale air while yanking up the commode lid and ripping out the white envelope pasted up beneath it. Suddenly the contents were spilling out in profusion, cascading onto his bed. With thudding heart he lifted one then another of the documents scattered there. His feverish eyes swam over the blurring print. Photographs and microdot-documents. Dossiers in which the name Grigori appeared with sickening frequency. Then it was all true. Grigori was alive. And Neiditch was Grigori.

Baumstein glanced up in the direction of the door, responding to what he did not know. For a moment he sat there at the edge of the bed, frozen, paralyzed—a hare startled by the scent of fox. There was no sound. Only a shattering silence. He continued to sit there, erect, unmoving, scarcely breathing, his eyes riveted to the door. Had he locked it? He thought he had but he could not be certain.

Suddenly there was a click, faint, but no less audible. This was followed by another, followed by the light, almost playful jiggle of a key turning deftly in a lock.

Baumstein waited there as if petrified in stone, living a nightmare, unable to scream. He heard tumblers slip and roll, then saw the doorknob slowly turn. There was a squeal of hinges as the door moved a crack and he heard a sound of breathing on the other side. The door swung open.

The two of them stood there framed in the doorway.

They had the gray, unreal look of a photographic negative—flat, featureless, and without dimensions. Gaping at them, he realized to his horror that his lips were moving yet no sound emerged. Fright had trapped the air in his mouth.

When they stepped into the room and closed the door quietly behind themselves, he knew he had no place left to run. Horst was still holding the hotel passkey in his hand. At the same time the other withdrew something from his pocket. Baumstein had a glimpse of something bright and metallic glinting in the light.

Alert, oddly reserved, with serpent fixity, he watched them approach. Suddenly Ludo's hand flashed forward. Baumstein saw the bright flashing object. It was a hypodermic syringe.

When they reached him, he no longer expected to live, and when Horst stuffed the wadded handkerchief into his mouth, he did not even struggle. In fact, he even opened his mouth docilely, like a dog accepting a biscuit, expecting to be patted on the head for good behavior. Such was his complicity in the act.

Then Ludo was pushing his sleeve up, twisting his arm at the same time. With the indignity of the filthy rag in his mouth and his position at the moment that of total subjugation, he gazed up at his tormentors. He did not want them to see any terror in his eyes and he feared that his expression might appear to beg for mercy. He did not wish to die ignobly.

He felt a slight prick just below the bicep of his twisted arm and then a sense of gray mist rolling like a scroll unfurling toward him. The last thing he recalled was a voice shrieking in his head. *"Links . . . Recht . . . Links . . . Recht. Links . . . Links."*

Shortly after dusk the three German gentlemen returned to the hotel and reported the accident. Herr

Krug did most of the talking. He described how they'd been on an outing to the Tronador with the lovely Viennese lady, how she had had too much wine to drink at lunch, and how she'd grown frivolous on the platform ledge overhanging the Vuriloches chasm. They had tried to reach her, but it was too late. She had gone over before anyone could reach her. Krug was overcome. There were tears in his eyes.

Doctor Neiditch was particularly distraught. He went directly to his room while the others made preparations to leave. For the Doctor to remain at the hotel another night was unthinkable. He had grown so fond of the young lady.

Ian Asher sat in a discotheque called the Ali Baba in downtown Bariloche. It was one of those hot, crowded little rooms, far too bright and noisy, and gotten up in Tyrolean gewgaws—stagheads and cuckoo clocks—to attract the largely Germanic clientele.

Asher sat at the bar drinking beer amid a festive crowd of young people in ski sweaters. He too wore a ski sweater and faded in unobtrusively with the surroundings. He had come there to receive a phone call from Asunción. Being one of the most visible and public places in Bariloche, it was also, for his purposes, one of the most unexpected places for such a dangerous transaction to occur.

He had been joking and drinking with a pretty Chilean girl. She appeared to like him very much. Then, at 7:40 sharp, he rose, excused himself and went to the pay phone. By the time he'd reached there it was already ringing. Closing the folding doors behind him, he picked up the receiver. For a moment he heard static and a high singing in the wires. The long-distance operator from Asunción asked him to identify himself. He did so. Then there was a click and a voice came on.

It did not identify itself or greet him. It merely said, "Rubens is dead. Dovia is dead. The operation is off. Repeat: OFF. Disperse your groups and get out fast." Only that, and in that order—terse, matter-of-fact, and unemotional—then rang off.

Asher sat there for a moment, still holding the receiver and hearing the wires singing once again in his ears. There was an odd, quizzical smile on his lips as if he were still listening to someone talking. Shortly a young man wanting to use the phone tapped with his ring on the glass. Asher murmured something into the dead phone and hung up. Smiling, he nodded to the young man waiting there and exited from the booth. Then, in the din of strobic lights and ear-shattering music, he threaded his way through the gyrating crowds to the door. When he passed the bar, the Chilean girl still holding his seat smiled and waved at him. He smiled and waved back, then left the place.

Back in the rented Ford Cortina, he drove immediately to the Llao Llao, his rapid mind clicking off a whole series of plausible revisions and alternatives to the original game plan. It would be difficult to describe what Asher was feeling or, for that matter, even to say with any certainty whether or not he felt anything at all. He was an ideologue. He had feelings about principles and causes. Not about individuals, save those who served causes to which he was committed. Dovia Safid was one of these. The overall emotion that he felt now was hate and a passion for personal vindication. He saw it all as a scorecard—and now the Doctor was up one.

At the main entrance of the Llao Llao, he spoke to the head bellman, identifying himself as an old friend of Fräulein Aldot. The bellman shook his head and recounted the sad events of that afternoon.

"What about Doctor Neiditch?" Asher inquired. Was he still at the hotel?

"El gran vencedor." The bellman nodded sadly and pointed to several suitcases waiting on a dolly under the porte cochere. "Yes, he is still here. But he will be leaving shortly. The poor man is quite broken up."

"How soon?" Asher asked.

Possibly an hour or so, the bellman informed him. Did the gentleman wish to have the Doctor paged?

"No, no," Asher assured him. He had no wish to disturb the Doctor during such a time of grief. He would see him later and pay his respects personally. Asher bid the bellman good evening, then wheeled the Cortina around and drove off into the night.

Within twenty minutes he was back at the deserted farmhouse. In short order he packed his long-barreled Berettas and few belongings into his haversack and was back out on the road to the Llao Llao.

In another twenty minutes he pulled back into the parking lot, turned off his lights, and waited. From where he was parked he had a clear prospect of the main entrance no more than one hundred feet or so away.

He smoked several cigarettes and checked his watch. Shortly he saw the long tan Mercedes pull around front under the porte cochere and then two bellmen come out and proceed to load its trunk. In the next moment Asher saw three men emerge from the entrance—a youngish, blond man; a short, oddly misshapen creature; and between them, Doctor Grigori in long cape and slouch hat. He appeared drunk and barely able to walk. Coming down the front steps he nearly stumbled. The bellman lunged to help him, and together they all managed to maneuver him into the back seat.

But something struck Asher as wrong or, at least, inconsistent. Dovia had spoken of four men with Grigori.

Here there were only two. Where were the other two? Had they left already? Or would they leave later? And why in God's name would they be separating? Of course, it was to confound any possible pursuers. But, in any event, this was the car that carried Grigori. Up ahead the Mercedes was already moving, and Asher had little recourse but to follow.

Almost two hours after Doctor Grigori's departure, with Asher in pursuit, Hans Rudel and Horst Matschke checked out, too. They were accompanied by a third gentleman, the American, Mr. John Gales, whom they had kindly offered a ride in their automobile back up to Asunción where he was due in two days on business. Mr. Gales, so Matschke informed the bewildered desk clerk, was so badly shaken by Fräulein Aldot's untimely demise that he could not even be relied upon to handle the simple paperwork of settling his bill. Herr Matschke had very kindly undertaken to handle all such matters for the American gentleman and see to his packing as well. Poor Gales was presently in his room too shattered to attend to any of these matters for himself. Matschke then presented the desk clerk with the keys to Herr Gales' safe-deposit box, along with a voucher receipt for reclaiming it, which the bewildered clerk quickly honored.

A half-hour later, when Rudel and Horst Matschke came down in the elevator, Herr Gales was with them. He wore the same American business suit he was wearing when he had checked in. He also wore a hat pulled down over his head and, oddly enough, because it was well past dusk, sunglasses.

The lobby at that hour was nearly deserted, most people being at the casino or in one of the many salons off the main lobby. Rudel and Matschke were therefore able to whisk their American friend out a side door to a waiting car without causing too much of a stir.

But the bellboy who took their bags down and who had also checked Mr. Gales in was puzzled, for the man they kept referring to so pointedly as "Herr Gales" was certainly not the same Herr Gales he had checked in. In fact, this Herr Gales, hiding beneath the slouch hat and the sunglasses, bore a striking resemblance to the man the bellboy had come to know as "Doctor Neiditch," *el gran vencedor* of the gambling casino.

When at last their car drove off, it was seen to be heading in an entirely different direction from that taken by the tan Mercedes nearly two hours before.

At about the same time, a search party of nearly a dozen men composed of police and volunteers from the village found the badly battered body of Nora Aldot. She had fallen nearly a thousand feet to her death from a cliff ledge above the rocky parapet of the Cerro Tronador. The body had been badly mangled from having struck and bounced down the jagged parapets projecting out beneath the ledge. During the several hours that it lay unprotected in the chasm, the remains had been mauled and the features disfigured by wild animals, evidently small rodents. But once the body had been carried out by stretcher to a waiting ambulance on the highway, and from there to a funeral parlor in the village, positive identification was quickly made. The police found much evidence inconsistent with a verdict of accidental death, but they were unwilling for some inexplicable reason to pursue the investigation. The death certificate therefore recorded that, just as the German gentleman had attested, the cause of death was emphatically and unequivocally accidental.

Part V

FLIGHT

When Baumstein awoke it was dawn. A shaft of sunlight lay like a warm, beneficent hand across his thudding brow, and he heard voices, sharp and contentious, droning in the distance. The gray twilight of drugged sleep turned into the lush green diffusion of a brilliant sunrise high in the Andes. Gradually consciousness came. He was sitting alone in the capacious rear seat of the big tan Mercedes and gradually growing aware of the tactile unfamiliarity of his limbs. Woozy and not yet fully oriented, he gaped down at the cape in which he was swathed and, with a faint sense of recoil, he remembered Grigori.

The swerving motion of the car on the winding mountain road had caused his head to roll about jarringly on his shoulder. He had been dreaming of his farm in the rolling Berkshire foothills of northwestern Connecticut. Edith and himself in rubber hipwaders casting for trout in the swift, frothy currents of the Housatonic. They were picking their way precariously over slippery rocks on the stream bottom, and he could even feel the numbing chill of the water through the insulation of the hipwaders. Edith wore a great, floppy straw sunbonnet, beneath which he could see clearly her scrubbed, pouting, and unremarkably pretty features. That was the waking vision he clung to in the lurching car—cherished and husbanded it as if his very sanity depended on it. And yet, even as he sat there, eyes still shut and feigning sleep, he felt a twinge of

243

pain, a premonition of impending loss, a certainty that he would never see her again.

The two men sat up front unaware he'd awakened. Von Rattenhuber—sullen, speechless—sat at the wheel, while the other, Krug, his large-domed head bobbing incessantly, hissed and spat an unending stream of obscenities in *hoch Deutsch*.

"I warned him. Christ if I didn't. I told him it was risky. Hazardous. But no, goddammit to Christ. He would come. He would have it his way. He would have it—" Krug's voice broke off into another boiling stream of invectives. "Now . . . Now what?" His head spun sharply about and he glanced warily back at Baumstein, still pretending to be unconscious.

"He can't go to Encarnación anymore," Von Rattenhuber muttered.

"There's no question. But how to stop him? He's determined to see Rolfe. Ach—it's past all reason."

"Can't they be headed off?" Von Rattenhuber pleaded. "Can't we reach Caffetti?"

"How? Tell me. If I knew where he was at this moment, don't you think I'd call or wire? He's en route someplace, right now, with the son."

"Call the Tyrol tonight. Leave a message for them with the desk clerk. Tell them plans have changed. We'll meet them elsewhere."

"No. No. No." Krug pounded his little mallet fist into his palm. "Don't you see? Are you stupid?"

"See what?" Von Rattenhuber smoldered at the wheel, his foot moving down harder on the accelerator. "I'm only trying to—"

"Don't you see?" Krug hissed like an angry kettle. "If this Asher person is trailing Gregor, do you think for a moment someone is not also trailing Caffetti? Didn't the experience of the Aldot woman teach you anything?" Krug paused a moment to permit the weight

of his words to register. Then he went on: "Just because you don't see them behind you, do you think that
means they're not there? Dumbhead—do they have to
put it right under your nose?"

The fiery little troll whirled suddenly around again.
This time he caught Baumstein's drowsy eyelids fluttering. "Ah, good morning, Herr Baumstein," he chirped
cordially. "How did you sleep? I trust well. I've just
been discussing with Herr Von Rattenhuber whether
to turn you and your portfolio of bearer bonds over to
the Paraguayan authorities, or to cut your throat and
sink your body fifty fathoms into the Paraná. Fishbait,
ay, Ludo?" he chuckled gleefully. "However, I think
for purposes of practicality, I have settled on the latter
course."

Baumstein cowered wordlessly in the back, as near to
tears as he had come in thirty years.

"But tell me, Herr Baumstein," Krug went on in his
extravagantly mocking way, "just to satisfy my own
curiosity, what in God's name is an Israeli agent of the
Mossad doing with a million dollars' worth of bearer
bonds?"

"An Israeli agent?" Baumstein nearly toppled out of
his seat.

"Well, you're certainly not an investment counselor,
as you told me." Krug smirked. "Did you mean to use
these bonds and securities to bribe people? Informers?
Police? Assassins?" A fine spray of spittle arched
gracefully from the dwarf's lips in Baumstein's direction, landing finally on his lapel. "You know, of course,
what happened to your foolish colleague?"

"My colleague?" Baumstein mumbled confusedly.

"The beautiful Fräulein Aldot—or should I say Safid
—with the fine legs and the splendid bosom. Ach—
what a pity."

Baumstein appeared more muddled than ever. The

aftereffects of hyoscine in his bloodstream had not yet worn off. "Safid? I'm afraid I . . ."

"I should tell you, my dear fellow," Krug fumed right on. "We know your little game. We've found you out. One of your top people in Asunción peached on the whole lot of you. Poor fellow's no longer with us. Had an accident. Just like poor Fräulein Aldot. Fatal, you know," Krug cackled.

Von Rattenhuber sat grim and sullen, his mouth set like the gash of an ax blade and fixed to the wheel as if he were an adjunct of the machinery.

"What do you mean?" Baumstein leaned suddenly forward, then clutched his head. "About Miss Aldot?"

Krug smirked. "About Miss Safid? Of course you couldn't have heard."

Baumstein's mouth was dry and his heart thumped.

"She had an accident, poor creature," Krug went on. "Stumbled from a ledge on the Tronador. Fell a thousand feet to her death."

"Fell?" Baumstein repeated the word as if it were in a foreign tongue. He felt as if he'd been kicked in the stomach.

"A fitting end for a lying, sneaking bitch agent." Krug winked mischievously at Baumstein. "Just like yourself."

"I am not an agent," Baumstein said again, this time more forcefully.

"Where, then, would you get a million dollars in negotiable bearer bonds if not from a government with that kind of resources? Such as the Israelis?" Krug's shrewd glance caught Baumstein's sudden apprehension. "Oh, don't worry. I have your portfolio. It's quite safe. But I do wish you would tell me how you came by them."

"I stole them," Baumstein remarked slowly.

Krug's eyes narrowed suspiciously. "Stole them?" He

burst into laughter. "Oh come, come, Herr Baumstein. Surely you can do better than that."

"I stole them, I tell you," Baumstein pleaded. "And I am not an Israeli agent. Until two night ago I'd never set eyes on Fräulein Aldot. I repeat, I am not an agent. I'm a common thief, and I don't know a blessed thing about what you're talking about."

Krug reached over the back of the seat and snatched Baumstein's wrist. Jerking up the sleeve in a single sweeping motion, he revealed the faded jagged numbers tattooed there. "Where did you get that?" he demanded. "Auschwitz, isn't it? I recognize the serials."

Baumstein nodded futilely after a pause.

Silent for so long, Von Rattenhuber suddenly laughed triumphantly at the admission.

"So," Krug continued with mounting pleasure. "Doctor Grigori is no stranger to you."

Baumstein could feel the net drawing inescapably around him. "Yes, I was at Auschwitz. And yes, I did know Doctor Grigori," he sighed. "Everyone did. But I have no interest in him. That was thirty years ago. Live and let live. I repeat, I am not an agent."

"Liar."

"I don't even know what the Mossad is."

The dwarf suddenly lunged over the rear of the seat and cracked Baumstein sharply across the face. Taken by surprise, Von Rattenhuber swerved and nearly lost control of the car. "Come, come, Herr Baumstein," Krug jeered. "No need to continue this little game of innocence—of naivete. You're fooling no one. You Mossad bastards have known for years Doctor Grigori's whereabouts. But I can assure you that if your plan had succeeded here, your Jewish brethren in Paraguay would be treated to a bloodbath the likes of which has not been seen since the Night of the Crystal."

Baumstein gaped incredulously at the dwarf, whose

features were twisted into a hateful grimace and violently animated by rage. He realized now that the man was quite mad. "Turn me over to the police," Baumstein said. "I'm a thief. I want to go to jail."

"No—no." Krug waved a fist beneath his nose. "That would be too good for you. Too easy."

"A moment ago you said—"

"I know what I said, but that would be too merciful. I've changed my mind now. You're going, Jew scum, where you belong. To the bottom of the Paraná. Ludo," he snapped. "Stop the car here."

The big Mercedes rolled to a halt at the crest of a boulder-strewn road, high up in the Cordillera. The sun of early morning blazed down, glistening on the ice-capped, wind-whipped peaks above.

In the next moment, Krug and Von Rattenhuber had gotten out and stormed round to the back. They yanked open the rear doors and converged on Baumstein from either side. The dwarf moved with almost acrobatic alacrity, pushing the cold, greasy barrel of a Luger hard up against the side of Baumstein's head. "No trouble please, Herr Baumstein."

Instantly Von Rattenhuber was there, once again pushing up Baumstein's sleeve and brandishing his hypodermic needle. There seemed little to do but accept the jab. Baumstein felt his body tauten, started to struggle; then came the momentary prick, and once again he felt himself yield almost willingly to the comfort and solace of those thick gray mists rolling inexorably toward him.

CHAPTER 37

"Impossible."

"I will."

"You will not. I won't hear of it."

Baumstein turned and woke to find himself lying in sour sheets in a cold bed. The room in which he lay was dark and smelled of cats. The shades were drawn and he could hear the sound of voluble argument from the room next door.

"I won't be responsible."

"Don't be. No one's asked you to."

"Ach scheiss."

Baumstein half rose, then clutched his head and pressed hard as if he felt it might suddenly blow apart. At once he realized that someone had taken his clothing off and left him sprawled there in his underwear on clammy sheets, unable to leave.

"They think they can intimidate me." He heard what he knew to be Grigori's muffled voice pouring through the plaster walls. "Well, they can't. They think they can drive me mad with fright. They can't. They think they can trick me into making a foolish move. Revealing myself. They can't. They think they can make me hate myself. They can't. They can't ..."

"Gregor!"

Baumstein heard a door slam and footsteps pounding in pursuit.

"Gregor," someone shouted again.

There was a brief scuffle outside in the hall. In the next moment the door of Baumstein's room burst open and a figure stood there looming large with a harsh white light streaming from the room behind it.

A switch clicked and suddenly the room flooded with light. Wincing with pain, Baumstein covered his eyes, aware of a tumult of movement all about him. Suddenly he felt rough hands on his arms, hauling him up, dragging him to his feet. Bright light and full consciousness came roaring back in upon him with the crooked, rage-reddened features of Doctor Grigori. The other four he knew as well. They circled around him. In the next moment a stinging crack of the Doctor's fist spun his head sideways, nearly snapping his neck.

"Why do you chase me?" Grigori shouted into Baumstein's pale gaping face. "Why do you hunt me down and try to harm me? How dare you?"

"I—" Baumstein's voice caught in his throat, and all he could think of was the indignity of cowering there in his underwear before four strangers and a maniac. How vulnerable one is without one's clothing, Baumstein thought ludicrously.

Grigori's features twisted into a horrible grimace. Suddenly he thrust his face up close to Baumstein's and bellowed: "Why do you stare at me that way?"

"Gregor," Rudel fretted. "This won't help anything."

"I did nothing to you. I don't harm you." The Doctor went on obliviously, his voice suddenly plaintive and whining—an aggrieved man terribly put upon. "Don't you see what I have here? What I am? Don't you see how I'm forced to live and with whom?" He flung his hand wildly round at his four companions, who hovered there now, gaping at him as well. "Is this not punishment enough?" he went on peevishly. "I no longer have a home. My home is a fortification. I have no wife or family. I live among savages. I'm at the mercy of thieves and cutpurses who suck around me like leeches. I don't have a single friend whose loyalty I can depend upon, or whose companionship I don't have to pay money for."

Krug glowered and Rudel's face darkened.

"What more do you people want from me?" Grigori wailed piteously. For a moment Baumstein thought that the Doctor was waiting for a reply, and in his mind he scrambled frantically to frame an answer that would be soothing and apposite. But instead all he could think of, peering into that twisted red mouth, was, This is the man who killed my brother. Did he look the same to David as he looked to Baumstein then?

Krug barged forward, appealing to the Doctor: "Gregor, we can't wait around here anymore. We've got to get out of this."

"Out of what?" the Doctor bellowed.

"Out of this." Krug pointed at Baumstein. "We don't know how many of them there are. Arganas says fourteen—possibly fifteen."

"*Ach scheiss,* Arganas." Grigori flung his hands up. When he turned back to Baumstein, he appeared subdued. Even oddly contrite. "What do you people want of me? Shall I give myself up so you can make a trial? So that you can beat your breasts and wring your hands and denounce me? So that the courts and the press can make another circus for the entertainment of the press —scum and rabble? Would that make it better? Would it make you sleep more comfortably at night? Would it improve my sleep? I don't sleep very comfortably, as it is, you know." Grigori sighed and turned away. "I am ashamed. Here, my own son is coming to see me. We have not seen each other for nine years, and in order for him to see me, he will have to be brought to some clandestine location where I will have to be in hiding like a thief. Like some cornered rat. I am ashamed to look my boy in the eye. Can you imagine that?" He spoke now as if he were appealing to Baumstein for mercy. "Have you children? Can you fathom that? Your own son looking at you with loathing and disgust?"

Yes, Baumstein nodded. He could well imagine Joel looking at him in that fashion. He felt a strange alliance with the man.

"Don't you see that?" Grigori went on.

Suddenly, unexpectedly, the Doctor whirled and grabbed Baumstein's wrist, lifting it up to the light. Squinting, he ran his fingers over the tattooed area, reading the numbers with his touch. "Auschwitz, ay?" he sighed wearily. "So you know me . . . Let's see," he said, rather like a college dean at a class reunion. "That must be thirty years ago." He appeared nostalgic.

"Gregor," Krug fumed impatiently. "We must be going if we're to reach the ferry by morning . . ."

Doctor Grigori waved him to silence. "Tell me, Herr Gales. Is that really your name?"

"No." Baumstein shook his head. "It's Baumstein. Jacob Baumstein."

"Ah, Baumstein," the Doctor mused aloud as if he were trying to recall the name. "When were you there, Baumstein?"

"From September of '44 to March of '45."

"Toward the end then? So the Russians liberated you?"

Yes, Baumstein nodded dumbly.

"Ach—it was a shithole, wasn't it?" Grigori cocked an eyebrow at him. "Had you family there?"

A picture of his brother David flashed momentarily in his mind. "No," he said instantly to his own profound disgust. "I was there alone."

Suspicion flickered in the Doctor's gaze. "No one at

all?" he asked. "Not a parent, or perhaps a brother or sister?"

"No one," Baumstein murmured, and his wet swimming eyes sought the floor.

The Doctor paused for a moment, dwelling inwardly on some nagging point. "During all that time," he said, "did I ever touch you, Baumstein? Hurt you? Molest you?" he added tentatively.

"No, never." Baumstein shook his head, his eyes still fixed on the floor.

"You must have been a child at the time. Nine? Ten?"

"Ten."

"Was I kind to you? Did I give you candy?"

"Yes," Baumstein mumbled. "You were kind."

Doctor Grigori beamed almost gratefully. "Yes, I was kind to the children. They used to call me 'Uncle.' Isn't that right, Baumstein?"

"Yes. That's right."

"You see? You see? Uncle." Grigori laughed triumphantly. He looked around at his companions. "You know, Baumstein," he went on warmly, "I have a boy your age. Early forties is it? Forty-one? Forty-two?"

"Forty-one."

"You would like him, Baumstein," Grigori went on. "He's much like you. I'm sorry I struck you. That was unfortunate. I am, as you well know, very pressed here at the moment." He appeared genuinely contrite. Then suddenly, that fierce, red grimace contorted his features again. "So! You're here to kill me, ay?" he snarled.

Baumstein reared back as if he were trying to avoid an on-rushing locomotive. "No—no such thing. I never—these men—" He flailed his hands hectically in the direction of the others. "These people here keep insisting—"

"That you're an agent of the Mossad?" Grigori added

smoothly and lit a cigarette. "Well, of course you are. We have absolute verification now to that effect."

Stupefied, Baumstein stared at the Doctor.

Grigori smiled. "You see, Baumstein. We're very well connected, as you must know, with the federal police forces of at least a half-dozen key nations. On my personal payroll are policemen not only in Paraguay but in Bonn, the U.S., and even Israel, too." Grigori's smile was sympathetic. "Yes, I did say Israel. We get wonderful information from Israel. Probably one of our most reliable sources."

"And the Israelis told you I was an agent of the Mossad?"

"Not at all. My sources in Asunción advised that there was a distinct possibility." Doctor Grigori puffed contentedly on his cigarette. "Later, Fräulein Aldot, or should I say Fräulein Safid, before her unfortunate accident, more or less verified this."

"Verified?" Baumstein gaped thunderstruck. "But she . . ."

"There's someone down there," Von Rattenhuber suddenly whispered. He was peering out of a corner of the curtain at the courtyard below.

Rudel strode quickly across the room and peered down. "Ach, for Christ's sake. That's no one," he remarked. "Only one of the farmhands."

"You're sure?" Ludo snapped.

"Of course I'm sure. I checked all that on the way up."

With a sigh, Krug turned back to the Doctor. "It's imperative we get you back up to 540 immediately."

"I told you, Alban, I don't move until I see my boy."

Krug fumed. "But you're in great peril every moment . . ."

"Gregor," Rudel appealed more reasonably. "Arganas expressly forbade—"

"Ach, fuck Arganas," the Doctor exploded. The others fell back before him as if from a rampaging lion. "Arganas can fuck off. I'm going to Encarnación to see my boy."

"When?" Krug demanded.

"Now. This minute. Hans . . . you and Horst come with me. I plan to reach there late tomorrow."

Krug thrust his jaw out at the Doctor. "And Ludo and I? What about us?"

Von Rattenhuber slouched out of the shadows near the window. *"Ja, Herr Doktor.* What about us?"

Grigori threw a raincoat capelike across his shoulders. "You and Krug go up by boat with our friend Baumstein here."

Krug smoldered. "And risk our necks?"

"You don't have to, Alban," the Doctor remarked obligingly. "Grigori Enterprises Ltd. can always make other arrangements for its Latin American franchises."

There was a lengthy pause while the enraged dwarf mentally calculated the catastrophic losses of such a contingency. He appeared to be on the verge of apoplexy.

"Very good, then." Grigori clapped his hands. "It's all settled. We'll meet you at the Tyrol."

"Madness," Krug choked. "Folly and madness. The Tyrol will be crawling with Mossad." He flung a hand in Baumstein's direction.

"If so" —the Doctor wheeled lightly on his heel, causing the hem of his raincoat to flare— "they won't find me there. I'll be at the Villa Antonio with Rolfe and Caffetti." He turned to Baumstein. "But they will find you." Grigori laughed, then stared hard into his eyes, realizing only then that the poor man was still standing there, shivering in his underwear. "For God's sake, Baumstein—put something on. You'll catch a draft. Besides, you look absurd." Then suddenly

Grigori's shifting, darting eyes lighted on a small pile of his own clothing—the clothing that Baumstein had worn during the ride up from Bariloche. It was draped across a chair, and now the Doctor strode across the room, retrieved the garments and brought them back to Baumstein. "Here—put these on. How do they fit you? Well, I hope. Take care of the cape. I'm particularly fond of it. I bought it in Madrid, you know. For the opera." He laughed engagingly, then in the next instant frowned. "I must say, I find *your* wardrobe somewhat limited. No flair. No panache, Herr Baumstein. What a drab little dormouse you must be."

Grigori moved back under the light, and only then did Baumstein recognize his own business suit draped on the Doctor. To his horror, oddly enough, it looked shabby and terribly misshapen.

"Horst—Hans," the Doctor snapped, and started for the door.

"Gregor," the dwarf cried. "What do you want us to do with him?" He nodded at Baumstein.

"Assuming the Israelis don't mistakenly kill him," *Den Schönen Doktor,* the Grand Selector, replied, "then *you* kill him."

CHAPTER **38**

The little ferry *Esperanza* bobbled at the dock, its tired diesels sputtering and wheezing. She was taking on passengers now, and a variety of people streamed up her ramps—farmers, planters, fat peasant wives with broods of yowling children, and Indians, en route with crowing hens and tethered goats that defecated on the scorched metal ramps.

Down on the dock a number of cars lined up in the suffocating heat and waited to have their papers and luggage compartments checked by the drowsy customs officials, then to drive on into the cavernous cargo hold below. About it all was a bleak, resolute air—a sense of smothered rage.

The big tan Mercedes had reached the dock before noon and had been waiting there in line nearly an hour to have its papers cleared. It was seventh in line and the three men inside smoldered dangerously in the noonday heat. There were perhaps another dozen vehicles behind it—automobiles and wagons, clanking carts with yams, melons, and bananas sloped up precariously within their holds—all moving with excruciating lassitude.

There was a brief altercation up front. Someone with imperfect papers was being turned away. There was shouting and a number of heavily armed police converged on the spot, ordering the offending car off the line. Now the tan Mercedes was waved ahead. When the customs official came to the window, Krug handed him papers. The official in khaki uniform with his enormous mustaches appeared to read the paper with his lips, straightening his back as he did so. Then he glanced at the men in the car. *"Y quien es el Doctor Neiditch?"*

Krug pointed with his thumb to the shawl-wrapped figure slumped in back beneath the huge slouch hat. *"Esta durmiendo,"* he whispered confidentially.

"Borracho?" the official inquired.

Krug winked. *"Un poquito."*

Both men chuckled. The official handed the papers back to Krug and flicked the brim of his hat. *"Bienvenidos a Paraguay, caballeros,"* he snapped and waved them on into the damp, cool hold.

Because it was growing late, the customs people worked a little more quickly now, and with good deal less care. Time was pressing and the inspections had become almost perfunctory. By the time they reached a rickety banana cart drawn by a sullen little donkey, their hearts were no longer in it. Now the official with the big mustaches merely glanced at the papers and up at the cartdriver—a dark, young *campesino* from the back country with a wide-brimmed straw hat. *"Ondivos, Carlos?"* he inquired.

"Si, soy Ondivos," replied the young man.

The official glanced at the cargo and at a bill of lading on his clipboard. *"Solamente bananas, Ondivos?"*

"Si, solamente."

"Bueno hombre. Abordo." He waved the young farmer on.

"Muchas gracias, amigo." The young farmer tipped his straw hat and, with a smart crack of the reins, brought his sullen mule awake. The cart creaked slowly forward.

By midafternoon the *Esperanza* was plying its way up-river against the current toward Encarnación, where it was scheduled to dock somewhere around midnight. Once out in midriver the weather had changed markedly. Winds sprang up out of the east and clouds passed over the sun. The water grew choppy and the day turned raw and mizzling.

Most of the passengers crowded themselves into the warmth of the noisome little salon below, with its little canteen that sold beer and coffee, doughnuts and soggy chips. The promenades above, therefore, remained rainwashed and empty—except for the two Germans, Krug and Von Rattenhuber, who preferred to sit above in deck chairs, aloof, secluded, drinking beer and playing poker, while Baumstein, still "under the weather," slumbered below in one of the few available cabins.

By evening the wind and rain had abated. Stars had come out and the Southern Cross hung upside down above the Brazilian jungle lying dark and inscrutable off to the right. Somewhere nearly directly beneath it, gliding upriver, the *Esperanza* moved as if in a dream through the close, stifling night, her muffled engines throbbing softly. She appeared to float weightless on the river, producing no wake, her still-life motion giving her some of the statuesque serenity of a large white swan sliding effortlessly over the surface of the water.

The ferry's position on the river just then was roughly twenty kilometers south and west of Posadas. Due to the odd configuration of the land there, the waters on the broad Paraná are uncommonly still at this point, virtually dead current, and at night flashing tentacles of moonlight dangle and writhe like iridescent serpents within its glassy surface.

It was slightly past 10 PM now. The *Esperanza* was scheduled to reach Encarnación in little less than two hours. Up forward near the bow Krug and Baumstein were conversing in the moving shadows near the rail. Von Rattenhuber had gone below to try and catnap. He was exhausted. He had not slept in nearly forty-eight hours.

Krug still wore his business suit and, for all the strain of the past two days, the gnomish little creature looked none the worse for wear. Standing there beside him, Baumstein was dressed quite casually in another set of Doctor Grigori's clothing—a white basque shirt, sandals, and a pair of outsized nankeen trousers. The huge trousers, baggy in the seat, gave Baumstein a bizarre, rather clownlike appearance, wholly incongruous for that time and place.

Leaning on the rail, his elbows barely reaching it,

Krug smoked a cigar and chatted incessantly. When he gestured with his hands, as he frequently did, his cigar would inscribe wide, lazy arcs of orange above the shimmering surface of the water. From time to time he would prod Baumstein with the barrel of a Taurus .38 revolver concealed in the pocket of his suit. Then once again they would amble a little farther down the rail like a pair of old friends conversing. Shortly they would light again at a point farther down the deck, and, while Krug continued to chat, Baumstein would stand there, head lowered, listening docilely like a child being castigated. Actually, he heard very little of what was being said to him. He was still full of hyoscine and moving about robotlike anywhere he was directed.

At a certain point, Baumstein stooped and leaned his head down toward Krug. It had occurred to him that he wanted to say something, but the thought, if there actually was one, quickly slipped his mind. Perhaps it was something about Edith, or his million dollars' worth of stolen bonds. All that seemed to matter very little now. He scarcely cared where his portfolio had gone. His mind was blank again—a series of flashing, insubstantial impressions. His rubbery legs were barely able to support him.

Where they stood just then the deck was deserted. Krug was talking heatedly, gesticulating with his pudgy little hands and scrawling hectically his orange calligraphy against the thick indigo night. He never even saw the young *campesino* step quickly out of the shadows, stride up purposefully, and plant himself squarely before them.

Baumstein made no gesture of recognition. His head merely dragged lower, lolling on his chest. But Krug looked up, an expression of grave disapproval for the impertinent young farmer with the temerity to approach him in this fashion. His mouth opened, about to let loose a barrage of invective. Then, at last, he saw the long shiny barrel of the Beretta pointing squarely at his paunch from beneath the fringed bottom of the farmer's poncho, and something approaching admiration registered in his blue, rheumy eyes.

The word "Oh" fell from his astonished lips, and in the next moment, the fierce, sputtering little creature was being lifted off his feet—kicking, thrashing, emitting a stream of guttural grunts while strong arms held him straight out above the dark, rushing water. When at last he dropped, or was let loose, he gave the curious impression of a doll being thrown from an open window. Then suddenly he was gone with a slight decorous splash into the swiftly receding darkness.

Ian Asher stood alone now, peering into the flaccid, loose-lipped face of J. Peter Baumstein. "So," he said, doffing his large-brimmed plantation hat, a rather courtly flourish, as if he were about to introduce himself. Then, suddenly, both men peered into each other's eyes.

What Baumstein saw through glazed vision was an open, rather boyish face, with cold predatory eyes from which, oddly enough, he felt no threat of danger.

What Asher saw was decidedly not the dark, asymmetrical features of Doctor Grigori, burned so sharply into his mind from the dozens of dossier photographs he'd carried about in his haversack for well over a year. It was, instead, the loose-grinning features of a stranger he suspected of being mildly drunk.

For a moment, while their eyes held each other, both men appeared to grasp the part the other had unwittingly played. Then, slowly, with a kind of stern forbearance, Asher put up his gun beneath the poncho.

Somewhere off to starboard, they could hear the shouts of the dwarf thrashing around out in the watery darkness. That, followed by the clamor of voices and the thudding of feet pounding up the steel ladders from the companionway below.

Asher started to turn, as if to fade back into the darkness out of which he'd come. But precisely at that moment, a ribbon of blue light like a huge jagged finger perforated the dark above the water. At first it appeared to be nothing more than a flash of static electricity. But in the next moment, the silhouette of the little ferry *Esperanza* stood out stark and white, lit up and nailed against the dark by the powerful beams of two crisscrossing searchlights.

Momentarily blinded by the glare of lights, the two men at the rail could see nothing. But suddenly, directly athwart the path of the ferry, Asher saw a gunboat looming out of the dark. It was long, gray, and squat— with the red and blue crossbars of a Paraguayan naval pack fluttering at its stern. The *Esperanza* was of Argentine registry and unarmed. But clearly visible atop the wheelhouse of the Paraguayan gunboat were three .50-caliber machine guns, their snub, brutal noses glinting silvery in the moonlight.

Suddenly there were shouts and pounding footsteps, the outraged growl of engines reversing, and then the night exploding into gunfire. A stream of tracer bullets showered up like cinders across the ferry's path, followed by a Klaxon whining and someone speaking over a bullhorn: "Mr. Asher," Colonel Félix Arganas' booming voice echoed across the watery darkness. "The man you're seeking is not on your boat. Give yourself up. You are surrounded."

Baumstein clung uncomprehending to the rail. He viewed the garish unreality of the scene through dim, unfocused eyes that turned the night into a million shards of colored, bursting glass. There were shouting and footsteps behind him, and through his badly garbled senses he had a brief glimpse of Von Rattenhuber, like a lean, sleek panther, slouching toward him.

"I repeat," Arganas boomed again. "Give yourself up. You are surrounded."

Suddenly Baumstein was aware of the man beside him—the *campesino* in the straw hat—mounting the rail, poised there momentarily, arms flung outward like an ascending angel, then gone, in a moment, noiselessly over the side.

Shortly, a white gash of light spurted across the water from the gunboat. As it did so, Baumstein staggered backward at the ferry rail, clutching his chest where bullets seeking Asher had found him instead. Legs splayed wide, arms flung outward against the taff, his body appeared suddenly to rise, to levitate balloonlike, then float languidly in the balmy air above the deck. Another gash of flame spat toward him from the gunboat, this time causing his feet to kick wildly in space. With the next blast, his head jolted backward. He did a somersault in midair, and then he was tumbling headfirst over the rail, hurtling downward toward the black, star-cluttered water. At the bottom of his descent, just as his head and torso slipped beneath the inky surface, the fall shuddered to a halt. His foot had caught in the last rung of the boarding ladder, and J. Peter Baumstein, limp and half-submerged, arms flung outward, inverted and crucified, hung there at the bottom of the ladder, twitching and jerking with the hectic animation of a hooked fish at the end of its line.

For several hours after, the ferry and the gunboat remained anchored in midstream. Krug had been retrieved from the water and taken unharmed aboard the gunboat, and a search of the area was begun for the man who'd been seen to jump over the side. One of the machine gunners maintained that he had seen a white, phantomlike figure cutting swiftly through the water and that he'd fired a long, withering barrage at it until he'd seen it go under. He watched the spot for several minutes thereafter but never saw the figure reappear on the surface again. Later, the big, wide-brimmed straw hat was recovered, floating on the slick water, and taken in evidence. The gunboat circled the area several times—moving first in large circles, then in ever-narrowing concentric circles, its searchlights sweeping broadly over the surface. They were fairly certain the swimmer was dead, but still there was no sign of a body.

On board the *Esperanza,* the ferry captain and Colonel Félix Arganas filled out a number of forms and depositions. Later, these would have to be submitted to the admiralties of both Paraguay and Argentina. The ferry captain was so badly shaken that Arganas had to help him complete his part of the forms.

When the Colonel finally left the ferry to proceed on its journey up to Encarnación, he took with him on the gunboat the body of J. Peter Baumstein to be returned to the American Consul in Asunción, where U.S. Treasury agents were already waiting to bring it back to the States. He would report to them later that he had conducted an exhaustive search of Baumstein's personal effects for the million dollars in stolen bonds and negotiable paper but, alas, found not a trace of either.

CHAPTER 39

"Well, where is he?"

"They are a bit late. Mechanical problems on the road, no doubt. They'll soon be here."

"Soon? He was due five hours ago. Something must be wrong."

"Then surely we'd have heard by now. A phone call. A wire. Don't worry. Nothing's wrong."

The two men sat in the lounge of the Hotel Tyrol in Encarnación. They had arrived there early that morning on the ferry from Buenos Aires, and it had been their understanding that Doctor Grigori would be there waiting for them. The desk clerk, a prickly, officious Latin, confirmed that the Doctor had been expected there the evening before, but as of yet he had not arrived. Nor had they received any message instructing them to cancel his reservations. They knew the Doctor well there, the clerk assured Rolfe Hupfauer. He had been their guest on numerous occasions, and in any event, they would hold his rooms until instructed otherwise.

Caffetti and Rolfe spent the rest of that day killing time—going in and out of the lounge for periodic refreshment, strolling around the parks and dusty plaza, and evading the importunate and unsightly mendicants that haunted the squares. They dared not stray too far from the hotel for fear Grigori might arrive and not find them there. Or lest he call with some urgent message of a change in plan.

As the day wore on and the temperature rose, Rolfe

Hupfauer grew increasingly peeved. Now, as dusk came on, peevishness turned to perturbation. Caffetti remained outwardly calm. Inwardly, however, he was apprehensive. This was very unlike the Doctor, whose habits of life were the soul of promptitude.

"I won't wait much longer," Rolfe fumed.

"I'm sure they'll be here any minute now."

"No call. No message. It's inexcusable."

"I admit I'm puzzled, unless . . ."

"I travel thirteen thousand miles to this godforsaken . . ."

"Unless they cabled a change of plans to us in Buenos Aires or at the ferry . . ."

"But they know we're at the Tyrol," Rolfe countered. "Even if there had been a change in plan, surely by this time they'd know something was wrong and cable us here."

"Unless . . ."

"Unless . . . Unless." Rolfe thumped the tabletop with a fist, looking just then very much like his father. "You always have another unless, Ricardo." The young man rose angrily to his feet, nearly upsetting their drinks.

"Where are you going?" Caffetti asked.

"To call home. I promised I'd call this evening. If anything happens, I'll be upstairs in my room." He turned and strode from the lounge.

Twenty minutes later he came back down to the lounge.

"Did you reach them?" Caffetti asked.

Rolfe settled himself before his tepid drink. "Ricardo, I'm leaving tomorrow."

"Leaving?" The older man gaped incredulously. "Without seeing him? Impossible!"

"Whether I see him or not, I'm going home. I should never have come here in the first place."

"But your father," Caffetti pleaded. "In his present state of mind—"

"I'm not interested in my father," Rolfe snapped. "Or his present state of mind. Quite frankly, I have no desire to ever see him again."

Caffetti's jaw fell open and hung that way for several moments. "For God's sake, Rolfe, how can you—"

"How I can is of no importance whatever." Rolfe Hupfauer was white as parchment. "The point is, I will. I'm leaving here first thing in the morning."

Caffetti slumped back in the leather banquette, defeated. "I suppose I knew all along," he sighed.

"Knew what?"

"Your feelings about your father."

Rolfe appeared to grow stronger, more resolute, as he went on. "In the past I've kept silent about my feelings. I won't any longer."

"I knew you'd come here under duress."

"My own self-imposed duress, I assure you. A sense of duty I no longer feel."

Rolfe sat quiet and grim, rolling an empty glass between his palms. Caffetti continued: "If you'd only known your father before the war, as I did. A young physician. Attractive. Kindly. Generous. Full of ideals and good works. Wishing only to help. And then a war, and something completely different emerges. Something none of us who'd known the man had ever suspected was there. Something . . ."

"Monstrous." Rolfe Hupfauer provided the word.

Caffetti nodded wearily. "I don't deny it. When the disclosures came—the family was mortified. I'm sure that's what killed the old man. He hadn't had a sick day until Nuremberg. He listened to the radio and read the papers each day, as if judging for himself. Looking for the truth. Hoping the whole thing would be disproved. Then one day he turned his face to the wall. He wouldn't get out of bed. That was the end of him. And as for his mother, your grandmother—well, as you very well know, to this day she refuses to believe. Yes, his acts were monstrous. Fiendish. Abhorrent. And whether or not he understands—even at this late date—what he did, I cannot truthfully say."

"My father's great talent has always been self-deception." Rolfe smiled sardonically. "Had he ever understood—really faced himself—as he should have, as any man of honor would have, he would have put a bullet through his head years ago."

For a long moment, Caffetti stared back. His shaved skull and heavy-lidded, gentle brown eyes gave him the look just then of a Florentine magistrate painted by some Quattrocento master.

Rolfe could see behind those eyes thoughts dashing hectically about, thoughts struggling to take shape and emerge—apologies, defenses, elaborate rationalizations. But nothing came. What had paralyzed Caffetti was his own realization that any defense he might offer for Doctor Grigori must of necessity become a defense of himself and the complicity he shared in the shielding of the man.

"What would you have had me do?" he suddenly blurted out. "Turn him in? Betray him? Your grandfather, old Grigori, was like a father to me. Treated me like one of his own." His lips moved aimlessly. He mouthed words, all meaningless and disjointed, then broke off, turned away, and gazed down defeated at his hands.

"You see, Ricardo," Rolfe Hupfauer said gently. "You're as doomed as I am. We ourselves did nothing, yet we will carry this curse to our graves. There's no answer for that, is there? No answer for you. No answer for me."

In the next moment, there was a small stir at the head

of the room. Caffetti looked up and saw the tall, stooped figure of Rudel, like a large, filthy crow, standing in the doorway. He was peering around, swiveling his neck from side to side, as if he were trying to locate someone in the shadows of the near-empty lounge.

"Over here." Caffetti waved.

Rudel nodded and signaled them to wait. Then, instead of coming in, he turned and went back out into the lobby. In the next moment Alban Krug, strutting and arrogant, appeared in the doorway. He started toward them, followed by Horst and Ludo, shortly to be followed by Rudel, all moving like a solid phalanx before a single slight figure flowing liquidly across the room. A smartly tailored trench coat thrown raffishly across his shoulders, Doctor Gregor Grigori waved, smiling at his son.

CHAPTER 40

Nearly two hours after he had dived off the bow of the *Esperanza,* Ian Asher emerged, sodden and dripping, from the murky Paraná River. It had taken him that long to cover the half-mile to the Paraguayan shore, for the gunboat moving about in wide, lazy circles, searchlight beams crisscrossing, had forced him to cover the distance mainly under water.

Once safely on shore he watched the movements of the gunboat still conducting its search for him. Concealed in the thick brush along the shore, Asher watched the lights sweep round and heard the occasional blasts of .50-caliber machine gun fire aimed principally at shadows and chimeras on the inky water. He had landed at exactly the point he had anticipated he would (for even if his mission had succeeded, his plan had always been to debark from the *Esperanza* over the side). Then, about a quarter of a mile in from where he'd landed, he'd found waiting for him the small cache of dry clothing and rudimentary rations he'd stored there several weeks before.

It was dark in the forest—swampy and fetid from the ceaseless decomposition of extravagant foliage. Fireflies like tiny meteors fled before him. Myriad crickets and giant tree toads intoned forlornly from every corner of the forest. It was through that dark labyrinth that Asher had to cut his way to the carefully concealed cache. One there, he stripped off his sodden peon garb and changed into fresh trousers, a basque shirt, and lightweight jacket. Then, after burying the old costume, he struck out through the forest toward a main road he knew to be several miles due west.

Passage through the forest was slow and arduous, but not at all impossible, if one were familiar, and Asher was, with the lumber trails that crisscrossed the area.

Moving through the cricket-haunted night, the darkness illuminated only by the ghostly flashing of fireflies, Asher consulted his compass and plowed ahead, the mind and soul and body of the man animated by a single thought. He had been duped (he was willing to accept that), and he smarted from the indignity of it. The man who had walked out of the Llao Llao in the slouch cap and cape, looking for all the world like Doctor Gregor Grigori, was not Grigori at all. Rather, it was some pitiful stooge into whose doomed eyes he had looked deeply for several seconds and seen fate written there. Even now, he could see the man's face quite clearly—dazed and baffled—the mark of the victim written unmistakably upon it. The eyes had a drugged, stuporous look, but there was terror within them and it was evident that they sensed the imminence of their own oblivion.

The man was dead now. There was no doubt of that. Asher had seen the bullets slice across his chest, the impact physically lifting him off his feet, off the deck, and tumbling him headfirst over the taffrail. By that time Asher was already in the water. Then once up on shore, in the light of swiveling beams, he could see them cutting the man down from where he dangled like slaughtered beef from the bottom rung of a boarding ladder. Once again the *Selektor* had struck. He had looked upon his candidate and thumbed him left, just as he no doubt had done with Rubens and with Dovia before him.

As he plowed ahead now, the memory of the girl gnawed at him. He had tried to put her aside, to bury her deep someplace where she could no longer prick and vex his conscience. But the image of the girl, lovely and youthful as it was, refused to be suppressed. He was actually furious with her. By getting herself killed, she had bungled his plan. So had Rubens, and the others too. Well, Rubens was dead now and the others all gone and he was alone. He didn't much mind that. He preferred being alone. He worked best that way. He was a solitary by nature and Fate had always fingered him for special destinies—trials to be sought and overcome by him and him alone.

Now it rankled him that Grigori had outfoxed him and that Dovia was dead. In death she seemed closer to him than she'd ever been in life. Martyrdom had put her in a special category. By virtue of her sacrifice, she was with him now, forever, solitary among the victims. He imagined them together, huddled in a sleeping bag somewhere in the Negev with the wild, almost festively colored calligraphy of rocks and tracer bullets bursting overhead.

That was all partially true. They had shared a sleeping bag. They had shared intimacies in a war zone. Only, in fact, it had been a still night. There had been no sense of impending doom. Only frantic, hasty embraces beneath a star-blown desert sky. There were no rockets or tracer bullets; no gorgeous vivid blooms of Egyptian artillery exploding overhead. He had added those elements to the canvas as a matter of his own personal taste. His own imagined violence, made so vivid that in recounting it in his mind, as he did over and over again, he could never again separate the fireworks from the actual scene.

Cutting ahead now through the itchy, suffocating night, his feverish imagination was fraught with images of destruction and holocaust. Flames leaped upward all about him—bright, lambent, and consuming. But he was not alone any longer in the shadows and the crematorium. He was with Dovia. Wedded, bonded, and sanctified by martyrdom. They had marched unbowed, unyielding into the cyanide showers.

Dovia's death would be repaid a thousandfold. Doctor Grigori lay ahead of him now—somewhere out there in the vast, clammy, star-filled night. It was just Grigori and himself now. Just the two of them alone, adversaries facing each other across the dark. And that, Asher thought consolingly, was precisely the way he wanted it.

CHAPTER 41

"Forgive me for behaving foolishly." Doctor Grigori wiped his eyes. "I loathe sentimentality." He laughed and kissed his son again. He was crying and slightly crapulous after three glasses of champagne. He had been driving hard all night and most of the day. He was exhausted now, he explained, and brimming over with a torrent of emotions.

The others had discreetly excused themselves, leaving father and son to their reunion. But while Grigori's colleagues were not visible, they were, nevertheless, very much present—guarding the front and rear entrances of the lounge, scrutinizing everyone who came and went.

"It's so strange," Grigori went on, flushed, dabbing his teary eyes with a handkerchief. "Seeing you sitting here before me. Like old times. As if we'd never been apart. You and I—as if nothing had ever happened. Tell me everything. Hedi? How is she? And my grandchildren. Freddy must be quite a young man by now. Thirteen, is it, or fourteen? And *Grossmutter*. How is she? How is the asthma? There's a fantastic new drug. I just read about it in the *International Journal*. Dilates the capillaries in the pleura. Relief almost instantaneous. I'll see that she gets some. Does she ask about me at all?"

Rolfe Grigori watched his father drink champagne and light another cigarette from the ashes of his last. He was vivacious, Rolfe thought, but artificially so, as if he were feigning it, creating the illusion at great expense to a rapidly depleting fund of energy. Unable to govern his emotions, he veered wildly from ecstatic happiness to grim despondency. Lighting another cigarette, he could barely bring the match to his tremulous fingers to do the job. He laughed a great deal—very loud and full of bravado, then grew flustered at the sober, judgmental cast of his son's mien. And all the while there were tears in his eyes, which seemed red and very tired, restless, and unable to stop their ceaseless wanderings round the room.

"Who are you looking for, Father?" Rolfe asked at one point.

"No one." Grigori laughed, and patted his son's hand. "No one. I'm searching no longer."

To Rolfe, who had not seen his father in nine years, the display of feeling seemed in some ways quite genuine; in others, unashamedly bogus. He could not escape the thought that what he was witnessing just then was a shrewd, carefully calculated performance, designed to put him off his guard, defuse all the resentment that Grigori knew had been welling up in his only child for years. It was the old Grigori charm put on to seduce him and, at the same time, a bald pitch for pity.

Over Rolfe's protests, Grigori ordered another bottle of champagne. Then he leaned toward him, placing a hand affectionately over his son's. "Tell me everything," he whispered. "I want to hear all about the old town. About everyone."

Rolfe cleared his throat. "It's very much as you left it, Father." He wanted to remove his father's hand but could not get himself to do it. "You heard old Schmieg died?"

"Yes. Von Sorgen wrote me. And Altmann too?"

"Yes—last winter. Very sudden."

"Vascular problems, I gather. I have a touch of that

myself. In the leg. Nothing very serious, mind you. But Schmieg lived to seventy-six. That's a good old age." Grigori pondered a moment, then laughed out loud. "I hope I do as well. And your mother? She's all right? You see her?"

"Yes—we all went down to Merano last spring. She wanted to see the children. She seemed quite well."

"And her marriage?" Grigori appeared momentarily embarrassed.

"He's a very nice chap. They're quite compatible."

Grigori poured his son another glass of champagne, then tossed off one of his own.

The younger man declined to drink but stared hard at his father. "And how are you, Father?"

"How am I?" The Doctor sighed and leaned back in the banquette. "Why, I'm splendid. Can't you see that?" He thumped his chest. "Vigorous. More energy today than I had twenty-five years ago. The outdoors. That's what does it. I don't pamper myself. Hunting. Fishing. A bit of convivial company from time to time." He winked raffishly at his son and burst out laughing. Then he frowned. "But you don't look so fine, *mein lieber Sohn*. Pale. Frazzled. Worried. Are you worried about something, Rolfe? Is everything all right at home?"

"Everything is fine, Father."

"And your work?"

"Fine. All fine."

"Do you need money? I'd be glad to . . ."

"I told you, I'm fine, Father." Rolfe Hupfauer's voice rose. "I don't need anything."

Grigori appeared momentarily baffled. Then he laughed out loud, pretending he had not heard the harsh edge in his son's voice. "Well, I'm going to take you under my wing here," he gushed. "You need some relaxation. I can see you work too hard. Nerves. Stress. It will kill you. Ricardo said you wouldn't enjoy hunting. But I'm going to take you up to the Chagras anyway, and . . ."

"I have no interest in hunting, Father," Rolfe said curtly.

"Oh?" The Doctor paused uncertainly. "Well, in that case, there's no need to go hunting. Perhaps you'd prefer some fishing, or possibly just to go out on the boat with me. Cruise upriver. Drink, swim, talk, and be alone."

"I'm here for a very short time, Father," Rolfe said quietly.

"Paraguay can be quite beautiful, you know." Grigori babbled on as if he had not heard a word. "Beastly climate, but there are marvelous things to see and do. I can take you down to Iguaçu to see the falls and San Bernardino. We can take a cabin and fish for dorado in the Ipacarai. Rolfe, I tell you, you'd really enjoy . . ."

"Father—I'm leaving here tomorrow."

"Yes, of course." Grigori laughed uneasily. "We'll be out of here first thing in the morning. Crack of dawn. I thought first we'd go up to Puerto Stroessner, stay a few days, then . . ."

"I mean, leaving Paraguay. I'm going home, Father."

"Home?" Grigori repeated the word as if he scarcely comprehended it. His eyes narrowed and he put down his champagne flute. "Home?"

"Yes, Father." Rolfe spoke with an ominous quiet. "To Günzburg. Back to Hedi and the children."

"But you've only just come. You can't really mean . . ."

"I'm going, Father. The only reason I came was because I'd heard you weren't well."

"Not well?" The Doctor's face flushed. "Who said I wasn't well. Who dared? Tell me, was it Caffetti?" He glared at his son. "Ah, so it was Caffetti."

"He believed he was doing the proper thing, and he was."

"How dare he? What's it his goddamned business? I'll see to him. What did he tell you? Come on, out with it."

Rolfe paused, anxious not to further upset his father. "He said only that you were tired and a bit nervous."

"Tired? Nervous?" Grigori laughed. "That stupid idiot. Do I look tired or nervous? Come, speak up. It had to be more than that to make you come all this way." Grigori's brow cocked. He appeared suddenly suspicious. "He didn't mention anything else?"

"About what?"

"About Enríquez?"

"Who's Enríquez?"

"My physician. He didn't say anything about that?"

Rolfe lied openly now. He denied he'd heard anything of his father's imaginary heart ailment or rectal polypomas. "No, Father." He tried to smile. "Only that of late you've been tired and nervous."

"*Ach scheiss.*" Grigori waved a hand in disgust. "Don't listen to Caffetti. Caffetti's an old woman. He's an Italian. You know Italians. They're all hysterics." He gulped more champagne and his face grew redder. "I'm neither tired nor nervous. You'd think I would be. I have good cause to be a little nervous. Only last night, some idiot tried to kill me."

Rolfe Hupfauer's glass paused halfway to his lips. "You're not serious?"

"Yes—quite serious."

"How? What happened? Tell me."

"It's of no consequence."

"Of no consequence?" Rolfe gaped. "You tell me someone just tried to kill you. And then you tell me it's of no consequence."

"It isn't." Grigori rummaged his pockets for a cigarette. "I don't care to talk about it. There have been so many attempts on my life. By now it's boring."

Rolfe frowned. "Tell me who. Do you know?"

"It wasn't actually me they shot at," Grigori said tentatively. "It was someone they thought was me. Fortunately, we'd been tipped off before. You see, there was this woman and a strange man."

"A strange man?"

Grigori caught the note of skepticism. "An accomplice. Agents," he tried again. "Oh, Christ. Forget it. It's too complicated." He looked away, trying to recover his composure. "For God's sake, Rolfe." His voice whimpered slightly and for the first time he permitted his son to see his exhaustion and fright. "Don't go home now. Don't leave me. I've been looking forward to this for so long." His hand raked hectically through his hair. "I'm a little tired now. Please spend some time with me. We don't have to hunt, or do anything, if you don't care to. Just stay with me. It's only a week or so out of your life. What's a week? You have a whole lifetime. Me—" He smiled wryly. "I'm nearly seventy. Time is at a premium for me. How do I know when, or if ever, you'll be back this way?"

Rolfe sat silently observing his father. What he saw before him now was a man—slight, suavely and expensively turned out, aging but still handsome and radiating an unmistakable air of well-being. But for all that, he could sense too that this was largely facade. Flesh sagged beneath his chin, the eyes wrinkled at the corners, and the lids were puffy with edema. He could see the handsome splashes of gray at his father's temple and realized with a shock of sadness that the vivid, youthful black hair above it was dyed. He stared at it fixedly for a moment, the way one stares at an obvious toupee or at cheap, ill-fitting dentures, then quickly he looked away.

"Don't go," Grigori went on, his voice husky with fatigue. "Give me at least a few days." Once again he covered the back of his son's hand with his own. This time Rolfe removed it.

"Father, I don't belong here. I'm needed home. I—"

"I need you here," Grigori snapped through gritted teeth, then almost immediately covered his eyes with his hands like a child mortified at having spoken a foul word. He spoke now from behind the screen of his hands. "I know what you think of me. I can imagine the kind of things you've heard. I understand what you're feeling. This loathesome man. This creature. This ogre. What does he want from me? You're embarrassed to be seen with me."

"Father—"

"Don't make me beg, Rolfe. Please—" Grigori's eyes glistened behind the suddenly parted hands. "Please."

Rolfe Grigori sat there regarding the tired, crumpled figure before him. He hated himself not for having caused his father to plead and abase himself, but because he had actively enjoyed it. Rolfe had always found it easy to despise the arrogant, vaunting Doctor Grigori. But this pathetic, pleading creature, sniveling before him, he was quite unable to deal with.

"Please, Rolfe."

The younger man shrugged and looked away. He could not bear to meet his father's overflowing eyes.

"You'll stay?" the Doctor whispered hoarsely.

Eyes lowered, Rolfe stared at his hands folded in his lap and nodded yes. When he looked up again, a huge, almost beatific smile radiated from his father's face.

CHAPTER 42

It was dawn when Asher stepped from the forest and onto the narrow third-class tarmac that sliced like an arrow through the upper Paraná. Aside from a pair of badly scuffed shoes, he appeared, for all that rough, inhospitable terrain he'd crossed, none the worse for wear. Fresh, cool, and eminently presentable. Now he brushed himself off and with that characteristic certitude of strong moral resolve, he set a course due north on the little jungle highway that crossed the Alto Paraná.

The sun was not yet full up, and so the forest was gray, still shrouded in thickly dappled shadows. The huge conifer and cypress soaring above the jungle brush cast large, misshapen shadows against the roseate morning sky.

Asher walked with a sense of exhilaration. He felt no fatigue from his exertions of the night before and as he moved, he did so with the conscious determination that each step brought him closer to Doctor Grigori.

Asher looked up, jolted from his long, rambling inward speculations, in time to see a 1947 REO pickup truck steam and putter to a halt beside him. The back of the truck was filled to the brim with a huge slope of maize shifting uneasily with the vehicle's lurching motion. Inside the cab a *campesino* with a broad, amiable face gazed quizzically down upon him.

"*Hey, amigo,*" he shouted above the idling motor.

"Que haces tu? What the hell are you doing out here this hour of the day?"

"My car broke down a few miles back," Asher shouted up in perfect demotic Spanish.

The *campesino* appeared doubtful. "I've been on this road six hours, *amigo*. I've seen no car."

"I drove it into the bush about ten miles back." Asher smiled. "Thought it would be safer there till I could get a tow truck to come and pull me out."

The explanation appeared to satisfy the farmer's doubts. After all, the fellow appeared decent, educated, pleasant enough. "Where are you going?" he inquired.

"Encarnación."

The *campesino* chewed his gum and nodded. "I can take you as far as Jablasco. You'll get a ride from there. Hop in."

They drove on for an hour or so, he and the driver, smoking and chatting amiably. The driver was going to meet his girl in Jablasco that night. They planned a big evening. Would he (Asher) care to come? The driver was certain his girl could find some pretty companion for the night.

"No thank you." Asher laughed. He had business in Encarnación.

"What exactly is your business?" the driver asked quizzically. Just then Asher saw the police cruiser straddling the highway up ahead. It was a roadblock.

The REO steamed and puttered to a halt. A *federal* sauntered round to the door of the cab.

"What's up?" the driver asked.

"There was a shooting on the ferry last night," the *federal* said, peering in at them. "We're looking for the bastard who may be involved. Papers please, *señores*."

The driver pulled his papers out and presented them. The *federal* scanned them, then looked next for the other fellow's. But instead of identity papers, what he saw was the muzzle of a long-barreled Beretta. It was the last thing he ever saw in this life.

With the *federal* dead, slumped on the ground with a shattered skull against the REO's running board, Asher now looked across at the driver, whose hands had automatically gone up above his head. With the muzzle of the gun pointing at him, he was too petrified to speak. He merely shook his head back and forth, as if to say, "No. Please. Not me."

Asher studied the man gravely. Suddenly he smiled and gave a helpless little shrug. *"Lo siento mucho, amigo,"* he murmured and patted the fellow on the knee, then he shot him between the eyes.

It was still quite early and no cars had come along. Asher took his time changing into the *federal*'s uniform. Then, taking the dead man's pistol and papers, he slipped in behind the wheel of the police cruise car, started the engine, and pointed himself resolutely toward Jablasco.

CHAPTER 43

Showered, shaved, anointed in talcum and cologne, Doctor Grigori slipped into freshly pressed evening clothes. In the adjoining room, Rolfe Hupfauer, sick at heart, was going through the same ritual of the toilette—despising himself and wishing to be far away. But Alban Krug had arranged for a banquet that night to celebrate the reunion of the Doctor and his son, and from that there was no escaping.

At 8:30 sharp, Hans Rudel knocked on his door.

Rolfe stepped out into the hall, where his father, resplendent in tie and tails, was waiting with his two lean panthers, flanking him on either side. Joined moments later by Caffetti, they descended *en masse* to the lobby, swept through in a matter of moments and exited discreetly through a side door. Outside, the big tan Mercedes awaited them.

Shortly they were out on the highway heading into the purple, velvety nighttime of the countryside. Climbing upward out of the river valley, they traversed the softly undulant hills outside the city, while the bright, tawdry lights of Encarnación sank slowly behind them.

Until they'd reached the hills, they were tense and silent. Then, once out of the city, Grigori laughed and chatted easily. He spoke mainly of the past, and his memory, Rolfe noted, was prodigious. The closer they got to the Café Bavaria, their destination, the more animated the Doctor became. But that was his nature, Rolfe thought—characteristically happiest in party clothes and going out for the evening.

At first, Rolfe tried to converse with his father, but finally he was forced to succumb to the torrent of words and memories that gushed irrepressibly from the man. Vanquished at last, the son sat utterly silent, hands folded in lap, grim and resigned to some inescapable sense of impending disaster.

The Café Bavaria was located out near the Obligado colony, some sixty kilometers from Encarnación. It was run by retired SS *Hauptsturmführer* Gearhardt Glenzmann and frequented primarily by fugitive and deracinated Wehrmacht veterans who'd stampeded to Paraguay in the wake of the war. That was in the bad old days when the future looked bleak for them or, at least, doubtful. Now they were all prosperous farmers, cattle ranchers, and land speculators with vast holdings in the mineral-wealthy Paraná region. Some pursued more questionable but nonetheless lucrative occupations. They were now the ruling class of Paraguay. They inhabited luxurious *estancias* attended by large staffs of pitifully underpaid natives, and their sources of income were as enigmatic as their way of life.

The Bavaria was a typical German country inn. Entering it, one might almost imagine himself somewhere in the Tyrol or the Black Forest. Squat, garishly carved Germanic furniture cluttered the place. Oak wainscoting darkened it and made it airless. At almost every foot of the way one was met by a cuckoo clock or a great staghead gazing down from the walls, its gentle dead eyes seemingly omniscient, but never judging.

When Grigori's party reached the Bavaria, the inn was gaudily lit up. An air of holiday festivity hung all about it. Myriad cars—Mercedeses and American Cadillacs—were drawn up all about the place.

Captain Glenzmann, unctuous and officious, greeted them at the door, shortly to be joined by Krug, the tyrannical dwarf in tuxedo, his pigeon-chest swelling, snappish and autocratic, puffing and self-important, barking orders at everybody.

Encarnación was Alban Krug's town. God help the man who would gainsay that. He owned most of its real estate; he was its Lord Mayor and, whether you liked it or not, he was the law of the land. He administered justice with the same high moral zeal with which he imposed punishment on wrongdoers—and for Alban Krug, a wrongdoer could be anything Krug wanted one to be. When Alban Krug threw a party in Encarnación, there might well be a good deal of muttering among those invited, but absolutely nobody dared to decline.

For Doctor Grigori's party Krug had conscripted nearly one hundred people drawn from the best German families in the area, as well as an obligatory sprinkling of Paraguayan aristocrats whom Krug thought of privately as "aboriginal." Nevertheless, he could see the public relations value of occasionally courting some of these "Hottentots," as he called them. Keep the natives pacified.

The people who attended the Krug banquet that night were largely mutual friends, past and present, of the Doctor and himself. A lofty gathering to say the least—ex-Wehrmacht chancellors, *Obersturmführers, Reich* ministers, a liberal scattering of Krupp and I. G. Farben types exported to the provinces for their own good—fellows who could not have survived a moment of scrutiny into their pasts. Here was literally the cream of the Third Reich—the zealots and true believers who were there only waiting it out until the Fourth Reich, which was inevitable, would rise like a phoenix on the ashes of the grand old order.

That evening, when Grigori and his party entered the banquet hall, the lights which had been dimmed suddenly went up. Everyone rose to his feet. Krug raised his fist like an imperial Caesar and a small Tyrolean band struck up the Horst Wessel. Champagne glasses were raised, and people cheered and clapped and stamped their feet as Doctor Grigori, followed by those in his party, marched triumphantly down the length of the room to a dais, above which hung an enormous swastika. Rolfe Hupfauer flushed angrily the moment he saw it.

There was cheering as they took their seats, and Doctor Grigori, basking in that spontaneous outpouring of love, waved around the room to old friends. Even Colonel Arganas had flown down from Asunción and embraced him there at the dais.

Bottles were decorked, champagne was served, and trays of Iranian caviar were wheeled around the room on large trolleys. Throughout the dinner there was entertainment—a strolling accordion player, Tyrolean jugglers and acrobats, a dancing bear, a Turkish belly-dancer, and a tall, saturnine magician attired in black cape and top hat, funereal and ominous as a vulture.

All throughout dinner a continuous stream of people came forward to pay their respects. Grigori, after all, was a legendary character. Now he was here, sitting there before them, a hero of the cause and a symbol of their own indestructibility.

Everybody wanted to meet him—touch him. But there was a screening process. In order to greet Doctor Grigori one had to pass first through Krug. Some people who had come forward he waved right up to see the Doctor. Others were unable to get past him. Those who were vouchsafed the supreme accolade of shaking Grigori's hand were also, as an added bonus, introduced to Rolfe. Many of those who came forward to pay their respects were old medical colleagues who'd served with Grigori in Auschwitz and Birkenau, or on the Russian front. When they reached him, they embraced him. They kissed each other on the cheeks. Shortly, Grigori's face was flushed with champagne and emotion. Tears glistened in his eyes.

All throughout the dinner they came, a steady parade of old friends and admirers, while strains of old Berlin cabaret tunes played on a strolling accordion lilted in the noisy background.

Of those whom Krug permitted to come forward, some brought their wives, some their children and grandchildren. To them, Grigori was an almost supernatural presence, illuminated by some inner mystical power. He was one of the chosen—a member of the supreme Wehrmacht pantheon. Everyone wanted only to be there in his presence.

It was all strangely primitive, Rolfe thought—atavistic, like the propitiation of some cruel divinity—feared, loathed and revered, but mostly feared. His father was to these people a god to whom one came prostrating oneself and making obeisance.

That is what Rolfe felt, sitting there watching people ushered forward by Krug, the all-powerful dwarf, to be presented to the all-powerful ogre-god. History had canonized his father as an ogre, and he could see now that people worshipped the ogre because they feared its wrath. They all knew what ghastly things the ogre was capable of, and their propitiation was part of a ritual to appease him. Some did this by presenting wives and children and grandchildren in a strange kind of symbolic sacrifice to the ogre.

At one point in this procession of supplicants, a gray, venerable gentleman who wore an iron cross around his neck and walked with a cane led forth his little grandson. The child was scarcely five or six, blond, cherubic, like the *putti* in a Tintoretto; the little rosy face was suffused with awe as he toddled forward to meet the god.

Rolfe watched, transfixed, as his father bent over the child, tousled its blond hair, then stooped to kiss it on each cheek. A chill coursed through him—a sense of desperation he felt recalling in a flash an open ditch he had been taken to behind Barracks 2 in Auschwitz, which was the medical dispensary. The Russian authorities seeking information as to his father's whereabouts had brought Rolfe there to the common grave heaped with the moldering, pathetic little bones of small children. These children, castrated, maimed, blinded and mutilated in the name of advanced medical research, had died horrible deaths at the hands of his father.

When that was first explained to him by the Russian colonel, with meticulous and unsparing detail, Rolfe could not comprehend it. Moreover, he refused to believe it. Then they brought him documentation and copious eyewitness accounts by far too many people reporting basically identical experiences for the whole thing to be a wicked fabrication of the Allies. And then there were the photographs—ghastly, haunted pictures of little Gypsy children, Slavic children, Jewish children—tiny victims. *Kindertoten—Racial detritus. Untermenschen. Human dross. Expendable.* Available for whatever uses might advance the cause.

For years after, the memory of that ghastly trench— the image of those tiny, sacrificial souls: malnourished; already half-dead; swollen abdomens; the blades of bones showing through their skin; eyes large, haunted, omniscient; sensing doom and accepting it sweetly— this memory pursued Rolfe Hupfauer down all the grieving years, compelling him to do retribution for the sins of his fugitive father.

Rolfe watched, with shrinking horror, the ogre kiss the cheeks of the little blond child and had a sudden urge to flee the table, and the awful room with the big swastika overhead, and the worshipful, cowering sycophants lining up all about him—all hating and fearing his father, nevertheless, all waiting their turn to do obeisance to him.

He was about to leave, but in the next moment Krug rose and tapped his champagne goblet with a butter knife. Suddenly the room was silent. A faint smile curling at his lips, an expression of cunning and arrogance in his eyes, Krug gazed round the room, then suddenly thrust his arm up and shouted "Sieg Heil."

Everyone in the room, including Grigori, rose to his feet and in thunderous unison roared back at the dwarf, "Sieg Heil." Having thus begun, the chant went on for ten minutes, thunderous, deafening, reverberating from the rafters, growing with each cheer in volume and intensity. Looking like some maniacal little toy doll, Krug stood before the roaring assembly, pumping his arms and shouting with fierce exultation. With each "Sieg Heil" he flung his little arm up and stamped his feet. His face grew red, transfixed with almost vindictive ecstasy. It was then that Rolfe realized that eyes—many eyes coming at him from all directions—were upon him. People stared questioningly at him, including his father. Then it suddenly dawned upon him that of all the people in the room, he was the only one still seated.

Rolfe had remained seated throughout this obscene ceremony. Everyone in the hall on his feet, chanting, shouting "Sieg Heils" glared at him. It was as if they were commanding him to rise and participate. Defying him to remain seated. Krug and Rudel and Caffetti, all standing beside him, stared. His father, mortified and swollen with anger, glowered down at him. His eyes, red and bleary from too much wine, commanded Rolfe to rise—to stand up for the Fatherland.

Rolfe Hupfauer never thought of himself as brave. With regard to his father in particular, he knew himself to be downright craven. He had always been a dutiful and obedient son. The thought of countermanding his father's wishes in any way would scarcely ever have occurred to him.

And now here he was at forty-three, still the weak-kneed and timorous little boy cringing before his father —waiting to drop his trousers and be strapped soundly across the buttocks.

Doctor Grigori's eyes burned into his son's, as if his great force of will could be conveyed through the intensity of his gaze. The Doctor "Sieg Heiled" as defiantly as ever, still commanding his son to rise.

A wave of panic swept over Rolfe. He knew he would never return to Paraguay—never after this nightmare set eyes upon his father again. Knowledge of that alone might have been expected to release him from any sense of obligation, but it didn't. With his eyes locked deep within his father's furious gaze, he sensed his own resolve weakening and the momentary rebellion passed. He felt himself beginning to rise. But it was an involuntary action, as if he were being dragged up from his seat by some invisible tether stretched taut between father and son. But still he remained seated.

The chanting and stamping of feet were now deafening. They roared in Rolfe's head while his father's look of outrage continued to batter him. Several times his resolve nearly crumbled. He felt his knees begin to flex, and the pressure of calf muscles tightening. The motion was automatic, uncontrollable. He was a person mesmerized by an evil wizard.

But each time he was about to capitulate, something within him, he knew not what, kept him seated in his chair.

His defiance appeared to goad the audience. They now appeared to sense the mortal combat between father and son, and they shouted and stamped even louder. In the next moment they had all raised their champagne glasses to Doctor Grigori and began to sing the Horst Wessel. Rolfe's gaze locked deep within his father's. But this time, instead of the arrogance and command he'd glimpsed there before, he saw naked pleading, and in that moment he was no longer interested in principle. Sick to his heart, he reached for his champagne flute and rose. A roar of acclamation went up. His father was beaming.

Later that evening, when the banquet was over and people gathered round the coat check room to say good night, Rolfe found himself face to face with Colonel Arganas.

The Colonel's manner was suave and assured. He wore a look of amusement as if he had just experienced something rare and infinitely pleasing. He was extremely amiable. Rolfe was curt and barely civil.

"I am informed that an attempt was made last evening on my father's life."

"That is correct," Arganas replied.

"I gather, too, that the immediate danger now seems past."

"Really?" Arganas cocked his brow. "I'm not aware that it is."

"Herr Krug told me that the assassin was shot in the water."

Arganas smiled indulgently at the young man.

"Is this true?" Rolfe demanded.

"It is quite true that the assassin was fired upon in the water."

"Well, then?"

The tone elicited a vaguely amused expression from Arganas. "We can't be certain the man was hit. We found no trace of the body."

"It could have sunk."

"Possibly." Arganas nodded patronizingly. "However, bodies that sink tend after several hours to rise again. As of yet, this one hasn't."

"Oh?" Rolfe hovered there, momentarily stymied. He studied Arganas now, taking the measure of the man, not at all sure if he was impressed or suspicious. "Then it is your feeling, Colonel, that the danger is still present?"

Arganas was silent a moment, framing a suitable reply. In his heart he might very well have suspected that Asher had perished in the Paraná. But as an eminently practical man, he knew it was to his distinct advantage to keep the threat of Asher alive for as long as possible. Without any real and present threat, it would be hard, he knew, to continue to extort those ever-escalating protection fees from the Doctor.

"This hired killer who has been stalking your father" —the Colonel spoke slowly and deliberately, as if he were pondering aloud—"is very accomplished at his work."

"You know the man?"

"I not only know him, but speaking as a professional, I have a great admiration for him. We have a dossier of several hundred pages on the fellow."

"He's an Israeli?"

"By birth. He's a Sabra. But even the Israelis have come to disavow him. He's more a man without a country. The fellow's an ex-commando and an ex-Mossad agent."

"Mossad?" Rolfe was perturbed. "What in God's name do they want with my father at this late date?"

"Hate dies hard, Herr Hupfauer." Arganas smiled sympathetically. "Your father's name shares a special place in the heart of world Jewry. Jews of a certain generation will never forget him."

"Yes, of course," Rolfe replied tersely. He had decided that, instead of being impressed, he would take a strong dislike to the small dark man in the Colonel's uniform.

"As I said," Arganas went on, "this man Asher . . ."

"Asher?"

"The man who is stalking your father."

"Yes?"

"He is skillful, professional, and very dangerous. The threat he poses is neither insubstantial nor imaginary. It's very real, I assure you. And . . . he has accomplices."

"Accomplices?"

"I've already dispensed with three of them," Arganas said, vaunting his own public relations unashamedly. "One a foolish bungler in Asunción who succumbed to the rigors of Tembuco prison; a second, a beautiful young woman in Bariloche who'd insinuated herself into your father's affections."

Rolfe's eyes narrowed warily. "And the third?"

"An unfortunate gentleman who had a fatal accident on the Paraná ferry last night."

"Is this the man whose body you failed to recover from the river?"

"No—that's Asher."

"Who may or may not still be alive," Rolfe muttered, his distaste mounting by the moment. "How many are there, then?"

"I'm sure I don't know." Arganas bristled. He did not at all care for the manner in which he was being addressed. "Could be one or two dozen."

"Then isn't it unwise for my father to be walking around here so brazenly—so openly?" Rolfe caught a glimpse of his father across the crowded room, basking in the glory of a circle of admirers.

"I would say he's safer here among large friendly crowds than he'd be cut off from his friends and isolated. Under no circumstances should you permit anyone to isolate your father again. The people in Bariloche nearly succeeded in doing just that. Well"—Arganas stiffened and came erect—"I'm afraid I must be going. I'm due in Asunción in the morning. But I would not have missed your father's party for the world."

"Going?" Rolfe was appalled. "Surely you're going to remain here by his side as long as this threat, as you say, still exists?"

The Colonel smiled more smugly than ever. He was prepared to be tolerant. "My dear Hupfauer," he sighed. "You can rest assured that my people here are under the strictest orders not to let your father out of their sight. There are perhaps fifty of my own personal staff circulating through the room at this very moment." Arganas patted Rolfe reassuringly on the arm. "Your father will be under surveillance twenty-four hours a day, every day, until he is back safely at the garrison of Carlos Antonio Lopez."

Arganas lit a cigarette and flung his coat rakishly across his shoulders.

"But what about this Asher?" Rolfe protested.

"Leave Asher to me." Arganas flashed a smile, seeing Doctor Grigori coming toward them. "Ah, here's the Doctor now." He nodded to Rolfe. "I'll say good night now and take my leave."

Arganas turned briskly on his heel and strode out. Gazing up, Rolfe saw his father threading his way through throngs of people, all of whom appeared to be straining to reach him—to make contact. Grigori had several old friends in tow, leading them across the room to his son. In the next moment his father, beaming, laughing, reeking of cognac and cigars, was embracing him.

Just at that moment the 12:45 AM coach from Jablasco was pulling into the depot in downtown Encarnación. Having driven through the heavy seasonal rains pelting downward high up in the mountains, the bus was dusty and mud-spattered. Its brakes squealed, and with a great wheeze of compressed air, its accordion doors folded open. A handful of passengers—hot, limp, bedraggled from eight hours of confinement—began to alight in desultory fashion. Shortly the flow accelerated, for Encarnación was the terminal point.

One of the last to descend was a man in the simple habit of a cleric. All of his earthly possessions he carried in a worn, tatty black leather bag. His manner was neat, quiet, unobtrusive. Emerging from the front entrance of the depot, the priest appeared to blend, chameleonlike, into the environment. A tired old porter, deeply honored by the chore, carried the priest's bag

out to the cab stand, hailed a taxi, and refused to take
a tip when one was proffered.

Ian Asher settled comfortably back in the rear seat
of the capacious old Mercedes cab and in his correct
and perfectly inflected Spanish, he asked the driver for
the best hotel in Encarnación. He knew which it was,
but he wished to appear to be a stranger.

The reply he wanted was, of course, the reply he got.
"The best is the Tyrol, *Padre.*"

"But it must be expensive."

"*Si, muy caro, Padre.*" The driver shrugged and
smiled apologetically at Asher in the rear-view mirror.

"Well, then, take me some place a bit cheaper,"
Asher said, and then added, "but make sure it's in the
same good neighborhood."

They both laughed.

CHAPTER 44

"I shall not be judged," Doctor Grigori cried across the
room at his son. "Never. And I do not have to justify
myself to anyone. Least of all to you. You are my son.
You're supposed to understand."

It was nearly four AM, and they were back at the
Tyrol now. The Doctor had removed his evening jacket,
black tie, and shoes. Now he paced the room attired
in socks, open shirt, and trousers with braces dangling
at the hips. He carried a large snifter of brandy that
sloshed on the furniture and carpets as he stormed up
and down, waving his arms and shouting. He and Rolfe
had been quarreling thus for at least an hour.

"What did I do that was so wrong?" Grigori ranted on. "I was making an honest inquiry. That's surely no crime, is it? I had two principal objectives—one, to make it possible for a woman to bear multiple offspring with each pregnancy, and two, to discover a way to control the physical traits of each offspring so that only the best racial characteristics of a people would be perpetuated. Was that wrong? Was that evil?"

Grigori paused to gulp his cognac greedily. Having drained his snifter, he wiped his mouth with the back of a hand. "My enemies make much of the fact that I tried to change the pigmentation of eyes and hair in some of the children I worked on. But what they fail to see is that I was only trying to transform and improve a less richly endowed people into the glorious Aryan mold of our forefathers.

"Therefore, my word on twins and triplets, as well as defective creatures such as dwarfs and hunchbacks, was, contrary to the distortions of my enemies, not motivated by cruelty at all. It was humanistic at heart. What else could be done with the poor things? They were doomed anyway.

"And this now brings me to the question of the Jews. I wish to stress I bear no malice toward Jews as such. I never did. Contrary to belief, and my actions in the past, I have never been an anti-Semite. The professional anti-Semite, the full-time hatemonger, ranting and raving, foaming at the mouth with his lunatic versions of Scripture and history, and his cheap bag of hate slogans, is the lowest form of scum to me. My father employed Jews in his factory in Günzburg. I numbered Jews among my closest friends. I have an enormous respect for Jews. They and the Germans are the only truly superior races. Unfortunately, the two could never coexist. One had to dominate and that had to be the Germans.

"Oh, yes, I do not deny that I executed Jews. That was unfortunate, but I was ordered to do so. It was a time of madness and war. One does things during such times of strife that one would have preferred not to have done. But, I insist, I did not kill Jews out of hate. I killed Jews on behalf of knowledge. If that sounds callous, very well then, so be it. And is it not now ironic—not to say vastly amusing—that the work I started in those first giddy, triumphant years of the early forties is carried on today by distinguished scientists, and funded by governments and wealthy foundations all working under a mantle of respectability and all cloaked with the most sanctimonious air of self-importance? Is this not laughable? To talk about racial purification is no longer horrific; on the contrary, it's fashionable. The 'coming thing.' Only now they have fancy names for it. They call it human engineering, behavioral conditioning, cloning, or some such lofty nonsense. These are only euphemisms for what I was doing in the forties. And men will win Nobel prizes tomorrow for doing those very same things I was called a 'monster' and a 'beast' for doing then.

"If you confront these 'distinguished, learned' men today with this simple truth, they will deny it. Cry 'outrage.' They will say that while their goals may be similar, their methods are totally different because they work with a chicken or a monkey rather than a child. Shameless and laughable casuistry. Mark my words, the chicken will soon enough become the child. And now, in their piety, in their disgusting self-serving, self-righteousness, they have even stripped me of my medical title and my philosophy degree. The university has disavowed me. Hypocrites all.

"No, I do not disavow my past. If anything, I am proud of it. If there is anything I regret in the past, if there is one mistake I made, my really big mistake was to have run. I should have stayed and faced the music. After all, I was only one of scores of 'camp' doctors. Why should the Allies have treated me any worse than the others? They would have tried me. They would have put me on the stand and shaken their fists in moral indignation. There would have been gnashings of teeth and wringing of hands. One of those public spectacles of moral fireworks, so beloved and revered by the so-called Western democracies. An exquisite opportunity for puritanical soul-shriving. The judges would have invoked the Lord God on High, shaken their wattles with wrath, and swooned with self-righteousness as they sentenced me to life imprisonment, then looked the other way as I slipped quietly out the back door of Spandau after four years; after all the drum-beating and chest-pounding had died down. And I would not be hiding out right now, pinned down forever, in this godforsaken pestiferous hellhole. I'd be a free man today."

Doctor Grigori paused in his pacing, suddenly aware once more that his son was in the room, watching him, staring at him oddly. The expression on Rolfe's face just then made him furious. "You look at me now as if I were some kind of monster. Oh, I know what you've heard." He glared at his son defiantly through his squinting eye. "I know what you've read. What's been attributed to me. I know how you've suffered from these stories. How your family and children—" He appeared to have run momentarily out of breath and stood now wiping his throat with a handkerchief. "Still, I maintain," Grigori went on, his speech becoming drunken and declamatory, "I never butchered, I never tortured, I never killed, I—"

Rolfe swung sharply about. "You never killed?"

"Never willfully." Grigori waved his finger as if to emphasize a significant point. "I was a soldier. A scientist. I had my duty. My code—"

"To abuse and torture, to maim and castrate. Were women and children part of your code?"

"Everyone. Everybody. We had our orders. A soldier does not distinguish . . . A soldier . . ." Grigori's voice trailed off as he saw the look of disgust on his son's face. "Oh, don't you see?" he pleaded. "It was a time of madness. Can you understand that? Madness. And possibly I was a little mad, too."

Grigori paused, exhausted by the effort of self-examination but exhilarated by it, too, as if, through it, he found comfort and release. "If I killed people," he went on now, "it was not the thousands I'm accused of killing. Nowhere near that. A mere handful actually. Possibly a dozen or so. No more." He waved his finger above his son again in self-justification and reeled forward, waving the brandy bottle. "And these few were diseased and moribund. Killing them was an act of mercy. Why has the press so exaggerated and lied?"

Rolfe spoke softly but emphatically. He no longer had any wish to spare his father. "It is all documented. I've seen records, photographs, sifted through endless testimony—"

"Portraying me as a monster?" Grigori went on, drowning out his son's refutations. "Why have they portrayed my past out of all proportion to the facts? We were scientists looking for the truth. Votive priests at the altar of knowledge. Why do they never speak of the countless acts of generosity and mercy I bestowed on these low creatures with whom I was forced to cohabit on a daily basis? Why do they not speak of how I brought sterilized equipment and the most hygienic practices to the surgical wards? Why do they not tell of how I single-handedly eliminated typhoid and cholera from the camps? How I helped Jewish mothers to have their babies painlessly and hygienically? Why do they not tell of this? Do you know why, my dear son?"

Rolfe gazed at his father quizzically, understanding now for the first time what Caffetti had been talking about when he'd spoken of his father's "illness."

"I'll tell you why," Grigori went on, animated by lunacy as well as drink. "Because the professional Zionists need a scapegoat. They need a scapegoat to whip up and maintain hate, and they have selected me. They have made a symbol of me. The symbol of an era. They've made a fund-raising device out of me."

Grigori collapsed into a chair, exhausted from his tirade and suddenly despondent. His chin drooped onto his chest. Sweat glistened on his forehead. Rolfe stood up now and walked to him. For a while he stood above the chair, staring down at his father. "Can I get you something?" he asked.

Doctor Grigori appeared not to have heard and Rolfe asked the question again. "My medicine," he murmured, at last. "In the bathroom in the leather case on the sink. The green pills. Please get them."

Rolfe found the pills exactly where they were supposed to be. For some reason he was alarmed, frightened that his father would take sick and possibly delay his own departure. Instantly he felt shame for his small selfish preoccupations. He brought the pills back out to his father along with a glass of water.

After Grigori had taken his medicine and sat quietly for a while, he grew talkative again, but this time rather wistfully so—full of a kind of sad, dreamy nostalgia. "When I first faced the awful truth of my exile," he began, "what it really meant in terms of my future life, what I had lost of my life and could never hope to regain, an awful depression took hold of me. That's quite typical of white men in the tropics. You know what they call it out here, Rolfe? They call it 'cafard.' I don't know the etymology of the word—only the symptoms, and I had them all. Depression. Anorexia. Apathy.

Sleeplessness. I read nothing, not even a newspaper. I put aside my music, and, most horrible of all, I put aside my work. I could see nothing ahead but a slow atrophy of mind and body. A steady irreversible descent into myself. An endless succession of empty days until oblivion." Grigori looked up and fixed his bleary eyes on his son. "And that is the way it has been for me these many years. But only recently, I don't know why, hope has come back and I've even started to work again. That's why I so wanted you to come. I wanted you to see me this way once more. Vital, involved, at the top of my power. So you might remember me this way."

Rolfe looked away, unable to confront his father's stricken eyes.

"Exile has cost me dearly, Rolfe," the Doctor went on, a tremor in his voice. "How dearly you'll never know. Oh, I don't complain, mind you. It's kept me alive these many years, and I'm grateful for that. But it is dismal to sit about in a godforsaken swamp with one's memories and the awful solitude. Nothing about for company but these filthy mongrel brutes, and I long for nights in the great, glittering capitals of the Continent—Berlin, Vienna, Paris. The good restaurants and the bright little cafés. The theater and the opera. Companionship and convivial talk. How I have longed for just good intelligent conversation. Oh, Rolfe, you have no idea—could never guess—what a steep price I've had to pay merely for life."

Grigori started to pour another brandy, but this time Rolfe stayed his hand. "Father, why don't you give it a rest?"

The Doctor regarded his son for a moment, then jerked the bottle roughly back. "Thank you." He stiffened and grew suddenly livid. "But I don't need you to tell me how much to drink. Yes—I have killed." He swelled then with something almost resembling pride.

"I admit it. But I have atoned for my sins. A thousand times over I have atoned. More than thirty years of running and hiding and being chased, of being banished to a filthy hut in a filthy swamp. Is that not atonement enough?"

For some time, Rolfe sat plunged in silence. He had been sitting in an overstuffed sofa that had the effect of bringing his knees up quite high. On one of these knees he balanced a glass of ice water with his hand, periodically sipping from it in order to fill the gaps of silence and his own embarrassment. Uncomfortable in formal dress, he appeared now rumpled, flushed and very tired. He wanted to go to bed—to get away from his father.

But the penultimate word of Grigori's last question still rang in his ears. "Atonement." He murmured the word beneath his breath. Shortly, he sighed, then put down his glass and rose to his feet. "I might possibly have believed in your atonement, Father"—he spoke slowly, buttoning his collar and straightening his tie—"had I not gone to this banquet tonight and seen you in front of that crowd of your admirers. I thought the swastika was a marvelous touch. How apposite. And when they sang the Horst Wessel and began the 'Sieg Heiling'—"

Grigori flushed.

"Trotting out all the old War Gods again, ay, Father?" Rolfe went on spitefully. "It could have been 1933 all over again."

"You take it too seriously."

Rolfe was amused. "Hardly, Father. I think I took it more as a joke. An obscene little joke coming from obscene little people. I only regret I was made a party to it."

"Oh, for Christ's sake." Grigori flung his hands up in despair. "It was harmless. A bit of simple nostalgia. Nothing more. Those people meant nothing more."

Rolfe shook his head despairingly. "Had you seen yourself up there 'Sieg Heiling' the way I did, Father, you'd have serious cause to question the quality of your atonement."

"By what right—"

"To this day I don't believe that you yet understand what you've done. You still see yourself as the victim of a terrible injustice."

"And was I not?" Grigori's roar was full of anguish. "I have suffered injustice. I have done my work. Good work. Honorable work. And I have been punished for it. I—"

"I want you to know, Father"—Rolfe cut him short—"that the only reason I stood up tonight, and for as long as I live I shall never be able to forgive myself for that, was to spare you any embarrassment before those people you call your friends."

Doctor Grigori's flush deepened. His jaws moved ponderously, as if he were chewing rubber, but no sound came.

Rolfe picked up his jacket now and flung it over his arm. "I'm going, Father."

"I don't want you to go."

"I should never have come here in the first place."

"I want you to stay."

"I came because I heard you were sick," Rolfe went on forcefully, gathering strength as he went. "You are sick, too, but not in the way I thought you were. Not in any way that I can help, and certainly not in any way that medicine can, either. Your pathology is historical, I'm afraid, and therefore quite incurable. It can be arrested for a while, but given the slightest opportunity, such as tonight amid that pack of champagne-swilling vultures, relapse is inevitable. Forgive me, Father, but in your mouth the word 'atonement' is laughable. I doubt you know the meaning of the word. Quite honestly"—

Rolfe slipped into his jacket—"I believe that if you had your way, we'd have the camps and the crematoria re-opened tomorrow, and you would once again resume your glorious, visionary and humanitarian medical research. Tell me, Father, was it sexual?"

"Sexual?"

"Yes—when you worked on the women and the children?"

"How dare you?"

"Were you that cool dispassionate scientist you like to portray yourself as, or was there something more basic, animalistic, going on instead?"

Grigori's face had gone an unhealthy purple. He appeared speechless. "Filth—" He spluttered cognac from his lips. "You filth—"

"If it were sexual," Rolfe went on ruthlessly, "I could understand—even forgive—what you did. If I could cling to the hope that those psychosexual horrors you inflicted on people were the result of pathology, sickness—I could forgive. But to maintain that what you were doing was in the lofty pursuit of knowledge; that you were a seeker after truth, a . . . a . . . what did you call yourself? A votive priest?" A burst of withering laughter broke from his lips. "Really, Father, I find that disgusting beyond all description."

The blast of Grigori's fist caught his son high up on the temple. It didn't hurt him so much as stun him. And the moment the Doctor had thrown the punch, he appeared to regret it. He stumbled forward now, as if he wished to retract the action. As if he could take back the last few moments. But by that time Rolfe had regained his composure as well as his resolve.

"Good night, Father." He spoke gently, sorrowfully, like a man resigned to defeat. "I'll be leaving here before breakfast. I'm quite certain I shall never see you again. I wish you well." He stared at the man for a moment as if he wished to say something more but questioned the wisdom of it. "If you're ever serious—I mean genuinely serious—about atonement, Father, come home. I'll get you the best legal counsel money can buy. It will probably cost you the rest of your life in prison, but, considering the horror of your crimes, that's quite cheap. Goodbye, Father."

Rolfe turned and started for the door. Grigori followed, no more than a step or two behind. "Come back here—I demand—Rolfe," he shouted, but in the next moment the door had closed irrevocably in his face.

"Rolfe," Grigori shouted once more. It was a shout not meant to command but, rather, one full of impotence and despair.

CHAPTER 45

Shortly before dawn Rolfe Hupfauer was up and moving about in his room. He packed his suitcase and called down to the desk for someone to come get his bags. He also instructed the clerk to call for a taxi to take him out to the airport.

He moved with a quiet urgency, a controlled haste powered by a premonition of danger, though of what he could not precisely say. Something about the way his father had looked that moment only several hours before when Rolfe had walked out on him—that stormy darkening look, the strangled cry behind the door—not so much one of defeat but more of outrage crying for vindication.

There was a knock, and the bellboy appeared with a

dolly cart to take his bags down. Rolfe followed not far behind, buttoning his coat and panting with the slight breathlessness of apprehension. Standing at the desk now, he waited for the drowsy, fumbling clerk to locate and then tabulate his bill.

After several minutes of inept fumbling, the man looked up, smiling with shy idiocy. "The bill has already been paid, *señor*."

"Paid?"

"Yes. The two gentlemen. About twenty minutes ago." The clerk held up the bill with the large rubber stamped cancellation mark reading "PAGADO."

"But I don't understand," Rolfe muttered, then had an awareness of movement about him. But his mind was slow. Still he did not grasp the situation.

In the next moment Horst and Ludo converged upon him from either side.

Von Rattenhuber smiled congenially. His eyes did not meet Rolfe's but were staring over his shoulder, at some point beyond. "Good morning, Herr Hupfauer. I trust you had a good night."

"Yes." Rolfe glanced uneasily at the two of them.

"Your bags are already out in the car," Matschke added. He made a sudden motion toward him, causing Rolfe to take a step back. "My bags?"

"Yes, we'll go right out now. The others are waiting."

"The others?"

The desk clerk beamed approvingly as the two men grasped Rolfe beneath the arms and half-jostled, half-guided him across the lobby to the exit.

Once outside through the swinging doors, Rolfe saw the tan Mercedes waiting at the foot of the steps, with a second car—a rented Buick roadster—directly preceding it. The morning sun glaring harshly into Rolfe's eyes momentarily blinded him, but even in that dazzling light he dimly perceived the silhouettes of two men sitting and waiting in the Buick.

"What is this? What's going on?"

"Right this way, Herr Hupfauer," Horst murmured soothingly in the way one speaks to the senile or the mildly deranged.

When he saw the back door of the Mercedes swing open, he started to resist, using his feet as brakes, but for the last four or five steps he was literally swept along, dragged across the pavement, the toes of his shoes scuffing along behind him.

Krug's huge domed head appeared like an ascending balloon at the rear window. He was beaming brightly when Rolfe reached there.

"Ah, good morning, Herr Hupfauer."

"What in God's name—" Rolfe sputtered at the open door, with Horst and Ludo attempting to cram him into the back seat.

"Take your hands off me," Rolfe shouted, flailing his arms out awkwardly. His hat was knocked from his head. Krug reached out from inside, a ghastly smile frozen on his features, and seized the sleeve of Rolfe's jacket. "Splendid, splendid, Herr Hupfauer." His face was red and his voice a lilting singsong. "Come right in."

There was a brief altercation at the open door as Horst and Ludo gently pushed from the outside and Krug pulled from the inside, attempting to get Rolfe into the back seat.

"What the hell is going on?" Rolfe bellowed in at Krug, then winced with pain as his forehead struck hard against the doorframe.

"Careful, you idiots," Krug snarled at the two men pushing from the outside. His face was red and glowering.

Rolfe sagged from the shock of the blow. Black

motes swarmed before his eyes and in that moment he was propelled into the rear seat. He fell grunting directly on top of Krug, whereupon the two men floundered for some time. In the next moment, Horst and Ludo leaped into the front seat.

Up ahead the Buick roadster carrying Rudel and Doctor Grigori slipped smoothly away from the curb. Instantly, Horst started the Mercedes and rolled out lurchingly behind them.

Several early-morning pedestrians, having observed the incident in front of the Tyrol, shook their heads disapprovingly. They thought they had witnessed a drunken scuffle and muttered a few pithy remarks about the unseemly behavior of boorish foreigners. Certainly, no one there noticed the small rented Chevrolet Impala, driven by a cleric, which had set out moments later from behind the small hotel across the way. Curiously enough, it was traveling in the same direction taken by the two cars that had just departed.

"What the hell's going on here?" Rolfe thundered. His head throbbed where he'd smashed it, but he'd regained his balance and clarity of vision.

"Nothing, Herr Hupfauer," Krug lilted on, full of bogus cordiality. "Nothing at all."

"I have a plane to catch. I'm expected home."

"Yes, of course."

"Stop this car at once."

"Certainly," the dwarf chirped, straightening his tie and jacket where they'd been rumpled in the brief scuffle. The car sped on through the narrow, unpeopled early-morning streets.

"Am I being kidnapped?"

"Kidnapped?" Krug was deeply aggrieved. "Certainly not." He inspected a liverish-colored mound beginning to rise on Rolfe's forehead. "That's a rather nasty bump you've got there. I regret the behavior of these two baboons." He glowered at the two men in the front seat, sitting wordless and staring stolidly forward. "Stupid dolts," he muttered through clenched teeth.

"But I'm being taken somewhere by force," Rolfe persisted. "Against my will."

"Not exactly, Herr Hupfauer. It's not as if—" The dwarf went on spinning elaborate casuistries as they pursued the green Buick up ahead. "You see, Herr Hupfauer, your father—"

"Is my father in that car up front?"

"Yes, he is." Krug nodded.

They were now trailing the Buick up a steep hill on the outskirts of town.

"I want to speak with him."

"Yes, of course." Krug smiled agreeably. "But not just yet."

"Now—I demand it."

"I regret that is not possible."

"I demand—"

"I'm sorry, Herr Hupfauer."

Rolfe sat back in his seat. He closed his eyes, permitting the darkness to calm him. Then at last, he sighed. "May I ask where I'm being taken?"

"Puerto Stroessner. Your father has a home there."

"I see. And am I to be kept a hostage there?"

"Why do you insist upon using words like kidnapped and hostage?" the dwarf protested amiably. "As I understand it, you're to be detained for only a few days—"

"A few days?"

"Three at the most. And you will have complete freedom within the house. The run of the place, in fact. You'll like it. It's quite pretty."

"You realize, of course," Rolfe interrupted, "my wife is expecting me to arrive tomorrow evening."

"Your wife has been cabled that you've been delayed

several days." Krug glowed with satisfaction. "You see, Herr Hupfauer. Not to worry. All is well."

They drove on through the morning. There seemed nothing more to say, and certainly nothing more to do. The car carrying Doctor Grigori, visible up ahead, but remote and inaccessible as a distant star, moved northward while the Mercedes followed unswervingly its every glide and turn, as if its destiny were inextricably linked to it.

It occurred to Rolfe now that he feared his father more in his absence than he did in his actual presence. Not that he believed that his father would intentionally harm him. But nevertheless, he'd come to fear the man in very specific ways—not the fear of the small errant boy for his father, but rather the fear of a defenseless and vulnerable law-abiding citizen, unaccustomed to violence, for a deranged and wholly unpredictable stranger.

Suddenly, with hope fluttering in his heart, Rolfe thought of Caffetti—a touch of sanity amidst this tide of lunacy. "Where is Caffetti?" he asked.

Krug stirred from some dark inner speculation and with a deep, rasping gargle spat a gout of phlegm out the window. "Señor Caffetti has gone back to Eldorado." A faint smirk, fleeting and furtive, creased Krug's face, as if he'd guessed Rolfe's intent. "I assure you, Herr Hupfauer, Ricardo could not have helped you."

"Helped me?" For some reason Rolfe found the words ominous.

"To avert this."

"To avert what?"

"We'll need gas soon." Horst proclaimed from up front.

"Never mind the gas," Krug snarled. "I'll inform you when to stop for gas." He turned back to Rolfe most charmingly—all smiles and conciliation. "To avert this unfortunate little side trip, so to speak. You see, your father has recently had some rather disturbing news."

"News?" Rolfe's ears perked. "What sort of news?"

Krug gazed out the window for a while at an immense vista of dry, flat plateau sliding past. "Two things actually." His tongue darted serpentlike across his thick, bluish lips. "The first is news received last evening that the Argentine government has agreed to extradite to Bonn an old friend of your father's and mine—Freddie Rothmann—who is accused of killing some forty thousand people at Mauthausen. We're not yet sure of this. We're awaiting verification from our own sources in Buenos Aires. If this is true"—Krug paused portentously—"it could have the most dire consequences for your father in Paraguay, since Paraguayan internal policy is quite often tied to that of the Argentine. Don't ask me why."

"So," Rolfe mused aloud. "And if Paraguay should follow suit—"

The dwarf made a clucking sound with his tongue. "That would be unfortunate. There are not too many places left in the world where your father is welcome."

"And the second?"

"The second?" Krug appeared puzzled.

"You mentioned *two* items of information."

"Ah, yes, of course. So I did. Well, then, the second and distinctly more ominous bit of news came from Colonel Arganas, who called shortly before dawn this morning to say that the hired assassin reported to have been shot to death in the Paraná River is now believed to be alive. A cache of clothing was just found buried not far from the banks of the river at precisely the point where the ferry incident occurred. A number of professional trackers using bloodhounds have picked up a trail through the forest. Arganas assures me that the situation is well in hand."

"Well in hand?" Rolfe felt more lost than ever.

"By that, I take it, he means they are close to an arrest."

"Then why, in God's name, does my father need me?"

Krug sighed and sat back in the deep leather upholstery. He lit one of his small, black, choking Di Nobili cigars. "I should have thought that would be obvious." Solicitude and impatience mingled in his voice. "Your father is in a state of nervous exhaustion. I've seen him this way before and it is not pleasant. He is, however, a remarkably resilient man, and I am certain that once we get him back up to the garrison of Carlos Antonio Lopez in Zone 540, where it is easier to manage his protection, his composure and good spirits will quickly return."

"Then why are we going to this Puerto Stroessner you speak of?"

"Because it's on the way, and he wants to."

"And then later, can you get him up to this 540 place? Will he go?"

"I'm afraid he has no choice," Krug announced rather woefully. "This morning on the phone Colonel Arganas ordered it. It appears that President Stroessner is outraged by the notoriety caused by the attempt the other night on your father's life. Already it's all about the country, and the embassies and foreign news services are beginning to ask questions. It can be very damaging, not to say embarrassing, to a country's credibility to maintain that you have no knowledge or records of a person's whereabouts within your national boundaries, while foreign agents and *provocateurs* enter with impunity and go directly to that person. Very embarrassing, indeed."

"I see," Rolfe replied, his mind racing forward in leaps and bounds.

Krug inhaled a puff of black smoke, then slowly exhaled it. "So for the time being, your presence here serves as a great moral support to your father. He has asked that you be detained a few days longer, and I wholeheartedly agree." The dwarf placed a hot paternal hand on Rolfe's knee. "After all, you are his son, and despite the"—he paused seeking the specific word—"*unpleasantness* of the past, some things are owed a father."

Sometime shortly after dusk the Buick and the tan Mercedes rolled up to Casa Sereno, the charming little white villa in Puerto Stroessner. Lights were glowing when they arrived and the Krausses, a pair of elderly housekeepers, had drawn baths, taken down beds, and prepared supper. But still Rolfe did not see his father, for immediately upon arrival Doctor Grigori went straight to his room and had supper served there. More anxious than ever to speak with his father and clarify his situation, Rolfe was, nevertheless, still deprived of his company. When he asked Krug when his father might conceivably be expected to give him an audience, the dwarf merely shook his head noncommittally.

"Your father has retired for the evening. He has a very busy day tomorrow, but I shall try to get to him first thing in the morning." Krug spoke in the manner of an office manager to a petitioner for a job.

For the remainder of the evening, Rolfe played backgammon with Matschke and Rudel while Herr Krauss shuffled about obsequiously on a large ungainly prosthetic shoe, serving coffee and brandy. Krug sequestered himself in the library, reading papers and catching up on mail. Periodically he would emerge from the room and, scowling, strut like a peacock about the players, then for no discernible reason, vanish back into the library, slamming the door behind him.

There was very little in the way of talk. Matschke and Rudel sat playing at the backgammon table, speechless and impassive, with pistol holsters strapped ostentatiously to their shoulders. Several times during the course of the evening, Herr Krauss would appear, looking solemn and formal like the officiary in a funeral parlor, and whisper something into Rudel's ear. Expressionless, Rudel would merely nod or rise and follow Krauss out into the hall, where Rolfe could hear them whispering heatedly.

It was all sinister and a little ludicrous.

Shortly before retiring Rolfe felt oppressed and in need of a bit of air. He rose, put on his jacket and started for the door. In the next moment Krug burst from the library. "Where do you think you're going?"

Rolfe stared oddly at the little man. "Just out to stretch my legs."

A series of significant glances were exchanged—Krug to Rudel, Rudel to Matschke, Matschke back to Krug. Without any conversation transpiring, they appeared to come to some mutually satisfactory solution.

"But, of course, Herr Hupfauer," Krug, as official spokesman for the group, remarked. "Ludo will be happy to accompany you."

"That won't be necessary." Rolfe slipped into his jacket. "I prefer to go alone."

Another series of glances ensued. "I'm afraid," Krug persisted, "that you are unaware of the customs of this country. It is unwise for foreigners to walk about here after dark, unprotected. Regretfully, we have our share here of wanton crime—cutpurses, muggers, hooligans, and the like. I have no objection to your having a walk this evening, but I'm afraid I must insist that Ludo go with you. Ludo," he bellowed over his shoulder.

The young man appeared instantly from one of the rooms above, buckling on a shoulder holster. There seemed little more to say. When they came back in a short time, Rolfe noticed that guards had been placed at every door, and several times during the night he awoke to hear voices murmuring below his window as the guard was being rotated.

CHAPTER 46

The following morning Doctor Grigori still had not appeared. Served by Frau Krauss, the others ate their breakfast in silence. It had rained all night and the only sound now was the sound of the large *lapacho* trees dripping dolefully outside the windows.

Horst and Ludo ate enormous quantities of sweet rolls and sausage and eggs, wolfing huge forkfuls of food, then washing it all down with draughts of steaming coffee. Rudel, on the other hand, scarcely ate. He pecked at his food and brooded more than ever. Periodically he would glare at Krug, who sat at the head of the table with a great napkin tucked under his chin, his avid little eyes riveted to the morning financial pages.

At the outer limits of his patience, Rolfe could contain himself no longer. "Will I be permitted to see my father this morning?" He'd addressed the question to Krug, and the note of exasperation in his voice had not gone unnoticed.

The heavy-lidded eyes of the dwarf rose slowly above the top of the financial page until gradually they came level with Rolfe's. "Your father is unwell this morning," he replied brusquely. "He asked me to convey his apologies for being unable to breakfast with you. He hopes he will be able to see you later in the day."

"What is the nature of his illness, may I inquire?" Rolfe said, exasperation mounting by the moment.

"I am afraid I am not at liberty—"

"Not at liberty?" Rolfe thundered across the table. The others at the table jumped, and Frau Krauss gaped through the small window at the kitchen door. "What do you mean, you're not at liberty? What is all this secrecy and mystery? May I remind you, I'm not at liberty either?" Rolfe boomed. His wrath was majestic. Even Krug was impressed. "Will you kindly convey that to my father?" he stormed on. "I'm kept here in my father's house like a prisoner. I'm not at liberty to go out without an armed guard. I'm not at liberty to shave or shower without some trained ape attending me, making certain I won't try to go out the window. What exactly is wrong with my father?" Rolfe smoldered. "Is he ashamed of the manner in which I was brought here? Shanghaied by thugs and brought here against my will. He ought to be ashamed. Is this my reward for coming all this distance to see him? Is he too frightened and ashamed to come down here now and face me?"

"Neither," Doctor Grigori proclaimed from the small balcony above the dining room. Attired in a silk lounging robe and freshly shaved and showered, the Doctor appeared quite fit. In the next moment he had turned sharply on his heel and was descending the stair with a swift and purposeful grace. Reaching the bottom, he strode across the room and planted himself squarely before his son. "I am neither frightened nor ashamed," he said, and glanced significantly at Krug. The dwarf snapped his finger and instantly the others rose and left the room, leaving the Doctor finally to confront his son.

When the doors were closed and they were at last

alone, Rolfe turned instantly to his father. But before
he could utter a word, Grigori held up a hand to silence
him. "I know what you're about to ask, and it is my
intention to send you home to your family as quickly
as possible. Believe me"—the Doctor seemed suddenly
distraught—"this was not the visit I had in mind for
us. I'm appalled at the manner in which you've been
treated here." Grigori rose and, wringing his hands
nervously, he started to pace the room. "I live a very
strange life here, as you can see—reclusive, secretive,
isolated as a leper. But that's the only way I can go on
living. There are people who would kill me in a minute.
My life hangs on a thread. In order to continue dangling, I must suffer the company of scum the likes of
which you see out there." He jerked his head in the
direction of the doors through which his colleagues had
just disappeared. "Several days ago in Bariloche," he
went on wistfully, "I met a young lady of whom I grew
quite fond—until I learned she was a paid operative
here with the express intention of dispatching me. As it
turned out, she died herself. She met a most untimely
end on the Tronador as did another of her colleagues
on the Paraná ferry several days ago. This was a quiet,
inoffensive gentleman who would never have struck you
as a hired assassin."

Limping slightly, Grigori paced, hectic and self-
absorbed. He appeared momentarily to have forgotten
the presence of his son in the room. Instead, he de-
claimed loudly, it seemed, for his own amusement.
Periodically he flung his arms out as if to embrace the
whole room. "There is a certain man following me right
now, at this very moment. I gather Krug has told you
something about him. They tell me this one is very
professional and very dangerous. Well and good. I welcome the challenge. I assure you I will dispose of him
the way I disposed of all the others—in the Paraná."

Grigori turned suddenly and scrutinized his son through the yellowing monocle that made his eye seem very large behind it. "I've detained you here for a few extra days, not as a son with any specific obligations to his father, but as a lawyer with specific duties to his client. In this matter, my dear son, I am your client."

"Father—" Rolfe half-rose, then fell back into his chair at the broad sweep of Doctor Grigori's arm.

"My will has not been reviewed since 1963 when Langbeine came here. I want you to review the old will, revise it wherever necessary, insert several codicils the nature of which I will describe to you in the days to come. In the new will you are to be sole executor with full power of attorney."

"But, Father, you have your solicitors."

"Ach." Grigori flung a hand out in disgust. "I don't trust any of them."

"Surely you trust Langbeine—he's been with the family for years."

"Langbeine is a paid lackey. A vulture like all the rest of them. He has not my interest at heart. I want you to draw my will."

For the first time since his arrival there, Rolfe felt a pang of pity for his father. The man appeared very much alone just then—blustering and frightened. A man around whom the net was slowly closing. The trapped, haggard, desperate look of the quarry all about him.

"This man—" Rolfe began.

"What man?"

"This agent. This assassin."

"I am not in the least concerned about him," Grigori snarled. "I will attend to him in my own way. You think I'm frightened?"

"Not at all, Father. I didn't say that—"

"Just because I want my will reviewed and redrawn.

I want my will redrawn now because I'm of an age where a man attends to such matters. I want my grandchildren and my surviving heirs to be well cared for." Grigori placed his gnarled, calloused hand over Rolfe's. He lowered his voice and spoke in a whisper. "I will not live much longer."

"Father, your doctors assure—"

Grigori flared instantly. "My doctors are idiots. There was blood in my stool again this morning. I have pain on elimination. I'm not able to hold my food. I'm losing weight. I know what Enríquez says, but remember —I am a doctor, too. Even if they have stripped me of my right to practice, I am still a physician. I know what I know."

Rolfe stared helplessly at his father. He knew it was useless to argue with him. Stubborn, irrational, sensing doom, he was a man to whom the *idée fixe* of imminent death attached itself like a leech. Whichever way he flailed or tossed, he could not rid himself of it. Quietly, he had capitulated and was now going about the orderly, mundane business of preparing for the event.

"I'm so sorry it worked out this way," Grigori went on sorrowfully. "I had such lovely plans for your visit."

"That's all right, Father."

"You'll draw up the will then?"

"Yes, of course."

"And the moment it's done, I'll see that you're driven to Asunción and put on the plane. It's only a matter of a day or two and you'll be out of here."

"Yes, of course, Father." Rolfe paused, then added, "I have one stipulation of my own, however."

Grigori cocked an eye warily at his son. "Stipulation?"

"If I draw up this will, as you ask"—Rolfe stared back at his father—"under no circumstances am I to be your heir."

CHAPTER 47

It was a lovely night in Puerto Stroessner, one of those languid tropical nights, the air redolent of jasmine and the sky strewn with stars. A group of men standing around the streetlamp before the Casa Sereno laughed and chatted in lowered voices, their figures casting large wavery shadows on the pavement.

It was past midnight, and Doctor Grigori and some friends had just come from a night on the town. Krug and Rudel were among the group of a half-dozen or so. Rolfe had chosen to remain home. Now, in this fashionable little suburb, they were saying their good nights before dispersing. Two automobiles—an American Lincoln Continental and the tan Mercedes 450—their headlights on, their motors idling, waited for them to break up.

A match flared. Someone laughed, and a head stooped toward the sudden ignition of light. Their voices, gruff and slurred, full of the harsh sibilants of foreigners speaking Spanish, carried on the swooning night breeze. Shortly, a side door just off the villa's verandah opened, and Herr Krauss emerged. He limped on his prosthetic shoe across the garden, and in the next moment he slipped behind the wheel of the Mercedes and drove it around to the renovated stable that served as a garage at the rear of the house.

Doctor Grigori and his retinue continued to chat lightheartedly in Spanish for several moments in the open driveway beneath the streetlamp, a clear sign that they anticipated no trouble. Colonel Arganas had assigned extra patrols around the house, and Grigori, always vigilant and distrustful, had increased his own personal staff of *Wachenhunde*.

Moments later Krauss had entered the house through a rear door, and the others, with a burst of raucous laughter, got into the waiting Lincoln and drove off. Krug and Rudel waited while the Doctor stood there a moment, puffing the last of his Egyptian cigarette and musing quietly. With the disappearance of his friends and with the night at an end, once more he was plunged in gloom.

Horst and Ludo emerged from the shadows and walked him quietly around to a side door, where at last he disappeared.

When the doors were all locked and the Doctor's private bodyguards had all disappeared into different parts of the villa, the street before the Casa Sereno was at last deserted. The other villas along the quiet, lime-shaded walks were all shrouded in darkness and seemingly untenanted. Several cars stood parked along the winding curbs. One of these was a late-model Chevrolet Impala with the license plates of a rented vehicle. It was parked diagonally across the way from the Casa Sereno. Within it, Ian Asher, still attired in the garb of a simple cleric, sat waiting behind the wheel. Although he was some three hundred feet from the villa, through the branches he could nevertheless see the soft orange lights flickering at its windows. He had been sitting there for several hours, moving only to lie on the floor beneath the wheel when the police patrols browsed through at regular intervals. He did not expect them to appear again for another twenty minutes. He sat perfectly still now, the long-barreled Beretta automatic strapped under his armpit and a bright new Uzi submachine gun in his lap. From time to time he thought of Dovia—imagined she was there beside him in the Negev, or was it Birkenau—the two of them standing upright and unflinching before the *Selektor,* the harsh, grim, metronomic chant of his voice exploding all about them. *"Links. Recht. Links. Recht. Links. Links. Links."*

When finally the last light in the villa had gone off and the house appeared to have retired for the night, Asher emerged from the car, leaving the motor running, for he fully intended to be back in just under four minutes.

Leaving the side door slightly ajar, so as to avoid the noise of closing it, Asher moved stealthily down a wooded path that wound around the side and into the rear of the Casa Sereno. When he reached the heavily shrubbed border of the garden, he could hear some of the guards chatting and laughing at their various posts about the house.

Asher huddled momentarily in the shadows, getting a fix on each—not only their location, but their degree of absorption in the job. Almost instantly, with a kind of feral cunning, he had chosen the most vulnerable spot and was at once slipping noiselessly across the open space and lighting, moments later, in the thick shadows against the wall of the house.

He crouched now beneath a rear window leading apparently to a pantry and silently slipped a glass cutter and a roll of adhesive tape from under the cleric's garb. He rose to examine the window but found it unlatched.

In the next instant, he had raised the window and swung himself pantherlike over the low sill, disappearing into the darkness of the house. He stood there for a moment in the darkness of the kitchen with the warmish vapors of the night's cooking still hovering above the place. It was on a white tile floor that he was standing, in a pantry of sorts, full of the shadowy outline of pots and pans depending from the walls. The place had a scrubbed, immaculate look.

A sudden explosion of lights momentarily blinded him. He whirled to face a startled guard standing in the doorway in his stockings and underwear, a pistol strapped across his shoulder. For a moment the guard stood there gaping at him, a look of amused astonishment on his stolid, brutal face. He had come down there, no doubt, for nothing more compelling than a drink of water. Now, however, he was peering down the barrel of Asher's submachine gun, and he made the fatal error of reaching for his pistol.

In the next moment, a blast of gunfire shattered the silence. It boomed off the cold white tiles of the kitchen. Looking stunned, like an ox surprised by predators at a waterhole, the guard reeled backward through a swinging door, still clutching his unfired pistol. It was as if the man had been picked up and tossed through space by some immense, supernatural force. The entire right side of his head had been torn away by a bullet.

Asher dashed across the living room in the direction of the stairway. A second guard, this time Horst Matschke, jerked open the door of a downstairs bedroom, saw the running figure, and slammed the door shut again. Asher sprayed a withering round of fire directly into the door, splintering it lengthwise. Moments after, a low agonized moan issued from somewhere behind it. Asher continued next into the hallway. The instant he appeared there he was met by a hail of fire from an unseen source at the top of the stairs. He heard shouting and the thudding of footsteps above, followed by a woman's scream, presumably Frau Krauss'—a prolonged and terrifying wail issuing from one of the upstairs rooms. Darting under cover of the stairway, Asher spurted a blast of fire straight up through a sharply angled wooden overhang at the invisible gunman crouched somewhere above.

It had only been a matter of seconds since Asher had entered the house, but already Doctor Grigori was nowhere to be seen. Asher instantly resolved to rush the stairs with guns blazing. Suddenly windows were shattering all about him, shards of glass showering inward from blasts of automatic gunfire coming from three directions outside the house. Despite meticulous surveillance and planning, there were undoubtedly a number of additional guards he had not even known about. The only comfort he had was in the knowledge that those outside had no way of knowing the number and size of the force carrying on the action inside.

Suddenly the sound of firing in the hallway stopped and a body came thumping down the stairs. It was Krug, looking outlandish in a nightshirt and clutching a Luger. He descended the steps on his back, bouncing gaily like a child's ball. An eerie quiet suddenly enveloped the rooms above, and the way to the second floor now seemed clear.

Hoping that his quarry was still above, Asher lunged through the hall and bounded up the stairs, taking them two at a time, shouting the word "Grigori" over and over again at the top of his lungs until that hoarse repetition conveyed the curious sense of a bell tolling. Shouting all the way, he darted from one room to the next, opening closet doors, looking under beds, ransacking through the attic storeroom. At one point he kicked open a door and found the Krausses cowering behind it, in their nightdress, clasping each other. He slammed the door shut and moved on, this time to the large sumptuous master bedroom. The huge king-sized bed had been taken down and a blue pastel Egyptian cigarette still burned in an ashtray on the night table beside it, but of Doctor Grigori there was no sign. He was gone, vanished, having fled undoubtedly through the open window at the end of the hallway where a gauzy voile curtain drifted languidly sideways in the cool evening breeze.

Plunging back down the stairs, Asher muttered furiously to himself. Gunfire still showered the house from outside. The sound of someone leaning frantically on an automobile horn blared up from the street below. Asher burst back into the kitchen, skipping over the riddled corpse he'd left there, blood seeping in little pools from its shattered skull. The Uzi submachine gun still blasting, Asher burst through the front door onto the verandah and sprinted through a hail of bullets to the Impala across the way.

Just as he reached for the door handle, a burst of submachine-gun fire scorched the air overhead, shattering the front windows of the villa opposite the Casa Sereno. In a moment the Impala was careening off down the street, its doors still open and swinging madly.

Lights began to go on in other villas along the sleeping street, and as the Impala tore through the night in the direction of Asunción, Asher heard the roar of a motorcycle behind him and the grumble of other cars starting up. Scattered fire continued for a few seconds more. Then, in the distance, he heard the wail of a police siren.

Part VI

RETRIBUTION

CHAPTER 48

It was a beautiful morning for flying, and Colonel Arganas found the prospect of the three-hour flight up into the Chagras distinctly pleasurable. They were going up to investigate reports of a tribe of poachers slipping over the Bolivian border into Paraguay and carrying off a fortune in jaguar pelts.

The day was bright and clear, winds moderate, visibility excellent, with long feathery sprays of cirrus clouds hanging motionless at altitudes of nineteen and twenty thousand feet.

Arganas stood at the runway, legs spread, arms crossed, trousers whipping backward from the gusty prop drafts. It was a cocky, rather proprietorial pose he struck there that morning as he watched a half-dozen mechanics and hangar attendants swarm all over the bright little Beechcraft Twin plane as they serviced and gassed her up. Engines humming, props pinging, her wings trembling with perky anticipation, she made a pretty picture there, Colonel Arganas thought, like a small, highly spirited puppy straining on its leash. The Colonel's small, furtive eyes darted here and there, observing with some satisfaction the special attention the runway crew afforded his prize pet.

It was a prize, too, for an itinerant cobbler's son who'd overcome the barrios of Asunción as well as the deeply entrenched prejudices of the Paraguayan Army officers corps—an elitist cadre, comprised almost exclusively of the feckless sons of Paraguayan aristocrats, dead-set against the advancement of the lower classes to commissioned rank. Despite the almost insurmountable obstacles, Arganas had advanced to the lofty rank of Colonel at an impressively early age—advanced to the point where his aristocratic colleagues, who had formerly either patronized or ignored him, had now come to fear him, for it was no secret that shortly he was to be breveted to brigadier. He had that promised him direct from *El Jefe,* with whom he enjoyed a most favored relationship. Yes, the plane was his and he was very proud of her.

It was right, therefore, that this crew of runway attendants should stroke and pamper his prize, cosset it and see to its every need. After all, was she not the special property of Colonel Arganas, Chief of the Police for Internal Security, and as such did she not deserve the extra-special treatment afforded to a favorite of *El Jefe?*

The Colonel stood now just behind the runway chief, peering down over his shoulder while they ran down the itemized list on the chief's clipboard. Smiling, the chief, somewhat awed by the importance of his client, pronounced the plane sound and ready to fly.

El Negrón too was particularly jolly that morning. He had done well at the casino the night before, and the thought of a small aeronautical jaunt up to the Chagras with the Colonel was always pleasurable. Ever so much more desirable than the rather tedious chores of the "collector."

At last the coils of gas line were retracted from the Beechcraft Twin's fuel tanks, and the plane, humming and purring, was wheeled out onto the runway and into the takeoff position. Shortly Arganas and *El Negrón* boarded and the glass fuselage was clamped down above them. In the next moment, Arganas was on the radio with the tower, checking his route and awaiting takeoff instructions and clearance.

Vibrating at the runway's edge, the Beechcraft Twin could scarcely contain herself. In the next moment, the clearances came, and Arganas, with that ineffable surge of excitement he invariably felt at the moment of flight—a kind of emancipation from earth, a shedding of "this mortal coil," a merging with angels—throttled forward.

Instantly the plane bounded ahead and proceeded to barrel down the runway at speeds of up to 250 knots. Coolly observing the low line of coconut palms racing at him from the runway's end, Arganas eased up on the stick and felt the plane lift off and start her climb. Just above the tips of the palms, where he could see the white, scorched skyline of Asunción and, beyond that, the dirty gray, unfurling ribbon he knew to be the Rio Paraguay, he glanced back and smiled into the radiant adoring face of *El Negrón,* glistening with sweat and transfixed into a kind of joy. It was at that moment that his life ended, or rather *their* lives ended—*El Negrón*'s, too—for the plane disintegrated above a plantain swamp, its various parts showering, drifting downward, rather as if it were caught within a camera's slow motion—wings, engine, housing, props, rudders, pipes, tanks, all blown to smithereens. Of the occupants of the plane there was no sign. They had simply been erased.

On the ground, the bemused tower dispatcher monitoring Arganas' ascent noted that the small white dot designating the Beechcraft Twin had simply vanished off the radar screen. One moment it was there, the next moment it was gone.

There was a great deal of confusion within the small terminal building. The moment they'd heard the explosion, people had come streaming out onto the runway tarmac. Several claimed they had seen a ball of fire in

the sky before they'd heard anything. A sudden, sound-
less illumination, as someone described it, rather pretty
to see, like a silent fireworks. And then the awful rum-
ble, like tenpins bowled over.

Suddenly there were sirens wailing and rescue crews
and fire trucks with ground crews swarming all over
them, racing out to the burning site.

The runway crew that had checked the plane was
among the first to go, piling into an old U.S. Army half-
track and already speeding to the spot glowing luridly
in the palm forest with great sparks crackling audibly
and flying upward into the burned, broken trees above
it. All of them, that is, except one crew member. Dressed
in the neatly pressed gray fatigues of an airlines mainte-
nance man, Ian Asher strolled unnoticed through the
small terminal, which had been virtually emptied of
passengers and desk personnel, all of whom had
streamed out onto the tarmac to witness this gaudy
disaster.

CHAPTER **49**

News of Colonel Arganas' death reached Zone 540
nearly a week after the incident. It came in the form of
a hand-delivered message sent by Caffetti in Eldorado.
It was delivered by a diminutive Indian with furtive eyes
who was anxious to go.

Doctor Grigori was taking breakfast beneath a striped
umbrella on the small stone patio just off his back yard.
He accepted the message, eyeing it warily as if it were
wired, or as if it were some child's prank that might

possibly sluice a stream of water into his eye. He fixed his monocle and read the message, moving his lips as he did so. He read slowly, forming each word with his mouth while his eyes grew very dark and still. The hand holding the small, yellow fragment of paper trembled slightly.

Esmeralda was there at the time. She refilled his coffee, noting, as she did, the darkening of his features—the way a cloud passes suddenly over the sun. When he finished reading, he sat there for a long moment, stony and immobile. All the color had drained from his face. She did not know what the message contained, but she sensed somehow that its contents were dire. In the next moment he crumpled the message in his fist and dropped it onto the table amid the soiled dishes. Then he pushed his chair from the table, nearly upsetting it, rose, turned, and walked stiffly back into the shed.

The Indian who'd brought the message shuffled uneasily, awaiting permission to withdraw. Esmeralda dismissed the fellow with a few *guaranís,* then gazing quickly around, snatched the small wadded ball of paper from the table, smoothed it out, and proceeded to read.

Characteristically Caffetti, the message was the very essence of the man—succinct and to the point: "ARGANAS DEAD. CIRCUMSTANCES INVESTIGATION UNDER WAY. CAUTION ADVISED. R.C."

Esmeralda took the message in to Rolfe.

It had been eight days that Rolfe Hupfauer had been up there. He had arrived with his father on that terrifying night, having come nearly fifteen miles through the jungle on foot. Rudel and Von Rattenhuber were with them. Filthy, muddy, scratched, close to exhaustion, they straggled up to the door in the early hours of the morning. Esmeralda understood at once from the excitement and their awful exhaustion that something bad had happened. She soon learned that Matschke and Krug were dead.

When they put the Doctor to bed that night, he was in a state of nervous collapse. He wept like a child and twitched and shivered under heavy blankets, although the temperature was hovering in the neighborhood of one hundred degrees. He went on a great deal in a garbled, fitful way about Günzburg and Freiburg, about *Grossvater* and something about "Tzigane," which he cried out several times. The drumming of some large flying insect at his window caused him to cringe beneath his blanket and scream terrifyingly that intruders were hovering outside his room.

Esmeralda whipped up a potent brew of brandy, hot milk, and Quaaludes. Shortly the spasms and twitching subsided, the babbling grew less, and he became drowsy.

But, true to form and as resilient as ever, Grigori was on his feet again in several days. Still shaking, but up taking thin gruels for nourishment and going about his business. He even started to play his records again— his beloved Strauss, Verdi, and Wagner. He took up his violin with a kind of wild, obsessed vigor.

Rudel left, promising to return within a fortnight, but privately, the ex-Luftwaffe ace had his doubts. For some time now he had been undergoing a growing dissatisfaction with his work. For whatever remuneration Grigori provided, regardless how handsome, it was not worth dragging about the country with him, a sitting target for every lunatic with a grudge. Loyalty, friendship, patriotism be damned, by this time Rudel had had a bellyful of the Doctor.

It might have been, too, the fact that this latest incident at the Casa Sereno had infuriated *El Jefe*, who had cautioned against Grigori's trip out of 540 but reluctantly yielded to it with the single caveat that it be *"chito."* Now the papers were full of the assassination attempt at Puerto Stroessner. The news services were burning up the wires with it. Embassies and international police organizations were already bombarding the Paraguayan government with inquiries regarding Doctor Grigori's whereabouts. This was a huge embarrassment, and *El Jefe* would not brook embarrassment. He was not a man to quickly forgive and forget. And so Rudel no doubt reasoned that it would be wise, not to say politic, that he disassociate himself from an increasingly unpopular cause.

When Esmeralda handed Rolfe the little yellow wadded ball of paper that morning, he was slow to react. Possibly he did not grasp the implications. Having read it, he put it aside and stared blankly ahead. He had been in 540 only slightly over one week, and already he had gone badly to seed. He hadn't shaved. His linen was soiled and his suit badly rumpled. The fabric, too, one of heavy, coarse wool, was totally wrong for the intense tropical heat. Nevertheless, he sat in it, smoldering in temperatures above one hundred degrees, tormented in his stolid, uncomplaining way by the myriad insects swarming all about him. The shriek of toucans, macaws, and squirrel monkeys tumbling in the dense green canopy overhead drove him to distraction. He could not bathe, he could not sleep, and he would not eat Esmeralda's food, which he thought of as barbaric. Consequently, he had grown listless and despondent. In two weeks' time he'd lost a good deal of weight, and he sat now morose, dirty, unshaven, his hair unkempt, his clothing disheveled, a bedraggled untidy sight, and certainly no longer recognizable as the same man who'd arrived in Paraguay, spruce and chipper, nearly two weeks before.

He had by now finished redrafting his father's will. But during most of that week Grigori had been in no condition to review the papers. Several times, however, as the Doctor's spirits lifted, he turned his attention to the will and each time found in the language something wanting or imprecise.

At first Rolfe tried to satisfy each criticism, but now he had come to take a very jaundiced view of them, seeing there the perfect device for detaining him indefinitely.

He did not trust his father one inch. He knew the man to be capable of any deception, any ruse to gain his ends. While being very little in the way of real physical protection, Rolfe was an enormous psychological comfort. His presence there amid a house of strangers, encircled by paid "friends" and an inept band of mercenaries, was Doctor Grigori's last anchor to reality.

So, for a time, Doctor Grigori appeared to recover, but news of Arganas' untimely demise set him drastically back. He issued one order to reinforce the barbed-wire fence and another to add additional searchlights to illuminate the compound at night. Then he took to his room with a vengeance. He refused to see anyone. Only Esmeralda was vouchsafed entry, coming and going with trays of food that remained untouched and decanters of cognac that were invariably drained.

Several times Rolfe tried to see his father—that is, to physically force entry to his room. All formal requests to see him had been summarily denied. Rolfe was now even forbidden to write or communicate in any way with his family. "A safety measure," Von Rattenhuber, smiling like a lean, hungry dog, assured him, while blocking passage to the Doctor's room.

In all that time, Grigori made no attempt to see his son. Instead, a large, impenetrable silence had begun to gather about him, until Rolfe commenced to doubt that his father was still there behind the door, or even anywhere within the shed. Several times he listened at the library door but heard no sound. Even though Esmeralda continued to go in and out with trays, Rolfe suspected this of being part of some elaborate ruse to create the illusion of Grigori's being there, while, in reality, he had no doubt retreated miles, possibly even oceans, away.

Rolfe could now see quite clearly, for all the hospitality of the house, that he was like a prisoner in a jail. He could not leave the compound unless in the presence of a *cuchillero,* who would let him in and out with an enormous set of padlock keys. It occurred to him that if he were kept there much longer against his will, he might try to escape. Then it occurred to him what a foolhardy thing that would be, for, assuming he did get outside the compound wire, presumably at night, where would he go? He had not the slightest notion of the way through the forest to the nearest village—Eldorado, about 120 kilometers away. If Grigori's dogs did not get him, surely the snakes or the swamp would. No— for Rolfe to set out through the forest by himself would be suicide.

One afternoon Ludo took him walking deep behind the compound. They had been walking nearly an hour and dusk was coming on when they broke out into a small clearing in the forest. It was unexpected and curiously incongruous—that sudden open space, that splash of sky in the midst of such cramped and profligate foliage. Like a raw scar, the ground sprawled there, as if it had been bulldozed.

The clearing was circular, about one hundred yards in diameter, and dotted with a multitude of narrow elliptical gashes in the earth. Above each gash had been piled a shallow mound. Some of these mounds appeared freshly dug. A disagreeable smell, as of bad drainage, hovered all about the place.

"What the devil is this?" Rolfe demanded.

"It's nothing. Come—let's go."

Ludo tried to steer him away, back into the forest, in the direction from which they had come, but Rolfe stood there rooted to the spot.

"What do you mean, nothing?" Rolfe's tone was querulous. "Obviously, it's something. It's been put here. Man-made. What's its purpose?"

"We dump trash here and bury it."

"Bury it? What on earth for?"

"If you don't, it draws rodents."

"Oh," Rolfe murmured thoughtfully. "I see."

"Come." Ludo tugged him. "Let's get back. It's growing dark."

Pacified, but still troubled with a nagging sense of unease, Rolfe permitted himself to be led off. Once away from the place he did not think of the clearing again.

CHAPTER **50**

Rolfe lay about all the next day in his room. He thought about his wife and family thousands of miles away. He wondered if Hedi suspected anything, what alarm she might be feeling, and what they might have told her to prevent her from going to the authorities. For instance, had they threatened her in any way? His father's reach, even in exile, he knew was still very long. That his father was mad he did not doubt. Dangerously, certifiably insane. And the more that realization grew, the more he questioned the possibility that his father would ever release him. His father, he now understood, had no intention of releasing him. Never had, in fact, but had brought him there to carry out some function, some role as of yet cryptic and undefined.

Frustration had turned to anger, and anger would shortly turn to panic, for Rolfe Hupfauer had good reason to suspect that he would never see his family again.

In Doctor Grigori's absence, Von Rattenhuber had assumed the management of the household. Administration was not Ludo's forte, and soon his stewardship became autocratic. Irrationally so. He imposed all sorts of rules and regulations, most of them mysterious as to design and worthless as to function. And all in the name of precaution against potential assassins. Greatly enjoying the imposition of rules, he insisted that meals be served at impossible hours for "efficiency" purposes. Hence, everyone in the house was to be up by five AM for breakfast, while dinner was to be served punctually at four PM. It was over by five, and then the long relentless jungle evening of heat and insects would spread out before them like some vast, arid waste that had, somehow, each night, to be crossed.

It was inevitable that Rolfe and Ludo should clash. With Grigori gone, his young companion did not hesitate to order Rolfe about and to dismiss brusquely any inquiries the son made regarding his father.

"Where is my father?" Rolfe demanded one evening.

"I'm sure I don't know."

"Do you know if he has yet read my new draft of his will?"

"I couldn't say."

Rolfe ground his teeth. "When will I be permitted to leave here?"

Von Rattenhuber shrugged and shook his head. "I'm afraid I couldn't say."

"Well, exactly what the hell could you say?" Rolfe bellowed, and they glowered at each other, poised like a pair of fighting cocks over a narrow space. It was then that Rolfe, exasperated to the point of tears, sprang toward the library door, only to find that Ludo had in one bound reached there before him, barring the way. A brief scuffle ensued. Rolfe made to raise his fist and, in a flash, received a crack on the jaw that spun his head about. It was at that point that Rolfe finally grasped the gravity of his situation.

Esmeralda lit candles each night and said her rosary. Never very communicative, she went about now muttering to herself. Hearing the low, rather plaintive cooing of some bird at night, she invariably read it as an evil augury and crossed herself. To Esmeralda everything was an evil augury. She still, however, came and went freely into the Doctor's library with her trays, muttering each time she emerged with the food untouched.

Once Rolfe accosted her there. "Is my father in there now?" he asked.

Her huge, frightened eyes evaded his, and she tried to move past him.

"Is my father in there, I say?" he fairly shouted.

She cringed against the wall, shaking her head back and forth, too frightened to speak. He was about to shake or throttle her, but Von Rattenhuber came and separated them, sending her packing into the kitchen. That's when Rolfe knew that his father was miles away from there—further back, deep in the bush, no doubt beyond Pirapo and the Japanese lumbermen laboring in the big mahogany forests up to the north.

Could it be, Rolfe reasoned, that he had been left there, intentionally unenlightened, uninformed, to serve as some kind of decoy perhaps, to confound any possible assailant who had tracked his father there. Was his father capable even of that? Why not? He was capable of so much else.

One night Rolfe lay in bed, sweltering in his sheets, while the big searchlights on the beacons around the compound glared into his room and the dogs bayed and the *cuchilleros* tramped up and down the gravel walks outside the house. Suddenly he heard the high whine of a truck turning laboriously around, then lumbering down the dirt road outside the compound wire. Next he heard voices moving toward the shed. One sounded like that of his father. Moments later he heard footsteps outside tramping in.

Instantly, he was up, out of bed, and crossing the room in great bounding strides. With a wild, almost desperate motion, he flung open the door and found himself standing face to face with his father.

For a brief time they regarded each other like strangers passing on a crowded thoroughfare—each struck by some resemblance, however fleeting, to a half-forgotten figure out of the shadowy distant past.

The man Rolfe saw there, trim, brisk, dressed in a bush jacket and chukka boots, was his father. There was not the slightest doubt of that. But he appeared nearly twenty years younger. At least that was the impression on first glance. His face, which had been scored by the normal complement of wrinkles and creases characteristic of men in the full flower of their seventh decade—that face had undergone a transformation as marvelous in some ways as it was grotesque. As if by sorcery the wrinkles had been erased, the creases and patches ironed out, and the skin suffused with a kind of boyish pink where the flesh was raw, as if bandages had been recently removed. The cheeks, which Rolfe recalled had begun to slip and sag into jowls, had been pinned up or glued back, forcing the pleat of flesh beneath his chin to strain backward. The eye that had always squinted, the eye that had so frightened and amazed Rolfe as a child, the eye that had needed a monocle to prop it open—that eye now stood open by itself, staring with beady fixity directly at him. What held it open Rolfe could not say, only that it now appeared several times larger than the other eye, which even heightened the impression of a face that was asymmetrical and grotesquely out of kilter.

The mouth had undergone a startling alteration. The lips, parted and protrusive, had been puckered into an unnatural position in which the teeth, constantly visible, were fixed into a leer. And when the mouth attempted speech, its parts were stiff and did not move properly in concert.

The triangular gap that had always been visible between the incisors had been closed by some kind of acrylic plug, and atop all this was a great lurid shock of dyed red hair. It was both laughable and hideous. The face, even the head, had been carpentered into something meant to simulate youth and vigor. Gaiety had been hammered into it, but it was the gaiety of a jack-o'-lantern grin on a rotting pumpkin, with its carved features already beginning to slip and slide, to crumble inward unto itself, collapsing down into the soft, putrescent flesh. The whole thing stank of perdition and corruption.

Suddenly the puckered mouth with the leering dental plate opened, and with a shudder of horror, Rolfe realized that his father had spoken something to him and now stood there smiling, with a curious air of expectation. He was awaiting a compliment.

Two men had come in with Doctor Grigori and hovered there like pillars, stolid and immobile on either side of him. Rolfe had never seen either of them before. Both were middle-aged and fleshy, brawny with the swollen paunches of insatiable beer drinkers. One had a short furze of blond hair and a thick pockmarked neck. Small dark eyes peered out of a coarse, fleshy face, like chips of coal embedded in raw dough.

The other was pink and epicene. A kind of dazed, undirected smile suffused his features, as if he were laughing inwardly at some private and immensely satisfying joke. There was something of the halfwit about him, made terrifying by the notion of brutal power coupled with mindless, irresponsible behavior.

Both of these men were looking at Rolfe, quizzically, almost defiantly. They appeared to be demanding that he justify his presence there. The pinkish one smirked, while the bull-necked, dough-faced fellow seemed to glower. He shifted on his feet, causing his jacket to fall open, thus revealing the butt end of a revolver. Then it occurred to Rolfe that these two men had come as replacements for manpower losses recently incurred by Grigori at Casa Sereno. Two new *Wachenhunde* for the Doctor. Hardly the sleek, lithe things that had been Horst and Ludo. They, at least, for all their lethality, had a kind of coltish grace and were not without traces of humor. These two new fellows were totally without any such redeeming graces. They were hardened professionals. Older and tougher. Mercenaries used to pledging their allegiance to any camp that paid the price of their ticket. The scum of the earth. God knows, Rolfe wondered, out of what sewer his father had plucked them.

Once again the stiff, puckered hole in the center of Grigori's face moved. Sounds issued from it, breathy, garbled, and not immediately comprehensible. But Rolfe gathered that they were words that framed greetings and pleasant observations of the day. Yet even as the words came, cheerful and breezy, the eyes that fixed him belied all that. They were dark and haunted, judgmental and oddly frightened. They searched his face for some telling reaction.

"So? What do you think?" the apparition asked.

Rolfe no longer thought of the person before him as his father. A separation, subtle but swift as the severing of cords, had taken place within him.

"Come, Rolfie." Grigori laughed. "The truth, boy. I can't wait to hear what you think."

The imposition of the new dental plate had altered his voice. It was higher now and slightly strangled, as if it came from the back of his throat, like the voice of a ventriloquist's dummy.

"I—I don't know," Rolfe stammered. The face was smiling disconcertingly at him. It was a proud, anticipatory smile, as if he were expecting wonder and delight at the sight of this magical transformation. Grigori doubtless believed in the miracle himself. The old snake had shed its skin and stood there now, all bright and shiny, born anew. He was delighted with his new self.

Rolfe's brain whirled, searching desperately for words to fill the gap. "It will take getting used to" was all he could manage. He swung between terror and pity, then recalled his own situation. "Father—" he blurted out, but Grigori, anticipating the question, hushed him before he could continue.

"Yes—yes. You will be able to leave very soon. The will seems fine. I have made all my arrangements now."

Ludo came in just then and hovered, arms folded, in the doorway, scrutinizing the situation. Grigori laughed and nodded toward his two new acquisitions. "Ah, Ludo," he cried. "Just in time. I was about to introduce Klaus and Putzi." He plunged ahead with desperate gaiety while the air all about them froze deeper into antagonism. "It will be so nice for us all. Klaus enjoys fishing. Perhaps we can take him upriver tomorrow and test him on dorado." One of those ghastly, strangled laughs issued from the twisted hole in the center of the Doctor's face. "Well, what do you think of me?" Grigori now pressed Ludo. "Am I not something to turn the ladies' heads?" He peacocked around the room, showing off his new face like a mannequin in a fashion salon.

CHAPTER **51**

The days that followed were a nightmare. Grigori was more solicitous of his son than ever, and just as secretive as to his plans for the future. Still, he would not permit Rolfe to go. Nor could he name a time in the foreseeable future when he would. All he would say, most cordially and sympathetically, was that eventually, yes, of course, Rolfe would be permitted to go.

Grigori would take Rolfe fishing on the Paraná, which, of course, he loathed, then made him play chess until all hours of the night and talked endlessly of his childhood in Bavaria. He read aloud to him from Goethe and Heine, and then one night, with the most elaborate ceremony, read to him from his monograph, twenty years in preparation, on the "Morphological Differences of the Jaw in Four Distinct Racial Types."

"This is my *magnum opus,*" he boasted, halfway through a decanter of cognac. "It will explode all of the pretty little bubbles—all of these naive, sophomoric ideas we currently subscribe to about race, the genetic transmission of racial information from one generation to the next. This will alter our whole conception of the evolutionary process. It will cast light on the most shadowy regions—"

Grigori grew more flushed and diffuse as he became more prophetic and grandiloquent. "This will be the crowning achievement of my life. It will be clear once and for all what I have been struggling to achieve. It will justify everything . . . everything . . ." His voice trailed off on that final word with a kind of choking sound. He fumbled for his brandy snifter, knocking it over and spilling its contents out onto the notepad with its cramped scribblings. He watched impassively the thick syrupy liquid flow freely over his "crowning achievement" of the past twenty years. He didn't even bother to blot it up.

Day followed day. A succession of torpid, uneventful hours spent in stultifying boredom and suffocating heat. It was inevitable that Von Rattenhuber should come to hate Klaus and Putzi, for it was obvious that they had supplanted him in order of importance within the Doctor's charmed circle.

Esmeralda resented Klaus and Putzi, too, but for different reasons. As a servant, a menial, and a black, they treated her with disdain. For her they had nothing but harsh words and gruff orders. She was not accustomed to being treated that way. The Doctor never treated her that way, nor had he ever permitted anyone to treat her that way. Nowadays, however, the Doctor was not himself.

Esmeralda thought of the Doctor's new companions as boorish. Their manners at the dinner table were execrable. The Doctor had dispensed with the rule of correct attire for dinner, and so Klaus and Putzi ate in their shirtsleeves with gun holsters strapped ostentatiously around their barrel chests. They ate like pigs at a trough, gorging themselves, guzzling copious amounts of beer and punctuating swallows with thunderous belches. When they finished, the table in the area of their plates and the floor beneath their chairs was littered with spilled food.

Rolfe was made physically ill at the spectacle of their eating. After a while, Ludo, smoldering with resentment, simply refused to come to the table. Even, it seemed, the Doctor found the sight of these two creatures at his table odious. Still, he insisted on at least a pretense of decorum at his table and tried to carry on a bit of civilized conversation during dinner. He would go on at great length about Björling's "stunning" "Nessun Dorma" and go into transports of ecstasy recalling the unforgettable night in Munich when he saw Flagstad give "the performance of her life" in *Siegfried*.

Putzi belched volubly and hoisted a joint of lamb to his grease-glistened mouth.

The next morning they woke and Von Rattenhuber was gone. His bedroom was stripped and his suitcase missing. The four-wheel drive overlander in the garage was also missing. In addition, nearly four hundred dollars in *guaranís* and *Deutschemarks* were taken from the household funds. Ludo left no note or forwarding address behind.

The Doctor spent a great deal of time with his new companions, showing them about and familiarizing them with the routine of the place. At night they would all drink a good deal, grow loud and boisterous and shout obscenities at the *cuchilleros* haunting the night outside the wire fences.

Sometimes during these drunken revels Grigori would play his violin. One night, dressed only in his tatty terry cloth robe, he played drunkenly for several uninterrupted hours while the *zwei Wachenhunde*, torpid and bloated from an excess of Kulmbacher beer, danced and reeled around the room like performing bears.

Late one afternoon Rolfe sat with his father in the garden. They sat opposite each other stiffly, awkwardly, saying little. A great gulf yawned between them—a gulf of thoughts unarticulated and reproaches poised dangerously on the tip of the tongue. The light at that particular moment had a lurid, violent quality—greenish and pewter with an imminence of rain. Great dark schooners of clouds scudded still and low above the compound. The air was so close and heavy that it bore down upon them with palpable weight.

Rolfe stared oddly at his father, or rather the frail vestige of the man he knew to be his father. Grigori had been drinking quite heavily that afternoon. He was reading the *Deutschen Soldaten* and his glasses had slipped down onto the tip of his nose. For a moment he appeared very old and fragile. Recalling the heroic image of his father being cheered at the Café Bavaria, Rolfe felt a twinge of pity.

At a certain point Rolfe became aware that his father was not reading, but only pretending to. Deliberately evading the accusatory gaze of his son.

"Father," Rolfe said. He whispered the way one might speak to a person just emerging from the ether of surgery.

Grigori did not stir.

"Father," he said again, this time louder and more insistent.

Grigori looked up and smiled, or rather, the mask moved ponderously into the shape of a smile.

"Father, I must leave here." Again Rolfe whispered, and even he was perplexed at why he felt constrained to whisper. "I shall become sick if I don't leave here."

Grigori said nothing but merely sat there smiling into the shadows, with a kind of blank, idiot radiance.

"If you continue to hold me here, Hedi will grow alarmed. She'll go to the police. To the Embassy. There'll be inquiries. They'll make a search. They'll come here. You don't want that, do you?"

Something like a frown passed momentarily over the Doctor's features. He shook his head as if in reply, not to Rolfe but to some dialogue he carried on within himself. He reached for his cognac decanter and with tremulous hands splashed a goodly quantity into a large stein out of which he drank almost continuously. Then his leaky red eyes returned almost gratefully to the pages of the *Deutschen Soldaten*.

A white gash of lightning splintered the torpid air, followed by a low growl of thunder rumbling across the Paraná from Brazil.

"Father." Rolfe started again. In place of the numbing terror he had been feeling for weeks, a curious calm had settled unaccountably upon him. He bore down on his father now with a gentle but quite relentless persistence. "You have no intention of ever permitting me to leave here, do you?"

For a moment the question hung in the air between them like a puff of foul air. Doctor Grigori's eyes never looked up but continued to move slowly up and down the columns of *Deutschen Soldaten*.

"Do you?" Rolfe persisted, for he knew he'd been heard.

Slowly the eyes rose and met his across the top of the page. The face, so drastically altered by the surgeon's scalpel, had a sinister, rather clownlike appearance. While the face smiled amiably, the eyes, narrow and steely like chips of flint, glinted with vicious delight. Others less intimate with the Doctor might have thought of it as a roguish look. Devilishly charming. The eyes of the charming young camp *Selektor,* Rolfe could not help thinking—eyes that examined and judged and decided. It was enough to turn the marrow of his bones to jelly.

Esmeralda's behavior had grown disturbingly erratic. More and more she stayed away from the house, appearing only to serve meals and clean up afterward. When she served Klaus and Putzi, her lips became twisted into a leer of contempt. When she looked at Grigori, her eyes appeared angry and reproachful. Going about her daily chores, she had a dazed stuporous look as if she were under the influence of some powerful drug, and then she mumbled a great deal to herself.

But when her chores were over for the day, she disappeared. Her comings and goings were as cryptic as the indecipherable mutterings she continually made as she moved about through the shed.

Once when Esmeralda had gone, Rolfe stumbled into her room. He'd discovered it inadvertently while rummaging about for needles and thread to mend his badly damaged suit. Entering the place, he had no idea it was her room, for so distraught was he after several weeks at 540 that it never dawned upon him till that moment that Esmeralda too was an occupant of the shed.

It was a small room at the rear of the compound— a cubicle actually, with a narrow cot, a small dresser and a cheval glass. It was as immaculate as it was austere—a novitiate's cell in a convent, right up to the plain wood crucifix that hung above the cot. With its windows and curtains shut against the heat of noon, the room hung in still, airless shadows. Above everything hovered a mustiness—the stench of burned incense mingled with the faintly repellent smell of old age.

Realizing his blunder, Rolfe turned at once, as if to leave, then turned back. His eye had caught something on the dresser top, reflected in the cheval glass. He could not make out what it was, only that it glinted slightly and compelled his gaze. Even then, before he knew exactly what it was, he was filled with a sense, a foreknowledge, a certainty that he was about to confront something repugnant.

It was very quiet in the shed. There was no one about. Grigori had gone out for a day of boating with Klaus and Putzi. Esmeralda had skulked off someplace into the forest to quietly nurse her grievances. She was not due back until late afternoon. If he wished to rifle through this pitiful little room, he had a clear field to do so. Still, Rolfe had a natural abhorrence of trespassing, violating the privacy of another individual.

He peered at the dresser again, squinting hard into the cool shadows. This time he realized that what he had seen reflected in the glass was not *one* thing, but rather a multitude of things—small, shapeless, indeterminate—set about on the dresser top in what appeared to be some fixed and carefully predetermined order.

Leaving the door ajar so as to seem less culpable if he were surprised there, Rolfe moved slowly across the room, coming at the dresser obliquely and on tiptoes, as if he were moving up on some unsuspecting prey.

What he found on the dresser top seemed, on the face of it, innocuous enough, yet for some unaccountable reason the display of it all there before him filled him with horror. There, set out in a variety of carefully assembled geometric patterns, was something not unlike a child's treasure trove. The patterns were composed of knickknacks, brummagem, and junk pickings. Here was a little figurine of a hump-backed creature—a dwarf or a troll with an old wen-scored face. Beside that was a scarecrow figure wrought of what appeared to be chicken bones and rag scraps. There were little Indian amulets and stone scarabs and several small reliquary boxes decorated with gaudy pinchbeck stones, which when opened sent up small puffs of some powdery substance that smelled of decay. He couldn't begin to guess what the powder was, only that he shuddered when his finger inadvertently touched it.

Then he saw the rocks. Why they arrested his gaze more so than any of the other rubbish there he couldn't say. Possibly because they had been assembled, or rather set up, with such terrifying obsessiveness. On each rock was indited some small drawing or calligraphy—petrographic figures such as one associates with primitive or prehistoric peoples, or like the little stick figures children draw when first they seek to represent the world around them. Other of the rocks contained a strange, indecipherable writing composed of figures that appeared not unlike cuneiform characters, but different from anything Rolfe had ever seen. The figures, bald and elemental as they were, conveyed no special meaning, nor did the strange wedgelike letters all scratched there by some sharp object such as a nail. But for him, the most chilling of the displays erected there was a small shrinelike structure no more than three inches high made of camphor wood and Indian beading. Within the shrine reposed a tiny altar on which Rolfe recognized a small portrait of his father, taken some thirty years ago in the uniform of an *Obersturmbannführer* of the Waffen-SS. It was a photograph that his mother had carried in a gold locket around her neck, a portrait she had often proudly shown him as a child whenever he'd inquire after the whereabouts of his father.

He stared at it, perplexed and a little queasy, uncertain of what it signified. On first glance it all appeared to smack of the most childish and primitive form of necromancy. Laughable, actually, but still it filled him with some cold, creeping dread.

On closer inspection he found within the shrine a

small heap of what appeared to be bones. They were small, jagged, as if broken violently, and seemingly feral, like the bones of a small cat—an ocelot, or possibly a margay. He paused there, puzzled, strangely uneasy, his mind careening ahead at sickening speeds. He had a sudden need to get away from the place. He started to turn as if to go, then turned back, his eyes drawn irresistibly to the shrine. In that moment a vision of the small, dank clearing in the back of the compound flashed through his head. He could almost smell the fecal stench of leaching and poor drainage that hovered above that place. Then what he saw before him was one of those narrow, elliptical scars hewn out of the earth there, with the shallow mound of earth heaped above it. And he knew, just as he had known thirty years before, when the Russian authorities had led him to the huge, open slag pit behind Barracks 2 at Auschwitz and confronted him with the spectacle of his father's "scientific work"—that abattoir, that charnel house of small bones—that once again, he was in the presence of the bones of small children.

Suddenly, hearing a *cuchillero* bark commands outside, he turned abruptly and fled the place.

After that he resolved to attempt a break. Whatever the risks and dangers of the forest, they were preferable to the horrors of the compound. The following day, the opportunity came.

It was late afternoon and Rolfe was taking his daily stroll about the grounds. The day had been hotter than usual and after a while he noted that the place was strangely deserted. No one from the household appeared to be about, and the shutters were drawn tight against the heat of day. Not even the ubiquitous *cuchilleros* were around. The blazing sun had no doubt driven them far back into the protection of the trees. In any event, the front gate had been left unguarded. Not only unguarded, but unlocked and slightly ajar.

Rolfe stared at the gate hanging open and, beyond that, a mere two or three steps, at the freedom beyond. It was simply a question of stepping out. Still, he distrusted that. He eyed the gate as if he suspected he was being tested. He imagined thousands of eyes observing his every move from the forest. For a moment he had a vision of snakes, lethal vipers, and quaking ooze. He imagined himself lost and driven mad by thirst into some vast, trackless wilderness, the huge quavering foliage closing forever behind him.

Contemplating certain doom, he hovered there a moment longer, baffled and immobile. Then in the next moment he was out beyond the gate and striding toward the cover of the forest.

He walked casually, like a man out strolling with neither purpose nor destination. Yet the affectation of the casual stroll cost him dearly in terms of an expenditure of nerve and will he could barely afford.

Having crossed the open space, some seventy-five yards between the fence and the brush, he entered the cool solitude of the forest. The moment he stepped under the canopy, branches and foliage appeared to enfold him like a cool embrace. Then, suddenly, he was running, dashing through that moist green diffusion of light, like a fish darting under water.

He did not care particularly where he was going. He only meant to put distance—and a great deal of it—between himself and the compound. He would worry about destination later. Running, leaping logs, dodging branches, he marveled at the soundness of his wind and the resilience of his legs. The more he ran, the more he seemed able to, his speed goaded primarily by visions of Hedi and the children, the cool, green Alpine lake sparkling below his balcony in Bavaria.

Instead of exhausting him, the run had the startling effect of exhilaration. So much so that he never heard the barking of pursuing dogs and the shouting of the *cuchilleros* all around him.

He had really not gotten very far. With the heady intoxication of sudden, unexpected freedom, he had been circling blindly around the compound rather than getting away from it.

They brought him back to the shed and left him there with his father. When the door of the library had closed behind the *cuchilleros,* and Rolfe and his father were at last alone, there was a long stretch of embarrassed silence in which the Doctor merely sat at his desk, his eyes lowered, scribbling rather fiercely into his diaries. For a long time he refused to acknowledge the presence of his son. When at last he deigned to speak, he laid his glasses down on the desk top, just above the diary papers, then leaned back in his chair with a tired resignation.

"So," he sighed wearily.

"So," Rolfe muttered.

"That was stupid."

"What choice did I have? You have no intention of letting me leave here." Rolfe glowered down at his father. He was filthy and scratched, overheated and panting from his futile dash. Furious, he thought for a moment of flinging in his father's face the question of the little cemetery out back and the bones in Esmeralda's room. Then he thought better of it and remained silent.

Grigori folded his hands across his stomach and regarded his son through narrowing eyes. "If you ever try that again, *mein lieb*"—his voice lilted ominously—"if you ever dare—believe me, I'll have you shot on the spot."

CHAPTER 52

One morning Rolfe woke to a great fracas outside his window. When he looked out he saw a tall black man attired bizarrely in stovepipe pants and a battered derby hat. He was quarreling loudly with one of the *cuchilleros*. Doctor Grigori stood between them, trying to mediate. The black man was Sabané, the old cacique from the Aché reservation up north beyond Pirapo. The *cuchillero*, a mean, licey-looking fellow, kept prodding the sorcerer with the barrel of his gun. Sabané, however, would give no quarter, and now they were shouting and berating each other. Grigori was shouting too, at Putzi, to try and separate Sabané and the *cuchillero*. Esmeralda stood by watching impassively, a faint, rather cryptic smile playing about her lips.

Rolfe rose from bed, sluiced his face with water, pulled on a pair of rumpled trousers, and wandered barefoot out into the dusty compound. They were still arguing there, but now Grigori was conversing more soothingly with the old cacique, who had been deeply offended by the *cuchillero*. Rolfe saw now that the garish costume Sabané wore was simply cast-off garments, no doubt begged, borrowed, or stolen from the European colonists in the area. In addition to the stovepipe trousers and the old derby, he wore a vest, a lady's blouse, a pair of filthy old tennis shoes, and a gaudy red bandmaster's frock coat, replete with epaulettes, gold frogging, all topped off with the rotting corpse of a small gray field mouse pinned to the velvet lapels. Around the old cacique's neck hung ropes of cheap necklaces and Aché beads that rattled and jangled as he spoke.

"Capezius come," Sabané chanted over and over again. "Capezius come now."

Grigori spoke in his stiff, guttural Spanish, trying to extract from the Indian some plausible account of what had happened at the reservation. Rolfe could not understand a word of what was being said, but from the heat and rapid fire of the exchange, he had gathered that there was some kind of an emergency up there.

"Capezius come. Capezius come." Sabané waved his arms and shifted quickly on his feet, almost dancing as he spoke.

"What's he saying?" Rolfe asked the *cuchillero* standing beside him. But the *cuchillero* only smiled slyly and shrugged, pointing at his tongue to indicate he could not speak German.

"Typhus." Esmeralda suddenly spoke, pronouncing the word portentously. She had been silent up until that moment but now she answered Rolfe's question, not looking at him but staring straight ahead into space. "There is typhus on the reservation. Three have already died, and the sickness is spreading. He must go at once." She nodded toward Grigori, who was still conversing with the old cacique. Now suddenly he turned and saw Rolfe.

"What are you doing here?" he asked belligerently.

Rolfe gaped, unable to make any plausible reply.

"Come with me," Grigori snapped, moving toward the shed.

Rolfe stumbled after him. "Where?"

"To the reservation. I need help. Klaus. Putzi," he bellowed over his shoulder. "Get out the jeep. I'll want my bag and medicines, too," he snapped at Esmeralda as he wheeled past. He fired off a steady stream of instructions to Rolfe, stumbling along beside him. "You'll

want some old trousers and boots. We'll be going quite
a distance on foot. Wear a hat, too. The sun is brutal
this time of day. I don't need any heat stroke on my
hands out there. Ask Esmeralda. She'll rig you up."

Grigori swept past into the shed, leaving Rolfe
stunned and speechless behind him. He was still standing there when the Doctor emerged again from the shed,
dressed in his long white Carmelite robes. The spectacle
of his father standing there in monk's vestments with his
dyed red hair and his plastic face all puckered into the
lurid grin of a wax museum mannequin was more unreal and nightmarish than anything Rolfe had ever
seen.

Grigori stood there beaming radiantly at his son. He
appeared exalted, almost triumphant in the white flowing robes. Cleansed he was, and in a state of incon-
testable grace. "Come," he said. "I want you to see
what I do for these people. How I am loved." Suddenly
he realized that Rolfe had still not changed for the
journey. "What? Still in those clothes? Esmeralda—
bring boots and old trousers. Hurry, Rolfe, for Christ's
sake. These people need me up there. Hurry now. I'll
be waiting outside with the others."

When Rolfe had changed and gone back out, he found
the jeep drawn up outside the compound fence and the
others already in it and waiting for him. Klaus, Putzi,
Sabané, his father and the *cuchillero,* who was to go
along for added protection. Sabané sat up front with
Klaus and Putzi on either side of him, both carrying
big Mauser rifles. Grigori sat in back with the *cuchillero,* who carried an Uzi machine gun slung across his
shoulder. A handful of the other *cuchilleros* hovered
around the jeep, joking and laughing, holding the nervous Dobermans on short, taut leashes.

Two crates of medical supplies had been strapped onto the rear bumper.

When Sabané saw Rolfe, he honked the horn and guffawed loudly. In the next moment, Rolfe had squeezed in between his father and the *cuchillero,* and with Klaus driving, they swung out onto the narrow dirt road heading north into the Chagras.

The windy, gutted, potholed little trench over which they bumped and lurched through the forest for several hours had originally been designed for the donkey carts that hauled lumber down out of the north. So narrow was the road and so thick the forest on either side of it that a vehicle coming down from the opposite direction would have caused an insoluble problem. Monkeys jabbered and leapt in the vines and branches overhead. Great vivid splashes of color, followed by loud squawkings, marked the paths of parrots, toucans, and macaws, darting in the forest before them.

The jeep moved at speeds of four to five miles an hour at best. Periodically they were forced to stop in order to haul fallen logs and other obstacles out of the road. At one point they had to stop in order to remove the maggoty, half-consumed carcass of a peccary from their path. Sabané, sitting up front, laughed heartily as Klaus and Putzi and the *cuchillero* wrestled the fuming object off to the side.

Shortly, Rolfe grew sick from the heat and lurching motion of the car. All the while his father kept up a stream of animated chatter, pointing out sights of particular interest and unusual specimens of flora and fauna.

Grigori was in fine fettle that morning. The trip out to the reservation was providential—precisely what he needed to take his mind off things. He welcomed now the opportunity to show his son how needed, how revered, he was by these primitive people. At last Rolfe would see what a selfless and dedicated man his father

really was—a scientist and a humanitarian laboring to
eliminate suffering amongst these inferior mongrel black
races, and not the monster sadist he was depicted as
at the close of the war.

In several hours' time they reached a narrow finger
of the Paraná some dozen miles or so upriver from
540. The jeep rumbled to a stop beside a small dock
sloping precariously out into the water and supported
there by a series of rotten, crumbling spiles. To that
a flat barge had been tied. It was a ferry station, but
there was nothing there to mark it as such.

An ancient boatman drowsed in the cool, dark foliage lining the shore. When they drove up, honking their
horn, the old ferryman rose halfway on his elbows,
lifted the torn, wide-brimmed raffia hat which had been
pushed over his forehead, and surveyed them through
dozy eyes.

Sabané stood up and jabbered at the man in Guaraní.
For the next few moments they stood there arguing—
settling on a price to ferry them over the water. The
negotiations were loud and heated. Shouting and berating the ferryman, Sabané pointed to the "holy man"
in white robes and appealed brazenly to the old fellow's
sense of piety. Would he rob God? the cacique demanded. Would he cheat the man doing God's work
on the troubled Aché reservation?

At last the old boatman capitulated. Hauling his long
bamboo pole out of the dense brush where he had it
concealed, he led Doctor Grigori and his party through
a broken wooden turnstile and out onto the rickety
dock.

They left the jeep drawn up on the shore, taking only
the two crates of medications onto the barge with them.
In a matter of moments they had untied from the dock
and, listing perilously in the still brown water, the barge

creaked out of its slip and edged its cumbersome way into the stream.

Out on the water, away from the protective cover of the forest's canopy, the sun blazed with murderous incandescence, raining spikes of heat down through the scorched air. There was no sign of life out on the river. Even the birds had fled deep into the forest, and the myriad insects, always rattling and buzzing, even they were still. There was no breeze, no movement on the water—only the tortuous creaky motion of the barge winding like a small disabled creature upstream.

Foolishly, Rolfe had set out without a hat, and now the sun pounded down on his head as if it were a hammer. He sat drooping over a rail, listless and swooning in the stern, listening to the old boatman gasp and grunt each time he poled the barge forward.

There was no place on the barge to hide from the sun, and now most of the others huddled forward, buried deep in their shirts. They dipped their handkerchiefs in the river, then wrung the tepid water out over their heads, achieving only the most ephemeral relief from the sledgehammer sun. In a few minutes' time the deck was like a griddle. The air was a blast furnace. Even Sabané was at last subdued—squatting silent on his haunches, he cringed forward, his bilious yellow eyes scanning the distant shore.

But, mysteriously, Grigori was unaffected. More alert, more animated than ever, he jibed and taunted everyone. He called them weaklings for submitting to the tyranny of the sun and offered them all cognac from his flask. He laughed heartily when there were no takers and, as a fitting gesture, took a long draught himself.

Perhaps it was the white robes that protected him, Rolfe thought. Perhaps the sun could not reach down in there and gnaw at his flesh the way it did the others. But more than that even, the white robes appeared to invest the Doctor with some mysterious source of power that enabled the flesh to transcend any earthly discomfort.

About a mile or so up the muddy tributary, the barge bumped the bottom and discharged its passengers onto a spit of shore. The ancient ferryman held out his hand and accepted the meager fistful of *guaranís* placed there by Doctor Grigori. Then he did something curious. He took several steps backward, bowed his head, and made the sign of the cross on the incinerated air before him. In the next moment he turned, hobbled onto the barge and with bent back poled himself out into the center of the stream.

The Aché reservation was about two miles from this point, and once again the small band of men set off into the forest. By now it was well past noon. They were weary and wet beneath their clothing. Their movement through the dense brush was like that of an inchworm, tortuous and desultory. Thickets studded with lethally sharp thorns ripped and tore at their clothing. Klaus and Putzi each staggered along beneath a crate of medication. Shortly they were all fuming and sputtering with the heat and the bugs and the exasperation—all, that is, except Doctor Grigori. Only he remained cool and seemingly unflappable, surging ahead and keeping up a stream of light banter.

At a certain point, as they plowed through the bush, Grigori was telling a slightly bawdy story of his student days in Frankfurt. "This strumpet—this whore—would come to my rooms at night." He laughed in his monk's frock. "Absolutely bottomless. Insatiable—I tell you, gentlemen—" He went on merrily until he heard the sound of whistling over his shoulder only several feet behind him. The whistling in itself was not strange, but it did strike him as incongruous hearing whistling out there in the bush. He did not know who was whistling or how long the person had been at it, only that the sound had, almost unnoticed, penetrated his consciousness. And even more extraordinary, the tune being whistled was from *Siegfried.*

Hearing it there just then, his heart leapt, and he smiled, not knowing exactly why. But no sooner had he smiled than the blood froze in his veins and he turned slowly, almost unwillingly, to see the short, brutal barrel of the Uzi machine gun leveled at his chest, and behind that the *cuchillero,* whistling.

At first Grigori didn't grasp the significance of the scene. He thought it was some kind of joke. Then, with the slow descent of his heart into his stomach, everything became all too clear—the *cuchillero* and the whistling, and *Siegfried*—everything.

Without even being told, Grigori turned and raised his hands above his head. "Not again," he murmured softly, followed by a cold, clipped *"Scheiss."* There in the great still noonday heat of the forest, the epithet fell swift and emphatic like a judge's gavel. It was a sound full of disgust and aggrievement, and the knowledge that fate had finally caught up with him.

The others had been walking up ahead, unawares. Now they turned and stood paralyzed, gaping at the scene about twenty yards behind them. It was a curious scene, too—Grigori in his white robes with his hands held high above his head. And the *cuchillero,* hatless and smiling, the barrel of the Uzi trained directly on him.

Ian Asher whispered something at Grigori in German. Instantly, without removing his staring, panicked eyes from the barrel of the gun, the Doctor shouted over his shoulder at the others to drop their weapons and, with hands raised above their heads, to march slowly toward them single-file.

They did as they were told. Klaus came first, dropping his Mauser on the ground and marching stiffly toward them. When he came abreast of Grigori, Asher halted him by sinking his gun barrel into the man's soft paunch. Then, with a lightning motion, he reached into Klaus' shirt and yanked out the Luger concealed beneath there. All in the same motion he cracked him so hard against the jaw with the gun butt that Klaus' head spun and blood proceeded to leak from his shattered teeth.

"No more tricks." Asher smiled, and whispered again at Grigori in perfect German. "Please." He was the soul of politeness.

The Doctor had turned white, the color of parchment. He was terribly rattled. "No tricks, please," he shouted again over his shoulder at the others.

Next came Putzi, who had very quickly divested himself of a Mauser as well as a machine pistol. He was a model of obedience and docility. Rolfe followed after, more confused than frightened. But as for Sabané, the old sorcerer had vanished without a word into the vast, encroaching wilderness. He had simply gone, and Asher, who had no doubt seen him go, had made no move to stop him. It was then that Grigori realized that the old shaman had sold him out to the Israeli, possibly for a few paltry *guaranís*.

Now Asher ordered them to stand in a single line before him. At his command they fumbled obediently into place, all the while eyeing the barrel of the Uzi pointed at them—first Klaus, holding his bleeding jaw, then Putzi, who had begun to whimper softly, then Rolfe, and finally Grigori, stolid and arrogant, carriage erect, like a man who sensed he had been reserved for a special fate.

"Forward," Asher commanded his first victim. Klaus stood there dazed and baffled, a beast of burden uncertain of what was expected of him.

"Forward," Asher commanded again, this time louder and more harshly. Klaus stumbled a few steps ahead and, at a signal from Asher, fell to his knees before him. The others, several yards behind, watched breathless and terrified, mesmerized by the curious, almost ritualistic movements of the two men before them.

Now he drew a long-barreled Beretta pistol and appeared to study the man on his knees before him. He studied him from a number of angles as if he were judging a variety of factors. And all the while he studied and judged, he was whistling little snatches of light breezy things from *Die Fledermaus* and *The Magic Flute*. The effect of this little charade was not lost on Doctor Grigori.

The inspection of Klaus was thorough. It appeared to go on interminably, exquisitely drawn out by the judge, all the while the kneeling man oozed blood from his shattered jaw down his shirtfront. Suddenly Asher appeared to shrug and stop whistling. Then, with an almost weary air of tedium, he uttered the word *"Links."* In the next moment a swift, dull thud from the Beretta pistol tore through the clearing. When the dust had cleared, the body of Klaus Hummel lay in a bloody hump at Asher's feet. At the impact of the bullet he had stumbled backward over a log, landing squarely on top of it. The log had the effect of arching his back high, and his head swung free below it. The right side of the skull had been torn away and a mass of gray-white cortical matter throbbed out onto the forest floor.

Asher took several steps sideward and cried out once again, "Forward."

"Don't do this," Grigori shouted.

"Forward," Asher snapped again, remorseless and unheeding.

Putzi, pale and trembling, stumbled forward, nearly fell, then recovered his balance. He made pathetic little whining sounds like a child who is about to be whipped. In the next moment, Asher started to whistle.

Standing in line while the judge's inspection went on, Rolfe imagined himself entrapped in a nightmare. All the while he kept struggling to awake, while thoughts of Hedi and the children flashed wildly through his head. He heard the awful whistling coming at him, as if over great distances, and thought of running, but he was paralyzed.

"Links," came the second judgment, loud and clear, ringing through the forest clearing above the mad, incessant buzz of crickets. And then the swift, dull thud and Putzi slumping sideways—slipping toward earth like a vase of flowers accidentally dislodged from a table.

"Forward," came the cry again, now almost mechanical.

Rolfe looked around, not realizing that it was himself who was now being called.

"Not him." Grigori made a lunge toward his son.

"Halten sie," Asher thundered, and leveled the Beretta directly at the Doctor.

"Let him go," Grigori sputtered and started backing off. "He's innocent. He's done nothing."

"Forward," the judge called out again.

"I have money. I'll pay you. Anything you want." Grigori reached under his monk's frock and proceeded to pull out wads of bills—*guaranís, Deutschemarks,* dollars and Swiss *francs*. He tore frantically at a sagging money belt tied round his middle, unhooking it and peeling off reams of money. "Here. Take it. Take it all." He flung the money belt at the *cuchillero*. It opened and its contents fluttered languidly all about the clearing, landing in branches and thickets, wafting downward into the alluvial ooze.

The man with the Beretta never glanced at the notes. "Forward," he cried again, pitiless and unyielding.

"Not him. Not him." Something approaching a sob choked off Grigori's final words. "Take me."

"Forward," Asher barked again.

Grigori fell back. For the first time, it appeared he was now truly frightened. Up until that moment he had remained confident that he would somehow handle the situation.

Rolfe staggered forward. Dazed and mute, his terrified eyes rolling in his head, he slumped to his knees before the judge, scarcely aware of what was going on around him.

Whistling tunefully, Asher commenced his examination. His eyes swept up and down the kneeling figure. Weighing, evaluating, searching out any defects in the quality of the specimen, his manner was coldly thorough. Several feet beyond, Doctor Grigori sat huddled on the earth, clutching and gathering his white robes all about him. "He's done nothing to you," he shouted. "Let him be. What kind of beast are you? Take me. I'll do what you want. Go where you want. Anything. Just let him be."

Asher appeared to hear not a word of this plea. He merely whistled, now something from the *Meistersinger,* and went blithely on with his examination. The procedure went on maddeningly long, as if the examiner wished to draw out interminably the awful moment of decision.

"*Links.*" At last the judgment came, loud and final, booming like a clap of thunder. Looking up, Rolfe saw for a moment the eyes of his executioner. They were stern but not unkind. Strangely, he bore the man no malice. He knew what was coming and lowered his head, almost gratefully, to accept it. He was like a man taking to his bed after great exertions, eager to find rest.

Grim and unprotesting, Grigori squatted in a crouching position on the ground and stared frozenly at the scene taking place before him.

Then followed the burst of fire. One shot—swift, impersonal, deadly. No malice in it whatsoever. Rolfe toppled backward, landing with his arms outstretched and staring wide-eyed at the sky above.

Asher stood now amid the carnage in the center of the clearing. His gaze traveled slowly around from one bloodied ruin to the next and lighted finally on Doctor Grigori. The Doctor huddled on the earth several feet off, his white robes muddied and gathered up around him like a lady's skirt, a pair of khaki trousers worn ludicrously beneath. The red dye of his hair had begun to leak down from his scalp and seep into the creases of his face. He stared numbly across at the shattered ruin of his only child, making a feeble motion to go to him, then inexplicably settling backward again onto his haunches. It had an air of resignation to it, as if he never intended to rise again.

Once again Asher's strange, mocking whistle sounded in the clearing. Grigori, crouching on his knees, shot him a look of pure terror.

"Forward," Asher cried.

Grigori didn't move.

"Forward," came the cry again, harsher and more insistent.

Grigori never budged.

"Forward." Asher repeated the command, then realized suddenly that the Doctor couldn't rise, that his legs had gone from beneath him. Slowly he started to pace toward the kneeling figure, cautiously, for he knew the Doctor to be capable of anything.

Reaching Grigori, Asher stood above him for several moments. The sun stood now directly overhead and burned through the canopy of the forest bathing everything in a soft green light. A shadow had fallen across Grigori's ashen face and he lowered his head now, awaiting the judgment he had successfully eluded for so many years. On his knees, he slouched slightly to the left, a tilt of awful weariness to his sagging frame. In his robes, within that peaceful setting, he looked suddenly like an ancient votive in a primitive rite. His eyes were closed tightly, as if he were resolved not to watch the moment of his own conclusion.

Asher, standing above him, whistled softly the Doctor's favorite aria from *Rienzi*. He could see the man trembling beneath his robes. Grigori had clasped his hands and started to pray under his breath and, as he did so, a large wet stain of urine began to blossom across his trouser front.

The Doctor waited patiently, but nothing happened. He waited several moments more, hearing the whistling above him. Still nothing happened. He concluded something was wrong and opened his eyes.

Asher was still there standing above him, the barrel of the Beretta pointed down directly at his head. "I want you to know," Asher said in German that was tinged with a strong trace of Bavarian, "I had nothing personal against your son. In the past two weeks that I've had an opportunity to observe him, I found him actually quite a decent fellow."

With a thrust of his head Asher gestured toward the clearing where the three slaughtered bodies lay. "Nor had I anything against them. This was merely in the way of a scientific experiment. I wanted to observe the effect of mindless violence on a criminally psychopathic sensibility such as your own. I wanted to see if such an act could arouse grief within even the dimmest and most primitively evolved moral consciousness. I think now I have my answer."

Asher recited all this with the most chilling detachment, as if he were reading aloud from a grocery list. "It should be a comfort for you to know, Doctor Grigori, that your son died in the service of scientific enlightenment. I know that you above all can appreciate the significance of that."

Grigori appeared to shrivel and turn gray. *"Jude."* He spat the word as if it were venom. Asher smiled wickedly down at the glowering figure crouching in the monk's robes, and suddenly flung his hand rightward. *"Recht,"* he whispered softly and nearly laughed as he did so. In the next instant he turned and vanished into the forest.

For some time Grigori sat there, not certain exactly what had happened. He knew only that he had been spared. For how long he knew not, only that he must go about now carrying with him this awful cargo of sorrow and loss, and that was precisely the reason he had been spared.

When at last he realized that he was still alive, he was infuriated. Rage turned him wild. He felt as if he had been cheated, betrayed. One of the Lugers that had been tossed into the clearing lay within several feet of him. He lunged for it, nearly tripping over the hem of his robes. Stumbling forward, he snatched it up and brandished it above his head. He whirled about several times, his mad eyes rolling in his head, trying to get a visual fix on the point where Asher had vanished into the forest. Directly at that point he fired the Luger, then went crashing off into the brush as if in pursuit of the spent bullet. Waving the gun above his head, he started to run, stumbling and lurching, tripping over the hem of his robes, and firing at the spectral images that whirled and danced all round him.

"Jude," he bellowed into the brush. *"Verdammte*

Jude." He fired again into the vast uncaring wilderness, waving his arms so that his robes fluttered madly behind him. Echoes rolled back at him across the bush, and a monkey jabbered in the branches above. But as for Asher, there was not a trace of him. He had vanished like a phantom. He was quite gone.